PRAISE FOR IAN RANKIN

'Arguably no Scottish novelist since Sir Walter Scott has had the commercial and critical success that Ian Rankin now enjoys. He may even be said to have invented modern Scotland, or at least modern Edinburgh, for his readers, just as Scott did in his time . . . *A Question of Blood* is the 14th full-length Rebus novel, and one of the best . . . Rebus lives. So does Rankin's Edinburgh . . . The crime novel has moved far beyond mere entertainment, and he is one of the novelists who have taken it there'

Allan Massie, *Spectator*

'One savage book gnawing at the heart of another. Ostensibly it's an inquiry into the fatal shooting of two seventeen-year-old pupils . . . But at the same time it is a psychological fix . . . an extended portrait of Rebus, who rages through the action like a man in torment, his mind and his hands on fire . . . *A Question of Blood* is skilfully composed and powerfully written, with a vein of compassion that Rankin taps to startling and justified effect'

Philip Oakes, *Literary Review*

'It exemplifies the enhanced craftsmanship of the author's recent work; the sheer number of handicaps Rebus overcomes and of the puzzles he solves evinces a relishable virtuosity'

John Dugdale, *Sunday Times*

'His novels flow as smoothly as the flooded Forth, and come peppered with three-dimensional characters who actually react to and are changed by events around them . . . this is Rankin at his raw-edged, page-turning best . . . With Rankin, you can practically smell the fagsmoke and whisky fumes' Martin Radcliffe, *Time Out*

'Real life and fiction blur in this cynical, bleak tale. You'll love every second of it'
Andrea Henry, *Daily Mirror*

'[Rankin's] consistent level of excellence is unmatched in the field of British crime writing' *The Times*

'Rankin is a master at what, for me, is one of the important aspects of a crime novel: the integration of setting, plot, characters and a theme which, for Rankin, is the moral dimension never far from his writing' *Guardian*

'Crimemaster Rankin is back . . . a powerful book brimming with genuine social comment'
Sunday Express

'As always, Rankin proves himself the master of his own milieu. He brings the dark underside of Edinburgh deliciously to life' *Daily Mail*

'Top notch . . . the bleakness is unrelenting, but it quite suits Mr Rankin who does his best work in the dark' *New York Times*

'Rankin weaves his plot with a menacing ease . . . His prose is understated, yet his canvas of Scotland's criminal underclass has a panoramic breadth. His ear for dialogue is as sharp as a switchblade. This is, quite simply, crime writing of the highest order'
Daily Telegraph

Born in the Kingdom of Fife in 1960, Ian Rankin graduated from the University of Edinburgh in 1982, and then spent three years writing novels when he was supposed to be working towards a PhD in Scottish Literature. His first Rebus novel was published in 1987, and the Rebus books are now translated into thirty-six languages and are bestsellers worldwide. Ian Rankin has been elected a Hawthornden Fellow, and is also a past winner of the Chandler-Fulbright Award. He is the recipient of four Crime Writers' Association Dagger Awards including the prestigious Diamond Dagger in 2005. In 2004, Ian won America's celebrated Edgar Award for *Resurrection Men*. He has also been short-listed for the Anthony Award in the USA, won Denmark's Palle Rosenkrantz Prize, the French Grand Prix du Roman Noir and the Deutscher Krimipreis. Ian Rankin is also the recipient of honorary degrees from the universities of Abertay, St Andrews, Edinburgh, Hull and the Open University. A contributor to BBC2's *Newsnight Review*, he also presented his own TV series, *Ian Rankin's Evil Thoughts*. Rankin is a number one bestseller in the UK and has received the OBE for services to literature, opting to receive the prize in his home city of Edinburgh, where he lives with his partner and two sons.

Find out more by visiting Ian's website at www.ianrankin.net or by following him on Twitter @Beathhigh

BY IAN RANKIN

The Inspector Rebus series

Knots and Crosses
Hide and Seek
Tooth and Nail
Strip Jack
The Black Book
Mortal Causes
Let It Bleed
Black and Blue
The Hanging Garden
Death Is Not the End (*novella*)
Dead Souls
Set in Darkness
The Falls
Resurrection Men
A Question of Blood
Fleshmarket Close
The Naming of the Dead
Exit Music
Standing in Another
   Man's Grave

The Inspector Fox series

The Complaints
The Impossible Dead

Other novels

The Flood
Watchman
Westwind
Doors Open

Writing as Jack Harvey

Witch Hunt
Bleeding Hearts
Blood Hunt

Short stories

A Good Hanging and Other
   Stories
Beggars Banquet

Non-fiction

Rebus's Scotland

Omnibus editions

Rebus: The Early Years
(Knots and Crosses,
Hide and Seek, Tooth and Nail)

Rebus: The St Leonard's Years
(Strip Jack, The Black Book,
Mortal Causes)

Rebus: The Lost Years
(Let It Bleed, Black and Blue,
The Hanging Garden)

Rebus: Capital Crimes
(Dead Souls, Set in Darkness,
The Falls)

All Ian Rankin's titles are available on audio.

Also available: *Jackie Leven Said* by Ian Rankin and Jackie Leven.

IAN
RANKIN
A QUESTION
OF BLOOD

An Orion paperback

First published in Great Britain in 2003
by Orion Books
This paperback edition published in 2017
by Orion Books,
an imprint of The Orion Publishing Group Ltd,
Carmelite House, 50 Victoria Embankment,
London EC4Y 0DZ

An Hachette UK company

10 9 8 7

Copyright © 2003 John Rebus Ltd
Introduction copyright © 2017 John Rebus Ltd

The right of Ian Rankin to be identified as the author
of this work has been asserted by him in accordance
with the Copyright, Designs and Patents Act 1988.

All rights reserved. No part of this publication may be
reproduced, stored in a retrieval system, or transmitted,
in any form or by any means, electronic, mechanical,
photocopying, recording or otherwise, without the
prior permission of the copyright owner.

All the characters in this book are fictitious, and any
resemblance to actual persons, living or dead, is purely
coincidental.

A CIP catalogue record for this book
is available from the British Library.

ISBN 978 1 4091 7576 6

Printed and bound in Great Britain by
Clays Ltd, Elcograf S.p.A.

MIX
Paper from
responsible sources
FSC® C104740
FSC
www.fsc.org

www.orionbooks.co.uk

Ita res accendent lumina rebus.
Anonymous

There is no prospect of an end.
James Hutton, scientist, 1785

In Memoriam –
St Leonard's C.I.D.

Introduction

The problem with writing about the real world is this: the real world sometimes bites.

Take the dedication page of this book: 'In Memoriam St Leonard's CID'. When I had made the decision to move John Rebus from a fictitious police station (Great London Road – no such street exists in Edinburgh) to a real one (St Leonard's), I had imagined he would be based there for the rest of his working life. But then a cop of my acquaintance phoned me with the information that St Leonard's was going to cease to have a CID facility. With the opening of the Scottish Parliament, detectives were going to be moved closer to that site. Which is why I gave St Leonard's the last rites and shifted Rebus to Gayfield Square. Thing is, my contact was misinformed. Either that or plans changed. St Leonard's kept its CID and I'd written it off unnecessarily.

Like I say, reality has teeth.

Let's take a second example, a gentleman by the name of Peacock Johnson. For a time, I had been offering character opportunities to charities. There'd be a ball or similar event and one of the auction prizes would be a role in one of my future books. One such winner was Peacock Johnson. I was given his name and e-mail address and duly got in touch. I said he had an interesting name and I wasn't sure what I was going to do with him. He replied that I could make him good guy or baddie but could I also add a friend of his called Wee Evil Bob. I'd looked at Peacock Johnson's website and seen mention of this fellow. I'd also seen a photo of Peacock himself – slicked-back hair; Hawaiian shirt; Elvis-in-Vegas shades. So I scratched my head and thought for a while and came up with a solution. I needed an illegal arms trader. Peacock sounded just the part, and his fictional sidekick would be his sidekick in real life.

Here's the thing though, I loved that character. So when the book was finished I e-mailed Peacock to see if I could use him in a future instalment. That e-mail bounced back. His website seemed to have been deleted, too. Curiouser and curiouser. So I turned sleuth. A well-known Scottish band, Belle and Sebastian, had been at the charity event . . . and their bassist Stuart David was a bit of a practical joker. So I contacted him and he owned up. Peacock Johnson was Stuart's invention. I had made a fictional character fictional! And now that he was in print, Stuart was going to write a novel about him – one in which he would be framed for murder and look to the author Ian Rankin for help. (Google Peacock Johnson and you should find it available online.)

Reality, you see, can also be stranger than fiction . . .

There were three things that brought the plot of *A Question of Blood* into focus. One was a TV documentary series I'd made on the subject of evil. What do we mean when we use the word? Where does 'evil' come from? And what do we do about it? I was still mulling these questions over as I began planning the book.

One thing we had explored was school shootings, mostly in the US. I had been asked at an event in Edinburgh why I'd never used the city's fee-paying schools in my work. They are part of the city's fabric after all, as well as being an anomaly in Scotland (there being so many of them in this one locale). A friend of mine – in fact, the very person who had introduced me to the Oxford Bar when we were both students – taught at a private school in Edinburgh and mentioned to me the access the pupils had to arms and ammunition. Basically, the Official Training Corps were taught how to shoot live rounds. Rifles and ammo were kept locked on the premises. With access to guns, I started to wonder why school shootings were not an apparent concern. The Dunblane massacre had happened, of course, but there seemed little fear of copycats – Thomas Hamilton had been an unhinged loner.

I had also become interested in Post-Traumatic Stress Disorder and the soldiers who suffered its effects. It was a truth that squaddies often found it hard to return to civilian life. Many who had taken part in conflicts on foreign soil suffered breakdowns or could not hold down a job and ended up homeless. I reckoned Rebus would sympathise, having had a breakdown himself as a result of his time in the armed forces.

Good and evil.

A private school with access to guns.

And an ex-soldier suffering PTSD.

I had enough components to make a start.

I decided to move the action out of Edinburgh, however, so that no real-life schools would feel they were being portrayed. Having decided on nearby South Queensferry, I went for a recce. It's a lovely spot. You can take a ferry out to the islands in the Firth of Forth, or enjoy a rest-stop at the atmospheric Hawes Inn, famously an inspiration to Robert Louis Stevenson who got the idea for *Kidnapped* while staying there. There's also a marina at Port Edgar on the edge of the town. Well, I reckoned I could make use of that, too.

I did have one overarching idea when I began the book. The reader would know from the start what had happened and who had been responsible. The only question remaining would be the why, and *A Question of Blood* would be a whydunit rather than whodunit.

But stories have minds of their own, as I was about to find out. Because just as the real world can have teeth with which to bite the unwary, so too can the novel . . .

Day One

Tuesday

1

'There's no mystery,' Detective Sergeant Siobhan Clarke said. 'Herdman lost his marbles, that's all.'

She was sitting by a hospital bed in Edinburgh's recently opened Royal Infirmary. The complex was to the south of the city, in an area called Little France. It had been built at considerable expense on a green-field site, but already there were complaints about a lack of useable space inside and car-parking space outside. Siobhan had found a bay eventually, only to discover that she would be charged for the privilege.

This much she had told Detective Inspector John Rebus on her arrival at his bedside. Rebus's hands were bandaged to the wrists. When she'd poured him some tepid water, he'd cupped the plastic beaker to his mouth, drinking carefully as she watched.

'See?' he'd chided her afterwards. 'Didn't spill a drop.'

But then he'd spoilt the act by letting the beaker slip as he tried to manoeuvre it back on to the bedside cabinet. The rim of its base hit the floor, Siobhan snatching it first bounce.

'Good catch,' Rebus had conceded.

'No harm done. It was empty anyway.'

Since then, she'd been making what both of them knew was small-talk, skirting questions she was desperate to ask and instead filling him in on the slaughter in South Queensferry.

Three dead, one wounded. A quiet coastal town just north of the city. A private school, taking boys and girls from age five to eighteen. Roll of six hundred, now minus two.

The third body belonged to the gunman, who'd turned his weapon on himself. No mystery, as Siobhan had said.

Except for the why.

'He was like you,' she was saying. 'Ex-army, I mean. They reckon that's why he did it: grudge against society.'

Rebus noticed that her hands were now being kept firmly in the pockets of her jacket. He guessed they were clenched and that she didn't know she was doing it.

'The papers say he ran a business,' he said.

'He had a power-boat, used to take out water-skiers.'

'But he had a grudge?'

She shrugged. Rebus knew she was wishing there was a place for her at the scene, anything to take her mind off the other inquiry – internal, this time, and with her at its core.

She was staring at the wall above his head, as if there was something there she was interested in other than the paintwork and an oxygen outlet.

'You haven't asked me how I'm feeling,' he said.

She looked at him. 'How are you feeling?'

'I'm going stir-crazy, thank you for asking.'

'You've only been in one night.'

'Feels like more.'

'What do the doctors say?'

'Nobody's been to see me yet, not today. Whatever they tell me, I'm out of here this afternoon.'

'And then what?'

'How do you mean?'

'You can't go back to work.' Finally, she studied his hands. 'How're you going to drive or type a report? What about taking phone calls?'

'I'll manage.' He looked around him, his turn now to avoid eye contact. Surrounded by men much his age and sporting the same greyish pallor. The Scots diet had taken its toll on this lot, no doubt about it. One guy was coughing for want of a cigarette. Another looked like he had

4

breathing problems. The overweight, swollen-livered mass of local manhood. Rebus held up one hand so he could rub a forearm over his left cheek, feeling the unshaven rasp. The bristles, he knew, would be the same silvered colour as the walls of his ward.

'I'll manage,' he repeated into the silence, lowering the arm again and wishing he hadn't raised it in the first place. His fingers sparked with pain as the blood pounded through them. 'Have they spoken to you?' he asked.

'About what?'

'Come on, Siobhan . . .'

She looked at him, unblinking. Her hands emerged from their hiding place as she leaned forwards on the chair.

'I've another session this afternoon.'

'Who with?'

'The boss.' Meaning Detective Chief Superintendent Gill Templer. Rebus nodded, satisfied that as yet it wasn't going any higher.

'What will you say to her?' he asked.

'There's nothing to tell. I didn't have anything to do with Fairstone's death.' She paused, another unasked question hanging between them: *Did you?* She seemed to be waiting for Rebus to say something, but he stayed silent. 'She'll want to know about you,' Siobhan added. 'How you ended up in here.'

'I scalded myself,' Rebus said. 'It's stupid, but that's what happened.'

'I know that's what you say happened . . .'

'No, Siobhan, it's what *happened*. Ask the doctors if you don't believe me.' He looked around again. 'Always supposing you can find one.'

'Probably still combing the grounds for a parking space.'

The joke was weak enough, but Rebus smiled anyway. She was letting him know she wouldn't be pressing him any further. His smile was one of gratitude.

'Who's in charge at South Queensferry?' he asked her, signalling a change of subject.

'I think DI Hogan's out there.'

'Bobby's a good guy. If it can be wrapped up fast, he'll do it.'

'Media circus by all accounts. Grant Hood's been drafted in to handle liaison.'

'Leaving us short-changed at St Leonard's?' Rebus was thoughtful. 'All the more reason for me to get back there.'

'Especially if I'm suspended . . .'

'You won't be. You said it yourself, Siobhan – you didn't have anything to do with Fairstone. Way I see it, it was an accident. Now that something bigger's come along, maybe it'll die a natural death, so to speak.'

' "An accident".' She was repeating his words.

He nodded slowly. 'So don't worry about it. Unless, of course, you really did top the bastard.'

'John . . .' There was a warning in her tone. Rebus smiled again and managed a wink.

'Only joking,' he said. 'I know damned fine who Gill's going to want to see in the frame for Fairstone.'

'He died in a fire, John.'

'And that means I killed him?' Rebus held up both hands, turning them this way and that. 'Scalds, Siobhan. That's all, just scalds.'

She rose from the chair. 'If you say so, John.' Then she stood in front of him, while he lowered his hands, biting back the sudden rush of agony. A nurse was approaching, saying something about changing his dressings.

'I'm just going,' Siobhan informed her. Then, to Rebus: 'I'd hate to think you'd do something so stupid and imagine it was on my behalf.'

He started shaking his head slowly, and she turned and walked away. 'Keep the faith, Siobhan!' he called after her.

'That your daughter?' the nurse asked, making conversation.

'Just a friend, someone I work with.'

'You something to do with the Church?'

6

Rebus winced as she started unpeeling one of his bandages. 'What makes you say that?'

'The way you were talking about faith.'

'Job like mine, you need more than most.' He paused. 'But then, maybe it's the same for you?'

'Me?' She smiled, her eyes on her handiwork. She was short and plain-looking and businesslike. 'Can't hang around waiting for faith to do anything for you. So how did you manage this?' She meant his blistered hands.

'I got into hot water,' he explained, feeling a bead of sweat beginning its slow journey down one temple. Pain I can handle, he thought to himself. The problem was everything else. 'Can we switch to something lighter than bandages?'

'You keen to be on your way?'

'Keen to pick up a cup without dropping it.' Or a phone, he thought. 'Besides, there's got to be someone out there needs the bed more than I do.'

'Very public-minded, I'm sure. We'll have to see what the doctor says.'

'And which doctor would that be?'

'Just have a bit of patience, eh?'

Patience: the one thing he had no time for.

'Maybe you'll have some more visitors,' the nurse added.

He doubted it. No one knew he was here except Siobhan. He'd got one of the staff to call her, so she could tell Templer that he was taking a sick day, maybe two at the most. Thing was, the call had brought Siobhan running. Maybe he'd known it would; maybe that's why he'd phoned her rather than the station.

That had been yesterday afternoon. Yesterday morning, he'd given up the fight and walked into his GP's surgery. The locum doctor had taken one look and told him to get himself to hospital. Rebus had taken a taxi to A&E, embarrassed when the driver had to dig the money for the fare out of his trouser pockets.

7

'Did you hear the news?' the cabbie had asked. 'A shooting at a school.'

'Probably an air-gun.'

But the man had shaken his head. 'Worse than that, according to the radio . . .'

At A&E, Rebus had waited his turn. Eventually, his hands had been dressed, the injuries not serious enough to merit a trip to the Burns Unit out at Livingston. But he was running a high temperature, so they'd decided to keep him in, an ambulance transferring him from A&E to Little France. He thought they were probably keeping an eye on him in case he went into shock or something. Or it could be they feared he was one of those self-harm people. Nobody'd come to talk to him about that. Maybe that's why they were hanging on to him: waiting for a psychiatrist with a free moment.

He wondered about Jean Burchill, the one person who might notice his sudden disappearance from home. But things had cooled there a little. They managed a night together maybe once every ten days. Spoke on the phone more frequently, met for coffee some afternoons. Already it felt like a routine. He recalled that a while ago he'd dated a nurse for a short time. He didn't know if she still worked locally. He could always ask, but her name was escaping him. It was a problem: he had trouble sometimes with names. Forgot the odd appointment. Not a big deal really, just part and parcel of the ageing process. But in court he found himself referring to his notes more and more when giving evidence. Ten years ago he hadn't needed a script or any prompts. He'd acted with more confidence, and that always impressed juries – so lawyers had told him.

'There now.' His nurse was straightening up. She'd put fresh grease and gauze on his hands, wrapped the old bandages back round them. 'Feel more comfortable?'

He nodded. The skin felt a little cooler, but he knew it wouldn't last.

'You due any more painkillers?' The question was

rhetorical. She checked the chart at the bottom of his bed. Earlier, after a visit to the toilet, he'd looked at it himself. It gave his temperature and medication, nothing else. No coded information meant to be understood only by those in the know. No record of the story he'd given when he was being examined.

I'd run a hot bath . . . slipped and fell in.

The doctor had made a kind of noise at the back of his throat, something that said he would accept this without necessarily believing it. Overworked, lacking sleep – not his job to pry. Doctor rather than detective.

'I can give you some paracetamol?' the nurse suggested.

'Any chance of a beer to wash them down?'

She smiled that professional smile again. The years she'd worked in the NHS, she probably didn't hear too many original lines.

'I'll see what I can do.'

'You're an angel,' Rebus said, surprising himself. It was the sort of thing he felt a patient might say, one of those comfortable clichés. She was on her way, and he wasn't sure she'd heard. Maybe it was something in the nature of hospitals. Even if you didn't feel ill, they still had an effect, slowing you down, making you compliant. Institutionalising you. It could be to do with the colour scheme, the background hum. Maybe the heating of the place was complicit, too. Back at St Leonard's, they had a special cell for the 'maddies'. It was bright pink, and was supposed to calm them down. Why think a similar psychology wasn't being employed here? Last thing they wanted was a stroppy patient, shouting the odds and jumping out of bed every five minutes. Hence the suffocating number of blankets, tightly tucked in to further hamper movement. Just lie still . . . propped by pillows . . . bask in the heat and light . . . Don't make a fuss. Any more of this, he felt, and he'd start forgetting his own name. The world outside would cease to matter. No job waiting for him. No

Fairstone. No maniac spraying gunfire through the classrooms . . .

Rebus turned on his side, using his legs to push free the sheets. It was a two-way fight, like Harry Houdini in a straitjacket. The man in the next bed along had opened his eyes and was watching. Rebus winked at him as he levered his feet into fresh air.

'Just you keep tunnelling,' he told the man. 'I'll go for a walk, trickle the earth out of my trouser-leg.'

The reference seemed lost on his fellow prisoner . . .

Siobhan was back at St Leonard's, loitering by the drinks machine. A couple of uniforms were seated at a table in the small canteen, munching on sandwiches and crisps. The drinks machine was in the adjoining hallway, with a view out to the car park. If she were a smoker, she would have an excuse to step outside, where there was less chance of Gill Templer finding her. But she didn't smoke. She knew she could try ducking into the under-ventilated gym further along the corridor, or she could take a walk to the cells. But there was nothing to stop Templer using the station's PA system to hunt down her quarry. Word would get around anyway that she was on the premises. St Leonard's was like that: no hiding place. She yanked on the cola can's ring-pull, knowing what the uniforms at the table would be discussing – same thing as everyone else.

Three dead in school shoot-out.

She'd scanned each of the morning's papers. There were grainy photos of both the teenage victims: boys, seventeen years old. The words 'tragedy', 'waste', 'shock' and 'carnage' had been bandied about by the journalists. Alongside the news story, additional reporting filled page after page: Britain's burgeoning gun culture . . . school security shortfalls . . . a history of suicide killers. She'd studied the photos of the assassin – apparently, only three different snaps had so far been available to the media. One was very blurry indeed, as if capturing a ghost rather than something made of flesh and blood. Another showed a man in overalls, taking hold of a rope as he made to board a small boat. He was smiling, head turned towards the camera. Siobhan got the feeling it was a publicity shot for his water-skiing business.

The third was a head-and-shoulders portrait from the man's days in military service. Herdman, his name was. Lee Herdman, aged thirty-six. Resident in South Queensferry, owner of a speedboat. There were photos of the yard where his business operated from. 'A scant half-mile from the site of the shocking event', as one paper gushed.

Ex-forces, probably easy enough for him to get a gun. Drove into the school grounds, parked next to all the staff cars. Left his driver's-side door open, obviously in a hurry. Witnesses saw him barge into the school. His first and only stop, the common room. Three people inside. Two now dead, one wounded. Then a shot to his own temple, and that was that. Criticisms were already flying – how was it possible, post-Dunblane, for Christ's sake, for someone just to walk into a school? Had Herdman shown any signs that he might be about to crack? Could doctors or social workers be blamed? The government? Somebody, anybody. It had to be someone's fault. No point just blaming Herdman: he was dead. There had to be a scapegoat out there. Siobhan suspected that by tomorrow they'd be wheeling out the usual suspects: violence in modern culture . . . films and TV . . . pressures of life . . . Then it would quieten down again. One statistic she *had* taken notice of – since the laws on gun ownership had been tightened after the Dunblane massacre, gun offences in the UK had actually risen. She knew what the gun lobby would make of that . . .

One reason everyone at St Leonard's was talking about the murders was that the survivor's father was a Member of the Scottish Parliament – and not just any MSP. Jack Bell had found himself in trouble six months back, apprehended by police during a trawl of the kerb-crawling

11

district down in Leith. Residents had been holding demonstrations, petitioning the constabulary to take action against the problem. The constabulary had reacted by swooping down one night, netting Jack Bell MSP amongst others.

But Bell had protested his innocence, putting his appearance in the area down to 'fact-finding'. His wife had backed him up, as had most of his party, with the result that Police HQ had decided to let the matter drop. But not before the media had had their fun at Bell's expense, leading the MSP to accuse the police of being in cahoots with the 'gutter press', of hounding him because of who he was.

The resentment had festered, leading Bell to make several speeches in parliament, usually remarking on inefficiency within the force and the need for change. All of which, it was agreed, might lead to a problem.

Because Bell had been arrested by a team from Leith, the very station now in charge of the shooting at Port Edgar Academy.

And South Queensferry just happened to be his constituency . . .

As if this wasn't enough to get tongues wagging, one of the murder victims happened to be the son of a judge.

All of which led to the second reason why everyone at St Leonard's was talking. They felt left out. Being a Leith call rather than St Leonard's, there was nothing to do but sit and watch, hoping there might be a need to draft officers in. But Siobhan doubted it. The case was cut and dried, the gunman's body laid out in the mortuary, his two victims somewhere nearby. It wouldn't be enough to deflect Gill Templer from—

'DS Clarke to the Chief Super's office!' The squawked imperative came from a loudspeaker attached to the ceiling above her head. The uniforms in the canteen turned to look at her. She tried to appear calm, sipping from her can. Her insides suddenly felt cold – nothing to do with the chilled drink.

'DS Clarke to the Chief Super!'

The glass door was ahead of her. Beyond it, her car sat obediently in its bay. What would Rebus do, run or hide? She had to smile as the answer came to her. He'd do neither. He'd probably take the stairs two at a time on his way to the boss's office, knowing *he* was right, and she, whatever she had to say to him, was wrong.

Siobhan dumped her can and headed for the stairs.

'You know why I wanted you?' Detective Chief Superintendent Gill Templer asked. She was seated behind the desk in her office, surrounded by the day's paperwork. As DCS, Templer was responsible for the whole of B Division, comprising three stations on the city's south side, with St Leonard's as Divisional HQ. It wasn't as hefty a workload as some, though things would change when the Scottish Parliament finally moved into its purpose-built complex at the foot of Holyrood Road. Templer already seemed to spend a disproportionate amount of time in meetings focused on the needs of the parliament. Siobhan knew that she hated this. No police officer joined the force because of a fondness for paperwork. Yet more and more, budgeting and finances were the topics of the day. Officers who could run their cases or their stations on-budget were prized specimens; those who could actually underspend were seen as altogether rarer and more rarefied beings.

Siobhan could see that it was taking its toll on Gill Templer. She always had a slightly harried look about her. Glints of grey were showing in her hair. Either she hadn't noticed, or couldn't find time these days to get them done. Time was defeating her. It made Siobhan wonder what price *she* would be asked to pay for climbing the career ladder. Always supposing that ladder was still visible after today.

Templer seemed preoccupied with a search of her desk drawer. Eventually she gave up and closed it, focusing her attention on Siobhan. As she did so, she lowered her chin.

This had the effect of hardening her gaze, but also, Siobhan couldn't help noticing, of accentuating the folds of skin around the throat and mouth. When Templer moved in her chair, her suit jacket creased below the breasts, showing that she'd gained some weight. Either too much fast food, or too many dinners at evening functions with the brass. Siobhan, who'd been in the gym at six o'clock that morning, sat a little more upright in her own chair, and lifted her head a little higher.

'I'm assuming it's about Martin Fairstone,' she said, beating Templer to the opening jab of the bout. When Templer stayed quiet, she went in again. 'I had nothing to do with—'

'Where's John?' Templer interrupted sharply.

Siobhan just swallowed.

'He's not at his flat,' Templer continued. 'I sent someone round there to check. Yet according to you he's taken a couple of days' sick leave. Where is he, Siobhan?'

'I . . .'

'The thing is, two nights ago Martin Fairstone was seen in a bar. Nothing unusual in that, except that his companion bore a striking resemblance to Detective Inspector John Rebus. Couple of hours later, Fairstone's being fried alive in the kitchen of his semi.' She paused. 'Always supposing he *was* alive when the fire started.'

'Ma'am, I really don't—'

'John likes to look out for you, doesn't he, Siobhan? Nothing wrong in that. John's got this knight-in-tarnished-armour thing, hasn't he? Always has to be looking for another dragon to fight.'

'This doesn't have anything to do with DI Rebus, ma'am.'

'Then what's he hiding from?'

'I'm not aware that he's hiding at all.'

'But you've seen him?' It was a question, but only just. Templer allowed herself a winning smile. 'I'd put money on it.'

'He's really not well enough to come in,' Siobhan parried, aware that her punches were losing much of their previous force.

'If he can't come here, I'm quite willing for you to take me to him.'

Siobhan felt her shoulders sag. 'I need to talk to him first.'

Templer was shaking her head. 'This isn't something you can negotiate, Siobhan. According to you, Fairstone was stalking you. He gave you that black eye.' Siobhan raised an involuntary hand towards her left cheekbone. The marks were fading; she knew they were more like shadows now. They could be hidden with make-up, or explained by tiredness. But she still saw them when she looked in the mirror.

'Now he's dead,' Templer was continuing. 'In a house fire, possibly suspicious. So you can see that I have to talk to anyone who saw him that night.' Another pause. 'When was the last time *you* saw him, Siobhan?'

'Which one – Fairstone or DI Rebus?'

'Both, if you like.'

Siobhan didn't say anything. Her hands went to clasp the metal arms of her chair, but she realised it had no arms. A new chair, less comfortable than the old one. Then she saw that Templer's chair was new, too, and set an inch or two higher than before. A little trick to give her an edge over any visitor . . . which meant the Chief Super felt the need of such props.

'I don't think I'm prepared to answer, ma'am.' Siobhan paused. 'With respect.' She got to her feet, wondering whether she'd sit down again if told to.

'That's very disappointing, DS Clarke.' Templer's voice was cold; no more first names. 'You'll tell John we've had a word?'

'If you want me to.'

'I expect you'll want to get your stories straight, prior to any inquiry.'

Siobhan acknowledged the threat with a nod. All it needed was a request from the Chief Super, and the Complaints would come shuffling into view, bringing with them their briefcases full of questions and scepticism. The Complaints: full title, the Complaints and Conduct Department.

'Thank you, ma'am,' was all Siobhan said, opening the door and closing it again behind her. There was a toilet cubicle along the hall, and she went and sat there for a while, taking a small paper bag from her pocket and breathing into it. The first time she'd suffered a panic attack, she'd felt as if she was going into cardiac arrest: heart pounding, lungs giving out, her whole body surging with electricity. Her doctor had said she should take some time off. She'd entered his surgery thinking he would recommend her to the hospital for tests, but instead he'd told her to buy a book about her condition. She'd found one in a pharmacy. It listed every single one of her symptoms in its first chapter, and made a few suggestions. Cut down on caffeine and alcohol. Eat less salt and fat. Try breathing into a paper bag if an attack seems imminent.

The doctor had said her blood pressure was a bit high, suggested exercise. So she'd started coming into work an hour early, spending that time in the gym. The Commonwealth Pool was just down the road, and she'd promised herself she'd start swimming there.

'I eat fine,' she'd told her doctor.

'Try making a list over the course of a week,' he'd said. So far, she hadn't bothered. And she kept forgetting her swimsuit, too.

All too easy to blame Martin Fairstone.

Fairstone: in court on two charges – housebreaking and assault. One of the neighbours challenging him as he left the flat he'd just looted; Fairstone smashing the woman's head into a wall, stamping on her face so hard the sole of one trainer left its impression. Siobhan giving evidence, doing her best. But they hadn't recovered the shoe, and

16

none of the haul from the flat had turned up in Fairstone's home. The neighbour had given a description of her attacker, then had picked out Fairstone's mug-shot, later on choosing him again at the ID parade.

There were problems, which the Procurator Fiscal's office had been quick to identify. No evidence at the scene. Nothing to link Fairstone to the crimes except an ID and the fact that he was a known housebreaker with several convictions for assault.

'The shoe would have been nice.' The Fiscal Depute had scratched at his beard and asked if they might try dropping either of the charges, maybe do a deal.

'And he gets a cuff round the ear and heads back home?' Siobhan had argued.

In court it was pointed out to Siobhan by the defence that the neighbour's original description of her attacker bore little resemblance to the figure in the dock. The victim herself fared little better, admitting to a margin of uncertainty which the defence exploited to the full. When giving her own evidence, Siobhan used as many hints as she could to let everyone know that the defendant had a history. Eventually, the judge couldn't ignore the remonstrations by the defence counsel.

'You're on a final warning, Detective Sergeant Clarke,' he had said. 'So unless you have some reason why you wish to scupper the Crown's chances in this case, I suggest you choose your answers more carefully from now on.'

Fairstone had just glared at her, knowing full well what she was trying to do. And afterwards, the not guilty verdict delivered, he'd bounded out of the court building as if there were springs in the heels of his brand-new trainers. He'd grabbed Siobhan by the shoulder to stop her walking away.

'That's assault,' she'd told him, trying not to show how furious and frustrated she felt.

'Thanks for helping me get off in there,' he'd said.

'Maybe I can return the favour some day. I'm off to the pub to celebrate. What's your poison?'

'Drop down the nearest sewer, will you?'

'I think I'm in love.' A grin spreading to cover his narrow face. Someone called to him: his girlfriend. Bottle-blonde hair, black tracksuit. Pack of cigs in one hand, mobile phone to her ear. She'd provided his alibi for the time of the attack. So had two of his friends.

'Looks like you're wanted.'

'It's *you* I want, Shiv.'

'You want me?' She waited till he nodded. 'Then invite me along next time you're going to beat up a complete stranger.'

'Give me your phone number.'

'I'm in the book – under "Police".'

'Marty!' His girlfriend's snarl.

'Be seeing you, Shiv.' Still grinning, he walked backwards for a few paces, then turned away. Siobhan had headed straight back over to St Leonard's to reacquaint herself with his file. An hour later, the switchboard had put through a call. It was him, phoning from a bar. She'd put the receiver down. Ten minutes later, he'd called again . . . and then another ten after that.

And the next day.

And the whole of the following week.

Unsure at first how to play it. She didn't know if her silences were working. They just seemed to make him laugh, made him try all the harder. She prayed he would tire, find something else to occupy him. Then he turned up at St Leonard's, tried following her home. She'd spotted him that time, led him a dance while summoning help on her mobile. A patrol car had pulled him up. Next day, he was kerbside again, just outside the car park at the back of St Leonard's. She'd left him there, exiting on foot instead by the front door, taking a bus home.

Still he wouldn't give up, and she realised that what had started – presumably – as a joke had turned into a more serious form of game. So she'd decided to bring one of her stronger pieces into play. Rebus had noticed anyway: the calls she wasn't taking; the time she spent by the office window; the way she kept glancing around her when they were out on a call. So eventually she'd told him, and the pair of them had paid a visit to Fairstone's council semi in Gracemount.

It had started badly, Siobhan soon realising that her 'piece' played to his own set of rules rather than anyone else's. A struggle, the leg snapping from a coffee-table, pine veneer yielding to the MDF within. Siobhan feeling worse than ever afterwards – weak, because she had brought Rebus in rather than deal with it herself; trembling, because at the back of her mind lurked the thought that she'd known what would happen, and had wanted it to happen. Instigator and coward.

They'd stopped for a drink on the way back into town. 'Think he'll do anything?' Siobhan had asked.

'He started it,' Rebus told her. 'If he keeps on hassling you, he knows now what he's in for.'

'A hiding, you mean?'

'All I did was defend myself, Siobhan. You were there. You saw.' His eyes fixing hers until she nodded. And he was right. Fairstone had lunged at him. Rebus had pushed him down on to the coffee-table, trying to hold him there. Then the leg snapped and both men slid to the floor, rolling and struggling. It had all been over in a matter of seconds, Fairstone's voice shaking with rage as he told them to get out. Rebus pointing a warning finger, repeating his order to 'back off from DS Clarke'.

'Just clear out, the pair of you!'

Her hand touching Rebus's arm. 'It's finished. Let's go.'

'You think it's finished?' Flecks of white saliva spitting from the corners of Fairstone's mouth.

Rebus's final words: 'It better be, pal, unless you really want to start seeing some fireworks.'

She'd wanted to ask him what he'd meant, but instead

had bought a final round of drinks. In bed that night, she'd stared at the dark ceiling before falling into a doze, waking with a sudden feeling of terror, leaping to her feet, adrenalin surging through her. She'd crawled on hands and knees from her bedroom, believing that if she got to her feet, she would die. Eventually it passed, and she used her hands on the hallway wall as she rose up from the floor. She walked slowly back to bed and lay down on her side, curled into a ball.

More common than you might think, her doctor would eventually tell her, after the second attack.

Between times, Martin Fairstone made a complaint of harassment, dropping it eventually. And he'd also kept on calling. She'd tried to keep it from Rebus, didn't want to know what he meant by 'fireworks' . . .

The CID office was dead. People were out on calls, or busy at court. It seemed you could spend half your life waiting to give evidence, only for the case to collapse or the accused to make a change of plea. Sometimes a juror went AWOL, or someone crucial was sick. Time seeped away, and at the end of it all the verdict was not guilty. Even when found guilty, it might be a question of a fine or suspended sentence. The prisons were full, and seen more than ever as a last resort. Siobhan didn't think she was growing cynical, just realistic. There'd been criticism recently that Edinburgh had more traffic wardens than cops. When something like South Queensferry came up, it stretched things tighter. Holidays, sick leave, paperwork and court . . . and not nearly enough hours in any given day. Siobhan was aware that there was a backlog on her desk. Due to Fairstone, her work had been suffering. She could still feel his presence. If a phone rang, she would freeze, and a couple of times she caught herself heading for the window, to check if his car was out there. She knew she was being irrational, but couldn't help it. Knew, too, that it wasn't the kind of thing she could talk to someone about . . . not without seeming weak.

The phone was ringing now. Not on her own desk, but on Rebus's. If no one answered, the switchboard might try another extension. She crossed the floor, willing the sound to stop. It did so only when she picked up the receiver.

'Hello?'

'Who's that?' A male voice. Brisk, businesslike.

'DS Clarke.'

'Hiya, Shiv. It's Bobby Hogan here.' Detective Inspector Bobby Hogan. She'd asked him before not to call her Shiv. A lot of people tried it. Siobhan, pronounced Shi-vawn, shortened to Shiv. When people wrote her name down, it turned into all sorts of erroneous spellings. She remembered that Fairstone had called her 'Shiv' a few times, attempting familiarity. She hated it, and knew she should correct Hogan, but she didn't.

'Keeping busy?' she asked instead.

'You know I'm handling Port Edgar?' He broke off. 'Course you do, stupid question.'

'You come over well on TV, Bobby.'

'I'm always open to flattery, Shiv, and the answer is "no".'

She couldn't help smiling. 'I'm not exactly snowed under here,' she lied, glancing across at the folders on her desk.

'If I need an extra pair of hands, I'll let you know. Is John around?'

'Mr Popular? He's taken a sickie. What do you want him for?'

'Is he at home?'

'I can probably get a message to him.' She was intrigued now. There was some urgency in Hogan's voice.

'You know where he is?'

'Yes.'

'Where?'

21

'You never answered my question: what do you want him for?'

Hogan gave a long sigh. 'Because I need that other pair of hands,' he told her.

'And only his will do?'

'So far as I know.'

'I'm suitably crushed.'

He ignored her tone. 'How soon can you let him know?'

'He might not be well enough to help.'

'If he's anywhere short of an iron lung, I'll take him.' She rested her weight against Rebus's desk. 'What's going on?'

'Just get him to call me, eh?'

'Are you at the school?'

'Best if he tries my mobile. Bye, Shiv.'

'Hang on a sec!' Siobhan was looking towards the doorway.

'What?' Hogan failed to mask his exasperation.

'He's just here. I'll put him on.' She stretched the receiver out towards Rebus. His clothes all seemed to be hanging awkwardly. At first, she thought he must be drunk, but then she realised what it was. He'd struggled to get dressed. His shirt was tucked into his waistband, but only just. His tie hung loose around his neck. Instead of taking the phone from her, he came forward and leaned his ear against it.

'It's Bobby Hogan,' she explained.

'Hiya, Bobby.'

'John? Connection must be breaking up . . .'

Rebus looked at Siobhan. 'Bit closer,' he whispered. She angled the mouthpiece so it rested against his chin, noting that his hair needed washing. It was plastered to his scalp at the front, but sticking up at the back.

'That better, Bobby?'

'Fine, yes. John, I need a favour.'

When the phone dipped a little, Rebus looked up at

Siobhan. Her gaze was directed at the doorway again. He glanced round and saw Gill Templer standing there.

'My office!' she snapped. 'Now!'

Rebus ran the tip of his tongue around his lips. 'I think I'm going to have to call you back, Bobby. Boss wants a word.'

He straightened up, hearing Hogan's voice becoming tinny and mechanical. Templer was beckoning for him to follow. He gave a little shrug in Siobhan's direction, and began to leave the room again.

'He's gone,' she told the mouthpiece.

'Well get him back!'

'I don't think that's going to be possible. Look . . . maybe if you could give me a clue what this is all about. I might be able to help . . .'

'I'll leave it open if you don't mind,' Rebus said.

'If you want the whole station to hear, that's fine by me.'

Rebus slumped down on the visitor's chair. 'It's just that I'm having a bit of trouble with door-handles.' He lifted his hands for Templer to see. Her expression changed immediately.

'Christ, John, what the hell happened?'

'I scalded myself. Looks worse than it is.'

'Scalded yourself?' She leaned back, fingers pressing the edge of the desk.

He nodded. 'There's no more to it than that.'

'Despite what I'm thinking?'

'Despite what you're thinking. I filled the kitchen sink to do some dishes, forgot I hadn't added cold and plunged my hands in.'

'For how long exactly?'

'Long enough to scald them, apparently.' He tried for a smile, reckoned the dishes story was easier to swallow than the bathtub, despite which Templer looked far from convinced. Her phone started ringing. She picked up the receiver and dropped it again, cutting the connection.

23

'You're not the only one having some bad luck. Martin Fairstone died in a fire.'

'Siobhan told me.'

'And?'

'Accident with a chip-pan.' He shrugged. 'It happens.'

'You were with him Sunday night.'

'Was I?'

'Witnesses saw you together in a bar.'

Rebus shrugged. 'I did chance to bump into him.'

'And left the bar with him?'

'No.'

'Went back to his place?'

'Says who?'

'John . . .'

His voice was rising. 'Who says it wasn't an accident?'

'The fire investigators are still looking.'

'Good luck to them.' Rebus made to fold his arms, realised what he was doing, and dropped them to either side again.

'That probably hurts,' Templer commented.

'It's bearable.'

'And it happened on Sunday night?'

He nodded.

'Look, John . . .' She leaned forward, elbows on the desktop. 'You know what people are going to say. Siobhan claimed Fairstone was stalking her. He denied it, then countered that you'd threatened him.'

'A charge he decided to drop.'

'But now I hear from Siobhan that Fairstone attacked her. Did you know about that?'

He shook his head. 'The fire's just a stupid coincidence.'

She lowered her eyes. 'It doesn't look good though, does it?'

Rebus made a show of examining himself. 'Since when have I been interested in looking good?'

Despite herself, she almost smiled. 'I just want to know that we're clean on this.'

'Trust me, Gill.'

'Then you won't mind making it all official? Get it down in writing?' Her phone had started ringing again.

'I'd answer it this time,' a voice said. Siobhan was standing in the hallway, arms folded. Templer looked at her, then picked up the receiver.

'DCS Templer speaking.'

Siobhan caught Rebus's eye and gave a wink. Gill Templer was listening to whatever the caller was telling her.

'I see . . . yes . . . I suppose that would be . . . Care to tell me why him exactly?'

Rebus suddenly knew. It was Bobby Hogan. Maybe not on the phone – Hogan could have gone over Templer's head, got the Deputy Chief Constable to make the call on his behalf. Needing that favour from Rebus. Hogan had a certain measure of power right now, power gifted him along with his latest case. Rebus wondered what sort of favour he wanted.

Templer put down the phone. 'You're to report to South Queensferry. Seems DI Hogan needs his hand holding.' She was staring at her desktop.

'Thank you, ma'am,' Rebus said.

'Fairstone won't be going anywhere, John, remember that. Soon as Hogan's finished with you, you're mine again.'

'Understood.'

Templer looked past him to where Siobhan was still standing. 'Meantime, maybe DS Clarke will shed some light—'

Rebus cleared his throat. 'Might be a problem there, ma'am.'

'In what way?'

Rebus held up his arms again and turned his wrists slowly. 'I might be all right for holding Bobby Hogan's hand, but I'll need a bit of help for everything else.' He half turned in the chair. 'So if I could just borrow DS Clarke for a little while . . .'

'I can get you a driver,' Templer snapped.

'But for writing notes . . . making and taking calls . . . needs to be CID. And from what I saw in the office, that narrows things down.' He paused. 'With your permission.'

'Get out then, the pair of you.' Templer made a show of reaching for some paperwork. 'Soon as there's news from the fire investigators, I'll let you know.'

'Very decent of you, boss,' Rebus said, rising to his feet.

Back in the CID room, he had Siobhan slide a hand into his jacket pocket, bringing out a small plastic jar of pills. 'Bastards measured them out like gold,' he complained. 'Get me some water, will you?'

She fetched a bottle from her desk and helped him wash down two tablets. When he demanded a third, she checked the label.

'Says to take two every four hours.'

'One more won't do any harm.'

'Not going to last long at this rate.'

'There's a prescription in my other pocket. We'll stop at a chemist's once we're on the road.'

She screwed the top of the jar back on. 'Thanks for taking me with you.'

'No problem.' He paused. 'Want to talk about Fairstone?'

'Not particularly.'

'Fair enough.'

'I'm assuming neither of us is responsible.' Her eyes bored into his.

'Correct,' he said. 'Which means we can concentrate on helping Bobby Hogan instead. But there's one last thing before we start . . .'

'What?'

'Any chance you could do my tie properly? Nurse hadn't a clue.'

She smiled. 'I've been waiting to get my hands around your throat.'

'Any more of that and I'll throw you back to the boss.'

But he didn't, even when she proved incapable of following his instructions for knotting a tie. In the end, the woman at the chemist's did it for him, while they waited for the pharmacist to fill his prescription.

'Used to do it for my husband all the time,' she said. 'God rest his soul.'

Outside on the pavement, Rebus looked up and down the street. 'I need cigarettes,' he said.

'Don't expect me to light them for you,' Siobhan said, folding her arms. He stared at her. 'I'm serious,' she added. 'This is the best chance of quitting that you're ever likely to have.'

He narrowed his eyes. 'You're enjoying this, aren't you?'

'Beginning to,' she admitted, opening the car door for him with a flourish of her arm.

2

There was no quick route to South Queensferry. They headed across the city centre and down Queensferry Road, picking up speed only when they hit the A90. The town they were approaching seemed to nestle between the two bridges – road and rail – which spanned the Firth of Forth.

'Haven't been out here in years,' Siobhan said, just to fill the silence inside the car. Rebus didn't bother answering. It seemed to him as if the whole world had been bandaged, muffled. He guessed the tablets were to blame. One weekend, a couple of months back, he'd brought Jean to South Queensferry. They'd had a bar lunch, a walk along the promenade. They'd watched the lifeboat being launched – no urgency about it, probably an exercise. Then they'd driven to Hopetoun House, taking a guided tour of the stately home's ornate interior. He knew from the news that Port Edgar Academy was near Hopetoun House, thought he remembered driving past its gates, no building visible from the road. He gave Siobhan directions, only for them to end up in a cul-de-sac. She did a three-point turn and found Hopetoun Road without further help from the passenger seat. As they neared the gates to the school, they had to squeeze past news vans and reporters' cars.

'Hit as many as you like,' Rebus muttered. A uniform checked their ID and opened the wrought-iron gates. Siobhan drove through.

'I thought it would be on the waterfront,' she said, 'with a name like Port Edgar.'

'There's a marina called Port Edgar. Can't be too far away.' As the car climbed a winding slope, he turned to look back. He could see the water, masts seeming to rise from it like spikes. But then it was lost behind trees, and turning again he saw the school coming into view. It was built in the Scots baronial style: dark slabs of stone topped with gables and turrets. A saltire flew at half-mast. The car park had been taken over by official vehicles, people milling around a Portakabin. The town boasted only a single, tiny police sub-station, probably not big enough to cope. As their tyres crunched over gravel, eyes turned to check them out. Rebus recognised a few faces, and those faces knew him, too. Nobody bothered to smile or wave. As the car stopped, Rebus made an attempt to pull the door-handle, but had to wait for Siobhan to get out, walk around to the passenger side, and open the door.

'Thanks,' he said, easing himself out. A uniformed constable walked over. Rebus knew him from Leith. His name was Brendan Innes, an Australian. Rebus had never got round to asking him how he'd ended up in Scotland.

'DI Rebus?' Innes was saying. 'DI Hogan's up at the school. Told me to tell you.'

Rebus nodded. 'Got a cigarette on you?'

'Don't smoke.'

Rebus looked around, seeking out a likely candidate.

'He said you're to go right up,' Innes was stressing. Both men turned at a noise from the Portakabin's interior. The door flew open and a man stomped down the three exterior steps. He was dressed as if for a funeral: sombre suit, white shirt, black tie. It was the hair Rebus recognised, in all its silvery back-combed glory: Jack Bell MSP. Bell was in his mid-forties, face square-jawed, permanently tanned. Tall and wide-bodied, he had the look of a man who'd always be surprised not to get his own way.

'I've every right!' he was yelling. 'Every bloody right in the world! But I might've known to expect nothing from you lot but utter bloody downright obstructiveness!' Grant Hood, liaison officer on the case, had come to the doorway.

'You're welcome to your opinion, sir,' he tried remonstrating.

'It's not an opinion, it's an absolute, undeniable fact! You got egg all over your faces six months ago, and that's not something you're ever likely to forget or forgive, is it?'

Rebus had taken a step forward. 'Excuse me, sir . . .?'

Bell spun round to face him. 'Yes? What is it?'

'I just thought you might want to keep your voice down . . . out of respect.'

Bell jabbed a forefinger at Rebus. 'Don't you dare start playing *that* card! I'll have you know my son could have been killed at the hands of that maniac!'

'I'm well aware of that, sir.'

'But I'm here representing my constituents, and as such I *demand* to be allowed inside . . .' Bell paused for breath. 'Who are you anyway?'

'The name's DI Rebus.'

'Then you're no bloody good to me. It's Hogan I need to see.'

'You'll appreciate that Detective Inspector Hogan's up to his eyes at the minute. It's the classroom you want to see, is that right?' Bell nodded, looking around as if seeking out anyone more useful to him than Rebus. 'Mind if I ask why, sir?'

'None of your business.'

Rebus shrugged. 'It's just that I'm on my way to talk to DI Hogan . . .' He turned away, started walking. 'Thought I might be able to put a word in on your behalf.'

'Hold on,' Bell said, voice immediately losing some of its stridency. 'Maybe you could show me . . .'

But Rebus was shaking his head. 'Best if you wait here, sir. I'll let you know what DI Hogan says.'

Bell nodded, but he was not to be placated for long. 'It's scandalous, you know. How can someone just walk into a school with a gun?'

'That's what we're trying to find out, sir.' Rebus looked

the MSP up and down. 'Got a cigarette on you, by any chance?'

'What?'

'A cigarette.'

Bell shook his head, and Rebus started heading towards the school again.

'I'll be waiting, Inspector. I won't be budging from this spot!'

'That's fine, sir. Best place for you, I dare say.'

There was a sloping lawn to the front of the school, playing fields to one side. Uniformed officers were busy on the playing fields, turning away trespassers who had climbed the perimeter wall. Media maybe, but more likely just ghouls: you got them at every murder scene. Rebus caught a glimpse of a modern building behind the original school. A helicopter flew over. He couldn't see any cameras aboard.

'That was fun,' Siobhan said, catching him up.

'Always a pleasure to meet a politician,' Rebus agreed. 'Especially one who holds our profession in such esteem.'

The school's main entrance seemed to be a carved wooden double-door with glass panels. Inside was a reception area with sliding windows leading on to an office, probably the school secretary's. She was in there now, giving a statement from behind a large white handkerchief, presumably belonging to the officer seated opposite her. Rebus knew his face but couldn't put a name to it. Another set of doors led into the body of the school. They'd been wedged open. A sign on them stated that ALL VISITORS SHOULD REPORT TO THE OFFICE. An arrow pointed back towards the sliding windows.

Siobhan gestured towards a corner of the ceiling, where a small camera was fitted. Rebus nodded and passed through the open doors, into a long corridor with stairs off to one side and a large stained-glass window at the far end. The floor was polished wood, creaking under his weight. There were paintings on the walls: robed figures of past

31

teachers, captured at their desks or reaching towards a bookcase. Further along were lists of names – duxes of the school; headmasters; those who'd gone on to die in service of their country.

'Wonder how easy it was for him to get in,' Siobhan said quietly. Her words reverberated in the silence and a head appeared round a door halfway down the corridor.

'Took you long enough,' boomed the voice of DI Bobby Hogan. 'Come and have a look.'

He had retreated back inside the sixth-year common room. It was about sixteen feet by twelve, with windows high up on the external wall. There were about a dozen chairs, and a desk with a computer on it. An old-looking hi-fi sat in one corner, CDs and tapes scattered about. Some of the chairs had magazines on them: *FHM, Heat, M8*. A novel lay open and face down near by. Backpacks and blazers hung on hooks below the windows.

'You can come in,' Hogan told them. 'The SOCOs have been through this lot with a fine-toothed comb.'

They edged into the room. Yes, the SOCOs – the scene of crime officers – had been here, because this was where it had happened. Blood spatters on one wall, a fine airbrushing of dull red. Larger drops on the floor, and what looked like skid-marks from where feet had slid across a couple of pools. White chalk and yellow adhesive tape showed where evidence had been gathered.

'He entered through one of the side doors,' Hogan was explaining. 'It was break-time, they weren't locked. Walked down the corridor and straight in here. Nice sunny day, so most of the kids were outside. He only found three . . .' Hogan nodded towards where the victims had been. 'Listening to music, flicking through magazines.' It was as if he was talking to himself, hoping if he repeated the words often enough they would start answering his questions.

'Why here?' Siobhan asked. Hogan looked up as if seeing

her for the first time. 'Hiya, Shiv,' he said with just a trace of a smile. 'You here out of curiosity?'

'She's helping me,' Rebus said, raising his hands.

'Christ, John, what happened?'

'Long story, Bobby. Siobhan asked a good question.'

'You mean, why this particular school?'

'More than that,' Siobhan said. 'You said yourself, most of the kids were outdoors. Why didn't he start with them?'

Hogan answered with a shrug. 'I'm hoping we'll find out.'

'So how can we help, Bobby?' Rebus asked. He hadn't moved far into the room, content to stay just inside the threshold while Siobhan browsed the posters on the walls. Eminem seemed to be giving the world the benefit of his middle finger, while a group next to him, boiler-suited and rubber-masked, looked like extras from a mid-budget horror film.

'He was ex-army, John,' Hogan was saying. 'More than that, he was ex-SAS. I remember you telling me once that you'd tried for the Special Air Service.'

'That was thirty-odd years ago, Bobby.'

Hogan wasn't listening. 'Seems like he was a bit of a loner.'

'A loner with some sort of grudge?' Siobhan asked.

'Who knows.'

'But you want me to ask around?' Rebus guessed.

Hogan looked at him. 'Any buddies he had are likely to be like him – armed forces cast-offs. They might open up to someone who's been the same road as them.'

'It was thirty-odd years ago,' Rebus repeated. 'And thanks for grouping me with the "cast-offs".'

'Ach, you know what I mean . . . Just for a day or two, John, that's all I'm asking.'

Rebus stepped back into the corridor and looked around him. It seemed so quiet, so peaceful. And yet the work of a few moments had changed everything. The town, the school would never be the same. The lives of everyone involved would stay convulsed. The school secretary might never emerge from behind that borrowed handkerchief. The families would bury their sons, unable to think beyond the terror of their final moments . . .

'What about it, John?' Hogan was asking. 'Will you help?'

Warm, fuzzy cotton wool . . . it could protect you, cushion you . . .

No mystery . . . Siobhan's words . . . *lost his marbles, that's all* . . .

'Just one question, Bobby.'

Bobby Hogan looked tired and slightly lost. Leith meant drugs, stabbings, prossies. Those, Bobby could deal with. Rebus got the feeling he'd been summoned here because Bobby Hogan needed a friend by his side.

'Fire away,' Hogan said.

'Got a cigarette on you?' Rebus asked.

There were too many people fighting for space in the Portakabin. Hogan loaded Siobhan's arms with paperwork, everything they had on the case, the copies still warm from the machine in the school office. Outside, a group of herring gulls had gathered on the lawn, seemingly curious. Rebus flicked them his cigarette butt and they sprinted towards it.

'I could report you for cruelty,' Siobhan told him.

'Ditto,' he said, looking the amount of paperwork up and down. Grant Hood was finishing a phone call, tucking his mobile back in his pocket. 'Where did our friend go?' Rebus asked him.

'You mean Dirty Mac Jack?' Rebus smiled at the nickname, which had graced the front page of a tabloid the morning after Bell's arrest.

'That's who I mean.'

Hood nodded down the hill. 'A member of the press corps called him, offering a TV slot at the school gates. Jack was off like a flash.'

'So much for not budging from the spot. Are the press boys behaving themselves?'

'What do you think?'

Rebus responded with a twitch of the mouth. Hood's phone sounded again, and he turned away to take the call. Rebus watched Siobhan manoeuvre the car boot open, some of the sheets slipping on to the ground. She picked them up again.

'That everything?' Rebus asked her.

'For now.' She slammed shut the boot. 'Where are we taking them?'

Rebus examined the sky. Thick, scudding clouds. Probably too windy for rain. He thought he could hear the distant sounds of rigging clanging against yacht-masts. 'We could get a table at a pub. Down by the rail bridge, there's a place called The Boatman's . . .' She stared at him. 'It's an Edinburgh tradition,' he explained with a shrug. 'In times past, professionals ran their businesses from the local howff.'

'We wouldn't want to mess with tradition.'

'I've always preferred the old-fashioned methods.'

She didn't say anything to this, just walked round to the driver's side and opened the door. She'd closed it and put the key in the ignition before she remembered. Cursing, she reached across to open Rebus's door for him.

'Too kind,' he said, smiling as he got in. He didn't know South Queensferry that well, but he knew the pubs. He'd been brought up on the other side of the estuary, and remembered the view from North Queensferry: the way the bridges seemed to drift apart as you looked south. The same uniformed officer opened the gates to let them out. Jack Bell was in the middle of the road, saying his piece to camera.

'A nice long blast on the horn,' Rebus ordered. Siobhan obliged. The journalist lowered his microphone, turned to glower at them. The cameraman slid his headphones down around his neck. Rebus waved at the MSP, gave him what might pass for an apologetic smile. Sightseers blocked half the carriageway, staring at the car.

'I feel like a bloody exhibit,' Siobhan muttered. A line of traffic was passing them at a crawl, wanting a look at the school. Not professionals; just members of the public who'd brought their families and video cameras with them. As Siobhan made to pass the tiny police station, Rebus said he would get out and walk.

'I'll meet you at the pub.'

'Where are you going?'

'I just want to get a feel for the place.' He paused. 'Mine's a pint of IPA if you get there first.'

He watched her drive away, taking her place in the slow procession of tourist traffic. Rebus stopped and turned to look up at the Forth Road Bridge, hearing its swoosh of cars and lorries, something almost tidal about it. There were tiny figures up there, standing on the footpath, looking down. He knew there would be more at the side of the opposite carriageway, where there was a better view of the school grounds. Shaking his head, he started walking.

Commerce in South Queensferry took place on a single thoroughfare, stretching from the High Street to the Hawes Inn. But change was coming. Driving past the town recently, headed for the road bridge, he'd noticed a new supermarket and business park. A sign tempting the tailback: TIRED OF COMMUTING? YOU COULD BE WORKING HERE. The message telling them that Edinburgh was full to the brim, the traffic slowing every year. South Queensferry wanted to be part of the movement away from the city. Not that you'd know it from the High Street: locally owned small shops, narrow pavements, tourist information. Rebus knew some of the stories: a fire at the VAT 69 distillery, hot whisky running down the streets, people drinking it and ending up in hospital; a pet monkey which, teased to distraction, ripped open the throat of a scullery-maid; apparitions such as the Mowbray Hound and the Burry Man . . .

There was a celebration every year to commemorate the Burry Man, bunting and flags put up, a procession through the town. It was months away yet, but Rebus wondered if there'd be a procession this year.

Rebus passed a clock-tower, Remembrance Day wreaths still pinned to it, untouched by vandals. The road grew so narrow, traffic had to use passing-places. Every now and then he caught glimpses of the estuary behind the buildings on the left. Across the road, the single-storey row of shops was topped with a terrace, itself fronted by houses. Two elderly women were standing by an open front door, their arms folded as they shared the latest rumours, eyes flitting towards Rebus, knowing him for a stranger. Their scowls dismissed him as just another ghoul.

He walked on, passing a newsagent's. Several people had gathered inside, sharing information from the evening paper's early printing. A news crew passed him on the other side of the road – a different crew from the one outside the school gates. The cameraman carried his camera in one hand, tripod slung over the other shoulder. Sound man with his rig hanging by his side, headphones round his neck, boom held like a rifle. They were on the recce for a good spot, led by a young blonde woman who kept peering down vennels in her search for the perfect shot. Rebus thought he'd seen her on TV, reckoned the crew were probably from Glasgow. Her report would start: *'A shattered community is today trying to come to terms with the horror which visited this once peaceful haven ... questions are being asked, but as yet the answers seem to be eluding everyone. ..* Blah blah. Rebus knew he could write the script himself. With the police offering no leads, the media had nothing to do but harass the locals, seeking droplets of news and prepared to squeeze them out of any rock or stone that might yield.

He'd seen it at Lockerbie, and didn't doubt Dunblane had been the same. Now it was South Queensferry's turn. He came to a curve in the road, beyond which was the esplanade. Stopping for a moment, he turned back to view the town, but most of it was hidden: behind trees, behind other buildings, beyond the arc he'd just travelled. There was a sea-wall here, and he decided it was as good a place as any to light the spare cigarette Bobby Hogan had gifted him. The cigarette was tucked behind his right ear, and he pawed at it, not quite catching it as it fluttered to the ground, a gust sending it rolling. Stooped, eyes down, Rebus started following, and almost collided with a pair of legs. The cigarette had come to rest against the pointed toe of a gloss-black, ankle-high stiletto. The legs above the shoes were covered in ripped black fishnet tights. Rebus stood up straight. The girl could have been anything from thirteen to nineteen years old. Dyed black hair lay like straw against her head, Siouxsie Sioux style. Her face was deathly white, the eyes and lips painted black. She was wearing a black leather jacket over layers of gauzy black material.

'Did you slash your wrists?' she asked, staring at his bandages.

'I probably will if you crush that cigarette.'

She bent down and picked it up, leaned forward to place it between his lips. 'There's a lighter in my pocket,' he said. She fished it out and lit the cigarette for him, cupping her hand expertly around the flame, keeping her eyes fixed on his as if to gauge his response to her nearness.

'Sorry,' he apologised, 'this is my last one.' It was hard to smoke and speak at the same time. She seemed to realise this, because after a couple of inhalations, she plucked the cigarette from his mouth, then placed it in her own. Inside her black lace gloves, her fingernails were black, too.

'I'm no fashion expert,' Rebus said, 'but I get the feeling you're not just in mourning.'

She smiled enough to show a row of small white teeth. 'I'm not in mourning at all.'

'But you go to Port Edgar Academy?' She looked at him, wondering how he knew. 'Otherwise you'd probably still be in class,' he explained. 'It's only kids from Port Edgar who're off just now.'

'You a reporter?' She returned the cigarette to his mouth. It tasted of her lipstick.

'I'm a cop,' he told her. 'CID.' She didn't seem interested. 'You didn't know the kids who died?'

'I did.' She sounded hurt, not wanting to be left out.

'But you don't miss them.'

She caught his meaning, nodding as she remembered her own words: *I'm not in mourning at all.* 'If anything, I'm jealous.' Again, her eyes were boring into his. He couldn't help wondering how she would look without the make-up. Pretty, probably; maybe even fragile. Her painted face was a mask, something she could hide behind.

'Jealous?'

'They're dead, aren't they?' She watched him nod, then gave a shrug of her own. Rebus looked down at the cigarette, and she took it from him, placing it in her mouth again.

'You want to die?'

'I'm just curious, that's all. I want to know what it's like.' She made an O of her lips and produced a swirling circle of smoke. 'You must have seen dead people.'

'Too many.'

'And how many's that? Ever watched someone die?'

He wasn't about to answer. 'I've got to be going.' She made to give him what little was left of the cigarette, but he shook his head. 'What's your name, by the way?'

'Teri.'

'Terry?'

She spelt it for him. 'But you can call me Miss Teri.'

Rebus smiled. 'I'll assume that's an assumed name. Maybe I'll see you around, Miss Teri.'

'You can see me whenever you like, Mr CID.' She turned and started walking into town, confident in her inch-and-a-half heels, hands brushing her hair back and letting it fall, then giving a little wave of one lace-gloved hand.

39

Knowing he was watching, enjoying playing the role. Rebus reckoned she qualified as a Goth. He'd seen them in town, hanging around outside record shops. For a time, anyone who fitted the description had been banned from entering Princes Street Gardens: a council edict, something to do with a trampled flowerbed and the knocking over of a litter-bin. When Rebus had read about it, he'd smiled. The line stretched back from punks to Teddy boys, teenagers undergoing their rites of passage. He'd been pretty wild himself before he'd joined the army. Too young for the first wave of Teddy boys, but growing into a secondhand leather jacket, a sharpened steel comb in the pocket. The jacket hadn't been right – not biker goods but three-quarter length. He'd cut it shorter with a kitchen knife, threads straggling from it, the lining showing.

Some rebel.

Miss Teri disappeared around the bend, and Rebus headed for The Boatman's, where Siobhan was waiting with the drinks.

'Thought I was going to have to drink yours,' she said, by way of complaint.

'Sorry.' He cupped the glass in both hands and lifted it. Siobhan had found them a corner table, nobody close by. Two piles of paperwork sat in front of her, alongside her lime-soda and an open packet of peanuts.

'How are the hands?' she asked.

'I'm worried I may never play the piano again.'

'A tragic loss to the world of popular music.'

'You ever listen to heavy metal, Siobhan?'

'Not if I can help it.' She paused. 'Maybe a bit of Motorhead to get the party started.'

'I was thinking of the newer stuff.'

She shook her head. 'You really think we're all right here?'

He looked around. 'Locals don't seem interested. It's not like we're going to be flashing autopsy photos or anything.'

'There are pictures of the crime scene though.'

'Keep them tucked away for now.' Rebus swallowed another mouthful of beer.

'You sure you can drink with those tablets you're taking?'

He ignored her, nodded towards one of the piles instead. 'So,' he said, 'what have we got, and how long can we stretch this assignment out for?'

She smiled. 'Not keen on another meeting with the boss?'

'Don't tell me you're looking forward to it?'

She seemed to give this some thought, then offered a shrug.

'You glad Fairstone's dead?' Rebus asked.

She glared at him.

'Just curious,' he said, thinking again of Miss Teri. He made a show of trying to slide one of the top sheets towards him, until Siobhan took the hint and did it for him. Then the two of them sat side by side, not noticing the light outside waning as the afternoon slurred towards evening.

Siobhan went to the bar for more drinks. The barman had tried asking her about the paperwork, but she'd deflected the conversation and they'd ended up talking about writers instead. She hadn't known of The Boatman's connection with the likes of Walter Scott and Robert Louis Stevenson.

'You're not just drinking in a pub,' the barman had explained. 'You're drinking in history.' A line he'd used a hundred times before. It made her feel like a tourist. Ten miles from the city centre, but everything felt different. It wasn't just to do with the murders – about which, she suddenly realised, her barman hadn't said anything. Denizens of the city tended to lump the outlying settlements together – Portobello, Musselburgh, Currie, South Queensferry . . . they were regarded as just 'bits' of the city. Yet even Leith, connected to the city centre by the ugly umbilical cord of Leith Walk, worked hard to preserve a separate identity. She wondered why anywhere else should be different.

Something had brought Lee Herdman here. He'd been born in Wishaw, joined the army at seventeen. Service in Northern Ireland and further abroad, then SAS training. Eight years in that regiment before finding himself back, as he would probably have put it, 'on civvy street'. He abandoned his wife, leaving her with two kids in Hereford, home of the SAS, and headed north. The background information was patchy. No mention of what happened to the wife and kids, or why he broke from them. He'd moved to South Queensferry six years ago. And he'd died here, aged thirty-six.

Siobhan looked across to where Rebus was studying another sheet of paper. He'd been in the army, and she'd often heard rumours that he'd trained for the SAS. What did she know about the SAS? Only what she'd read in the report. Special Air Service, based in Hereford, motto: Who Dares Wins. Selected from the best candidates the army could muster. The regiment had been founded during World War Two as a long-range reconnaissance unit, but had been made famous by the Iranian Embassy siege in 1980 and the 1982 Falklands campaign. A pencilled footnote to one sheet stated that Herdman's previous employers had been contacted and asked to provide what information they could. She'd mentioned this to Rebus, who'd just snorted, indicating that he didn't think they would be very forthcoming.

Sometime after his arrival in South Queensferry, Herdman had started his boat business, towing water-skiers and such like. Siobhan didn't know how much it cost to buy a speedboat. She'd made a note to this effect, one of dozens listed on the pad back at the table.

'You're not in a hurry then,' the barman said. She hadn't noticed him coming back.

'What?'

He lowered his eyes, directing her to the drinks in front of her.

'Oh, right,' she said, trying for a smile.

'Don't worry about it. Sometimes a dwam's the best place to be.'

She nodded, knowing that 'dwam' meant dream. She seldom used Scots words, they jarred with her English accent. That she'd never tried altering her accent was testament to its usefulness. It could wind people up, which had proved handy in some interviews. And if people occasionally mistook her for a tourist, well, they sometimes dropped their guard, too.

'I've figured out who you are,' the barman was saying now. She studied him. Mid-twenties, tall and broad-shouldered with short black hair and a face which would retain its sculpted cheekbones for a few years yet, booze, diet and cigarettes notwithstanding.

'Impress me,' she said, leaning against the bar.

'At first I took you for a pair of reporters, but you're not asking any questions.'

'You've had a few reporters in then?' she asked.

He rolled his eyes in reply. 'Way you've been sifting through that lot,' he said, nodding towards the table, 'I'm thinking detectives.'

'Clever lad.'

'He came in here, you know. Lee, I mean.'

'You knew him?'

'Oh aye, we chatted . . . just the usual stuff, football and that.'

'Ever go out on his boat?'

The barman nodded. 'Brilliant, it was. Scudding underneath both the bridges, craning your neck to look up . . .' He angled his head now to show her what he meant. 'He was a boy for the speed was Lee.' He stopped abruptly. 'I don't mean drugs. He just liked going fast.'

'What's your name, Mr Barman?'

'Rod McAllister.' He held out a hand, which she shook. It was damp from washing glasses.

'Pleased to meet you, Rod.' She withdrew her hand and reached into her pocket, bringing out one of her business cards. 'If you think of anything that might help us . . .'

He took the card. 'Right,' he said. 'Right you are, Seb . . .'

'It's pronounced Shi-vawn.'

'Christ, is that how it's spelt?'

'But you can call me Detective Sergeant Clarke.'

He nodded and tucked the card into the breast pocket of his shirt. Looked at her with renewed interest. 'How long will you be in town?'

'As long as it takes. Why?'

He shrugged. 'Lunchtimes we do a mean haggis, neeps and tatties.'

'I'll bear that in mind.' She picked up the glasses. 'Cheers, Rod.'

'Cheers.'

Back at the table, she stood Rebus's pint glass next to the open notebook. 'Here you go. Sorry it took a while, turns out the barman knew Herdman, could be he's got . . .' By now she was sitting down. Rebus wasn't paying any attention, wasn't listening. He was staring at the sheet of paper in front of him.

'What is it?' she asked. Glancing at the sheet, she saw it was one she'd already read. Family details of one of the victims. 'John?' she prompted. His eyes rose slowly to meet hers.

'I think I know them,' he said quietly.

'Who?' She took the sheet from him. 'The parents, you mean?'

He nodded.

'How do you know them?'

Rebus held his hands up to his face. 'They're family.' He saw that she didn't understand. '*My* family, Siobhan. They're *my* family . . .'

3

It was a semi-detached house at the end of a cul-de-sac on a modern estate. From this part of South Queensferry there was no view of the bridges, and no inkling of the ancient streets only a quarter of a mile away. Cars sat in their driveways – middle-management models: Rovers and BMWs and Audis. No fences separating the homes, just lawn leading to path leading to more lawn. Siobhan had parked kerbside. She stood a couple of feet behind Rebus as he managed to ring the doorbell. A dazed-looking girl answered. Her hair needed washing and brushing, and her eyes were bloodshot.

'Your mum or dad in?'

'They're not talking,' she said, making to close the door again.

'We're not reporters.' Rebus fumbled with his ID. 'I'm Detective Inspector Rebus.'

She looked at the ID, then stared at him.

'Rebus?' she said.

He nodded. 'You know the name?'

'I think so . . .' Suddenly there was a man behind her. He held out a hand towards Rebus.

'John. It's been a while.'

Rebus nodded at Allan Renshaw. 'Probably thirty years, Allan.'

The two men were studying one another, trying to fit faces to their memories. 'You took me to the football once,' Renshaw said.

'Raith Rovers, wasn't it? Can't remember who they were playing.'

'Well, you better come in.'

'You understand, Allan, I'm here in an official capacity.'

'I heard you were in the police. Funny how things turn out.' As Rebus followed his cousin down the hall, Siobhan introduced herself to the young woman, who in turn said she was Kate, 'Derek's sister.'

Siobhan remembered the name from the case information. 'You're at university, Kate?'

'St Andrews. I'm studying English.'

Siobhan couldn't think of anything else to say, nothing that wouldn't sound trite or forced. So she just made her way down the long narrow hallway, past a table strewn with unopened mail, and into the living room.

There were photographs everywhere. Not just framed and decorating the walls, or arranged along the shelving units, but spilling from shoeboxes on the floor and coffee-table.

'Maybe you can help,' Allan Renshaw was telling Rebus. 'I'm having trouble putting names to some of the faces.' He held up a batch of black and white photos. There were albums, too, open on the sofa and showing the growth of two children: Kate and Derek. Starting with what looked like christening pictures, and progressing through summer holidays, Christmas mornings, days out and special treats. Siobhan knew that Kate was nineteen, two years older than her brother. She knew, too, that the father worked as a car salesman on Seafield Road in Edinburgh. Twice – in the pub and again on the drive here – Rebus had explained his connection to the family. His mother had had a sister, and that sister had married a man called Renshaw. Allan Renshaw was their son.

'You never kept in touch?' she had asked.

'That's not the way our family worked,' he'd replied.

'I'm sorry about Derek,' Rebus was saying now. He hadn't managed to find anywhere to sit, so was standing by the fireplace. Allan Renshaw had perched on the arm of the sofa. He nodded, but then saw that his daughter was about to clear a space so that their visitors could sit.

'We're not finished sorting them yet!' he snapped.

'I just thought . . .' Kate's eyes were filling.

'What about some tea?' Siobhan said quickly. 'Maybe we could all sit in the kitchen.'

There was just enough room for the four of them around the table, Siobhan squeezing past to deal with the kettle and the mugs. Kate had offered to help, but Siobhan had cajoled her into sitting down. The view from the window above the sink was of a handkerchief-sized garden, hemmed in by a picket fence. A single dishcloth was pegged to a whirligig drier, and two strips of lawn had been cut, the mower stationary now as the grass grew around it.

There was a sudden noise as the catflap rattled and a large black and white cat appeared, leapt on to Kate's lap, and glared at the newcomers.

'This is Boethius,' Kate said.

'Ancient Queen of Britain?' Rebus guessed.

'That was Boudicca,' Siobhan corrected him.

'Boethius,' Kate explained, 'was a medieval philosopher.' She stroked the cat's head. Its markings, Rebus couldn't help thinking, made it look like it was wearing a Batman mask.

'A hero of yours, was he?' Siobhan guessed.

'He was tortured for his beliefs,' Kate went on. 'Afterwards, he wrote a treatise, trying to explain why good men suffer—' She broke off, glancing towards her father. But he appeared not to have heard.

'While evil men prosper?' Siobhan guessed. Kate nodded.

'Interesting,' Rebus commented.

Siobhan handed out the teas and sat down. Rebus ignored the mug in front of him, perhaps unwilling to draw attention to his bandages. Allan Renshaw had tight hold of the handle of his own mug, but seemed in no hurry to try lifting it.

'I had a phone call from Alice,' Renshaw was saying. 'You remember Alice?' Rebus shook his head. 'Wasn't she a cousin on . . . Christ, whose side was it?'

'Doesn't matter, Dad,' Kate said softly.

'It matters, Kate,' he argued. 'Time like this, family's all there is.'

'Didn't you have a sister, Allan?' Rebus asked.

'Aunt Elspeth,' Kate answered. 'She's in New Zealand.'

'Has anyone told her?'

Kate nodded.

'What about your mother?'

'She was here earlier,' Renshaw interrupted, gaze fixed on the table.

'She walked out on us a year ago,' Kate explained. 'She lives with—' She broke off. 'She lives back in Fife.'

Rebus nodded, knowing what she'd been about to say: *she lives with a man* . . .

'What was the name of that park you took me to, John?' Renshaw asked. 'I'd only have been seven or eight. Mum and Dad had taken me to Bowhill, and you said you'd go for a walk with me. Remember?'

Rebus remembered. He'd been home on leave from the army, itching for some action. Early twenties, SAS training still ahead of him. The house had felt too small, his father too set in a routine. So Rebus had taken young Allan down to the shops. They'd bought a bottle of juice and a cheap football, then had headed to the park for a kickabout. He looked at Renshaw now. He would be forty. His hair was greying, with a pronounced bald spot at the crown. His face was slack, unshaven. He'd been all skin and bones as a kid, but was now heavily built, most of it around the waist. Rebus struggled for some vestige of the kid who'd played football with him, the kid he'd taken to Kirkcaldy to watch Raith playing some forgotten opponent. The man in front of him was ageing fast: wife gone, son now murdered. Ageing fast and struggling to cope.

'Is anyone looking in?' Rebus asked Kate. He meant

friends, neighbours. She nodded, and he turned back to Renshaw.

'Allan, I know this has been a shock for you. Do you feel up to answering a few questions?'

'What's it like being a policeman, John? You have to do this sort of thing every day?'

'Not every day, no.'

'I couldn't do it. Bad enough selling cars, watching the buyer driving off in this perfect machine, big smile on their face, and then you watch them coming back for a service or repairs or whatever, and you see the car losing that shine it once had . . . They're not smiling any more.'

Rebus glanced at Kate, who just shrugged. He guessed she'd been hearing a lot of her father's ramblings.

'The man who shot Derek,' Rebus said quietly, 'we're trying to work out why he did it.'

'He was a madman.'

'But why the school? Why that particular day? You see what I'm saying.'

'You're saying you won't let it lie. All we want is to be left alone.'

'We need to know, Allan.'

'Why?' Renshaw's voice was rising. 'What's it going to change? You going to bring Derek back? I don't think so. The bastard who did it's dead . . . I don't see that anything else matters.'

'Drink your tea, Dad,' Kate said, a hand reaching for her father's arm. He took it in his own hand, held it up to plant a kiss.

'It's just us now, Kate. Nobody else matters.'

'I thought you just told me family mattered. The Inspector's our family, isn't he?'

Renshaw looked at Rebus again, eyes filling with tears. Then he got up and walked from the room. They sat for a moment, hearing him climbing the stairs.

'We'll just leave him,' Kate said, sounding sure of her role, and comfortable with it. She straightened in her seat and pressed her hands together. 'I don't think Derek knew the man. I mean, South Queensferry's a village, there's always the chance he knew his face, maybe even who he was. But nothing other than that.'

Rebus nodded, but stayed quiet, hoping she would feel the need to fill the silence. It was a game Siobhan knew how to play, too.

'He didn't pick them out, did he?' Kate went on, going back to stroking Boethius. 'I mean, it was just the wrong place at the wrong time.'

'We don't know yet,' Rebus responded. 'It was the first room he went into, but he'd passed other doors to get to it.'

She looked at him. 'Dad told me the other boy was a judge's son.'

'You didn't know him?'

She shook her head. 'Not well.'

'Weren't you a pupil at Port Edgar?'

'Yes, but Derek's two years younger than me.'

'I think what Kate means,' Siobhan clarified, 'is that all the boys in his year were two years younger than her, so she wouldn't be disposed to have any interest in them.'

'Too true,' Kate agreed.

'What about Lee Herdman? Did you know him?'

She met Rebus's stare, then nodded slowly. 'I went out with him once.' She paused. 'I mean, I went out on his boat. A bunch of us did. We thought water-skiing would be glamorous, but it was too much like hard work, and he scared the shit out of me.'

'In what way?'

'If you were on the skis, he tried to freak you out, pointing the boat towards one of the bridge supports or Inch Garvie Island. You know it?'

'The one that looks like a fortress?' Siobhan guessed.

'I suppose they must have had guns there during the war, cannons or something to stop anyone coming up the Forth.'

'So Herdman tried scaring you?' Rebus asked, steering the conversation back on course.

'I think it was some sort of trial, to see if your nerve held. We all thought he was a maniac.' She stopped abruptly, hearing her own words. Some of the colour left her already pale face. 'I mean, I never thought he'd . . .'

'Nobody did, Kate,' Siobhan reassured her.

It took the young woman a few seconds to regain her composure. 'They're saying he was in the army, maybe even a spy.' Rebus didn't know where she was headed, but nodded anyway. She looked down at the cat, who now lay with eyes closed, purring loudly. 'This is going to sound crazy . . .'

Rebus leaned forward. 'What is it, Kate?'

'Well, it's just . . . the first thing that went through my mind when I heard . . .'

'What?'

She looked from Rebus to Siobhan and then back again. 'No, it's just too stupid.'

'Then I'm your man,' Rebus said, giving her a smile. She almost smiled back, then took a deep breath.

'Derek was in a car smash a year back. He was okay, but the other kid, the one who was driving . . .'

'He died?' Siobhan guessed. Kate nodded.

'Neither of them had a licence, and they'd both been drinking. Derek felt really guilty about it. Not that there was a court case or anything . . .'

'So what's it got to do with the shooting?' Rebus asked.

She shrugged. 'Nothing at all. It's just that when I heard . . . when Dad phoned me . . . I suddenly remembered something Derek told me a few months after the crash. He said the dead boy's family hated him. And that's why I thought what I did. Soon as I remembered that, the word that jumped into my head was . . . revenge.' She rose from her chair, holding on to Boethius, placing the cat on the vacant seat. 'I think I should check on Dad. I'll be back in a minute.'

Siobhan got up, too. 'Kate,' she said, 'how are you coping?'

'I'm fine. Don't worry about me.'

'I'm sorry about your mother.'

'Don't be. Her and Dad used to fight all the time. At least we don't have that any more . . .' And with another forced smile, Kate left the kitchen. Rebus looked to Siobhan, a slight raising of the eyebrows the only indication that he'd heard anything of interest in the past ten minutes. He followed Siobhan into the living room. It was dark outside now, and he switched on one of the lamps.

'Think I should close the curtains?' Siobhan asked.

'Reckon anyone would open them again come morning?'

'Maybe not.'

'Then leave them open.' Rebus switched on another lamp. 'This place needs all the light it can get.' He sifted through some of the photos. Blurred faces, backdrops he recognised. Siobhan was studying the family portraits lining the room.

'The mother's been erased from history,' she commented.

'Something else,' Rebus said casually. She looked at him. 'What?'

He waved an arm towards the shelf units. 'It may be my imagination, but seems like there are more photos of Derek than there are of Kate.'

Siobhan saw what he meant. 'What do we make of that?'

'I don't know.'

'Maybe some of the photos of Kate had her mother in them, too.'

'Then again, they sometimes say the youngest child becomes the parents' favourite.'

'You're speaking from experience?'

'I've got a younger brother, if that's what you mean.'

Siobhan thought about this. 'Do you think you should tell him?'

'Who?'

'Your brother.'

'Tell him he was always the apple of our dad's eye?'

'No, tell him what's happened here.'

'That would entail locating his whereabouts.'

'You don't even know where your own brother is?'

Rebus shrugged. 'That's the way it is, Siobhan.'

They heard footsteps on the stairs. Kate came back into the room.

'He's asleep,' she said. 'He's been sleeping a lot.'

'I'm sure it's the best thing,' Siobhan said, almost wincing as the cliché trickled out.

'Kate,' Rebus interrupted, 'we're going to leave you alone now. But I've got one last question, if that's all right with you.'

'I won't know till I've heard it.'

'It's just this: I'm wondering if you can tell us exactly when and where Derek's car crash took place?'

D Division headquarters was a venerable old building in the middle of Leith. The drive from South Queensferry hadn't taken too long – the evening traffic had been heading out of the city rather than in. The CID offices were quiet. Rebus reckoned everyone had been pulled to the school shooting. He found a member of the admin staff and asked her where the files might be kept. Siobhan was already stabbing at a keyboard, in case she could find anything that way. In the end, the file was tracked down to one of the storage cupboards, mouldering on a shelf alongside hundreds of others. Rebus thanked the admin clerk.

'Happy to help,' she said. 'This place has been a real graveyard today.'

'Just as well the villains don't know that,' Rebus said with a wink.

She snorted. 'It's bad enough at the best of times.' By which she meant understaffing.

'I owe you a drink,' Rebus told her as she turned to go. Siobhan watched her wave a hand, not looking back.

'You didn't even get her name,' she said.

'I won't be buying her a drink either.' Rebus placed the file on a desk, and sat down, making room so that Siobhan could slide a chair across to join him.

'Still seeing Jean?' she asked as he opened the file. Then she screwed up her face. Sitting on top of the sheets of paper was a glossy colour photograph of the accident scene. The dead teenager had been wrenched from the driving seat, so that the upper half of his body was sprawled across the car bonnet. There were more photos underneath: autopsy shots. Rebus slid them beneath the file and started to read.

Two friends: Derek Renshaw, sixteen, and Stuart Cotter, seventeen. They'd decided to borrow Stuart's dad's car, a nippy Audi TT. The father was on a business trip, due back later that night, flying in and taking a taxi home. The boys had plenty of time, and decided to drive into Edinburgh. They had a drink at one of the shoreside bars in Leith, then headed for Salamander Street. The plan had been to hit the A1, put the car through its paces, then head for home. But Salamander Street looked to them like a nice racing straight. It was calculated that they'd probably been doing seventy when Stuart Cotter lost control. The car had tried braking for lights, spun across the road, up on to the pavement and into a brick wall. Head-on. Derek had been wearing a seatbelt, and survived. Stuart, despite the airbag, had not.

'Do you remember this?' Rebus asked Siobhan. She shook her head. He didn't remember it either. Maybe he'd been away, or involved in a case of his own. If he'd come across the report . . . well, it was nothing he hadn't seen too many times before. Young men confusing thrills with stupidity, adulthood with risk. The name Renshaw might have clicked with him, but there were a lot of Renshaws out there. He sought the name of the officer in charge. Detective Sergeant Calum McLeod. Rebus knew him vaguely: a good cop. Meaning the report would be scrupulous.

'I want to know something,' Siobhan said.

'What?'

'Are we seriously considering that this was a revenge killing?'

'No.'

'I mean, why wait a whole year? Not even a year to the day . . . thirteen months. Why wait that long?'

'No reason at all.'

'So we don't think . . .'

'Siobhan, it's a motive. Right now, I think that's what Bobby Hogan wants from us. He wants to be able to say that Lee Herdman just lost it one day and decided to top a couple of schoolkids. What he doesn't want is for the media to get hold of a conspiracy theory or anything that could make it look as though we'd left some stone unturned.' Rebus sighed. 'Revenge is the oldest motive there is. If we clear Stuart Cotter's family, it's one thing less to worry about.'

Siobhan nodded. 'Stuart's father's a businessman. Drives an Audi TT. Probably got the money to pay for someone like Herdman.'

'Fine, but why kill the judge's son? And that other kid he wounded? Why kill himself, if it comes to it? That's not what a hired assassin does.'

Siobhan shrugged. 'You'd know more about that than me.' She flicked through more sheets. 'Doesn't say what line of business Mr Cotter is in . . . Ah, here it is: entrepreneur. Well, that covers a multitude of sins.'

'What's his first name?' Rebus had the notebook out, but couldn't hold the pen. Siobhan took it from him.

'William Cotter,' she said, writing it down and adding the address. 'Family lives in Dalmeny. Where's that?'

'Next door to South Queensferry.'

'Sounds posh: Long Rib House, Dalmeny. No street name or anything.'

'Things must be good in the entrepreneur business.' Rebus studied the word. 'I'm not even sure I could spell it.' He read a little further. 'Partner's name is Charlotte, runs two tanning salons in the city.'

'I've been thinking of trying one of those,' Siobhan said.

'Now's your chance.' Rebus was almost at the bottom of the page. 'One daughter, Teri, aged fourteen at the time of the crash. Making her fifteen now.' He frowned in concentration and tried as best he could to sift through the other sheets.

'What are you looking for?'

'A photo of the family . . .' He was in luck. DS McLeod had indeed been scrupulous, clipping newspaper stories about the case. One tabloid had got hold of a family snapshot, mum and dad on the sofa, son and daughter behind so that only their faces could be seen. Rebus was fairly sure he recognised the girl. Teri. Miss Teri. What was it she'd said to him?

You can see me whenever you like . . .

What the hell had she meant by that?

Siobhan had seen the look on his face. 'Not someone else you know?'

'Bumped into her when I was walking to The Boatman's. She's changed a bit though.' He studied the shining, make-up-free face. The hair seemed mousy-brown rather than jet-black. 'Dyed her hair, powdered her face white with big black eyes and mouth . . . black clothes, too.'

'A Goth, you mean? That's why you were asking me about heavy metal?'

He nodded.

'Think it has anything to do with her brother's death?'

'Might have. There's something else though.'

'What?'

'It was what she said . . . Something about not being sad they were dead . . .'

They got take-out food from Rebus's favourite curry house on Causewayside. While the order was being filled, an off-licence down the street yielded six bottles of chilled lager.

'Fairly abstemious really,' Siobhan said, hoisting the carrier bag from the counter.

'You don't honestly think I'm sharing these?' Rebus stated.

'I'm sure I can twist your arm.'

They took the provisions to his flat in Marchmont, parking the car in the last space going. The flat was two flights up. Rebus fumbled to slot the key into the lock.

'I'll do it,' Siobhan said.

Inside, the flat was musty. There was a fug which could have been bottled as *eau de bachelor*. Stale food, alcohol, sweat. CDs were scattered across the living-room carpet, marking out a trail between the hi-fi and Rebus's favourite chair. Siobhan left the food on the dining-table and went into the kitchen for plates and cutlery. There were few signs that anyone had been cooking of late. Two mugs in the sink, a margarine tub open on the draining-board, its contents spotted with mould. A shopping list in the form of a yellow Post-It note had been stuck to the refrigerator door: bread/milk/marge/bacon/b.sauce/w.up liq/lightbulbs. The note was beginning to curl, and she wondered how long it had been there.

When she returned to the living room, Rebus had managed to put on a CD. It was something she'd given him as a present: Violet Indiana.

'You like it?' she asked.

He shrugged. 'I thought you might.' Meaning he hadn't got round to playing it until now.

'Better than some of that dinosaur stuff you play in your car.'

'Don't forget, you're *speaking* to a dinosaur.'

She smiled and started lifting containers out of the bag. Glancing over to the hi-fi, she saw Rebus chewing on a bandage.

'You can't be that hungry.'

'Easier to eat with these things off.' He started unwinding the strips of gauze, first one hand and then the other. She noticed that he slowed down as he got closer to the end. Finally, both hands were revealed, red and blistered and hot-looking. He tried flexing his fingers.

'Time for some more tablets?' Siobhan suggested.

He nodded, came over to the table and sat down. She opened a couple of lagers and they started to eat. Rebus didn't have a strong grip on his fork, but he persevered, dripping dollops of sauce on to the table, but managing to avoid splashing his shirt. They ate in silence, other than to comment on the food. When they'd finished, Siobhan cleared the table and wiped it clean.

'Better add J-cloths to your shopping list,' she said.

'What shopping list?' Rebus sat down in his chair, resting a second bottle of lager on his thigh. 'Can you see if there's any cream?'

'Are we having dessert?'

'I mean in the bathroom – antiseptic cream.'

Dutifully, she checked the cabinet, noticing that the bath was full to its brim. The water looked cold. She came back holding a blue tube. 'For stings and infections,' she said.

'That'll do.' He took the tube from her and rubbed a thick layer of white cream over both hands. She'd opened her second bottle, rested against an arm of the sofa.

'Want me to let the water out?' she asked.

'What water?'

'The bath. You forgot to pull the plug. I'm assuming it's the one you say you fell into . . .'

Rebus looked at her. 'Who've you been talking to?'

'Doctor at the hospital. He sounded sceptical.'

'So much for patient confidentiality,' Rebus muttered. 'Well, at least he'll have told you they really are scalds, not burns?' Siobhan twitched her nose. 'Thanks for checking up on my story.'

'I just knew it wasn't very likely you'd be washing dishes. Now, about that bathwater . . .?'

'I'll do it later.' He sat back, took a swig from his bottle. 'Meantime, what are we going to do about Martin Fairstone?'

She shrugged, slid down on to the sofa proper. 'What are we supposed to do? Apparently, neither of us killed him.'

'Talk to any fireman, they'll all say the same thing: you want to do someone in and get away with it, you get them blind drunk and then turn on the chip-pan.'

'So?'

'It's something every cop knows, too.'

'Doesn't mean it wasn't an accident.'

'We're cops, Siobhan: guilty until proven innocent. When did Fairstone give you that shiner?'

'How do you know it was him?' The look on Rebus's face told her he felt insulted by the question. She sighed. 'The Thursday before he died.'

'What happened?'

'He must've been following me. I was unloading bags of groceries from the car, carrying them into the stairwell. When I turned round, he was biting into an apple. He'd lifted it from one of the bags sitting at the kerb. Had this big smile on his face. I walked right up to him . . . I was furious. Now he knew where I lived. I gave him a slap . . .' She smiled at the memory. 'The apple went flying halfway across the road.'

'He could have had you for assault.'

'Well, he didn't. He threw a fast right, caught me just below the eye. I staggered back and tripped over the step. Landed on my backside. He just walked away, picking up the apple again as he crossed the road.'

'You didn't report it?'

'No.'

'Tell anyone how it happened?'

She shook her head. She remembered Rebus asking her; she'd shaken her head then, too. But knowing ... knowing he wouldn't have to work too hard. 'Only after I found out he was dead,' she said. 'I went to the boss and told her.'

There was a silence between them. Bottles were raised to mouths, eyes meeting eyes. Siobhan swallowed and licked her lips.

'I didn't kill him,' Rebus said quietly.

'He made that complaint about you.'

'And withdrew it pronto.'

'Then it was an accident.'

He didn't say anything for a moment. Then: 'Guilty until proven innocent,' he repeated.

Siobhan lifted her drink. 'Here's to the guilty.'

Rebus managed a half-smile. 'That was the last time you saw him?' he asked.

She nodded. 'What about you?'

'Weren't you scared he'd come back?' He saw the look she gave him. 'Okay, not "scared" then ... but you must have wondered?'

'I took precautions.'

'What kind of precautions?'

'The usual: watched my back ... tried not to go in or out after dark unless someone else was around.'

Rebus rested his head against the back of his chair. The music had finished. 'Want to hear something else?' he asked.

'I want to hear you say that the last time you saw Fairstone was the time you had that fight.'

'I'd be lying.'

'So when did you see him?'

Rebus angled his head to look at her. 'The night he died.' He paused. 'But then, you already know that, don't you?'

She nodded. 'Templer told me.'

'I was just out for a drink, that's all. Ended up next to him in a pub. We had a bit of a chat.'

'About me?'

'About the black eye. He said it was self-defence.' He paused. 'Way you tell it, maybe it was.'

'Which pub was it?'

Rebus shrugged. 'Somewhere near Gracemount.'

'Since when did you start drinking so far from the Oxford Bar?'

He looked at her. 'So maybe I wanted to talk to him.'

'You went hunting for him?'

'Listen to Little Miss Prosecution!' Colour had risen to Rebus's face.

'And no doubt half the pub clocked you as CID,' she stated. 'Which is how Templer found out.'

'Is that called "leading the witness"?'

'I can fight my own battles, John!'

'And he'd have put you on the deck every time. This bastard had a history of thumping people. You saw his record . . .'

'That didn't give you the right—'

'We're not talking about rights here.' Rebus leapt from the chair and made for the dining-table, helping himself to a fresh bottle. 'You want one?'

'Not if I'm driving.'

'Your choice.'

'That's right, John. *My* choice, not yours.'

'I didn't top him, Siobhan. All I did was . . .' Rebus swallowed back the words.

'What?' She'd turned her body on the sofa to face him. 'What?' she repeated.

'I went back to his house.' She just stared, mouth open a fraction. 'He invited me back.'

'He *invited* you?'

Rebus nodded. The bottle-opener trembled in his hand. He delegated the job to Siobhan, who returned the opened bottle to him. 'Bastard liked playing games, Siobhan. Said we should go back and have a drink, bury the hatchet.'

'Bury the hatchet?'

'His exact words.'

'And that's what you did?'

'He wanted to talk . . . not about you, about anything but. Time he'd served, cell stories, how he grew up. Usual sob story, dad who thumped him, mum who didn't care . . .'

'And you sat there and listened?'

'I sat there thinking how badly I wanted to smack him.'

'But you didn't?'

Rebus shook his head. 'He was pretty dopey by the time I left.'

'Not in the kitchen though?'

'In the living room . . .'

'Did you see the kitchen?'

Rebus shook his head again.

'Have you told Templer this?'

He made to rub his forehead, then remembered that it would hurt like blazes. 'Just go home, Siobhan.'

'I had to pull the two of you apart. Next thing you're back at his house sharing a drink and a chat? You expect me to believe that?'

'I'm not asking you to believe anything. Just go home.'

She stood up. 'I can—'

'I know, you can look after yourself.' Rebus sounded tired all of a sudden.

'I was going to say, I can wash the dishes, if you like.'

'That's okay, I'll do them tomorrow. Let's just get some sleep, eh?' He walked across to the room's large bay window, stared down on to the quiet street.

'What time do you want picked up?'

'Eight.'

'Eight it is.' She paused. 'Someone like Fairstone, he must have had enemies.'

'Almost certainly.'

'Maybe someone saw you with him, waited till you'd left . . .'

'See you tomorrow, Siobhan.'

'He was a bastard, John. I keep expecting to hear you say that.' She deepened her voice. ' "World's better off without him." '

'I don't remember saying that.'

'You would have though, not so long ago.' She made towards the door. 'I'll see you tomorrow.'

He waited, expecting to hear the lock click shut. Instead, he could hear a background gurgling of water. He drank from the bottle of lager, staring from the window. She did not emerge on to the street. When the living-room door opened, he could hear the bath filling.

'You going to scrub my back, too?'

'Beyond the call of duty.' She looked at him. 'But a change of clothes wouldn't be a bad idea. I can help you sort some out.'

He shook his head. 'Really, I can manage.'

'I'll hang around till you're done in the bath . . . just to make sure you can get out again.'

'I'll be fine.'

'I'll wait anyway.' She'd walked towards him, plucked the lager from his loose grasp. Lifted it to her mouth.

'Better keep the water tepid,' he warned her.

She nodded, swallowed. 'There's just one thing I'm curious about.'

'What?'

'What do you do when you need the toilet?'

He narrowed his eyes. 'I do what a man's got to do.'

'Something tells me that's as much as I need to know.' She handed back the bottle. 'I'll check the water's not too hot this time round . . .'

Afterwards, wrapped in a towelling robe, he watched as she emerged at street level, looking up and down the pavement before making for her car. Looking up and down the pavement: checking her back, even though the bogey man had gone.

Rebus knew there were more of them out there. Plenty

of men like Martin Fairstone. Teased at school, becoming the 'runt', tagging along with gangs who would make jokes about him. But growing stronger for it, graduating to violence and petty theft, the only life he would ever know. He had told his story, and Rebus had listened.

'Reckon I need to see a head doctor, get myself checked out, like? See, what's on the inside of your head isn't always the same as what you do on the outside. Does that sound like pish? Maybe it's because I'm pished. There's more whisky when you need a top-up. Just say the word, I'm not used to doing the whole host bit, know what I'm saying? Just chantering away here, don't pay any heed ...'

And more ... so much more, with Rebus listening, taking small sips of whisky, knowing he was feeling it. Four pubs he'd been to before tracking Fairstone down. And when the monologue had finally dried up, Rebus had leaned forward. They were seated in squishy armchairs, coffee-table between them with a cardboard box beneath in place of the missing leg. Two glasses, a bottle, and an overflowing ashtray, and Rebus leaning forward now to say his first words in nearly half an hour.

'Marty, let's put all this shit with DS Clarke on the back-burner, eh? Fact is, I couldn't give a monkey's. But there is a question I've been meaning to ask ...'

'What's that?' Fairstone, heavy-lidded in his chair, cigarette held between thumb and forefinger.

'I heard a story that you know Peacock Johnson. Anything you can tell me about him?'

Rebus at the window, thinking about how many pain-killers were left in the bottle. Thinking about nipping out for a proper drink. Turning from the window and making for his bedroom. Opening the top drawer and pulling out ties and socks, finally finding what he'd been looking for.

Winter gloves. Black leather, nylon-lined. Never worn, until now.

Day Two

Wednesday

4

There were times when Rebus could swear he'd smelled his wife's perfume on the cold pillow. Impossible: two decades of separation; not even a pillow she'd slept on or pressed her head against. Other perfumes, too – other women. He knew they were an illusion, knew he wasn't really smelling them. Rather, he was smelling their absence.

'Penny for them,' Siobhan said, switching lanes in a half-hearted attempt to speed their progress through the morning rush-hour.

'I was thinking about pillows,' Rebus stated. She'd brought coffee for both of them. He was cradling his.

'Nice gloves, by the way,' she said now, by no means for the first time. 'Just the thing this time of year.'

'I can get another driver, you know.'

'But would they provide breakfast?' She floored the accelerator as the amber traffic light ahead turned red. Rebus worked hard to keep his coffee from spilling.

'What's the music?' he asked, looking at the in-car CD player.

'Fatboy Slim. Thought it might wake you up.'

'Why's he telling Jimmy Boyle not to leave the States?'

Siobhan smiled. 'You might just be mis-hearing that particular lyric. I can put on something more laid-back . . . what about Tempus?'

'Fugit, why not?' Rebus said.

Lee Herdman had lived in a one-bedroom flat above a bar on South Queensferry's High Street. The entrance was down a narrow, sunless vennel with an arched stone roof. A police constable stood guard by the main door, checking the names of visitors against a list of residents fixed to his clipboard. It was Brendan Innes.

'What sort of shifts are they making you work?' Rebus asked.

Innes checked his watch. 'Another hour, I'll be out of here.'

'Anything happening?'

'People heading to work.'

'How many flats apart from Herdman's?'

'Just the two. Schoolteacher and his girlfriend in one, car mechanic in the other.'

'Schoolteacher?' Siobhan hinted.

Innes shook his head. 'Nothing to do with Port Edgar. He teaches the local primary. Girlfriend works in a shop.'

Rebus knew that the neighbours would have been interviewed. The notes would be somewhere.

'You spoken to them at all?' he asked.

'Just as they come and go.'

'What do they say?'

Innes shrugged. 'The usual: he was quiet enough, seemed a nice enough guy . . .'

'Quiet *enough*, rather than just quiet?'

Innes nodded. 'Seems Mr Herdman hosted a few late-nighters for his friends.'

'Enough to rile the neighbours?'

Innes shrugged again. Rebus turned to Siobhan. 'We've got a list of his acquaintances?'

She nodded. 'Probably not comprehensive as yet . . .'

'You'll want this,' Innes was saying. He was holding up a Yale key. Siobhan took it from him.

'How messy is it up there?' Rebus asked.

'The search team knew he wasn't coming back,' Innes answered with a smile, lowering his head as he started adding their names to his list.

The downstairs hall was cramped. No sign of any recent

mail. They climbed two flights of stone steps. There were a couple of doors on the first landing, only one on the second. Nothing to identify its occupier – no name or number. Siobhan turned the key and they walked in.

'Plenty of locks,' Rebus commented. Including two bolts on the interior side. 'Herdman liked his security.'

Hard to say how messy the place had been before Hogan's team had made their search. Rebus picked his way across a floor strewn with clothes and newspapers, books and bric-a-brac. They were in the eaves of the building, and the rooms seemed claustrophobic. Rebus's head was barely two feet shy of the ceiling. The windows were small and unwashed. Just the one bedroom: double bed, wardrobe and chest of drawers. Portable black and white TV on the uncarpeted floor, empty half-bottle of Bell's next to it. Greasy yellow linoleum on the floor of the kitchen, foldaway table giving just enough room to turn. Narrow bathroom, smelling of mildew. Two hall cupboards, which looked to have been emptied and hastily rearranged by Hogan's men. Leaving only the living room. Rebus went back in.

'Homely, wouldn't you say?' Siobhan commented.

'In estate agent parlance, yes.' Rebus picked up a couple of CDs: Linkin Park and Sepultura. 'The man liked his metal,' he said, tossing them down again.

'Liked the SAS, too,' Siobhan added, holding up some books for Rebus to see. They were histories of the regiment, books about conflicts in which it had taken part, stories of survival by ex-members. She nodded to a nearby desk, and Rebus saw what she was pointing out: a scrapbook of news cuttings. These were all about soldiering, too. Whole articles discussing an apparent trend: American military heroes who were murdering their wives. Cuttings about suicides and disappearances. There was even one headed 'Space runs out in SAS cemetery', which Rebus paid most attention to. He knew men who'd been buried in the plots set aside in St Martin's churchyard, not far from the regiment's original HQ. Now a new cemetery site was being proposed near the current HQ at Credenhill. In the same piece, the deaths of two SAS soldiers were mentioned. They'd died on a 'training exercise in Oman', which could mean anything from a cock-up to assassination during covert operations.

Siobhan was peering into a supermarket carrier-bag. Rebus heard the chink of empty bottles.

'He was a good host,' she said.

'Wine or spirits?'

'Tequila and red wine.'

'Judging from the empty bottle in the bedroom, Herdman was a whisky man.'

'Like I say, a good host.' Siobhan took a sheet of paper from her pocket and unfolded it. 'Acording to this, forensics took away the remains of a number of spliffs, plus some traces of what looked like cocaine. Took his computer, too. They also removed a number of photographs from the inside of the wardrobe.'

'What sort of photos?'

'Guns. Bit of a fetish, if you ask me. I mean . . . putting them on the wardrobe door.'

'Which makes of gun?'

'Doesn't say.'

'What type of gun did he use again?'

She checked this. 'Brocock. It's an air-gun. The ME38 Magnum, to be precise.'

'So it's like a revolver?'

Siobhan nodded. 'You can buy one across the counter for just over a hundred quid. Powered by gas cylinder.'

'But Herdman's had been tweaked?'

'Steel sleeving inside the chamber. Means you can use live ammo, point-two-two. Alternative is to drill the gun out to take thirty-eight calibres.'

'He used point-two-two?' She nodded again. 'So someone did the work for him?'

'He might've done it himself. Dare say he'd have had the know-how.'

'Do we know how he came by the gun in the first place?'

'As an ex-soldier, I'm guessing he had contacts.'

'Could be.' Rebus was thinking back to the 1960s and '70s, arms and explosives walking off army bases the length and breadth of the land, mostly at the behest of both sides of the Northern Ireland Troubles . . . Plenty of soldiers had a 'souvenir' tucked away somewhere; some knew places where guns could be bought and sold, no questions asked . . .

'And by the way,' Siobhan was saying, 'it's guns plural.'

'He was carrying more than one?'

She shook her head. 'But one was found during a search of his boathouse.' She referred to her notes again. 'Mac 10.'

'That's a serious gun.'

'You know it?'

'Ingram Mac 10 . . . it's American. Thousand-round-a-minute job. Not something you'd be able to walk into a shop and buy.'

'Lab seems to think it had been deactivated at one time, meaning that's exactly what you could do.'

'He tweaked it, too?'

'Or bought it tweaked.'

'Thank Christ he didn't take that one to the school. It would have been carnage.'

The room went quiet as they considered this. They went back to their search.

'This is interesting,' she said, waving one of the books at him. 'Story of a soldier who cracked up, tried to kill his girlfriend.' She studied the jacket. 'Jumped from a plane and killed himself . . . True-life, by the look of it.' Something fell from between two pages. A snapshot. Siobhan picked it up, turned it round for Rebus to see. 'Tell me it's not her again.'

But it was. It was Teri Cotter, taken fairly recently. She was outdoors, other bodies edging into the picture. A street

71

scene, maybe in Edinburgh. She looked to be seated on a pavement, wearing much the same clothes as when she'd helped Rebus smoke his cigarette. She was sticking her studded tongue out towards the photographer.

'She looks cheery,' Siobhan commented.

Rebus was studying the photo. He turned it over, but the back was blank. 'She said she knew the boys who died. Never thought to ask if she knew their killer.'

'And Kate Renshaw's theory that Herdman might connect to the Cotters?'

Rebus shrugged. 'Might be worth looking at Herdman's bank account for signs of blood money.' He heard a door close downstairs. 'Sounds like one of the neighbours is home. Shall we?'

Siobhan nodded and they left the flat, making sure it was locked behind them. On the landing below, Rebus put an ear first to one door and then to the other, finally nodding at the second. Siobhan banged on it with her fist. By the time the door opened, she had her ID out.

Two surnames on the door: the teacher and his girlfriend. It was the girlfriend who answered. She was short and blonde, and would have been pretty were it not for a sideways jutting of her jaw which gave her what Siobhan guessed was a semi-permanent scowl.

'I'm DS Clarke, this is DI Rebus,' Siobhan said. 'Mind if we ask you a couple of questions?'

The young woman looked from one to the other. 'We already told the other lot everything we know.'

'We appreciate that, miss,' Rebus said. He saw her eyes drop to stare at his gloves. 'But you do live here, right?'

'Aye.'

'We understand that you got on fine with Mr Herdman, even though he could be a bit noisy sometimes.'

'Just when he had a party, like. It was never a problem – we raise the roof ourselves now and then.'

'You share his taste for heavy metal?'

She wrinkled her nose. 'More of a Robbie woman myself.'

'She means Robbie Williams,' Siobhan informed Rebus.

'I'd have worked it out eventually,' Rebus sniffed.

'Good news was, he only ever played that stuff when he was partying.'

'Did you ever get an invite?'

She shook her head.

'Show Miss . . .' Rebus was talking to Siobhan, but broke off and smiled at the neighbour. 'Sorry, I don't know your name.'

'Hazel Sinclair.'

He added a nod to his smile. 'DS Clarke, can you show Miss Sinclair . . .'

But Siobhan already had the photograph out. She handed it to Hazel Sinclair.

'It's Miss Teri,' the young woman stated.

'You've seen her around then?'

'Of course. Looks like she's just stepped out of *The Addams Family*. I often see her down the High Street.'

'But have you seen her here?'

'Here?' Sinclair thought about it, the effort further distorting her jawline. Then she shook her head. 'I always thought he was gay anyway.'

'He had kids,' Siobhan said, taking back the photo.

'Doesn't mean much, does it? Lot of gays are married. And he was in the army, probably a ton of gays in there.'

Siobhan tried to suppress a smile. Rebus shifted his feet.

'Besides,' Hazel Sinclair was saying, 'it was always guys you saw coming up and down the stairs.' She paused for effect. 'Young guys.'

'Any of them look as good as Robbie?'

Sinclair shook her head dramatically. 'I'd eat breakfast off his backside any day of the week.'

'We'll try to keep that out of our report,' Rebus said, dignity intact as both women cracked up with laughter.

*

In the car on the way to Port Edgar marina, Rebus looked at some photos of Lee Herdman. Mostly they were copied from newspapers. Herdman seemed tall and wiry, with a mop of curly greying hair. Wrinkles around his eyes, a face lined with the years. Tanned, too, or more likely weather-beaten. Glancing out, Rebus saw that the clouds had gathered overhead, covering the sky like a grubby sheet. The photos had all been taken outdoors: Herdman working on his boat, or heading out into the estuary. In one, he gave a wave to whoever had been left ashore. There was a broad smile on his face, as though this was as good as life could get. Rebus had never seen the point of sailing. He supposed the boats looked pretty enough from a distance, when watched from one of the pubs on the waterfront.

'Have you ever sailed?' he asked Siobhan.

'I've been on a few ferries.'

'I meant on a yacht. You know, hoisting the spinnaker and all that.'

She looked at him. 'Is that what you do with a spinnaker?'

'Buggered if I know.' Rebus looked up. They were passing beneath the Forth Road Bridge, the marina down a narrow road just past the huge concrete stanchions which seemed to lift the bridge skywards. This was the sort of thing that impressed Rebus: not nature, but ingenuity. He thought sometimes that all man's greatest achievements had come from a battle with nature. Nature provided the problems, humans found the solutions.

'This is it,' Siobhan said, turning the car through an open gateway. The marina comprised a series of buildings – some more ramshackle than others – and two long jetties jutting out into the Firth of Forth. At one of these, a few dozen boats had been moored. They passed the marina office and something called the Bosun's Locker, and parked next to the cafeteria.

'According to the notes, there's a sailing club, a sail-maker's, and somewhere that'll fix your radar,' Siobhan said, getting out. She started round to the passenger side, but Rebus was able to open his own door.

'See?' he said. 'I'm not quite at the knacker's yard yet.' But through the material of the gloves, his fingers stung. He straightened and looked around. The bridge was high overhead, the rush of cars quieter than he'd expected, and almost drowned out by the clanging of whatever it was on boats that made that clanging sound. Maybe it was the spinnakers . . .

'Who owns this place?' he asked.

'Sign at the gate said something about Edinburgh Leisure.'

'Meaning the city council? Which means that technically speaking, you and me own it.'

'Technically speaking,' Siobhan agreed. She was busy studying a hand-drawn plan. 'Herdman's boat-shed is on the right, past the toilets.' She pointed. 'Down there, I think.'

'Good, you can catch me up,' Rebus told her. Then he nodded towards the cafeteria. 'Coffee to go, and not too hot.'

'Not scalding, you mean?' She made for the cafeteria steps. 'Sure you can manage on your own?'

Rebus stayed by the car as she disappeared, the door rattling behind her. He took his time lifting cigarettes and lighter from his pocket. Opened the packet and nipped a cigarette out with his teeth, sucking it into his mouth. The lighter was a lot easier than matches, once he'd found a bit of shelter from the wind. He was leaning against the car, relishing the smoke, when Siobhan reappeared.

'Here you go,' she said, handing him a half-filled beaker. 'Lots of milk.'

He stared at the pale grey surface. 'Thanks.'

Together, they headed off, turning a couple of corners and finding no one around, despite the half-dozen cars parked alongside Siobhan's. 'Down here,' she said, leading them ever closer to the bridge. Rebus had noted that one of the long jetties was actually a wooden pontoon, providing tie-ups for visiting boats.

'This must be it,' Siobhan said, tossing her half-empty cup into a nearby bin. Rebus did the same, though he'd only taken a couple of sips of the warmish, milkyish concoction. If there was caffeine in there, he'd failed to find it. Bless the Lord for nicotine.

The shed was just that: a shed, albeit a well-fed example of the species. About twenty feet wide, knocked together from a mixture of wooden slats and corrugated metal. Half its width comprised a sliding door, which stood closed. Two sets of chains lay on the ground, evidence that police had forced their way in with bolt-cutters. A length of blue and white tape had replaced the chains, and someone had fixed an official notice to the door, warning that entry was prohibited under pain of prosecution. A handmade sign above announced that the shed was actually 'SKI AND BOAT – prop. L Herdman'.

'Catchy title,' Rebus mused, as Siobhan untied the tape and pushed the door open.

'Does exactly what it says on the tin,' she responded in kind. This was where Herdman ran his business, teaching fledgling sailors and scaring the wits out of his water-skiing clientele. Inside, Rebus could see a dinghy, maybe a twenty-footer. It sat on a trailer whose tyres needed some air. There were a couple of power-boats, too, again on trailers, their outboard motors gleaming, as was a new-looking jet-ski. The place was almost too tidy, as though swept and polished by an obsessive. Against one wall stood a workbench, the tools neatly arrayed on the wall above. A single oily rag gave the clue that mechanical work might actually go on here, lest the unwary visitor suspect they'd stepped into the marina's exhibit space.

'Where was the gun found?' Rebus asked, walking in.

'Cupboard under the workbench.'

Rebus looked: a neatly severed padlock lay on the

76

concrete floor. The cupboard door was open, showing only a selection of ratchets and spanners.

'Don't suppose there's much left for us to find,' Siobhan stated.

'Probably not.' But Rebus was still interested, curious as to what the space could tell him about Lee Herdman. So far it told him Herdman had been a conscientious worker, tidying up after himself. His flat had indicated a man who wasn't nearly so fussy in his personal life. But professionally . . . professionally, Herdman gave a hundred per cent. This chimed with his background. In the army, it didn't matter how messy your personal life might be, you didn't let it interfere with your work. Rebus had known soldiers whose marriages were collapsing, but still kept their kit immaculate, perhaps because, as one RSM had put it, *the army's the best fucking shag you'll ever have . . .*

'What do you think?' Siobhan asked.

'It's almost as if he was waiting for a visit from Health and Safety.'

'Looks to me like his boats are worth more than his flat.'

'Agreed.'

'Signs of a split personality . . .'

'How so?'

'Chaotic home life, quite the opposite at his place of work. Cheap flat and furnishings, expensive boats . . .'

'Quite the little psychoanalyst,' a voice boomed from behind them. The speaker was a stocky woman of about fifty, hair pulled back so tightly into a bun that it seemed to push her face forward. She was wearing a black two-piece suit and plain black shoes, olive-coloured blouse with a string of pearls at the neck. A black leather backpack was slung over one shoulder. Next to her stood a tall, broad-shouldered man maybe half her age, black hair cropped short, hands pressed together in front of him. He wore a dark suit, white shirt and navy tie.

'You'll be Detective Inspector Rebus,' the woman said, stepping forward briskly as if to shake hands, unfazed when Rebus didn't reciprocate. Her voice had dropped a single decibel. 'I'm Whiteread, this is Simms.' Her small, beady eyes fixed on Rebus. 'You've been to the flat, I take it? DI Hogan said you might . . .' Her voice drifted off as she moved just as briskly away from Rebus, into the interior of the shed. She circled the dinghy, inspecting it with a buyer's eye. English accent, Rebus was thinking.

'I'm DS Clarke,' Siobhan piped up. Whiteread stared at her, and gave the briefest of smiles.

'Of course you are,' she said.

Simms had walked forward meantime, repeating his name by way of introduction and then turning to Siobhan to go through the exact same procedure, but this time with a handshake. His accent was English, too, voice emotionless, the pleasantries a formality.

'Where was the gun found?' Whiteread asked. Then she noticed the broken padlock, and answered her own question with a nod, walking over to the cupboard and squatting down sharply in front of it, her skirt rising to just above the knees.

'Mac 10,' she stated. 'Notorious for jamming.' She stood up again, patted her skirt back down.

'Better than some kit,' Simms responded. Introductions over, he was standing between Rebus and Siobhan, legs slightly apart, back straight, hands again clasped in front of him.

'Care to show some ID?' Rebus asked.

'DI Hogan knows we're here,' Whiteread replied casually. She was examining the surface of the workbench now. Rebus followed her slowly.

'I asked you for ID,' he said.

'I'm well aware of that,' Whiteread said, her attention shifting to what looked like a small office at the rear of the building. She made off towards it, Rebus at her heels.

'You're marching,' he warned her. 'Dead giveaway.' She said nothing. The office had once sported a large padlock, but it, too, had been broken open, and the door fixed shut afterwards with more police-issue tape. 'Plus your partner used the word "kit",' Rebus went on. Whiteread peeled the tape away and looked inside. Desk, chair, a single filing-cabinet. No space for anything else, other than what looked like a two-way radio on a shelf. No computers or copiers or fax machines. The desk drawers had been opened, contents examined. Whiteread lifted out a sheaf and started flipping through.

'You're army,' Rebus stated into the silence. 'You might be in mufti, but you're still army. No women in the SAS as far as I know, so what does that make you?'

She snapped her head towards him. 'It makes me someone who can help.'

'Help what?'

'With this sort of thing.' She went back to her work. 'To stop it happening again.'

Rebus stared at her. Siobhan and Simms were standing just outside the door. 'Siobhan, call Bobby Hogan for me. I want to know what he knows about these two.'

'He knows we're here,' Whiteread said, not looking up. 'He even told me we might be bumping into you. How else would I know your name?'

Siobhan had the mobile in her hand. 'Make the call,' Rebus told her.

Whiteread stuffed the paperwork back into its drawer and pushed it shut. 'You never quite made it into the Regiment, did you, DI Rebus?' She turned slowly towards him. 'Way I hear it, the training broke you.'

'How come you're not in uniform?' Rebus asked.

'It scares some people,' Whiteread said.

'Is that it? Couldn't be that you don't want to add to all the bad publicity?' Rebus was smiling coldly. 'Doesn't look good when one of your own throws a maddie, does it? Last thing you want is to remind everybody that he was one of yours.'

'What's done is done. If we can stop it happening again, so much the better.' She paused, standing right in front of him. Half a foot shorter, but every bit his equal. 'Why should you have a problem with that?' Now she returned his smile. If his had been cold, hers came straight from the deep-freeze. 'You fell down, didn't make the grade. No need to let that get to you, Detective Inspector.'

Rebus heard 'Detective' as 'Defective'. Either her accent, or she'd been trying for the pun. Siobhan had been connected, but it was taking a few moments for Hogan to come to the phone.

'We should take a look in the boat,' Whiteread said to her partner, squeezing past Rebus.

'There's a ladder,' Simms said. Rebus tried to place the accent: Lancashire or Yorkshire maybe. Whiteread he wasn't so sure about. Home Counties, whatever that meant. A kind of generic English as taught in the posher schools. Rebus realised, too, that Simms didn't appear comfortable in either his suit or this role. Maybe it was a class thing again, or maybe he was new to both.

'First name's John, by the way,' Rebus told him. 'What's yours?'

Simms looked to Whiteread. 'Well, tell the man!' she snapped.

'Gav . . . Gavin.'

'Gav to your friends, Gavin when on business?' Rebus guessed. Siobhan was handing him the phone. He took it.

'Bobby, what the hell are you doing letting two numpties from Her Majesty's armed forces crawl all over our case?' He paused to listen, then spoke again. 'I used the word advisedly, Bobby, as they're about to start crawling over Herdman's boat.' Another pause. 'That's hardly the point though . . .' And then: 'Okay, okay. We're on our way.' He pushed the phone back into Siobhan's hand. Simms was steadying the ladder while Whiteread climbed.

'We're just away,' Rebus called to her. 'And if we don't see each other again . . . well, I'll be crying inside, believe me. The smile will just be for show.'

He waited for the woman to say something, but she was

80

aboard now and seemed to have lost interest in him. Simms was climbing the ladder, giving a backwards glance towards the two detectives.

'I've half a mind,' Rebus said to Siobhan, 'to grab the ladder and run for it.'

'I don't think that would stop her, do you?'

'Probably right,' he admitted. Then, raising his voice: 'One last thing, Whiteread – young Gav was looking up your skirt!'

As Rebus turned to leave, he shrugged at Siobhan, as if to acknowledge that the shot had been cheap.

Cheap, but worthwhile.

'I mean it, Bobby, what the hell's the matter with you?' Rebus was walking down one of the school's long corridors towards what looked very much like a floor-to-ceiling safe, the old kind with a wheel and some tumblers. It stood open, as did an interior steel gate. Hogan was staring inside.

'God almighty, man, those bastards have no place here.'

'John,' Hogan said quietly, 'I don't think you've met the principal . . .' He gestured into the vault, where a middle-aged man was standing, surrounded by enough guns to start a revolution. 'Dr Fogg,' Hogan said, by way of introduction.

Fogg stepped over the threshold. He was a short, stocky man with the look of a one-time boxer: one ear seemed puffy, and his nose covered half his face. A nick of scar tissue cut through one of his bushy eyebrows. 'Eric Fogg,' he said, shaking Rebus's hand.

'Sorry about my language back there, sir. I'm DI John Rebus.'

'Working in a school, you hear worse,' Fogg stated, making it sound like something he'd said a hundred times before.

Siobhan had caught up, and was about to introduce herself when she saw the contents of the vault.

'Jesus Christ!' she exclaimed.

'My thoughts exactly,' Rebus agreed.

'As I was explaining to DI Hogan,' Fogg began, 'most independent schools have something like this on the premises.'

'CCF, is that right, Dr Fogg?' Hogan added.

Fogg nodded. 'The Combined Cadet Force – army, navy and air force cadets. They parade each Friday afternoon.' He paused. 'I think a big incentive is that they can eschew school uniform that day.'

'For something slightly more paramilitary?' Rebus guessed.

'Automatic, semi-automatic and other weapons,' Hogan recited.

'Probably deters the odd housebreaker.'

'Actually,' Fogg said, 'I was just telling DI Hogan that if the school's alarm system is activated, the responding police units are instructed to make for the armoury first. It dates back to when the IRA and suchlike were looking for guns.'

'You're not saying the ammo's kept here, too?' Siobhan asked.

Fogg shook his head. 'There's no live ammo on the premises.'

'But the guns are real enough? They're not deactivated?'

'Oh, they're real enough.' He looked at the contents of the vault with something approaching distaste.

'You're not a fan?' Rebus guessed.

'I think the practice is . . . slightly in danger of outliving its useful application.'

'There speaks a diplomat,' Rebus said, forcing a smile from the principal.

'Herdman didn't get his gun from here?' Siobhan was asking.

Hogan shook his head. 'That's another thing I'm hoping the army investigators might help us with.' He looked at Rebus. 'Always supposing you can't.'

'Give us a break, Bobby. We've hardly been here five minutes.'

'Do you do any teaching, sir?' Siobhan asked Fogg, hoping to defuse any argument her two senior officers might be thinking of starting.

Fogg shook his head. 'I used to: RME – Religious and Moral Education.'

'Instilling a sense of morality in teenagers? That must've been tough.'

'I've yet to meet a teenager who started a war.' The voice rang slightly false: another prepared answer to an oft-put point.

'Only because we don't tend to give them the firepower,' Rebus commented, staring again at the array of arms.

Fogg was relocking the iron gate.

'So nothing's missing?' Rebus asked.

Hogan shook his head. 'But both victims were in the CCF.'

Rebus looked to Fogg, who nodded confirmation. 'Anthony was a very keen member . . . Derek a little less so.'

Anthony Jarvies: the judge's son. His father, Roland Jarvies, was well known in Scottish courts. Rebus had probably given evidence fifteen or twenty times in cases over which Lord Jarvies had presided with wit and what one lawyer had described as 'a gimlet eye'. Rebus wasn't sure what a gimlet eye was, but he got the idea.

'We were wondering,' Siobhan was saying, 'whether anyone's been looking at Herdman's bank or building society.'

Hogan studied her. 'His accountant's been very helpful. Business wasn't going to the wall or anything.'

'But no sudden deposits?' Rebus asked.

Hogan narrowed his eyes. 'Why?'

Rebus glanced in the principal's direction. He hadn't meant for Fogg to notice, but he did.

'Would you like me to . . .?' Fogg said.

'We're not quite finished, Dr Fogg, if that's all right.' Hogan's eyes met Rebus's. 'I'm sure whatever DI Rebus wants to say will be kept between us.'

'Of course,' Fogg stressed. He had locked the door of the vault, and now turned the combination wheel.

'The other kid who was killed,' Rebus started to explain to Hogan. 'He was in a car crash last year. The driver was killed. We're wondering if it's too far back for revenge to be a motive.'

'Doesn't explain why Herdman would top himself after.'

'Botched job maybe,' Siobhan said, folding her arms. 'Two other kids got hit, Herdman panicked . . .'

'So when you talk about Herdman's bank, you're thinking a big, recent deposit?'

Rebus nodded.

'I'll get someone to take a look. Only thing we've got from his business accounts is a missing computer.'

'Oh?'

Siobhan asked if it could be a tax dodge.

'Could be,' Hogan agreed. 'But there's a receipt. We've talked to the shop that sold him the set-up – top of the range.'

'Reckon he ditched it?' Rebus asked.

'Why would he do that?'

Rebus shrugged.

'Perhaps to cover something up?' Fogg suggested. When they looked at him, he lowered his eyes. 'Not that it's my place to . . .'

'Don't apologise, sir,' Hogan reassured him. 'You might have a good point.' Hogan rubbed a hand across his eyes, turned his attention back to Rebus. 'Anything else?'

'These army bastards,' Rebus began. Hogan held up the same hand.

'You just have to accept them.'

'Come on, they're not here to shed any light. If anything, it'll be the opposite. They want his SAS past forgotten, hence the plain-clothes. For Whiteread read "whitewash".'

'Look, I'm sorry if they're stepping on your toes—'

'Or trampling us to death,' Rebus interrupted.

'John, this investigation's bigger than you and me, bigger than *anything*!' Hogan's voice had risen, quavering slightly. 'Last thing I need is this sort of shit!'

'Language, please, Bobby,' Rebus said, glancing meaningfully towards Fogg.

As Rebus had hoped, Hogan started to remember Rebus's own recent outburst, and his face cracked into a smile.

'Just get on with it, eh?'

'We're on your side, Bobby.'

Siobhan took a step forward. 'One thing we'd like to do . . .' She ignored Rebus's gaze, a gaze which said this was the first he'd heard of it, '. . . is interview the survivor.'

Hogan frowned. 'James Bell? What for?' His eyes were on Rebus, but it was Siobhan who answered.

'Because he survived, and he's the only one in the room who did.'

'We've talked to him half a dozen times. Kid's in shock, God knows what else.'

'We'd go easy,' Siobhan insisted quietly.

'*You* might, but then it's not you that worries me . . .' His eyes were still on Rebus.

'It'd be good to hear it from someone who was there,' Rebus said. 'How Herdman acted, anything he said. Nobody seems to have seen him that morning: not the neighbours, no one at the marina. We need to fill in some of the blanks.'

Hogan sighed. 'First of all, listen to the tapes.' Meaning recordings of the interviews with James Bell. 'If you still think you need to see him face to face . . . well, we'll see.'

'Thank you, sir,' Siobhan said, feeling the moment merited a certain formality.

'I said we'll see: no promises.' Hogan raised a warning finger.

'And take another look at his finances?' Rebus added. 'Just in case.'

Hogan nodded tiredly.

'Ah, there you are!' a voice boomed. Jack Bell was marching down the corridor towards them.

'Oh, Christ,' Hogan muttered. But Bell's attention was focused on the principal.

'Eric,' he said loudly, 'what the hell's this I'm hearing that you won't go on the record about the school's inadequate security?'

'The school had adequate security, Jack,' Fogg said with a sigh, indicating that this was an argument he'd had before.

'Complete rubbish, and you know it. Look, all I'm trying to do is highlight that the lessons of Dunblane have not been learned.' He held up a finger. 'Our schools still aren't safe . . .' A second finger was raised. 'And guns are flooding the streets.' He paused for effect. 'And something's got to be done, you must see that.' His eyes narrowed. 'I could have lost my son!'

'A school is not a fortress, Jack,' the principal pleaded, but to no effect.

'Nineteen ninety-seven,' Bell steamrollered on, 'aftermath of Dunblane, hand weapons above point-two-two were banned. Legitimate owners surrendered their weapons, and what did that leave us?' He looked around, but no answer was forthcoming. 'The only people hanging on to their guns were the underworld, who seem to find it increasingly easy to get hold of any amount of armaments they desire!'

'You're preaching to the wrong audience,' Rebus stated.

Bell stared at him. 'Maybe I am,' he agreed, pointing a finger. 'Because you lot seem utterly incapable of tackling the problem to any degree whatsoever!'

'Now hang on, sir,' Hogan started to argue.

'Let him rattle on, Bobby,' Rebus interrupted. 'The hot air might help keep the school heated.'

'How dare you!' Bell snarled. 'What makes you think you can talk to me like that?'

'I suppose I just *elected* to,' Rebus retorted, stressing the word, reminding the MSP of the precarious nature of his calling.

In the silence that followed, Bell's mobile phone began to trill. He managed a sneer in Rebus's direction before turning on his heels, moving a few paces back down the corridor as he answered the call.

'Yes? What?' Glanced at his wristwatch. 'Is it radio or TV?' Listened again. 'Local radio or national? I'll only do national . . .' He kept walking, leaving his audience to relax a little, sharing looks and gestures.

'Right,' the principal was saying, 'I suppose I'd best get back to . . .'

'Mind if I walk you to your office, sir?' Hogan asked. 'Couple more things we need to talk about.' He nodded towards Rebus and Siobhan. 'Back to work,' he said.

'Yes, sir,' Siobhan agreed. Suddenly the corridor was empty, save for Rebus and her. She puffed out her cheeks, then exhaled noisily. 'Bell's a real piece of work.'

Rebus nodded. 'He's ready to exploit this whole thing to the hilt.'

'He wouldn't be a politician if he didn't.'

'Natural instincts, eh? Funny how things turn out. His career could have gone down the pan after he was nabbed in Leith.'

'Think he wants a spot of revenge?'

'He'll drag us down if he can. We have to make sure we're moving targets.'

'And that was you being a "moving target", was it? Answering him back like that?'

'Man's got to have a little fun, Siobhan.' Rebus stared down the empty corridor. 'You think Bobby's going to be okay?'

'He looked knackered, if I'm being honest. By the way . . . you don't think he needs to be told?'

'Told what?'

'That the Renshaws are your family.'

Rebus fixed her with his eyes. 'Might lead to complications. I don't think Bobby needs any more of those right now.'

'It's your decision.'

'That's right, it is. And we both know I'm never wrong.'

'I'd forgotten that,' Siobhan said.

'Happy to remind you, DS Clarke. Always happy to oblige . . .'

5

South Queensferry police station was a squat box, most of it single-storey, and sited across the road from an Episcopal church. A notice outside stated that the station was open for public enquiries between nine and five on weekdays, manned by a 'civilian assistant'. Another notice explained that there was, contrary to local rumours, a twenty-four-hour police presence in the town. This soulless spot was where the witnesses had been interviewed, all except James Bell.

'Cosy, isn't it?' Siobhan said, pulling open the front door. There was a short, narrow waiting area, its only inhabitant a constable who put down his bike magazine and lifted himself from his seat.

'At ease,' Rebus told him, while Siobhan showed her ID. 'We need to listen to the Bell tapes.'

The officer nodded and unlocked an interior door, leading them into a dispiriting, windowless room. The desk and chairs had seen better days. Last year's calendar – promoting the merits of a local shop – curled on one wall. There was a tape player on top of a filing cabinet. The uniform lifted it down and plugged it in, placing it on the desk. Then he unlocked the cabinet and found the correct tape, sealed in a clear plastic bag.

'This is the first of six,' he explained. 'You'll need to sign for it.' Siobhan did the necessary.

'Any ashtrays around here?' Rebus asked.

'No, sir. Smoking's not allowed.'

'That was more information than I needed.'

'Yes, sir.' The constable was trying not to stare at Rebus's gloves.

'Is there so much as a kettle?'

'No, sir.' The constable paused. 'Neighbours sometimes drop off a flask or a bit of cake.'

'Any chance of that happening in the next ten minutes?'

'Unlikely, I'd say.'

'Off you go and do some foraging then. See what marks you can get for initiative.'

The constable hesitated. 'I'm supposed to stay here.'

'We'll guard the fort, son,' Rebus said, sliding off his jacket and hanging it over the back of a chair.

The constable looked sceptical.

'I'll take mine white,' Rebus said.

'Me too, no sugar,' Siobhan added.

The constable stood there a moment or two longer, watching them get as comfortable as the room would allow. Then he backed out and closed the door slowly after him.

Rebus and Siobhan looked at one another and shared a complicit smile. Siobhan had brought the notes relevant to James Bell, and Rebus reread them while she took the tape out and slotted it home.

Eighteen ... son of the MSP Jack Bell and his wife Felicity, who worked as an administrator at the Traverse Theatre. The family lived in Barnton. James intended going to university to study politics and economics ... a 'competent pupil', according to the school: 'James goes his own way, not always outgoing, but can turn on the charm when necessary.' He preferred chess to sport.

'Probably not CCF material,' Rebus mused. A moment later, he was listening to James Bell's voice.

The interviewing officers identified themselves: DI Hogan, DC Hood. A shrewd move, involving Grant Hood: being press liaison officer on the case, he would need to know the survivor's story. Some of it might provide morsels which he could offer to the journos in return for favours. It was important to have the media on your side; important, too, to maintain as much control over them as possible. They wouldn't be getting near James Bell yet. They'd have to go through Grant Hood.

Bobby Hogan's voice identified the date and time – Monday evening – and the scene of the interview – A&E at the Royal Infirmary. Bell had been wounded in the left shoulder. A clean shot, ripping through flesh, missing bones, exiting again, the bullet lodged in the wall of the common room.

'*Are you up to talking, James?*'

'*I think so . . . hurts like buggery.*'

'*I'm sure it does. For the tape then, you are James Elliot Bell, is that correct?*'

'*Yes.*'

'Elliot?' Siobhan asked.

'Mother's maiden name,' Rebus explained, checking the notes again.

Very little background noise: had to be a private room at the hospital. A clearing of the throat from Grant Hood. The squall of a squeaky chair. Hood probably holding the mike, his chair closest to the bed. Turning the mike between Hogan and the boy, not always timing it right, so that a voice was sometimes muffled.

'*Can you tell me what happened, Jamie?*'

'*Please, my name's James. Could I have some water?*'

The sound of the mike being laid down on top of bedclothes, water poured.

'*Thank you.*' A pause until the cup was replaced on the bedside cabinet. Rebus thought of his own cup falling, Siobhan catching it. Like James Bell, on Monday night he, too, had been in hospital . . . '*It was mid-morning break. We get twenty minutes. I was in the common room.*'

'*Was that your usual hang-out?*'

'*Better there than the grounds.*'

'*It wasn't a bad day though: warm enough.*'

'I prefer to be inside. Do you think I'll be able to play the guitar when I get out of here?'

'I don't know,' Hogan said. 'Could you play before you came in?'

'You spoilt the patient's punchline. Shame on you.'

'Sorry about that, James. So how many of you were in the common room?'

'Three. Tony Jarvies, Derek Renshaw and me.'

'And what were you doing there?'

'There was some music on the hi-fi ... I think Jarvies was doing homework, Renshaw was reading the paper.'

'Is that how you talk to one another? Using surnames?'

'Most of the time.'

'The three of you were friends?'

'Not especially.'

'But you often spent time together in the common room?'

'More than a dozen of us use that room.' A pause. 'Are you trying to ask me if I think he targeted us deliberately?'

'It's one thing we're wondering about.'

'Why?'

'Because it was break time, lots of pupils outdoors ...'

'But he walked into the school, into the common room, before he started shooting?'

'You'd make a good detective, James.'

'It's not high on my list of career options.'

'Did you know the gunman?'

'Yes.'

'You knew him?'

'Lee Herdman, yes. Quite a lot of us knew him. Some of us took water-skiing lessons. And he was an interesting guy.'

'Interesting?'

'His background. The man was a trained killer, after all.'

'He told you that?'

'Yes. He was in Special Forces.'

'Did he know Anthony and Derek?'

'Quite possibly.'

'But he knew you?'

'We'd met socially.'

'Then you've maybe been asking yourself the same question we have.'

'You mean, why did he do it?'

'Yes.'

'I've heard that people with his sort of background ... they don't always fit into society, do they? Something happens, and it tips them over the edge.'

'Any idea what tipped Lee Herdman over the edge?'

'No.' A long pause followed, the mike muffled against the sheets as the two detectives seemed to confer. Then Hogan's voice again.

'So can you take us through it, James? You were in the room ...'

'I'd just put on a CD. One thing the three of us didn't share was musical taste. When the door opened, I don't think I even bothered looking round. Then there was this horrendous explosion, and Jarvies collapsed. I'd been crouching in front of the hi-fi, but I stood up again, turning. I saw this huge-looking gun. I mean, I'm not saying it was particularly large, but it seemed that way, pointing at Renshaw now ... There was a figure behind the gun, but I couldn't really see him ...'

'Because of the smoke?'

'No ... I don't remember smoke. The only thing I seemed to be able to focus on was the gun barrel ... I was sort of frozen. Then a second explosion, and Renshaw sort of collapsed like a puppet, just crumpled to the floor ...'

Rebus found that he'd closed his eyes. It wasn't the first time he'd pictured the scene.

'Then he turned the gun on me ...'

'Did you know who he was by this point?'

'Yes, I suppose so.'

'Did you say anything?'

'I don't know ... maybe I opened my mouth to say something ... I think I must have started moving, because when the shot came it ... well, it didn't kill me, did it? It was like a hard shove, pushing me back and over.'

'He hadn't said anything up to this point?'

'Not a word. Mind you, my ears were ringing.'

'Small room like that, I'm not surprised. Is your hearing okay now?'

'There's still a hissing, but they say that'll go away.'

'He didn't say anything?'

'I didn't hear him say anything. I just lay there, getting ready to play dead. And then there was the fourth shot . . . and for a split second I thought it was me . . . finishing me off. But when I heard the body fall, I sort of knew . . .'

'What did you do?'

'I opened my eyes. I was at floor level, and I could see his body through the legs of the chair. He still had the gun in his hand. I started to get up. My shoulder was feeling numb, and I knew there was blood pouring out, but I couldn't take my eyes off the gun. I know this'll sound ridiculous, but I was thinking of those horror films, you know?'

Hood's voice: 'Where you think the bad guy's dead . . .'

'And he keeps coming back to life, yes. And then there were people in the doorway . . . teaching staff, I suppose. They must have got a hell of a shock.'

'What about you, James? You bearing up?'

'To be honest, I'm not sure it's really hit me yet – pardon the pun. We're all being offered counselling. I suppose that'll help.'

'You've been through an ordeal.'

'I have, haven't I? Something to tell the grandkids, I suppose.'

'He's so calm about it,' Siobhan said. Rebus nodded.

'We really appreciate you talking to us. Would it be okay if we left you a notepad and pen? You see, James, you're probably going to find yourself going back over it time and again in your mind – and that's good, it's how we deal with things like this. But maybe you'll remember something, and want to write it down. Putting it all down is one more way of dealing with it.'

'Yes, I can see that.'

'And we'll want to talk to you again.'

Hood's voice: 'As will the media. It's down to you whether

you want to say anything to them, but I can talk you through it, if you like.'

'I won't be talking to anybody for a day or two. And don't worry, I know all about the media.'

'Well, thanks again for this, James. I think your mum and dad are waiting outside.'

'Look, I'm feeling a bit tired after everything. Do you think you could tell them I've nodded off?'

At which point the tape went dead. Siobhan let it run for a few more seconds, then switched off the machine. 'End of first interview – want to listen to another?' She nodded towards the filing-cabinet. Rebus shook his head.

'Not for now, but I'd still like to talk to him,' he said. 'He says he knew Herdman. That makes him relevant.'

'He also says he doesn't know why Herdman did it.'

'All the same . . .'

'He sounded so calm.'

'Probably the shock. Hood was right, it takes time to sink in.'

Siobhan was thoughtful. 'Why do you think he didn't want to see his parents?'

'Are you forgetting who his dad is?'

'Yes, but all the same . . . Something like that happens, doesn't matter what age you are, you want a hug.'

Rebus looked at her. 'Do you?'

'*Most* people would . . . most normal people, I mean.' A knock at the door. It opened a fraction and the constable's head appeared.

'No joy with the drinks,' he said.

'We're done here anyway. Thanks for trying.'

They left the constable to lock the tape away again and headed out squinting into daylight. 'James didn't tell us much, did he?' Siobhan said.

'No,' Rebus admitted. He was replaying the interview in his mind, seeking anything they could use. The only glimmer: James Bell had known Herdman. But so what? Plenty of people in the town had known Lee Herdman.

'Shall we head up the High Street, see if we can find a café?'

'I know where we can get a cuppa,' Rebus said.

'Where?'

'Same place we got one yesterday . . .'

Allan Renshaw hadn't shaved since the day before. He was alone in the house, having sent Kate out to see some friends.

'Not good for her being cooped up here with me,' he said as he led them through to the kitchen. The living room hadn't been touched, photos still waiting to be pored over, sorted, or shoved back into their boxes. Rebus noted that some remembrance cards had appeared on the mantelpiece. Renshaw picked up a remote from the arm of the sofa and switched off the TV. A video had been playing, homemade, family holiday. Rebus decided not to comment. Renshaw's hair stuck up in places, and Rebus wondered if he'd slept in his clothes. Renshaw sat down heavily on one of the kitchen chairs, leaving Siobhan to fill the kettle. Boethius was lying on the worktop, and Siobhan made to stroke him, but the cat leapt on to the floor and padded through to the living room.

Rebus sat down opposite his cousin. 'Just wondered how you were,' he said.

'Sorry I left you with Kate the other night.'

'No need to apologise. You sleeping okay?'

'Far too much.' A humourless smile. 'A way of shutting it all out, I suppose.'

'How are the funeral arrangements?'

'They won't let us have his body, not just yet.'

'It'll be soon, Allan. It'll all be over soon.'

Renshaw looked up at him with bloodshot eyes. 'You promise, John?' He waited till Rebus nodded. 'Then how come the phone keeps ringing, reporters wanting to talk to me? They don't think it's going to end soon.'

'Yes they do. That's why they're pestering you. They'll

move on somewhere else in a day or so, just you watch. Anyone in particular you want me to chase off?'

'There's a guy Kate's talked to. He seems to upset her.'

'What's his name?'

'It's written down somewhere . . .' Renshaw looked around as if the name might be right there under his nose.

'Next to the phone maybe?' Rebus guessed. He got up and walked back into the hall. The phone was on a ledge just inside the front door. Rebus picked it up, hearing only silence. He saw that the line had been disconnected at its wall point: Kate's work. There was a pen next to the phone, but no paper. He looked over towards the stairs and saw a pad. Scribbled names and numbers on its top sheet.

Rebus walked back through to the kitchen, placing the notepad on the table.

'Steve Holly,' he announced.

'That's the name,' Renshaw agreed.

Siobhan, who'd been pouring tea, paused and looked at Rebus. They both knew Steve Holly. He worked for a Glasgow tabloid, and had proved his nuisance value in the past.

'I'll have a word,' Rebus promised, reaching into his pocket for the painkillers.

Siobhan handed round the mugs and sat down. 'You okay?' she asked.

'Fine,' Rebus lied.

'What happened to your hands, John?' Renshaw asked. Rebus shook his head.

'Nothing, Allan. How's the tea?'

'It's fine.' But Renshaw made no move to drink. Rebus stared at his cousin, thinking of the tape, of James Bell's calm narrative.

'Derek didn't suffer,' Rebus said quietly. 'Probably didn't know anything about it.'

Renshaw nodded.

'If you don't believe me . . . well, one day soon you'll be able to ask James Bell. He'll tell you.'

Another nod. 'I don't think I know him.'

'James?'

'Derek had a lot of friends, but I don't think he was one of them.'

'He was friends with Anthony Jarvies though?' Siobhan asked.

'Oh aye, Tony was round here a lot. They'd help one another with homework, listen to music . . .'

'What sort?' Rebus asked.

'Jazz mostly. Miles Davis, Coleman something . . . I forget the names. Derek said he was going to buy a tenor sax, learn to play it when he went to university.'

'Kate was saying Derek didn't know the man who shot him. Did you know him, Allan?'

'I'd seen him in the pub. Bit of a . . . loner's not the right word. But he wasn't always in company. Used to disappear for days at a time. Hill-walking or something. Or maybe away on that boat of his.'

'Allan . . . if this is out of order, you've every right to say so.'

Renshaw looked at him. 'What?'

'I was wondering if I could maybe take a look at Derek's room . . .'

Renshaw climbed the stairs in front of Rebus, Siobhan at the rear. He opened the door for them, but stood aside to let them enter.

'Haven't really had a chance to . . .' he apologised. 'Not that the place is . . .'

The bedroom was small, dark with the curtains closed.

'Mind if I open them?' Rebus asked. Renshaw just shrugged, unwilling to cross the threshold. Rebus pulled the curtains apart. The window looked down on to the back garden, where the dishcloth still hung from the whirligig, the mower still stood on the lawn. There were prints on the walls: moody black and white shots of jazz players. Photos torn from magazines showing elegant young women in repose. Bookshelves, a hi-fi, a fourteen-inch TV with integral video. A desk with a laptop computer connected to a printer. Barely leaving space for the single bed. Rebus looked at the spines of some of the CDs: Ornette Coleman, Coltrane, John Zorn, Archie Shepp, Thelonious Monk. There was some classical stuff, too. Draped over a chair: a running-vest and shorts, a sheathed tennis racket.

'Derek was into sports?' Rebus remarked.

'Did a lot of jogging and cross-country.'

'Who did he play tennis with?'

'Tony . . . a few others. Didn't get any of it from me, I'll tell you that.' Renshaw looked down at himself, as if assessing his girth. Siobhan gave him the smile she felt was expected. She knew though that there was nothing natural about anything he said. It was coming from a small part of his brain, while the rest still reeled in horror.

'He liked dressing up, too,' Rebus said, holding up a framed photo of Derek with Anthony Jarvies, both in their CCF uniforms and caps. Renshaw stared at it from the safety of the doorway.

'Derek only joined because of Tony,' he said. Rebus remembered Eric Fogg saying much the same thing.

'Did they ever go out sailing together?' Siobhan asked.

'Might have done. Kate tried water-skiing . . .' Renshaw's voice died. His eyes widened slightly. 'That bastard Herdman took her out in his boat . . . her and some friends. If I ever see him . . .'

'He's dead, Allan,' Rebus said, reaching out to touch his cousin's arm. Football . . . down in the park in Bowhill . . . young Allan grazing his knee on the tarmac, Rebus rubbing a dock leaf over the broken skin . . .

I had a family, but I let them get away . . . His wife estranged, daughter in England, brother God knew where.

'See when they bury him,' Renshaw was saying, 'I've a good mind to dig him up and kill him again.'

Rebus squeezed the arm, watching the man's eyes brim with fresh tears. 'Let's go down,' he said, guiding Renshaw back to the top of the stairs. There was just enough room for them to stand side by side in the passageway. Two grown men, hanging on.

'Allan,' Rebus said, 'any chance we could borrow Derek's laptop?'

'His laptop?' Rebus stayed silent. 'What's the point of . . .? I don't know, John.'

'Just for a day or two. I'll bring it back.'

Renshaw seemed to be having difficulty making sense of the request. 'I suppose . . . if you think . . .'

'Thanks, Allan.' Rebus turned his head, nodding towards Siobhan, who retreated back up the staircase.

Rebus took Renshaw into the living room, seating him on the sofa. Renshaw immediately picked up a handful of photographs.

'I need to get these sorted,' he said.

'What about work? How long are you off for?'

'They said I could go back after the funeral. It's a quiet time of year.'

'Maybe I'll come and see you,' Rebus said. 'It's time I traded my junk-heap in.'

'I'll look after you,' Renshaw promised, looking up at Rebus. 'You see if I don't.'

Siobhan had appeared in the doorway, laptop tucked beneath her arm, trailing cables.

'We better be going,' Rebus said to Renshaw. 'I'll look in again, Allan.'

'You'll always be welcome, John.' Renshaw made the effort to stand up, reaching out a hand. Then he pulled Rebus to him in a sudden embrace, slapping his hands against Rebus's back. Rebus returned the gesture, wondering if he looked as awkward as he felt. But Siobhan had averted her eyes, studying the tips of her shoes as if to assess their need for a polish. When they walked out to the car, Rebus realised he was sweating, his shirt sticking to him.

'Was it hot in there?'

'Not especially,' Siobhan said. 'You still running a temperature?'

'Looks like it.' He mopped his brow with the back of one glove.

'Why the laptop?'

'No reason really.' Rebus met her look. 'Maybe to see if there's anything about the car crash. How Derek felt, whether anyone blamed him.'

'Apart from the parents, you mean?'

Rebus nodded. 'Maybe . . . I don't know.' He sighed.

'What?'

'Maybe I just want to go through it to get a sense of the lad.' He was thinking of Allan, perhaps even now switching the TV back on and settling down with the video remote, bringing his son back to life in colour and sound and movement. But only a facsimile, contained by the tight confines of the box.

Siobhan nodded and bent down to slide the laptop on to the back seat of the car. 'I can understand that,' she said.

But Rebus wasn't so sure that she could.

'You keep up with your family?' he asked her.

'A phone call every other weekend.' He knew both her parents were alive, lived down south. Rebus's mother had died young; he'd been in his mid-thirties when his father had joined her.

'Did you ever want a sister or brother?' he asked.

'Sometimes, I suppose.' She paused. 'Something happened to you, didn't it?'

'How do you mean?'

'I don't know exactly.' She thought about it. 'I think at some point you decided that a family was a liability, because it could make you weak.'

'As you've already surmised, I was never one for hugs and kisses.'

'Maybe so, but you hugged your cousin back there . . .'

He got into the passenger seat and closed his door. The

painkillers were coating his brain in bubble-wrap. 'Just drive,' he said.

She put the key in the ignition. 'Where?'

Rebus remembered something. 'Get your mobile out and call the Portakabin.' She pushed the numbers and relinquished the phone to his outstretched hand. When it was answered, Rebus asked to speak to Grant Hood.

'Grant, it's John Rebus. Listen, I need a number for Steve Holly.'

'Any particular reason?'

'He's been hassling one of the families. I thought I'd have a quiet word.'

Hood cleared his throat. Rebus remembered the same sound from the tape, and wondered if it was becoming a regular thing with Hood. When the number came, Rebus repeated it so Siobhan could note it down.

'Hold on a minute, John. Boss wants a word.' Meaning Bobby Hogan.

'Bobby?' Rebus said. 'News on that bank account?'

'What?'

'The bank account . . . any big deposits? Jog your memory at all?'

'Never mind that.' There was urgency in Hogan's voice.

'What is it?' Rebus prompted.

'Seems Lord Jarvies put away one of Herdman's old pals.'

'Oh aye? When was this?'

'Just last year. Guy by the name of Robert Niles – ring any bells?'

Rebus furrowed his brow. 'Robert Niles?' he repeated. Siobhan nodded, made a slashing motion across her neck.

'The guy who cut his wife's throat?'

'That's the one,' Hogan said. 'Found fit to plead. Guilty verdict, and life from Lord Jarvies. I got a call, seems Herdman's been a regular visitor to Niles ever since.'

'What was it . . . nine, ten months back?'

'They put him in Barlinnie, but he flipped, went for another prisoner, then started cutting at himself.'

'So where's he now?'

'Carbrae Special Hospital.'

Rebus was thoughtful. 'You think Herdman was after the judge's son?'

'It's a possibility. Revenge and all that . . .'

Yes, revenge. That word now hung over both the dead boys . . .

'I'm going to see him,' Hogan was saying.

'Niles? Is he fit to see anyone?'

'Seems like. Want to tag along?'

'Bobby, I'm flattered. Why me?'

'Because Niles is ex-SAS, John. Served alongside Herdman. If anyone knows the inside of Lee Herdman's head, it's him.'

'A killer locked up in a psycho ward? My, aren't we lucky.'

'The offer's there, John.'

'When?'

'I was thinking first thing tomorrow. It's a couple of hours by car.'

'Count me in.'

'Good man. Who knows, you might get stuff out of Niles . . . empathy and all that.'

'You think so?'

'Way I see it, one look at your hands, and he'll take you for a fellow sufferer.'

Hogan was chuckling as Rebus handed the phone to Siobhan. She ended the call.

'I got most of that,' she said. Her phone chirruped immediately. It was Gill Templer.

'How come Rebus never answers his phone?' Templer bellowed.

'I think he has it switched off,' Siobhan said, eyes on Rebus. 'He can't push the buttons.'

'Funny, I've always taken him for an expert at pushing buttons.' Siobhan smiled: *especially yours*, she thought.

'Do you want him?' she asked.

'I want the pair of you back here,' Templer said. 'Pronto, with no excuses.'

'What's happened?'

'You've got trouble, that's what. The worst kind ...' Templer let her words hang in the air. Siobhan saw what she must mean.

'The papers?'

'Bingo. Someone's on to the story, only they've added some bells and whistles that I'd like John to explain to me.'

'What sort of bells and whistles?'

'He was spotted leaving the pub with Martin Fairstone, walking home with him, in fact. Spotted leaving, too, a good while later, and just before the house went up in flames. The paper in question is getting ready to lead with it.'

'We're on our way.'

'I'll be waiting.' The phone went dead. Siobhan started the car.

'We've to go back to St Leonard's,' she informed Rebus, going on to explain why.

'Which paper is it?' was all Rebus said, at the end of a lengthy silence.

'I didn't ask.'

'Call her again.'

Siobhan looked at him, but made the call.

'Give me the phone,' Rebus ordered. 'Don't want you going off the road.'

He took the phone and held it to his ear, asked to be put through to the Chief Super's office.

'It's John,' he said, when Templer answered. 'Who's got the story?'

'Reporter by the name of Steve Holly. And the sod's like a terrier at a lamppost convention.'

'I knew it would look bad,' Rebus explained to Templer. 'That's why I didn't say anything.'

They were in Templer's office at St Leonard's. She was seated, Rebus standing. She held a sharpened pencil in one hand, manipulating it, studying its tip, maybe weighing it up as a weapon. 'You lied to me.'

'I just left out a few details, Gill . . .'

'*A few details?*'

'None of them relevant.'

'You went back to his house!'

'We had a drink together.'

'Just you and a known criminal who'd been threatening your closest colleague? Who'd made an allegation of assault against you?'

'I had a word with him. We didn't argue or anything.' Rebus began to fold his arms, but this served to increase the blood pressure in his hands, so he unfolded them again. 'Ask the neighbours, see if they heard raised voices. I'll tell you right now, they didn't. We were drinking whisky in the living room.'

'Not the kitchen?'

Rebus shook his head. 'I wasn't in the kitchen all night.'

'What time did you leave?'

'No idea. Gone midnight, easy.'

'Not long before the fire then?'

'Long enough.'

She stared at him.

'The man had had a skinful, Gill. We've all seen it: they get the munchies, turn on the chip-pan, and fall asleep. It's either that or the lighted cigarette down the side of the sofa.'

Templer tested the pencil's sharpness against her finger.

'How much trouble am I in?' Rebus asked, the silence getting to him.

'Depends on Steve Holly. He makes a song and dance, we have to be seen to be doing something about it.'

'Like putting me on suspension?'

'It had crossed my mind.'

'I don't suppose I could blame you.'

'That's awfully magnanimous, John. Why did you go to his house?'

'He asked me. I think he liked playing games. That's all Siobhan was to him. Then I came along. He sat there feeding me drink, spouting on about his adventures . . . I think it gave him a buzz.'

'And what did you think *you* were going to get out of it?'

'I don't know exactly . . . I thought it might distract him from Siobhan.'

'She asked you for help?'

'No.'

'No, I'll bet she didn't. Siobhan can fight her own battles.'

Rebus nodded.

'So it's a coincidence?'

'Fairstone was a disaster waiting to happen. It's a blessing he didn't take anyone else with him.'

'A blessing?'

'I won't be losing too much sleep, Gill.'

'No, I suppose that would be too much to ask.'

Rebus straightened his back, held on to the silence, embracing it. Templer flinched. She'd drawn a bead of blood from her finger with the pencil tip.

'Final warning, John,' she said, dropping her hand, unwilling to deal with the injury – that sudden fallibility – in front of him.

'Yes, Gill.'

'Final means final with me.'

'I understand. Want me to fetch a plaster?' His hand reached for the door-knob.

'I want you to leave.'

'If you're sure there's nothing—'

'Out!'

Rebus closed the door after him, feeling the muscles in his legs starting to work again. Siobhan was standing not ten feet away, one questioning eyebrow raised. Rebus gave her an awkward thumbs-up, and she shook her head slowly: *I don't know how you get away with it.*

He wasn't sure he knew either.

'Let me buy you a drink,' he said. 'Canteen coffee all right?'

'That's pushing the boat out.'

'I'm on a final warning. It's hardly the winning goal at Hampden.'

'More of a throw-in at Easter Road?'

She managed a smile from him. He felt an aching in his jaw, the feeling of sustained tension which a simple smile could displace.

Downstairs, however, it was chaos. People milled around, the interview rooms all seemed to be full. Rebus recognised faces from Leith CID, meaning Hogan's team. He grabbed an elbow.

'What's going on?'

The face glowered at him, then softened as he was recognised. The detective constable's name was Pettifer. He'd only been half a year in CID; already he was toughening up nicely.

'Leith's jam-packed,' Pettifer explained. 'Thought we'd use St Leonard's for the overflow.'

Rebus looked around. Pinched faces; ill-fitting clothes; bad haircuts ... the cream of Edinburgh's lower depths. Informers, junkies, touts, scammers, housebreakers, muscle, alkies. The station was filling with their mingled scents, their slurred, expletive-strewn protestations. They'd fight anyone, anytime. Where were their lawyers? Nothing to drink? Needing a pish. What was the game? What about human rights? No dignity in this fascist state . . .

Detectives and uniforms tried for a semblance of order, taking names, details, pointing to a room or a bench where a statement could be taken, everything denied, a muttered complaint made. The younger men had a swagger, not yet ground down by the constant attentions of the law. They smoked, despite the warning signs. Rebus bummed a roll-up from one of them. He wore a check baseball cap, its rim pointing skywards. Rebus reckoned one gust of Edinburgh wind would have the thing sailing from its owner's head like a frisbee.

'No' done nothing, like,' the youth said, twitching one shoulder. 'Just helping out, so they says. Dinne want nothing to do with shooters, chief, that's the gospel. Pass it along, eh?' He winked a snake's cold eye. 'One good turn and all that.' Meaning the rumpled cigarette. Rebus nodded, moved off again.

'Bobby's looking for whoever might have supplied the guns,' Rebus told Siobhan. 'Rounding up the usual desperadoes.'

'Thought I recognised some faces.'

'Aye, and not from judging any bonny baby contests.' Rebus studied the men – they were all men. Easy to see them as mere debris; work hard enough, and you might find a smear of sympathy somewhere in your soul. These were men on whom the fates had decided not to shine; men who'd been brought up to respect greed and fear; men whose whole lives had been tainted from the word go.

Rebus believed this. He saw families where the children ran wild, and would grow up indifferent to anything but the rules of survival in what they saw as a jungle. Neglect was almost in their genes. Cruelty made people cruel. With some of these young men, Rebus had known their fathers and grandfathers, too, criminality in their blood, ageing the one and only disincentive to their recidivism. These were basic facts. But there was a problem. By the time Rebus and his like had reason to confront these men, the damage was already done, and in many cases appeared irreversible. So there could be little room for sympathy. Instead, it came down to attrition.

And then there were men like Peacock Johnson. Peacock wasn't his real name, of course. It was down to the shirts he wore, shirts which could curdle any hangover an onlooker might be harbouring. Johnson was low-life masquerading as high. He made money, and spent it, too. The shirts were often custom-made by a tailor in one of the narrow lanes of the New Town. Johnson sometimes affected a homburg, and had grown a thin, black moustache, probably thinking he looked like Kid Creole. His dental work was good – which by itself would have marked him out from his fellow denizens – and he used his smile prodigally. He was a piece of work.

Rebus knew he was in his late thirties, but could pass either for ten years older or a decade younger, depending on his mood and outfit. He went everywhere with a runt of a guy called Evil Bob. Bob sported what was almost a uniform: baseball cap, tracksuit top, baggy black jeans and oversized trainers. Gold rings on his fingers, ID bracelets on both wrists, chains around his neck. He had an oval, spotty face with a mouth which hung open almost permanently, giving him a look of constant bewilderment. Some people said that Evil Bob was Peacock's brother. If so, Rebus guessed some cruel genetic experiment had taken place. The tall, nearly elegant Johnson and his brutish sidekick.

As for the 'Evil' in Evil Bob, so far as anyone knew it was just a name.

As Rebus watched, the two men were being separated. Bob was to follow a CID officer upstairs to where a space was newly available. Johnson was about to accompany DC Pettifer into Interview Room 1. Rebus glanced towards Siobhan, then pushed his way through the scrum.

'Mind if I sit in on this one?' he asked Pettifer. The young man looked flustered. Rebus tried for a reassuring smile.

'Mr Rebus . . .' Johnson was holding out his hand. 'What a pleasing surprise.'

Rebus ignored him. He didn't want a pro like Johnson to know just how new Pettifer was to the game. At the same time, he had to convince the detective constable that no dirty trick was being played, that Rebus wasn't going to be there as invigilator. All he had was his smile, so he tried it again.

'Fine,' Pettifer said at last. The three men entered the interview room, Rebus holding his index finger up in Siobhan's direction, hoping she'd know he wanted her to wait for him.

IR1 was small and stuffy and held the body odours of what seemed like its last half-dozen guests. There were windows high up on one wall, but they wouldn't open. On the small table sat a twin-tape deck. There was a panic button at shoulder height behind it. A video camera was trained on the room from a bracket above the door.

But there'd be no recording today. These interviews were informal, goodwill a priority. Pettifer carried nothing into the room but a couple of sheets of blank paper and a cheap biro. He would have studied the file on Johnson, but wasn't about to brandish it.

'Take a seat, please,' Pettifer said. Johnson brushed the chair's surface with a bright red handkerchief, before lowering himself on to it with showy deliberation.

Pettifer sat down opposite, then realised there was no chair for Rebus. He made to stand up again, but Rebus shook his head.

'I'll just stand here, if that's okay,' he said. He was leaning against the wall opposite, legs crossed at the ankles, hands resting in his jacket pockets. He'd found a spot where he was in Pettifer's line of vision, but where Johnson would have to turn to see him.

'You're sort of like a guest star, Mr Rebus?' Johnson obliged with a grin.

'VIP treatment for you, Peacock.'

'The Peacock always travels first class, Mr Rebus.' Johnson sounded satisfied, resting against the back of the chair, arms folded. His hair was jet black, slicked back from the brow, curling where it met the nape of his neck. He'd been known to keep a cocktail stick in his mouth, working it like a lollipop. Not today though. Today he was chewing a piece of gum.

'Mr Johnson,' Pettifer began, 'I assume you know why you're here?'

'You're asking all us cats about the shooter. I told the other cop, told anyone who'd listen, the Peacock doesn't do that sort of thing. Shooting kids, man, that's pure evil.' He shook his head slowly. 'I'd help you if I could, but you've got me here under false pretexts.'

'You've been in a spot of trouble before over firearms, Mr Johnson. We just wondered if you might be the sort of man who'd have his ear to the ground. Could be you've heard something. Maybe a rumour, someone new in the marketplace . . .'

Pettifer sounded confident. It could be ninety per cent front, inside he could be shivering like the last leaf on autumn's tree, but he sounded okay, and that was what mattered. Rebus liked what he saw.

'The Peacock isn't what you'd call a snitch, your honour. But in this case, it's a definite. If I hear something, I come straight to you. No worries on that bulletin board. And for the record, I deal in replica weapons – collectors' market, respectable gentlemen of industry and suchlike. When the powers above make such trade illegal, you can be sure the Peacock will cease operations.'

'You've never sold illegal firearms to anyone?'

'Never.'

'And don't happen to know of anyone who might?'

'As I said in a previous answer, the Peacock is not a snitch.'

'What about reactivating these collectors' guns of yours: know anyone who'd be able to do that?'

'Not a scooby, m'lud.'

Pettifer nodded and looked down at the sheets of paper, which were just as blankly white as they'd been when he'd placed them on the table. During the lull, Johnson turned his head to check on Rebus.

'What's it like back in cattle class, Mr Rebus?'

'I like it. The people tend to be that bit cleaner in their habits.'

'Now, now . . .' Another grin, this time accompanied by a wagging finger. 'I won't have uppity public servants soiling my VIP suite.'

'You're going to love in it Barlinnie, Peacock,' Rebus said. 'Put it another way: the guys in there are going to love you to absolute bits. Dressing up always tends to go down well in the Bar-L.'

'Mr Rebus . . .' Johnson lowered his head and produced a sigh. 'Vendettas are ugly things. Ask the Italians.'

Pettifer shifted in his chair, its legs scraping the floor. 'Maybe if we could get back to the question of where you think Lee Herdman could have sourced those guns . . .?'

'They're mostly made in China these days, aren't they?' Johnson said.

'I mean,' Pettifer went on, an edge creeping into his voice, 'how would someone go about getting hold of them?'

Johnson gave an exaggerated shrug. 'By the grip and the trigger?' He laughed at his own joke, laughed alone into the room's silence. Then he shifted in his seat, tried for a solemn face. 'Most armourers are Glasgow-based. They're the cats you should be talking to.'

'Our colleagues in the west are doing just that,' Pettifer said. 'But meantime, you can't think of anyone in particular we should be asking?'

Johnson shrugged. 'Search me.'

'You should do that, DC Pettifer,' Rebus said, making for the door. 'You should definitely take him up on that . . .'

Outside, the situation was no calmer and there was no sign of Siobhan. Rebus guessed she'd retreated to the canteen, but instead of looking for her, he headed upstairs, glancing in at a couple of rooms before finding Evil Bob, who was being interviewed by a shirt-sleeved DS called George Silvers. Around St Leonard's, Silvers was known as 'Hi-Ho'. He was a time-server, awaiting the oncoming pension with all the anticipation of a hitch-hiker at a truck stop. He didn't so much as nod when Rebus entered the room. There were a dozen questions on his list, and he wanted them asked and answered, so that the specimen in front of him could be deposited back on to the street. Bob watched as Rebus pulled a chair between the two men and sat down, his right knee only inches from Bob's left. Bob squirmed.

'I've just been in with Peacock,' Rebus said, ignoring the fact that he was interrupting one of Silvers's questions. 'He should change his name to canary.'

Bob stared at him dully. 'Why's that then?'

'Why do you think?'

'Dunno.'

'What do canaries do?'

'Fly around . . . live in trees.'

'They live in your grannie's fucking birdcage, you moron. And they sing.'

Bob thought about this; Rebus could almost hear the cogs grinding. With a lot of low-lifes, it was an act. Many of them were clever enough, wise not just in the ways of the street. But Bob was either Robert de Niro in full method mode, or else he was no actor at all.

'What sort of stuff?' he asked. Then he saw Rebus's look. 'I mean, what sort of stuff do they sing?'

Not de Niro then . . .

'Bob,' Rebus said, elbows on knees, leaning close to the

squat young man, 'you hang around with Johnson, you're going to spend half your life behind bars.'

'So?'

'Doesn't that bother you?'

Stupid question, Rebus realised as the words came out. The arch look from Silvers told him as much. Prison would be just another sleepwalking session for Bob. It would have no effect on him whatsoever.

'Peacock and me, we're partners.'

'Oh aye, and I'm sure he's splitting it right down the middle. Come on, Bob . . .' Rebus smiled conspiratorially. 'He's ripping you off. Big grin on his face, blinding you with dental work. But he's stitching you up. And when things start going wrong, guess who'll be taking the fall? That's why he keeps you around. You're the guy in the panto who gets the custard pie in his face every performance. The pair of you buy and sell guns, for Christ's sake! Think we're not on to you?'

'Replicas,' Bob stated, as if remembering a lesson and repeating it rote. 'For collectors to hang on their walls.'

'Oh aye, everybody wants a bunch of fake Glock 17s and Walther PPKs above the fireplace . . .' Rebus straightened up. He didn't know if it was possible to get through to Bob. There had to be something, a weakness to be exploited. But the guy was like so much wet dough. You could knead him, twist him all out of shape . . . you'd only ever end up with a spongy mass. He decided on one last try.

'One of these days, Bob, a kid's going to draw one of your replicas and someone'll take him down, thinking the gun's real. It's only a matter of time.' Rebus was aware that he was allowing some emotion to creep into his voice. Silvers was studying him, beginning to wonder what he was up to. Rebus looked at him, then shrugged, started to push up from the chair.

'Think about it, Bob, just do that for me.' Rebus tried for eye contact, but the young man was staring at the ceiling lights, as if at a firework display.

'I've never been to a panto . . .' he was starting to tell Silvers as Rebus left.

Siobhan, dumped by Rebus, had gone upstairs to CID. The main office was busy, detectives seated at borrowed desks, facing their interviewees. At her own desk, the computer monitor had been pushed to one side, her in-tray relegated to the floor. Detective Constable Davie Hynds was taking notes as a young man, pupils reduced to pinpoints, droned on.

'What's wrong with your own desk?' Siobhan asked.

'DS Wylie pulled rank on me.' Hynds nodded towards where Detective Sergeant Ellen Wylie sat at his desk, preparing for her next interview. She looked up at mention of her name and smiled. Siobhan smiled back. Wylie was based at the West End station. Same rank as Siobhan, but more years on her clock. Siobhan knew they might become rivals in the promotion stakes. She decided to squeeze her in-tray into one of the desk drawers, didn't like the idea of this invasion. Each police station was a fiefdom of sorts. No telling what the raiders could take away with them . . .

When she picked up the in-tray, she saw the corner of a white envelope, poking out from beneath a series of stapled reports. She eased it out, then placed the in-tray in the desk's single deep drawer, closing and locking it. Hynds was looking at her.

'Nothing you need, is there?' Siobhan asked him. He shook his head, wondering if an explanation was on its way. But all Siobhan did was walk away, heading back downstairs to the drinks machine. It was more peaceful down here. A couple of the visiting detectives were on a break, smoking and sharing some joke in the car park. She didn't see Rebus there, so stayed by the machine, opening the ice-cold can. The sugar hit her teeth and then her stomach. She found the can's list of contents, reminding herself that the panic-attack books said to lay off caffeine.

She was trying to find room in her affections for decaf coffee, and she knew there were caffeine-free soft drinks out there somewhere. Salt: that was another one to avoid. High blood pressure and all that. Alcohol was all right in moderation. She wondered if a bottle of wine in the evening after work could be classed as 'moderate', doubted it somehow. Thing was, if she drank half a bottle, the rest tasted foul next day. Memo to self: explore possibility of buying half-bottles of wine only.

She remembered the envelope, lifted it from her pocket. Handwritten, more of a scrawl really. She put her can down on top of the machine, already getting a bad feeling as she peeled the envelope open. Just a single sheet of paper, she was sure of that. No razor blades, no glass . . . Plenty of nutters out there keen to share their thoughts with her. She unfolded the letter. Big scrawled capitals.

LOOK FORWARD TO SEEING YOU AGAIN IN HELL – MARTY.

The name was underlined. Her heart was racing. She didn't doubt who Marty was: Martin Fairstone. But Fairstone was a tub of cinders and bone on a shelf in someone's lab. She studied the envelope. Address and postcode perfect. Somebody's idea of a joke? But who could it be? Who knew about her and Fairstone? Rebus and Templer . . . anyone else? She thought back a few months. Someone had left messages on her screensaver, had to be CID, one of her so-called colleagues. But the messages had stopped. Davie Hynds and George Silvers: they worked beside her. Grant Hood, too, most of the time. Others came and went. But she hadn't told any of them about Fairstone. Hold on . . . when Fairstone had made his complaint, had any of it become a matter of record? She didn't think so. But cop shops were hives of gossip; hard to keep any secrets.

She realised she was staring through the glass outer doors, and the two detectives in the car park were staring back at her, wondering what it was about them that she was finding so mesmeric. She tried for a smile and a shake of the head, as if to say she'd been in a 'dwam'.

For lack of anything else to do, she took out her mobile, intending to check for messages. But started to make a call instead, punching in the number from memory.

'Ray Duff speaking.'

'Ray? You busy?'

Siobhan knew what the initial answer would be: an intake of breath preceding an elongated sigh. Duff was a scientist, working for the forensics lab at Howdenhall.

'You mean apart from checking that all the Port Edgar bullets came from the same gun, then examining blood spatter configurations and powder residues, ballistic angles, all that?'

'At least we keep you in a job. How's the MG?'

'Running like a dream.' The last time the two had spoken, Duff had just finished rebuilding a '73 special. 'That offer of a spin some weekend still stands.'

'Maybe come the better weather.'

'There's a hood, you know.'

'Not the same though, is it? Look, Ray, I know you're up to your eyes in work from the school, but I was wondering if I could ask a wee favour . . .'

'Siobhan, you know I'm going to say no. Everyone wants this done and dusted.'

'I know. I'm working Port Edgar too.'

'You and every other cop in the city.' Another sigh. 'Just out of curiosity, what is it exactly?'

'Between you and me?'

'Of course.'

Siobhan looked around. The detectives outside had lost interest in her. Three constables sat together at a table in the canteen, eating sandwiches and drinking tea, maybe twenty feet away from her. She turned her back on them, so she was facing the machine.

'I just got this letter. Anonymous.'

'Threatening?'

117

'Sort of.'

'You should show it to someone.'

'I was thinking of showing it to you, see if you can take anything from it.'

'I meant show it to your boss. Gill Templer, isn't it?'

'I'm not exactly her star pupil right now. Besides, she's snowed under.'

'And I'm not?'

'Just a quick recce, Ray. It could be something or nothing.'

'But on the q.t., am I right?'

'Right.'

'Which is wrong. Someone's threatening you, you need to report it, Shiv.'

That nickname again: *Shiv.* More and more people seemed to be using it. She decided this wasn't the time to tell Ray how much she disliked it.

'Thing is, Ray, it's from a dead man.'

There was a pause on the line. 'Okay,' Duff drawled at last. 'You've got my attention.'

'Council house in Gracemount, chip-pan fire . . .'

'Ah yes, Mr Martin Fairstone. I've been trying to get some work done on him, too.'

'Come up with anything?'

'Bit early to tell . . . Port Edgar came straight in at number one. Fairstone dropped a few places.'

She had to smile at the analogy. Ray liked his charts. Their conversations usually contained top threes and fives. And right on cue:

'By the way, Shiv – top three Scottish rock and pop acts?'

'Ray . . .'

'Humour me. No thinking allowed, just off the top of your head.'

'Rod Stewart? Big Country? Travis?'

'No room for Lulu? Annie Lennox?'

'I'm not much good at this, Ray.'

'Rod's an interesting choice though.'

'Blame DI Rebus. He loaned me the early albums . . .' She attempted a sigh of her own. 'So are you going to help me or not?'

'How soon can you get it to me?'

'Within the hour.'

'I suppose I could stay late. Wouldn't *that* make a change?'

'Have I ever mentioned your good looks, wit and charm?'

'Only every time I agree to do you a favour.'

'You're an angel, Ray. Call me a.s.a.p.'

'Come for a drive sometime,' Duff was telling her as she ended the call. She carried the letter through the canteen, into the booking area beyond.

'Got an evidence bag, by any chance?' she asked the custody sergeant. He opened a couple of drawers. 'I could get one from upstairs,' he said, admitting defeat.

'What about one of the possessions envelopes?'

The custody sergeant stooped again and produced an A4-sized manila envelope from below the counter.

'That'll do,' Siobhan said, dropping her own envelope in. She wrote Ray Duff's name on the front, adding her own name as reference and the word URGENT, then walked back through the canteen and out into the car park. The smokers had gone back inside, meaning she wouldn't have to apologise for her earlier fit of the stares. Two uniforms were getting into a patrol car.

'Hey, guys!' she called. Getting closer, she recognised the passenger as PC John Mason, his station nickname the utterly obvious 'Perry'. The driver was Toni Jackson.

'Hiya, Siobhan,' Jackson said. 'Missed you Friday night.'

Siobhan shrugged an apology. Toni and some of the other female uniforms liked to let off steam once a week. Siobhan was the only detective allowed into their fold.

'I'm assuming I missed a good night?' she asked.

'A great night. My liver's still recovering.'

Mason looked interested. 'So what did you get up to?'

'Wouldn't you like to know?' his partner responded with a wink. Then, to Siobhan: 'You wanting us to play postman?' She nodded towards the envelope.

'Could you? It's for forensics at Howdenhall. Delivered into this guy's hands if at all possible.' Siobhan tapped Duff's name.

'We've a couple of calls to make . . . it's not much of a detour.'

'I promised it'd be there inside an hour.'

'Way Toni drives, that won't be a problem,' Mason offered.

Jackson ignored this. 'Rumour has it you've been relegated to chauffeur, Siobhan.'

Siobhan twitched her mouth. 'Only for a few days.'

'How did he manage to hurt his hands?'

Siobhan stared at Jackson. 'I don't know, Toni. What do the bush drums say?'

'They say all sorts of things . . . Everything from fist-fights to fat-fryers.'

'Not that the two are mutually exclusive.'

'Nothing's mutually exclusive where DI Rebus is concerned.' Jackson smiled wryly, holding her hand out for the envelope. 'You're on a yellow card, Siobhan.'

'I'll be there Friday, if you want me.'

'Promise?'

'Cross my CID heart.'

'In other words, it depends.'

'It always does, Toni, you know that.'

Jackson was looking over Siobhan's shoulder. 'Talk of the devil,' she said, getting back behind the steering-wheel. Siobhan turned round. Rebus was watching from the doorway. She didn't know how long he'd been there. Long enough to see the envelope change hands? The engine caught, and she stepped away from the car, watching it depart. Rebus had opened his cigarette packet and was pulling one out with his teeth.

'Funny how the human animal can adapt,' Siobhan said, walking towards him.

'I'm thinking of extending my repertoire,' Rebus told her. 'Might try playing the piano with my nose.' He got the lighter to work at the third attempt, started puffing.

'Thanks for leaving me out in the cold, by the way.'

'It's not cold out here.'

'I meant—'

'I know what you meant.' He looked at her. 'I just wanted to hear what Johnson had to say for himself.'

'Johnson?'

'Peacock Johnson.' He saw her eyes narrow. 'He calls himself that.'

'Why?'

'You saw the way he dresses.'

'I meant why did you want to see him?'

'I'm interested in him.'

'Any particular reason?'

Rebus just shrugged.

'Who is he anyway?' Siobhan asked. 'Should I know him?'

'He's small time, but those can be the most dangerous. Sells replica guns to anyone who wants them . . . might even deal in a few examples of the real thing. Fences stolen goods, dispenses soft drugs, just the odd bit of hash . . .'

'Where does he operate?'

Rebus looked like he was thinking. 'Out Burdiehouse way.'

She knew him too well to be conned. 'Burdiehouse?'

'That direction . . .' The cigarette flexing in his mouth.

'Maybe I could go look in the files.' She held his gaze, waited until he blinked.

'Southhouse, Burdiehouse . . . somewhere out there.' Smoke spilled down his nostrils, reminding her of a cornered bull.

'In other words, next door to Gracemount?'

He shrugged. 'It's just geography.'

'It's where Fairstone lived . . . his patch. What are the chances of two scumbags like that not knowing one another?'

'Maybe they did.'

'John . . .'

'What was in the envelope?'

Her turn to try for the poker face. 'Don't change the subject.'

'Subject's closed. What was in the envelope?'

'Nothing for you to worry your pretty little head about, DI Rebus.'

'Now you've got me worried.'

'It was nothing, honest.'

Rebus waited, then nodded slowly. 'Because you can take care of yourself, right?'

'That's right.'

He tipped his head, let the remains of the cigarette fall to the ground. Crushed it under the toe of his shoe. 'You know I won't need you tomorrow?'

She nodded. 'I'll try to while away the hours.'

He tried to think of a comeback; gave up eventually. 'Come on then, let's skedaddle before Gill Templer can find another excuse for a bollocking.' He started walking towards her car.

'Good,' Siobhan said. 'And while I'm driving, you can be telling me all about Mr Peacock Johnson.' She paused. 'By the way: top three Scottish rock and pop acts?'

'Why do you ask?'

'Come on, off the top of your head.'

Rebus thought for a moment. 'Nazareth, Alex Harvey, Deacon Blue.'

'Not Rod Stewart?'

'He's not Scottish.'

'You're still allowed him if you want.'

'Then I'll get to him eventually, probably right after Ian Stewart. But first I need to go through John Martyn, Jack

Bruce, Ian Anderson . . . not forgetting Donovan and the Incredible String Band . . . Lulu and Maggie Bell . . .'

Siobhan rolled her eyes. 'Is it too late for me to say I wish I'd never asked?'

'Far too late,' Rebus said, getting into the passenger side. 'Frankie Miller's another . . . Simple Minds in their heyday . . . I always had a soft spot for Pallas . . .'

Siobhan stood by the driver's-side door, gripping the handle but making no further effort. From inside, she could hear the catalogue continuing, Rebus's voice rising, making sure she didn't miss a single name.

'Not the sort of place I'd normally drink,' Dr Curt muttered. He was tall and thin, often described behind his back as 'funereal'. Late fifties, with a long, slack face and baggy eyes. He reminded Rebus of a bloodhound.

A funereal bloodhound.

Which was apt in its way, considering he was one of Edinburgh's most highly respected pathologists. Under his guidance, corpses could tell their stories, sometimes revealing secrets: suicides who turned out to be murder victims; bones which turned out not to be human. Curt's skill and intuition had helped Rebus solve dozens of cases down the years, so it would have been churlish to turn the man down when he called and asked Rebus to join him for a drink, adding, as a postscript: 'Somewhere quiet, mind. Somewhere we can talk without tongues wagging all around us.'

Which was why Rebus had suggested his regular haunt, the Oxford Bar, tucked away in an alley behind George Street and a long way from both Curt's office and St Leonard's.

They were seated in the back room, at the table at the far end. No one else about. Midweek and mid-evening, the main bar boasting only a couple of suits who were about to go home, and one regular who'd just come in. Rebus brought the drinks to the table: a pint for him, gin and tonic for the pathologist.

'Slainte,' Curt said, raising his glass.

'Cheers, Doc.' Rebus still couldn't lift his beer with just the one hand.

'It's like you're holding a chalice,' Curt commented. Then: 'Do you want to talk about how it happened?'

'No.'

'The rumours are flying.'

'They can be stacking up air miles for all I care. What's intriguing me is your phone call. Do you want to talk about that?'

Rebus had arrived home, soaked in a tepid bath and phoned out for a curry. Jackie Leven on the hi-fi, singing about the romantic hard men of Fife – how could Rebus have forgotten to put him on the list? And then Curt's phone call.

'Can we talk? Maybe in person? Tonight . . .?'

No hint as to why, just an arrangement to be in the Oxford Bar at half past seven.

Curt savoured his drink. 'How's life been treating you, John?'

Rebus stared at him. With some men, men of a certain age and class, there had to be this preamble. He offered a cigarette, which the pathologist accepted.

'Take one out for me, too,' Rebus asked. Curt did so, and both men smoked in silence for a moment.

'I've been hunky-dory, Doc. How about yourself? Often get this urge to phone cops up of an evening and arrange assignations in dingy back rooms?'

'I believe the "dingy back room" was your choice rather than mine.'

Rebus acknowledged as much with a slight bow of the head.

Curt smiled. 'You're not a man of great patience, John . . .'

Rebus shrugged. 'Actually, I can sit here all night, but I'll be a lot more relaxed once I know what this is about.'

'It's about what's left of a man called Martin Fairstone.'

'Oh, yes?' Rebus moved a little in his chair, crossing one leg over the other.

'You know him, of course?' When Curt sucked on the cigarette, his whole face seemed to collapse inward. He'd only become a smoker in the past five years, as if keen to test his own mortality.

'I knew him,' Rebus said.

'Ah yes . . . past tense, unfortunately.'

'Not too unfortunate. I can't see him being missed.'

'Be that as it may, Professor Gates and myself . . . well, we think there are grey areas.'

'Ash and bone, you mean?'

Curt shook his head slowly, refusing to see the joke.

'Forensics will tell us more . . .' His voice drifted off. 'DCS Templer has been persistent. I think Gates will talk to her tomorrow.'

'And what's this got to do with me?'

'She thinks you may have been involved in some way in this man's murder.'

The final word lay in the smoky air between them. Rebus didn't need to repeat it aloud; Curt heard the unspoken question.

'We think maybe murder,' he said, nodding slowly. 'Some evidence that he was tied to the chair. I have photos . . .' He reached into a briefcase which was on the floor next to him.

'Doc,' Rebus was saying, 'you probably shouldn't be showing me these.'

'I know, and I wouldn't if I thought there was the slightest chance that you were involved.' He looked up. 'But I know you, John.'

Rebus was looking towards the briefcase. 'People have been wrong about me before.'

'Maybe.'

The manila file was on the table between them, resting on damp beer-mats. Rebus picked it up, opened it. There were a couple of dozen photographs of the kitchen, wisps of smoke still evident in the background. Martin Fairstone was barely recognisable as human. More like a blackened, blistered store mannequin. He was lying face down. A chair lay behind him, reduced to a couple of stumps and part of the seat. What got Rebus was the cooker. For some reason, its surface had been left mostly untouched. He could see the chip-pan sitting on one of its rings. Christ, clean it up and it might still be usable . . . Hard to think that a chip-pan could survive where a human couldn't.

'What you'll see from this is the way the chair has fallen. It's tipped forward, taking the victim with it. It's almost like he fell on his knees, pitched that way, and then later slid into a completely prone position. And you see how his arms are positioned? Flat by his sides?'

Rebus saw, but wasn't sure what he was supposed to take from any of it.

'We think we found the remains of some rope . . . a plastic clothes-rope. The covering has melted, but the nylon was pretty resilient.'

'You often get a clothes-rope in a kitchen,' Rebus said, playing devil's advocate now because suddenly he knew where this was leading.

'Agreed. But Professor Gates . . . well, he's got the forensics people looking at it . . .'

'Because he thinks Fairstone was tied to the chair?'

Curt just nodded. 'The other photos, in some of them . . . the close-ups . . . you can see the bits of rope.'

Rebus saw.

'And there's this train of events, you see. A man is unconscious, tied to a chair. He wakes up, fire is raging around him, the fumes already deep in his lungs. He's trying to wrestle himself free, the chair tips, and he starts to suffocate. It's the smoke that's killing him . . . he's dead before the flames can break his bonds . . .'

'It's a theory,' Rebus said.

'Yes, it is,' the pathologist said quietly.

Rebus sorted through the pictures again. 'So suddenly it's murder?'

'Or culpable homicide. I suppose a lawyer could argue that tying him up wasn't what killed him . . . that it was meant merely as a warning, say.'

Rebus looked at him. 'You've been giving this some thought.'

Curt lifted his glass again. 'Professor Gates will talk to Gill Templer tomorrow. He'll show her these photos. Forensics will have their say . . . People are whispering that you were there.'

'Has a reporter been in touch by any chance?' Rebus watched Curt nod. 'Name of Steve Holly?' Another nod. Rebus cursed out loud, just as Harry the barman came in to clear the empty glasses. Harry was whistling, a sure sign that he had a woman on the go. Probably wanted to brag about it, but Rebus's outburst had him beating a retreat.

'How are you going to . . .?' Curt couldn't find the right words.

'Fight it?' Rebus suggested. Then he smiled sourly. 'I can't fight something like this, Doc. I was *there*, whole world knows it, or will do soon.' He made to gnaw at a fingernail, then remembered he couldn't. He felt like punching the table, but couldn't do that either.

'It's all circumstantial,' Curt was saying. 'Well, almost . . .' He reached across the table and found one particular photograph, a close-up of the skull, its mouth gaping. Rebus felt the beer churning in his stomach. Curt was pointing to the neck.

'Might look like skin to you, but there's something . . . there's *been* something hanging around the throat. The deceased didn't wear a cravat or anything?'

The idea was so ridiculous that Rebus burst out laughing. 'This was a council house in Gracemount, Doc, not a gentlemen's club in the New Town.' Rebus started to pick his drink up, but found he didn't want it. He was still shaking his head at the notion of Martin Fairstone in a cravat. Why not a smoking jacket, too? A butler to roll him his cigarettes . . .

'The thing is,' Dr Curt was saying, 'if he wasn't wearing something around his throat, a neckerchief or something, then what this begins to look like is a gag of some sort. Maybe a handkerchief stuffed into his mouth, knotted behind the head. Only he was able to slip it off . . . maybe too late by then to call out. It slid down around his neck, you see.'

And again, Rebus saw.

He saw himself trying to talk his way out of it.

Saw himself failing.

7

Siobhan had this idea.

The panic attacks often came when she was asleep. Maybe it was to do with her bedroom. So she decided to try sleeping on the sofa: perfect arrangement really. Duvet thrown over her, TV in the corner, coffee and a box of Pringles. Three times during the evening, she'd found herself standing by the window, looking out on to her street. If the shadows seemed to have movement to them, she'd watch the same spot for a few minutes until reassured. When Rebus had called to tell her about his meeting with Dr Curt, she'd asked him a question.

Had the body been properly ID'd?

He'd asked what she'd meant.

'Charred remains . . . the ID will be down to DNA, right? Has anyone done that yet?'

'Siobhan . . .'

'Just for the sake of argument.'

'He's dead, Siobhan. You can start to forget about him.'

Biting her bottom lip, less reason than ever now to bother him with the letter. His plate was already heaped.

He'd rung off. Reason for calling her: if the shit hit the fan next day, he wouldn't be around for it, and Templer might go looking for a surrogate.

Siobhan decided to make more coffee – decaf instant. It left a sour taste in her mouth. She stopped by the window, a quick glance out before she headed for the kitchen. Her doctor had asked her to write down a list of her 'menus' for a typical week, then had circled everything he thought might be contributing to her attacks. She tried not to think about the Pringles . . . problem was, she liked them. Liked wine, too, and fizzy drinks, and takeaways. As she'd reasoned with her doctor, she didn't smoke, took regular exercise. She had to let off steam some time . . .

'Booze and fast food are how you let off steam?'

'They're how I wind down at day's end.'

'Maybe you should try not getting wound up in the first place.'

'You're going to tell me you've never smoked or had a drink?'

But of course he wasn't going to say that. Doctors had higher stress levels than cops. One thing she had done – her own initiative – was try getting into ambient music. Lemon Jelly, Oldsolar, Boards of Canada. Some hadn't worked – Aphex Twin and Autechre; not enough meat on their bones.

Meat on their bones . . .

She was thinking of Martin Fairstone. The way he smelled: male chemicals. His discoloured teeth. Standing by her car, chewing his way into her shopping, casual in his aggression, *secure* in it. Rebus was right: he had to be dead. The note was a sick joke. Problem was, she couldn't seem to find a candidate. There had to be someone out there, someone she was failing to remember . . .

Bringing her coffee through from the kitchen, she wandered over to the window again. There were lights on in the tenement across the way. A while back, someone had spied on her from there . . . a cop called Linford. He was still on the force, working at HQ. At one time, she'd thought about moving, but she liked this place, liked her flat, the street, the area. Corner shops, young families and professional singles . . . most of the 'families' were younger than her, she realised. She was always being asked: when you going to find a fellah? Toni Jackson seemed to ask every time the Friday Club met. She would point out eligible men in the bars and clubs, not taking no for an answer, leading them over to the table where Siobhan sat with her head in her hands.

Maybe a boyfriend *was* the answer, keep away the prowlers. But then, a dog would do just as well. Thing about a dog was . . .

Thing about a dog was, she didn't want one. Didn't want a boyfriend either. She'd had to stop seeing Eric Bain for a while, when he'd started talking about taking their friendship 'to the next stage'. She missed him: he would arrive late of an evening, sharing pizza and gossip, listening to music, maybe playing a computer game on his laptop. Soon she'd try inviting him round again, see how it went. Soon, but not yet.

Martin Fairstone was dead. Everyone knew it. She wondered who would know if he wasn't. The girlfriend maybe. Close friends or family; he had to be staying with someone, making money to keep himself together. Maybe this Peacock Johnson would know. Rebus said the guy was a magnet for local gen. She didn't feel sleepy, could be a drive would do her good. Ambient on the car hi-fi. She picked up her phone, called Leith cop-shop, knowing the Port Edgar case was financed to the hilt, meaning there'd be bodies on the night shift, keen to top up their bank accounts. She got through to one, asked for some details.

'Peacock Johnson . . . I don't know his first name, not sure anybody else does. He was interviewed earlier today at St Leonard's.'

'What is it you need, DS Clarke?'

'For the moment, just his address,' Siobhan said.

Rebus had taken a taxi – easier than driving. Even then, opening the passenger door had required a hard squeeze of his thumb on the catch, and the thumb was still burning. His pockets bulged with change. Small change was hard for him to deal with. He was using notes for every possible transaction, filling his pockets with the residual coins.

His conversation with Dr Curt was still echoing at the

back of his mind. A murder inquiry was all he needed right now, especially with himself as prime suspect. Siobhan had asked him about Peacock Johnson, but he'd managed to keep his answers vague. Johnson: the reason he was standing here, ringing the doorbell. The reason he'd gone back to Fairstone's house that night, too . . .

The door was opened to him, bathing him in light.

'Ah, it's you, John. Good man, come in.'

A mid-terraced house, new-build, off Alnwickhill Road. Andy Callis lived there on his own, his wife dead a year past, cancer snatching her too young. A framed wedding photo hung in the hall. Callis a good stone and a half lighter, Mary radiant, haloed by light, flowers in her hair. Rebus had been at the graveside, Callis placing a posy on the coffin. Rebus had accepted the role of pall-bearer, one of six, including Andy himself, keeping his eyes on the posy as the coffin was lowered into the earth.

A year back. Andy seeming to be getting over it, but then this . . .

'How are you doing, Andy?' Rebus asked. The electric fire was on in the living room. Leather chair and matching footstool facing the TV. The room tidy, fresh-smelling. The garden outside well-tended, its borders free of weeds. Another picture above the mantelpiece: Mary's portrait, done in a studio. Same smile as in the wedding photo, but a few lines around the eyes, the face fuller. A woman growing into maturity.

'I'm fine, John.' Callis settled into his chair, moving like an old man. He was early forties, hair not yet grey. The chair creaked as it adjusted itself to him.

'Help yourself to a drink, you know where it is.'

'I might have a nip.'

'Not driving?'

'Taxi brought me.' Rebus went to the drinks cabinet, raised a bottle, watched Callis shake his head. 'Still on those tablets?'

'Not supposed to mix them with drink.'

'Me too.' Rebus poured himself a double.

'Is it cold in here?' Callis was asking. Rebus shook his head. 'What's with the gloves then?'

'I hurt my hands. That's why I'm on tablets.' He lifted the glass. 'And other non-prescribed painkillers.' He brought his drink over to the sofa, made himself comfortable. The TV was playing silently, some sort of game show. 'What's on?'

'Christ knows.'

'So I'm not interrupting?'

'You're fine.' Callis paused, keeping his eyes on the screen. 'Unless you've come here to try pushing me again.'

Rebus shook his head. 'I'm past that, Andy. Though I'm bound to admit, we're stretched to the limit.'

'That school thing?' From the corner of his eye, he watched Rebus nod. 'Terrible thing to happen.'

'I'm supposed to be working out why he did it.'

'What's the point? Give people . . . the opportunity, it's going to happen.'

Rebus reflected on the pause after 'people'. Callis had been about to say 'guns', but had swallowed the word back. And he'd called it 'that school thing' . . . 'thing' rather than 'shooting'.

Not out of the woods yet then.

'You still seeing the shrink?' Rebus asked.

Callis snorted. 'Fat lot of good.'

She wasn't really a shrink, of course. It wasn't lying on the sofa and talking about your mother. But Rebus and Callis had turned it into this joke. Joking made it easier to talk about.

'Apparently there are worse cases than me,' Callis said. 'Guys who can't so much as pick up a pen or a bottle of sauce. Everything they see reminds them . . .' His voice faded.

Rebus finished the sentence in his head: *of guns.* Everything reminded them of guns.

'Bloody odd when you think about it,' Callis went on. 'I

mean, we're supposed to be scared of them, isn't that the whole point? But then someone like me reacts, and suddenly it's a problem.'

'It's a problem when it affects the rest of your life, Andy. Having any trouble pouring sauce on to your chips?'

Callis patted his stomach. 'Not so you'd notice.'

Rebus smiled, leaned back against the sofa, whisky glass resting on the arm. He wondered if Andy knew about the tic in his left eye or the slight catch in his voice. It had been nearly three months since he'd taken sick leave from the force. Up until then, he'd been a patrol officer, but with specialist training in firearms. Lothian and Borders had only a handful of such men. They couldn't just be replaced. Edinburgh only had the one Armed Response Vehicle.

'What does your doctor say?'

'John, doesn't matter what he says. The force isn't going to let me back in without a battery of tests.'

'You're scared you might fail?'

Callis stared at him. 'I'm scared I might pass.'

They sat in silence after that, watching the TV. It looked to Rebus like one of those survival programmes: strangers cooped up together, whittled down each week.

'So tell me what's been happening,' Callis said.

'Well . . .' Rebus considered his options. 'Not much really.'

'Apart from the school thing?'

'Apart from that, yes. The guys keep asking for you.'

Callis nodded. 'The odd face pops round now and then.'

Rebus leaned forward, elbows on knees. 'You're not coming back then?'

A tired smile from Callis. 'You know I'm not. They'll call it stress or something. Invalided out . . .'

'How many years is it, Andy?'

'Since I joined?' Callis's lips puckered in thought. 'Fifteen . . . fifteen and a half.'

'One incident in all that time, and you're ready to call it a day? Not even really an "incident" . . .'

'John, look at me, will you? Notice anything? The way the hands tremble?' He raised a hand for Rebus to see. 'And this vein that seems to keep pulsing in my eyelid . . .' Raised the same hand to his eye for effect. 'It's not me that's calling time, it's my body. All these warning signs, you saying I just ignore them? Know how many call-outs we had last year? Not far short of three hundred. We drew weapons three times more often than in the previous year.'

'World's toughening up all right.'

'Maybe so, but I'm not.'

'No reason you should.' Rebus was thoughtful. 'So let's say you don't go back on gun duty. Plenty of desks need filling.'

Callis was shaking his head. 'That's not for me, John. The paperwork always got me down.'

'You could go back on the beat . . .?'

Callis was staring into space, not really listening. 'The thing that gets me is, I sit here with the shakes, and those little bastards are still out there, carrying guns and getting away with it. What sort of system is that, John?' He turned to stare at Rebus. 'What the hell use are we if we can't stop that happening?'

'Sitting here and getting maudlin's not going to change things,' Rebus said quietly. There was as much anger as defeat in his friend's eyes. Slowly, Callis lifted both feet from the stool and eased himself upright. 'I'm going to put the kettle on. Can I get you anything?'

On the television, several contestants were arguing over some task. Rebus checked his watch. 'I'm fine, Andy. I should really be going.'

'It's nice of you to keep dropping in, John, but you shouldn't feel you have to.'

'It's only a pretext for raiding your drinks cabinet, Andy. Soon as that's empty, you won't see me for dust.'

Callis tried smiling. 'Phone for a cab, if you like.'

'I've got my mobile.' And he could use it, too – albeit by pushing each key with a pen.

135

'Sure I can't get you something else?'

Rebus shook his head. 'Busy day tomorrow.'

'Me too,' Andy Callis said.

Rebus obliged him with a nod. Their conversation always finished this way: *Busy tomorrow, John? Always busy, Andy. Aye, me too* . . . He thought of things he could say – about the shooting, about Peacock Johnson. He didn't think they would do any good. In time, they'd be able to talk – talk properly, rather than the games of ping-pong which so often passed for conversation between them. But not yet.

'I'll see myself out,' Rebus called towards the kitchen.

'Stay till the taxi gets here.'

'I need a breath of air, Andy.'

'What you mean is, you need a ciggie.'

'Instincts like that, I can't believe they never made you a detective.' Rebus opened the front door.

'Never wanted to be one,' came Andy Callis's closing words.

In the cab, Rebus decided on a detour, telling the driver to head towards Gracemount, then directing him to Martin Fairstone's house. The windows had been boarded up, door padlocked against vandals. It would only take a couple of junkies to turn the place into a crack den. There were no scorch marks on the exterior walls. The kitchen was to the back of the property. That was where the damage would be. The fire crew had dragged some fittings and furnishings out on to the overgrown lawn: chairs, a table, a broken-down upright hoover. Left there, not even worth looting. Rebus told the driver they could go. Some teenagers had gathered at a bus stop. Rebus didn't think they were waiting for a bus. The shelter was their gang hut. Two of them stood on top of it, three others lurked in its shadows. The driver came to a stop.

'What's up?' Rebus asked.

'I think they've got rocks. We drive past, they'll pelt us.'

Rebus looked. The boys on top of the shelter were standing stock-still. He couldn't see anything in their hands.

'Give me a second,' Rebus said, getting out.

The driver turned. 'You off your head, pal?'

'No, but I'll be mad as hell if you drive off without me,' Rebus warned. Then, leaving the cab door open, he walked towards the bus stop. Three bodies stepped out of the shelter. They wore hooded tops, the hoods pulled tight around their faces to ward off the night chill. Hands tucked into pockets. Thin, wiry specimens in baggy denims and trainers.

Rebus ignored them, kept his eyes on the two atop the shelter. 'Collecting rocks, eh?' he called. 'It was birds' eggs with me.'

'Fuck are you talking about?'

Rebus lowered his eyes, meeting the hard stare of the leader. Had to be the leader: flanked either side by his lieutenants.

'I know you,' Rebus said.

The youth looked at him. 'So?'

'So maybe you remember me.'

'I ken you all right.' The youth made a snorting noise, in imitation of a pig.

'Then you'll know how much damage I can do you.'

One of the boys on top of the shelter let out a laugh. 'There's five of us, ya wanker.'

'Good on you, you've learned to count to five.' A car's headlights appeared, and Rebus could hear his taxi's engine start to whine. He glanced back, but the driver was only moving it closer to the kerb. The approaching car slowed, but then sped up, unwilling to get involved. 'And I take your point,' Rebus continued. 'Five against one, you'd probably kick the shit out of me. But that's not what I meant. What I meant was what happens after. Because the one thing you can be sure of is that I'd see you charged, sentenced and stuck in jail. Young offenders? Fine: you'd

137

get a spell in some cushy institution. But before that, they'd have you banged up in Saughton. Adult wing. And that, believe me, would be an absolute pain in the arse.' Rebus paused. *Your* arses, to be precise.'

'This is our fucking ground,' one of the others spat. 'Not yours.'

Rebus gestured back towards the taxi. 'Which is why I'm leaving . . . with your permission.' His eyes were back on the leader again. His name was Rab Fisher. He was fifteen, and Rebus had heard his gang called the Lost Boys. Plenty of arrests under their belts, no actual prosecutions. Mums and dads at home who would say they'd done their best – 'battered the life out of him' first few times he was caught, according to Fisher's dad. *But what can you do?*

Rebus had a few answers. Too late for them though. Easier just to accept the Lost Boys as another statistic.

'Do I have your permission, Rab?'

Fisher was still staring, relishing this moment of power. The world waited on his say-so. 'I could do with some gloves,' he said at last.

'Not these ones,' Rebus told him.

'They look comfy.'

Rebus shook his head slowly, started sliding one glove off, trying not to flinch. He held up a blistered hand. 'Yours if you want, Rab, but this has been inside it . . .'

'That's fucking gross,' one of the lieutenants stated.

'Which is why you wouldn't want to wear them.' Rebus slipped the glove back on, turned and headed back to the cab. He got in and shut the door after him.

'Drive past them,' he ordered. The cab moved forward again. Rebus kept his eyes front, though he knew five separate stares were on him. As the cab speeded up, there was a thud on the roof, and a half-brick bounced across the road.

'Just a shot across our bows,' Rebus said.

'Easy for you to say, chief. It's not your fucking cab.'

Back on the main road, they paused at a red light. A car

had stopped across the road, its interior light on as the driver pored over a street-plan.

'Poor sod,' the cabbie commented. 'Wouldn't like to get lost around here.'

'Do a U-turn,' Rebus ordered.

'What?'

'Do a U-turn and pull over in front of it.'

'What for?'

'Because I'm asking,' Rebus snapped.

The driver's body language told Rebus he'd had easier fares. As the lights turned green, he signalled for a right turn, and executed the manoeuvre, pulling up to the kerb. Rebus already had the money ready. 'Keep the change,' he said, getting out.

'I've earned it, pal.'

Rebus walked back to the parked car, opened the passenger door and slid inside. 'Nice night for a drive,' he told Siobhan Clarke.

'Isn't it?' The street-plan had disappeared, probably beneath her seat. She was watching the cabbie getting out, examining the roof of his vehicle. 'So what brings you to this part of the world?'

'I was visiting a friend,' Rebus told her. 'What's your excuse?'

'Do I need one?'

The cabbie was shaking his head, casting a baleful look in Rebus's direction before geting back into the driving seat and heading off, executing another U-turn so he could make for the safety of town.

'Which street is it you're looking for?' Rebus asked. She looked at him and he smiled. 'I saw you studying the A to Z. Let me guess: Fairstone's house?'

It took her a moment to answer. 'How did you know?'

He shrugged. 'Call it a man's intuition.'

She raised an eyebrow. 'I'm impressed. I'm also guessing that's where you've just come from?'

'I was visiting a friend.'

'Does this friend have a name?'

'Andy Callis.'

'I don't think I know him.'

'Andy was one of the woolly-suits. He's on sick leave.'

'You say "was" . . . makes me think he's not coming back from sick leave.'

'Now it's my turn to be impressed.' Rebus shifted in the seat. 'Andy's lost it . . . mentally, I mean.'

'Lost it for good?'

Rebus shrugged. 'I keep thinking . . . Ach, never mind.'

'Where does he live?'

'Alnwickhill.' Rebus had answered without thinking. He glared at Siobhan, knowing it had been no innocent question. She was smiling back at him.

'That's near Howdenhall, isn't it?' She reached under her seat, produced the street-plan. 'Bit of a distance from here . . .'

'All right, so I took a detour on the way back.'

'To look at Fairstone's house?'

'Yes.'

She seemed satisfied, closed the map.

'I'm in the frame for this, Siobhan,' Rebus said. 'That gives me a reason to be nosy. What's yours?'

'Well, I just thought . . .' She was struggling, tables effectively turned.

'Thought what?' He held up a gloved hand. 'Never mind. It's painful watching you trying to come up with a story. Here's what I think . . .'

'What?'

'I think you weren't looking for Fairstone's house.'

'Oh?'

Rebus shook his head. 'You were going to do some sniffing. See if you could conduct a little private investigation, maybe track down friends, people who'd known him . . . Maybe someone like Peacock Johnson. How am I doing?'

'Why would I do that?'

'I get the feeling you're not convinced Fairstone's dead.'

'Male intuition again?'

'You hinted as much when I phoned you.'

She gnawed her bottom lip.

'Want to talk about it?' he offered quietly.

She looked down into her lap. 'I got a message.'

'What sort of message?'

'It was signed "Marty", waiting for me at St Leonard's.'

Rebus was thoughtful. 'Then I know just the thing to do.'

'What?'

'Head back into town and I'll show you . . .'

What he had to show her was the High Street, and Gordon's Trattoria, where they stayed open late, serving strong coffee and pasta. Rebus and Siobhan slid into an empty booth, either side of the tight-fitting table, ordering double espressos.

'Make mine decaf,' Siobhan remembered to say.

'What's with the unleaded?' Rebus asked.

'I'm trying to cut down.'

He accepted this. 'Anything to eat, or is that *verboten*, too?'

'I'm not hungry.'

Rebus decided that he was, and ordered a seafood pizza, warning Siobhan that she'd have to help him out with it. The back half of Gordon's comprised the restaurant, only one voluble table left sitting, polishing off *digestifs*. Where Rebus and Siobhan sat, near the front door, it was all booths and snacks.

'So tell me again what the message said.'

She sighed and repeated it for him.

'And the postmark was local?'

'Yes.'

'First- or second-class stamp?'

'What does it matter?'

Rebus shrugged. 'Fairstone struck me as definitely

141

second class.' He watched her. She looked tired and wired at the same time, a potentially fatal conjunction. Unbidden, the image of Andy Callis came to his mind.

'Maybe Ray Duff will shed some light,' Siobhan was saying.

'If anyone can, it's Ray.'

The coffees arrived. Siobhan lifted hers to her lips. 'They're going to string you up tomorrow, aren't they?'

'Maybe,' he said. 'Whatever happens, I think you should keep well clear. That means not talking to Fairstone's friends. If the Complaints catch you, they'll smell a plot.'

'You definitely think it was Fairstone who died in that fire?'

'No reason not to.'

'Apart from the message.'

'It wasn't his style, Siobhan. He wouldn't have posted a letter, he'd have come straight to you, same as all the other times.'

She considered this. 'I know,' she said at last.

There was a lull in the conversation, both of them sipping the strong, bitter coffee. 'Sure you're all right?' Rebus eventually asked.

'Fine.'

'Sure?'

'Do you want it in writing?'

'I want you to mean it.'

Her eyes had darkened, but she didn't say anything. The pizza arrived, and Rebus cut it into slices, cajoling her into taking one. There was silence again as they ate. The drunken table was leaving, laughing noisily all the way into the street. Closing the door, their waiter raised his eyes to heaven, giving thanks that the restaurant was quiet again.

'Everything okay over here?'

'Fine,' Rebus said, eyes on Siobhan.

'Fine,' she repeated, holding his gaze.

*

Siobhan said she'd give him a lift home. Getting into the car, Rebus glanced at his watch: eleven o'clock.

'Can we get the news headlines?' he asked. 'See if Port Edgar's still the main story.'

She nodded, switched on the radio.

'... where a candlelit vigil is being held tonight. Our reporter, Janice Graham, is at the scene ...'

'Tonight, in South Queensferry, the residents are making their voices heard. Hymns will be sung, and the local Church of Scotland minister will be joined by the school chaplain. Candles may be a problem, however, as there's a stiff breeze blowing from the Firth of Forth. For all of that, a sizeable crowd is already beginning to gather, with local MSP Jack Bell in attendance. Mr Bell, whose son was wounded in the tragedy, is hoping to gather support for his gun legislation campaign. Here's what he said earlier ...'

Stopped at a red light, Rebus and Siobhan shared a look. Then she nodded, no words needed between them. When the light changed to green, she drove across the junction, pulled into the side of the road, and waited for traffic to clear before doing a U-turn.

The vigil was being held outside the school gates. A few flickering candles were managing to stay lit, but most people knew better and had brought torches. Siobhan double-parked next to a news van. The crews were out in force: TV cameras, microphones, flash-bulbs. But they were outnumbered ten to one by singers and the merely curious.

'Got to be four hundred people here,' Siobhan said.

Rebus nodded. The road was completely blocked by bodies. A few uniformed constables were standing on the periphery, hands behind their backs in what was probably meant as a gesture of respect. Rebus saw that Jack Bell had been pulled to one side so that he could share his views with half a dozen journalists, who were busily nodding and scribbling, filling sheet after sheet of their notebooks as he talked.

'Nice touch,' Siobhan said. Rebus saw what she meant: Bell was wearing a black armband.

'Subtle, definitely,' he agreed.

At that moment, Bell looked up and noticed them, eyes staying on them as he continued his oration. Rebus started winding his way through the crowd, standing on tiptoe to view the scene immediately in front of the gates. The church minister was tall, young, and in good voice. Next to him stood a much smaller woman of similar age. Rebus guessed that this was the chaplain of Port Edgar Academy. A hand tugged at his arm, and he looked to his immediate left, where Kate Renshaw was standing, well-wrapped against the cold, a pink woollen scarf muffling her mouth. He smiled and nodded. A couple of men near by, their singing enthusiastic but off-key, looked to have come directly from one of South Queensferry's hostelries. Rebus could smell beer and cigarettes in the air. One man jabbed his friend in the ribs, nodding towards a roving TV camera. They straightened up, and sang all the louder.

Rebus didn't know if they were local or not. Sightseers possibly. Hoping to catch a glimpse of themselves on the box over tomorrow morning's breakfast . . .

The hymn finished, and the chaplain started saying a few words, her voice faint, hardly carrying as a strong wind started gusting in from the coast. Rebus looked at Kate again and gestured towards the back of the crowd. She followed him to where Siobhan was standing on the periphery. A cameraman had climbed up on to the school's perimeter wall to get an overview of the crowd, and was being told to come down again by one of the uniforms.

'Hi there, Kate,' Siobhan said. Kate pulled her scarf down.

'Hello,' she said.

'Your dad not here?' Rebus asked. Kate shook her head.

144

'He'll hardly set foot outside the house.' She folded her arms around herself, bounced on her toes, feeling the chill.

'Good turn-out,' Rebus said, eyes on the crowd.

Kate nodded. 'I'm amazed how many of them know who I am. They keep saying how sorry they are about Derek.'

'Something like this, it can bring people together,' Siobhan said.

'If it didn't . . . well, what would that say about us?' Someone else had caught her attention. 'Sorry, I've got to . . .' She started walking over towards the huddle of journalists. It was Bell; Bell who had gestured for her to join him. He put an arm around her shoulder as more flash-guns lit the hedgerow behind them. Wreaths and bunches of flowers had been left there, with fluttering messages and snapshots of the victims.

'. . . and it's thanks to the support of people like her that I think we stand a chance. More than a chance, in fact, because something like this can – and should – never be tolerated in what we like to call a civilised society. We never want to see it happen again, and that's why we're taking this stand . . .'

When Bell paused to show the journalists the clipboard he was holding, the questions started. He kept a protective arm on Kate's shoulders as she answered them. Protective, Rebus wondered, or proprietorial?

'Well,' Kate was saying, 'the petition's a good idea . . .'

'An excellent idea,' Bell corrected her.

'. . . but it's only the start. What's really needed is action, action from the authorities to stop guns getting into the wrong hands.' At the word 'authorities', she glanced towards Rebus and Siobhan.

'If I can just give you some figures,' Bell interrupted again, brandishing the clipboard, 'gun crime is on the increase – we all know that. But the statistics don't begin to tell the story. Depending on who you listen to, you'll hear that gun crime is rising at ten per cent a year, or twenty per

145

cent, or even forty per cent. Any rise whatsoever is not only bad news, not only a shameful blot on the records of police and intelligence-gathering resources, but, more importantly—'

'Kate, if I could just ask you,' one of the journalists butted in, 'how do you think you can get the government to listen to the victims?'

'I'm not sure I can. Maybe it's time to ignore the government altogether and appeal directly to the people who're actually doing the shooting, the people selling these guns, bringing them into the country . . .'

Bell pitched his voice even louder. 'As far back as 1996, the Home Office reckoned that two thousand guns per week – per *week* – were coming into the UK illegally . . . many of them through the Channel Tunnel. Since the Dunblane ban came into force, handgun crimes have increased forty per cent . . .'

'Kate, if we could ask you for your opinion of . . .'

Rebus had turned away, walking back to Siobhan's car. When she caught up with him, he was lighting a cigarette, or trying to. The wind meant his lighter kept sputtering.

'Going to help me?' he asked.

'No.'

'Cheers.'

But she relented, holding her coat open so that he could shelter long enough to get the cigarette lit. He nodded his thanks.

'Seen enough?' she asked.

'Reckon we're every bit as bad as the ghouls?'

She considered this, then shook her head. 'We're interested parties.'

'That's one way of putting it.'

The crowd was beginning to disperse. Many were lingering to study the hedgerow's makeshift shrine, but others started passing the spot where Rebus and Siobhan stood. The faces were solemn, resolute, tear-stained. One woman was hugging both her pre-teenage children to her, the kids bemused, perhaps wondering what they'd done to bring on their mother's sobs. An elderly man, leaning heavily on a walking-frame, seemed determined to walk the route home without any other help, shaking his head at the many who offered.

A group of teenagers had come dressed in their Port Edgar uniforms. Rebus didn't doubt they'd been captured by a few dozen cameras since their arrival. The girls' mascara had run. The boys looked awkward, as if regretting coming. Rebus looked for Miss Teri, but didn't see her.

'Isn't that your friend?' Siobhan said, gesturing with her head. Rebus studied the crowd again, saw immediately who she meant.

Peacock Johnson, part of the procession heading back into town. And beside him, a full foot shorter, Evil Bob. Bob had removed his baseball cap for the duration, showing the balding crown of his head. Now, he was fixing the cap back into place. Johnson had dressed down for the occasion: a grey shimmering shirt, silk maybe, beneath a full-length black raincoat. There was a black string-tie around his neck, fixed with a silver clasp. He, too, had removed his headgear – a grey trilby – which he held in both hands, running his fingers around its rim.

Johnson seemed to sense that he was being stared at. When his eyes met Rebus's, Rebus crooked a finger at him. Johnson said something to his lieutenant, the pair of them threading their way through the throng.

'Mr Rebus, paying your respects like the true gentleman you doubtless perceive yourself to be.'

'That's my excuse . . . what's yours?'

'The self-same, Mr Rebus, the self-same.' He made a little bow at the waist in Siobhan's direction.

'Lady-friend or colleague?' he asked Rebus.

'The latter,' Siobhan answered.

'No requirement for the two to be, as they say, mutually exclusive.' He grinned at her while sliding his hat back on.

'See that guy over there?' Rebus said, nodding towards

where Jack Bell was finishing his interview. 'If I told him who you are and what you do, he'd have a field day.'

'Mr Bell, you mean? First thing we did when we got here was sign his petition, isn't that right, wee man?' Looking down at his companion. Bob didn't seem to understand, but nodded anyway. 'Clear conscience, you see,' Johnson continued.

'Doesn't begin to explain what you're doing here . . . unless that conscience of yours is guilty rather than clear.'

'A low blow, if you don't mind me saying.' Johnson winced for effect. 'Say goodnight to the nice detectives,' he said, patting Evil Bob's shoulder.

'Goodnight, nice detectives.' A wet smile appearing on the over-fed face. Peacock Johnson had joined the crowd again, head bowed as if in Christian contemplation. Bob fell in a couple of paces behind his master, for all the world like a pet being taken for a walk.

'What do we make of that?' Siobhan asked.

Rebus shook his head slowly.

'Maybe your comment about guilt isn't wide of the mark.'

'Be nice to nail the bastard for something.'

She gave him a questioning look, but his attention had turned to Jack Bell, who was whispering something in Kate's ear. Kate nodded, and the MSP gave her a hug.

'Reckon she's got a future in politics?' Siobhan mused.

'I hope to Christ that's the attraction,' Rebus muttered, showing his cigarette stub little mercy as he ground it under his heel.

Day Three

Thursday

8

'Is this country the pits or what?' Bobby Hogan asked.

Rebus felt it was an unfair question. They were on the M74, one of the most lethal roads in Scotland. Articulated lorries were lashing Hogan's Passat with a spray which was nine parts grit to one of water. The wipers were on at high speed, and still not coping, despite which Hogan was trying to do seventy. But doing seventy meant getting past the trucks, and the HGV drivers were enjoying an extended game of leapfrog, leading to a queue of cars waiting to overtake.

Dawn had brought milky sunshine to the capital, but Rebus had known it wouldn't last. The sky had been too hazy, blurred like a drunk's good intentions. Hogan had decided they should rendezvous at St Leonard's, by which time fully half of Arthur's Seat's great stone outcrop had vanished into the cloud. Rebus doubted David Copperfield could have pulled the trick off with any more brio. When Arthur's Seat started disappearing, rain was sure to follow. It had started before they reached the city boundary, Hogan flipping the wipers to intermittent, then to constant. Now, on the M74 south of Glasgow, they were flying to and fro like Roadrunner's legs in the cartoon.

'I mean, the weather . . . the traffic . . . why do we put up with it?'

'Penitence?' Rebus offered.

'Suggesting we've done something to deserve it.'

'Like you say, Bobby, there must be a reason we stay put.'

'Maybe we're just lazy.'

'We can't change the weather. I suppose it's in our power to tweak the amount of traffic, but that never seems to work, so why bother?'

Hogan raised a finger. 'Exactly. We simply can't be arsed.'

'You think that's a fault?'

Hogan shrugged. 'It's hardly a strength, is it?'

'I suppose not.'

'Whole country's gone to cack. Jobs up the khyber, politicians with their snouts in the trough, kids with no . . . I don't know.' He exhaled noisily.

'Touch of the Victor Meldrews this morning, Bobby?'

Hogan shook his head. 'I've been thinking this for ages.'

'And I thank you for inviting me into the confessional.'

'Know something, John? You're more cynical than I am.'

'That's not true.'

'Give me a for instance.'

'For instance, I believe in an afterlife. What's more, I think the pair of us are going to be entering it sooner than expected if you don't ease the foot off . . .'

Hogan smiled for the first time that morning, signalled to pull into the middle lane. 'Better?' he asked.

'Better,' Rebus agreed.

Then, a few moments later: 'You really believe there's something there after we die?'

Rebus considered his answer. 'I believe it was a way of getting you to slow down.' He pushed in the button for the car's cigarette lighter, then wished he hadn't. Hogan noticed him flinch.

'Still giving you gyp?'

'It's getting better.'

'Tell me again how it happened.'

Rebus shook his head slowly. 'Let's talk about Carbrae instead. How much are we really going to get from Robert Niles?'

'With a bit of luck, more than his name, rank and serial number,' Hogan said, pulling out again to overtake.

Carbrae Special Hospital was sited, as Hogan himself described it, in 'the sweaty armpit of who-knows-where'. Neither man had been there before. Hogan's directions were to take the A711 west of Dumfries and head towards Dalbeattie. They seemed to miss a turn-off, Hogan cursing the solid wall of lorries in the inside lane, reckoning they'd hidden a signpost or slip-road from view. As a result, they didn't come off the M74 till Lockerbie, heading west into Dumfries.

'Were you at Lockerbie, John?' Hogan asked.

'Just for a couple of days.'

'Remember that fuck-up with the bodies? Laying them out on the ice-rink?' Hogan shook his head slowly. Rebus remembered: the bodies had stuck to the ice, meaning the whole rink had to be defrosted. 'That's what I mean about Scotland, John. That just about sums us up.'

Rebus disagreed. He thought the quiet dignity of the townspeople in the aftermath of Pan Am 103 said a hell of a lot more about the country. He couldn't help wondering how the people of South Queensferry would cope, once the three-ring circus of police, media and mouthy politicians had moved on. He'd watched fifteen minutes of morning news while slurping down a coffee, but had to turn the sound off when Jack Bell appeared, snaking one arm around Kate, whose face shone a ghostly white.

Hogan had picked up a bundle of newspapers between his home and Rebus's. Some had managed to get photos from the vigil into their later editions: the minister leading the singing; the MSP holding up his petition.

'I can't sleep at all,' one resident was quoted as saying, 'for fear of who else might be out there.'

Fear: the crucial word. Most people would live their whole lives untouched by crime, yet they still feared it, and that fear was real and smothering. The police force existed to allay such fears, yet too often was shown to be fallible, powerless, on hand only after the event, clearing up the mess rather than preventing it. Meantime, someone like Jack Bell began to look as if he was at least trying to do something . . . Rebus knew the terms they trotted out at seminars: proactive rather than reactive. One of the tabloids had latched on to this. They were backing Bell's campaign, whatever it might be: *If our forces of law and order can't deal with this very real and growing problem, then it's up to us as individuals or organised groups to take a stand against the tide of violence which is engulfing our culture . . .*

An easy enough editorial to write, Rebus surmised, the author merely dictating the MSP's words. Hogan glanced towards the newspaper.

'Bell's on a roll, isn't he?'

'It won't last.'

'I hope not. Sanctimonious bastard gives me the boak.'

'Can I quote you on that, Detective Inspector Hogan?'

'Journalists: now there's another reason this country's the pits . . .'

They stopped for coffee in Dumfries. The café was a dreary combination of formica and bad lighting, but neither man cared once they'd taken a bite from the thick bacon butties. Hogan looked at his watch and calculated that they'd been on the road the best part of two hours.

'Least the rain's stopping,' Rebus said.

'Put out the flags,' Hogan responded.

Rebus decided to try a change of subject. 'Ever been this way before?'

'I'm sure I must've driven through Dumfries; doesn't ring a bell though.'

'I came on holiday once. Caravan on the Solway Firth.'

'When was this?' Hogan was licking melted butter from between his fingers.

'Years back . . . Sammy was still in nappies.' Sammy: Rebus's daughter.

'You ever hear from her?'

'A phone call now and then.'

'She still down in England?' Hogan watched Rebus nod. 'Good luck to her.' He opened his roll and peeled some of the fat from the bacon. 'Scottish diet: that's another thing we're cursed with.'

'Christ, Bobby, shall I just drop you off at Carbrae? You could sign yourself in, play Mr Grumpy to a captive audience.'

'I'm just saying . . .'

'Saying what? We get shit weather and eat shit food? Maybe you should have Grant Hood stage a press conference, seeing how it's going to come as news to every bugger who lives here.'

Hogan concentrated on his snack, chewing without seeming to swallow. 'Too long cooped up in that car, maybe?' he finally offered.

'Too long on the Port Edgar case,' Rebus countered.

'It's only been—'

'I don't care how long it's been. Don't tell me you're getting enough sleep? Putting it all behind you when you go home at night? Switching off? Delegating? Letting others share the—'

'I get the point.' Hogan paused. 'I brought you in, didn't I?'

'Just as well, or I suspect you'd have been driving down here on your lonesome.'

'And?'

'And there wouldn't have been anybody to moan at.' Rebus looked at him. 'Feel better for letting it all out?'

Hogan smiled. 'Maybe you're right.'

'Well, wouldn't that be a first for the books?'

Both men ended up laughing, Hogan insisting on picking up the tab, Rebus leaving a tip. Back in the car, they found the road to Dalbeattie. Ten miles out of Dumfries, a single signpost pointed right, taking them up a narrow, winding track with grass growing in the middle.

'Not much traffic then,' Rebus commented.

155

'Bit out of the way for visitors,' Hogan agreed.

Carbrae had been purpose-built in the forward-looking 1960s, a long box-shaped structure with annexes off. None of which could be seen until they had parked the car, identified themselves at the gate, and been met and escorted within the thick, grey concrete walls. There was an outer perimeter, too, a wire fence twenty feet high, topped here and there with security cameras. At the gatehouse they'd been given laminated passes, hung by a red ribbon from the neck. Signs warned visitors of forbidden items within the complex. No food or drink, newspapers or magazines. No sharp objects. Nothing was to be passed to a patient without prior consultation with a member of staff. Mobile phones were not permitted: 'Our patients can be upset by the slightest thing, no matter how harmless it may seem to you. If in doubt, please ASK!'

'Any chance we might upset Robert Niles?' Hogan asked, his eyes meeting Rebus's.

'Not in our nature, Bobby,' Rebus said, switching off his phone.

And then an orderly appeared, and they were in.

They walked down a garden path, neat flowerbeds to either side. There were faces at some of the windows. No bars on the windows themselves. Rebus had expected the orderlies to be thinly disguised bouncers, huge and silent, dressed in hospital whites or some other form of uniform. But their guide, Billy, was small and cheery-looking, casually clothed in T-shirt, jeans and soft-soled shoes. Rebus had a horrible thought: the lunatics had taken over the asylum, the real staff locked away. It would explain Billy's beaming, rosy-cheeked countenance. Or maybe he'd just been dipping into the medicine locker.

'Dr Lesser is waiting in her room,' Billy was saying.

'What about Niles?'

'You'll talk to Robert there. He doesn't like strangers going into his own room.'

'Oh?'

'He's funny that way.' Billy shrugged his shoulders, as if to say: don't we all have our little foibles? He punched numbers into a keypad by the front door, smiling up at the camera trained on him. The door clicked open, and they entered the hospital.

The place smelled of . . . not exactly medicine. What was it? Then Rebus realised: it was the aroma of new carpets – specifically the blue carpet which stretched before them down the corridor. Fresh paint, too, by the look of it. Apple green, Rebus guessed it had said on the industrial-sized tins. Pictures on the walls, stuck there with Blu-tack. Nothing framed, and no drawing-pins. The place was quiet. Their shoes made no noise on the carpet. No piped music, no screams. Billy led them down the hall, stopping before an open door.

'Dr Lesser?'

The woman inside was seated at a modern desk. She smiled and peered over her half-moon glasses.

'You got here then,' she stated.

'Sorry, we're a few minutes late,' Hogan began to apologise.

'It's not that,' she reassured him. 'It's just that people miss the turn-off, and then phone to say they're lost.'

'We didn't get lost.'

'So I see.' She had come forward to greet them with handshakes. Hogan and Rebus introduced themselves.

'Thanks, Billy,' she said. Billy gave a little bow and backed away. 'Won't you come in? I won't bite.' She offered her smile again. Rebus wondered if it was part of the job description for working at Carbrae.

The room was small, comfortable. A yellow two-seat sofa; bookshelf; hi-fi. No filing cabinets. Rebus guessed the patient files would be kept well away from prying eyes. Dr Lesser said they could call her Irene. She was in her late twenties or early thirties, with chestnut-brown hair falling to just below her shoulders. Her eyes were the same colour

157

as the clouds which had obscured Arthur's Seat earlier that morning.

'Please, sit yourselves down.' Her accent was English. Rebus thought Liverpudlian.

'Dr Lesser . . .' Hogan began.

'Irene, please.'

'Of course.' Hogan paused, as if weighing up whether to use her first name. If he did, she might start using *his* first name, and that would be way too cosy. 'You understand why we're here?'

Lesser nodded. She had pulled over a chair so she could sit in front of the detectives. Rebus was aware that the sofa was a tight fit: Bobby and him, probably thirty stones between them . . .

'And you understand,' Lesser was saying, 'that Robert has the right to say nothing. If he starts to get upset, the interview is over and that's final.'

Hogan nodded. 'You'll be sitting in, of course.'

She raised an eyebrow. 'Of course.'

It was the answer they'd expected, but disappointing all the same.

'Doctor,' Rebus began, 'maybe you could help prepare us. What can we expect from Mr Niles?'

'I don't like to pre-empt—'

'For example, is there anything we should avoid saying? Maybe trip-words?'

She looked appraisingly at Rebus. 'He won't talk about what he did to his wife.'

'That's not why we're here.'

She thought for a moment. 'He doesn't know his friend is dead.'

'He doesn't know Herdman's dead?' Hogan repeated.

'News doesn't interest the patients, on the whole.'

'You'd prefer it if we kept it that way?' Rebus guessed.

'I'm assuming you don't need to tell him why you're so interested in Mr Herdman . . .'

'You're right, we don't.' Rebus looked to Hogan. 'Just have to watch we don't slip up, eh, Bobby?'

As Hogan nodded, there was a knock on the still-open door. All three of them stood up. A tall, muscular man was waiting there. Bull neck, tattooed arms. For a moment, Rebus thought: now that's what orderlies are supposed to look like. Then he saw Lesser's face, and realised that this giant was Robert Niles.

'Robert . . .' The doctor's smile was back in place, but Rebus knew she was wondering how long Niles had been there, and how much he'd taken in.

'Billy said . . .' The voice was like a rumble of thunder.

'That's right. Come in, come in.'

As Niles entered the room, Hogan made to close the door after him.

'Not in here,' Lesser commanded. 'The door is always open.'

Two ways of taking that: openness, nothing to hide; or meaning an attack was more likely to be spotted.

Lesser was gesturing for Niles to take her chair, while she retreated behind her desk. As Niles sat down, so did the two detectives, wedging themselves back into the sofa.

Niles stared at them, face angled downwards, eyes hooded.

'These men have a few questions they'd like to ask you, Robert.'

'What sort of questions?' Niles was wearing a dazzling white T-shirt and grey jogging bottoms. Rebus was trying not to stare at the tattoos. They were old, probably dated back to his army days. When Rebus had been a soldier, he'd been the only recruit not to celebrate joining up by getting a few tattoos on his first home leave. Niles's specimens included a thistle, a couple of writhing snakes, and a dagger with a banner wrapped around it. Rebus suspected the dagger was something to do with his time in the SAS, even though the regiment frowned upon ornamentation: tattoos were like scars – means of identification.

Which meant they could be used against you if you were ever captured . . .

Hogan had decided to take the initiative. 'We want to ask you about your friend Lee.'

'Lee?'

'Lee Herdman. He visits you sometimes?'

'Sometimes, yes.' The words came slowly. Rebus wondered how much medication Niles was on.

'Have you seen him lately?'

'Few weeks back . . . I think.' Niles swung his head towards Dr Lesser. Time probably didn't mean much in Carbrae. She nodded encouragingly.

'What do you talk about when he comes to see you?'

'The old days.'

'Anything in particular?'

'Just . . . the old days. Life was good back then.'

'Was that Lee's opinion, too?' Hogan ended the question and sucked in air, realising he'd just used the past tense about Herdman.

'What's all this about?' Another look towards Lesser, reminding Rebus of a trained animal seeking some instruction from its owner. 'Do I have to be here?'

'Door's open, Robert.' Lesser waved a hand in its direction. 'You know that.'

'Lee seems to have gone, Mr Niles,' Rebus said, leaning forward a little. 'We just want to know what happened to him.'

'Gone?'

Rebus shrugged. 'It's a long drive down here from Queensferry. The pair of you must be pretty close.'

'We were soldiers together.'

Rebus nodded. 'SAS Regiment. You were the same unit?'

'C Squadron.'

'That was nearly me once.' Rebus tried a smile. 'I was a Para . . . tried for the Regiment.'

'What happened?'

160

Rebus was trying not to think back. There were horrors lurking there. 'Flunked the training.'

'How soon did you drop?'

Easier to tell the truth than to lie. 'I passed everything up until the psychological stuff.'

A smile broke Niles's face wide open. 'They cracked you.'

Rebus nodded. 'I cracked like a fucking egg, mate.' Mate: a soldier's word.

'When was this?'

'Early seventies.'

'Bit before me then.' Niles was thinking. 'They had to change the interrogations,' he remembered. 'Used to be a lot harder.'

'I was part of that.'

'You cracked under interrogation? What did they do to you?' Niles's eyes narrowed. He was more alert now, having a conversation, someone else answering *his* questions.

'Kept me in a cell ... constant noise and light ... screams from the other cells ...'

Rebus knew he had everyone's attention now. Niles clapped his hands together. 'The chopper?' he asked. When Rebus nodded, he clapped again, turned to Dr Lesser. 'They put a sack over your head and take you up in a chopper, then say they'll drop you if you don't give them what they want. When they dump you out, you're only eight feet above the ground, only you don't know that!' He turned back to Rebus. 'It really fucks you up.' Then he thrust forward a hand for Rebus to shake.

'It really does,' Rebus agreed, trying to ignore the searing pain of the handshake.

'Sounds barbaric to me,' Dr Lesser commented, her face paler than before.

'It breaks you or it makes you,' Niles corrected her.

'It broke me,' Rebus agreed. 'But you, Robert ... did it make you?'

'For a while it did.' Niles grew a little less agitated. 'It's when you get out . . . that's when it hits you.'

'What?'

'The fact that all the things you . . .' He fell silent, as still as a statue. Some new set of chemicals kicking in? But behind Niles's back, Lesser was shaking her head, meaning there was nothing to worry about. The giant was just lost in thought. 'I knew some Paras,' he said at last. 'Right hard bastards, they were.'

'I was Rifle Company, 2 Para.'

'Saw time in Ulster then?'

Rebus nodded. 'And elsewhere.'

Niles tapped the side of his nose. Rebus imagined those fingers gripping a knife, drawing the blade across a smooth white throat . . . 'Mum's the word,' Niles said.

But the word Rebus had been thinking of was 'wife'. 'Last time you saw Lee,' he asked quietly, 'did he seem okay? Maybe he was worried about something?'

Niles shook his head. 'Lee always puts on a brave face. I never get to see him when he's down.'

'But you know there are times when he *is* down?'

'We're trained not to show it. We're *men*!'

'Yes, we are,' Rebus confirmed.

'Army doesn't have any place for cry-babies. Cry-babies can't shoot a stranger dead, or lob a grenade at him. You've got to be able to . . . what you're trained for is . . .' But the words wouldn't come. Niles twisted his hands together, as though trying to choke them into existence. He looked from Rebus to Hogan and back again.

'Sometimes . . . sometimes they don't know how to switch us off . . .'

Hogan sat forward. 'Does that apply to Lee, do you think?'

Niles stared at him. 'He's done something, hasn't he?'

Hogan swallowed back a response, looked to Dr Lesser for guidance. But it was too late. Niles was rising slowly from his chair.

162

'I'm going to go now,' he said, moving towards the door. Hogan opened his mouth to say something, but Rebus touched his arm, stilling him, knowing he was probably about to toss a grenade into the room: *Your pal's dead, and he took some schoolkids with him* . . . Dr Lesser got up and walked to the doorway, reassuring herself that Niles wasn't hiding just out of sight. Satisfied, she took the chair he'd just vacated.

'He seems pretty bright,' Rebus commented.

'Bright?'

'In control. Is that the medication?'

'Medication plays its part.' She crossed one trousered leg over the other. Rebus noticed that she wore no jewellery at all, nothing on her wrists or around her neck, and no earrings that he could see.

'When he's . . . "cured" . . . does he go back to jail?'

'People think coming to a place like this is a soft option. I can assure you it isn't.'

'That's not what I was getting at. I just wondered—'

'From what I remember,' Hogan interrupted, 'Niles never explained why he cut his wife's throat. Has he been any more forthcoming with you, Doctor?'

She looked at him, unblinking. 'That has no relevance to your visit.'

Hogan shrugged. 'You're right, I'm just curious.'

Lesser turned her attention to Rebus. 'Maybe it's a kind of brainwashing.'

'How so?' Hogan asked.

Rebus answered him. 'Dr Lesser agrees with Niles. She thinks the army trains men to kill, then does nothing to switch them off before they're returned to civvy street.'

'Plenty of anecdotal evidence to suggest just that,' Lesser said. She leaned her hands on her thighs, the gesture telling them the session was over. Rebus got up, same time she did, Hogan more reluctant to follow her lead.

'We came a long way, Doctor,' he said.

'I don't think you'll get any more from Robert, not today.'

'I doubt we can afford the time to come back.'

'That's your decision, of course.'

Finally, Hogan rose from the sofa. 'How often do you see Niles?'

'I see him every day.'

'I mean, one-to-one.'

'What is it you're asking?'

'Maybe next time, you could ask him about his friend Lee.'

'Maybe,' she conceded.

'And if he says anything . . .'

'Then that would be between him and me.'

Hogan nodded. 'Patient confidentiality,' he agreed. 'But there are families out there who've just lost their sons. Maybe you could try thinking of the victims for a change.' Hogan's tone had hardened. Rebus started steering him towards the door.

'I apologise for my colleague,' he told Lesser. 'A case like this, it takes its toll.'

Her face softened slightly. 'Yes, of course . . . If you'll wait a second, I'll call Billy.'

'I think we can find our own way out,' Rebus said. But as they entered the corridor, he saw Billy approaching. 'Thanks for your help, Doctor.' Then, to Hogan: 'Bobby, say thank you to the nice doctor.'

'Cheers, Doc,' Hogan grudgingly managed. Freeing himself from Rebus's grip, he started down the corridor, Rebus making to follow.

'DI Rebus?' Lesser called. Rebus turned to her. 'You might want to talk to someone yourself. Counselling, I mean.'

'It's thirty years since I left the army, Dr Lesser.'

She nodded. 'A long time to be carrying any baggage.' She folded her arms. 'Think about it, will you?'

Rebus nodded, backing away. He offered her a parting

wave, then turned and started walking, feeling her eyes still on him. Hogan was ahead of Billy, and seemed in no need of company. Rebus fell into step with the orderly.

'That was helpful,' he commented, speaking to Billy but knowing Hogan could hear.

'I'm glad.'

'Well worth the trip.'

Billy just nodded, satisfied that someone else's day was turning out as bright as his own.

'Billy,' Rebus said, laying a hand on the young man's shoulder, 'do we look at the visitors' book here, or over at the gatehouse?' Billy looked baffled. 'Didn't you hear Dr Lesser say?' Rebus ploughed on. 'We just need the dates for Lee Herdman's visits.'

'The book's kept at the gatehouse.'

'Then that's where we'll give it the once-over.' Rebus fixed the orderly with a winning smile. 'Any chance of a coffee while we're at it?'

There was a kettle in the gatehouse, and the guard made two mugs of instant. Billy headed back into the hospital.

'Think he'll go straight to Lesser?' Hogan said in an undertone.

'Let's be as quick as we can.'

Not easy when the guard was so interested in them, asking about life in CID. Probably stir-crazy, cooped up in his box all day, a bank of CCTV monitors, a few cars to process every hour . . . Hogan offered him tidbits, most of which Rebus suspected he was making up. The visitors' book was an old-fashioned ledger, broken up into columns for date, time, visitor's name and address, and person visited. This last was subdivided, so that both patient's and doctor's name could be recorded. Rebus started with visitors' names and ran his finger quickly down three pages until he found Lee Herdman. Almost exactly a month back, so Niles's estimate hadn't been far out. A month further back, another visit. Rebus jotted the details into his notebook, holding the pen lightly. At least they'd be taking something back to Edinburgh.

He paused to take a sip from the chipped, flower-patterned mug. It tasted like one of those cheap supermarket mixtures, more chicory than coffee. His father used to buy the same stuff, saving a few pence. One time, the teenage Rebus had brought home a more expensive substitute, which his father had shunned.

'Good coffee,' he said now to the guard, who looked pleased with the compliment.

'We about done here?' Hogan asked, tiring of telling stories.

Rebus nodded, but then let his eyes glance down the columns one final time. Not visitors this time, but patients visited . . .

'Company's on its way,' Hogan warned. Rebus looked up. Hogan was pointing at one of the TV screens. Dr Lesser, accompanied by Billy, striding out of the hospital building and down the path.

Rebus went back to the ledger, and saw R. Niles again. R.Niles/Dr Lesser. Another visitor, not Lee Herdman.

We didn't ask her! Rebus could have kicked himself.

'We're out of here, John,' Bobby Hogan was saying, putting down his mug. But Rebus wasn't moving. Hogan stared at him, and Rebus just winked. Then the door flew open and Lesser was standing there.

'Who gave you permission,' she spat, 'to go trawling through a confidential record?'

'We forgot to ask about other visitors,' Rebus told her calmly. Then his finger tapped the ledger. 'Who's Douglas Brimson?'

'That's none of your business.'

'How do you know?' Rebus was jotting the name into his notebook as he spoke.

'What are you doing?'

Rebus closed the notebook, slipping it into his pocket. Then he nodded towards Hogan.

166

'Thanks again, Doc,' Hogan said, preparing to leave. She ignored him, glaring at Rebus.

'I'll be reporting this,' she warned him.

He shrugged. 'I'll be suspended by the end of the day anyway. Thanks again for all your help.' He squeezed past her, following Hogan to the car park.

'I feel better,' Hogan said. 'It might have been cheap, but we ended up scoring a point.'

'A cheap point is always worth scoring,' Rebus agreed.

Hogan stopped at the Passat, fumbling in his pocket for the keys. 'Douglas Brimson?' he asked.

'Another of Niles's visitors,' Rebus explained. 'With an address at Turnhouse.'

'Turnhouse?' Hogan frowned. 'You mean the airport?'

Rebus nodded.

'Is there anything else out there?'

'Apart from the airport, you mean?' Rebus shrugged. 'Might be worth finding out,' he said, as the car's central locking clunked open.

'What's this about you waiting to be suspended?'

'I had to say something.'

'But why pick on that?'

'Jesus, Bobby, I thought the analyst had left the building.'

'If there's anything I should know, John . . .'

'There isn't.'

'I brought you in on this, I can dump you just as quickly. Remember that.'

'You're a real motivator, Bobby.' Rebus pulled the passenger-side door closed. It was going to be a long drive . . .

9

MAKE MY DAY (C.O.D.Y.).

Siobhan stared at the note again. Same handwriting as yesterday, she was sure of that. Second-class post, but it had only taken a day to reach her. The address was perfect, down to the St Leonard's postcode. No name this time, but she didn't need a name, did she? That was the point the writer was making.

Make my day: a reference to Clint Eastwood's Dirty Harry? Who did she know called Harry? Nobody. She wasn't sure whether she was meant to get the C.O.D.Y. reference, but straight off she knew what it meant: Come On, Die Young. She knew it because it was the title of a Mogwai album, one she'd bought a while back. A piece of American gang graffiti, something like that. Who did she know, apart from her, who liked Mogwai? She'd loaned Rebus a couple of CDs, months ago. Nobody in the station really knew her taste in music. Grant Hood had been to her flat a few times . . . so had Eric Bain . . . Maybe she hadn't been meant to get the meaning, not without working at it. She guessed most fans of the band were younger than her, teens and early twenties. Probably mostly male, too. Mogwai played instrumentals, mixing ambient guitar with ear-wrenching noise. She couldn't remember if Rebus had ever given her back the CDs . . . Had one of them been *Come On Die Young*?

Without realising it, she'd walked from her desk to the window, peering out on to St Leonard's Lane. The CID room was dead, all the Port Edgar interviews concluded. Transcripts would be typed up, collated. It would be someone's job to feed it all into the computer system, see if technology could find connections missed by the merely mortal . . .

The letter-writer wanted her to make his day. *His* day? She studied the writing again. Maybe an expert could tell if it was a masculine or feminine hand. She suspected the writer had disguised their real handwriting. Hence the scrawl. She went back to her desk and called Ray Duff.

'Ray, it's Siobhan – got anything for me?'

'Morning to you too, DS Clarke. Didn't I say I'd get back to you when – *if* – I found something?'

'Meaning you haven't?'

'Meaning I'm up to my neck. Meaning I haven't yet got round to doing very much about your letter, for which I can only offer an apology and the excuse that I'm flesh and blood.'

'Sorry, Ray.' She gave a sigh, pinched the bridge of her nose.

'You've had another one?' he guessed.

'Yes.'

'One yesterday, one today?'

'That's right.'

'Want to send me it?'

'I think I'll hang on to this one, Ray.'

'As soon as I've got news, I'll call you.'

'I know you will. Sorry I've bothered you.'

'Speak to someone, Siobhan.'

'I already have. Bye, Ray.'

She cut the call, tried Rebus's mobile, but he wasn't answering. She didn't bother with a message. Folded the note, put it back in its envelope, slipped the envelope into her pocket. On her desk sat a dead teenager's laptop, her task for the day. There were over a hundred files in there. Some would be computer applications, but most were documents created by Derek Renshaw. She'd already looked at a few: correspondence, school essays. Nothing about the car crash in which his friend had died. Looked like he'd been trying to set up some sort of jazz fanzine. There were pages of layout, photos scanned in, some of them lifted from the net. Plenty of enthusiasm, but no real talent for writing. *Miles was an innovator, no question, but later on he acted more as a scout, finding the best new talent around and embracing it, hoping something would rub off on himself* . . . Siobhan just hoped Miles had wiped himself clean afterwards. She sat in front of the laptop and stared at it, trying to concentrate. The word CODY was bouncing around her head. Maybe it was a clue . . . leading to someone with that surname. She didn't think she knew anyone called Cody. For a moment she had a jarring thought: Fairstone was still alive, and the charred corpse belonged to someone called Cody. She shook the notion aside, took a deep breath, got back to work.

And hit an immediate brick wall. She couldn't log on to Derek Renshaw's e-mail account without his password. She picked up the phone and called South Queensferry, thankful that Kate answered rather than her father.

'Kate, it's Siobhan Clarke.'

'Yes.'

'I've got Derek's computer here.'

'Dad told me.'

'But I forgot to ask for his password.'

'What do you need that for?'

'To look at any new e-mails.'

'Why?' Sounding exasperated, wanting it all to be finished.

'Because that's what we do, Kate.' Silence on the line. 'Kate?'

'What?'

'Just checking you hadn't hung up on me.'

'Oh . . . right.' And then the line went dead. Kate Renshaw had hung up on her. Siobhan gave a silent curse, decided she'd try again later, or get Rebus to do it. He was family after all. Besides, she had the folder with all Derek's old e-mails – no code needed to access that. She scrolled back, found that there were four years' worth of e-mails in the folder. She hoped Derek had been neat and tidy, hoped he'd erased all the junk. She was five minutes into the task and bored of rugby scores and match reports when her phone rang. It was Kate.

'I'm really sorry,' the voice said.

'Don't be. It's all right.'

'No, it's not. You're just trying to do your job.'

'Doesn't mean *you* have to like it. If I'm being honest, *I* don't always like it either.'

'His password was Miles.'

Of course. It would have taken Siobhan only a few minutes of lateral thinking.

'Thanks, Kate.'

'He liked to go on-line. Dad complained for a while about the phone bills.'

'You were close, weren't you, you and Derek?'

'I suppose so.'

'Not every brother would share his password.'

A snort, something almost like a laugh. 'I guessed it. Only took me three goes. He was trying to guess mine, and I was trying to guess his.'

'Did he get yours?'

'Bugged me for days about it, kept coming up with new ideas.'

Siobhan's left elbow rested on the desktop. She bunched the fist and rested her head against it. Maybe this was going to turn into a long call, a conversation Kate needed to have.

Memories of Derek.

'Did you share his taste in music?'

'God, no. His stuff was all shoe-gazing. Sat in his room for hours, and if you went in he was cross-legged on the bed, head in the clouds. I tried dragging him to a few clubs in town, but he said they just depressed him.' Another snort. 'Different strokes, I suppose. He got beaten up once, you know.'

'Where?'

'In town. I think that's when he started sticking close to home. Some kids he bumped into didn't like his "posh" accent. There's a lot of that, you know. *We're* all snobs, because our parents are rich shits who pay for our education; *they're* all schemies who'll end up on the dole . . . that's where it starts.'

'Where what starts?'

'The aggression. I remember my last year at Port Edgar, we got a letter "advising" us not to wear our uniform in town, unless we were on a supervised trip.' She gave a long sigh. 'My parents pinched and scraped so we could go private. It might even be what broke them up.'

'I'm sure that's not true.'

'A lot of their fights were to do with money.'

'Even so . . .'

There was silence on the line for a moment. 'I've been going on the net, looking up stuff.'

'What sort of stuff?'

'All sorts . . . trying to work out what made him do it.'

'Lee Herdman, you mean?'

'There's this book, it's by an American. He's a psychiatrist or something. Know what it's called?'

'What?'

'*Bad Men Do What Good Men Dream*. Do you think there's any truth in that?'

'Maybe I'd have to read the book.'

'I think he's saying we've all got it in us, the potential to . . . well, you know . . .'

'I don't know about that.' Siobhan was still thinking of Derek Renshaw. The beating was another thing he hadn't mentioned so far in his computer files. So many secrets . . .

'Kate, is it all right if I ask . . .?'

'What?'

'Derek wasn't depressed or anything, was he? I mean, he liked sports and stuff.'

'Yes, but when he came home . . .'

'He'd rather sit in his room?' Siobhan guessed.

'With his jazz and his surfing.'

'Any sites in particular? Any favourites?'

'He used a couple of chat rooms, message boards.'

'Let me guess: sport and jazz?'

'Bullseye.' There was a pause. 'You know what I said about Stuart Cotter's family?'

Stuart Cotter: the crash victim. 'I remember,' Siobhan said.

'Did you think I was crazy?' Kate trying for a lightness of tone.

'It'll be looked into, don't worry.'

'I didn't really mean it, you know. I don't really think Stuart's family would . . . would do something like that.'

'Fair enough, Kate.' Another silence on the line, longer this time. 'Have you hung up on me again?'

'No.'

'Anything else you want to talk about?'

'I should let you get back to work.'

'You can always call again, Kate. Any time you want to chat.'

'Thanks, Siobhan. You're a pal.'

'Bye, Kate.' Siobhan ended the call, stared at the screen again. She pressed a palm to her jacket pocket, felt the shape of the envelope.

C.O.D.Y.

Suddenly it didn't seem so important.

She got back to work, plugged the laptop into a phone socket and used Derek's password to access a slew of new e-mails, most of which turned out to be junk, or regular sports updates. There were a few from names she recognised from the folder. Friends Derek had probably never met, except when on-line, friends around the globe who shared his passions. Friends who didn't know he was dead.

She straightened her back, feeling vertebrae crackle. Her neck was stiff, and her watch told her it was going to be a late lunch. She didn't feel hungry but knew she should eat.

What she really felt like was a double espresso, maybe with a side order of chocolate. That double-combo sugar-caffeine rush that made the world go round.

'I won't give in,' she said to herself. Instead, she'd go to the Engine Shed, where they served organic meals and fruit teas. She fished a paperback and her mobile phone out of her shoulder-bag, then locked the bag in the bottom drawer of her desk – you could never be too careful in a police station. The paperback was a critique of rock music by a female poet. She'd been trying to finish it for ages. George 'Hi-Ho' Silvers came into the office as she was leaving.

'Just off to lunch, George,' Siobhan told him.

He looked around the empty office. 'Mind if I join you?'

'Sorry, George, I'm meeting someone,' she lied blithely. 'Besides, one of us has to hold the fort.'

She walked downstairs and out of the station's main entrance, turning left into St Leonard's Lane. Her eyes were on the tiny screen of her phone, checking for messages. A hand landed heavily on her shoulder. A deep voice growled: 'Hey.' Siobhan spun round, dropping both phone and paperback. She grabbed at a wrist, twisted it hard, pulling down so that her attacker dropped to his knees.

'Jesus fuck!' the man gasped. She couldn't see much more than the top of his head. Short dark hair, gelled to stand up in little spikes. Charcoal suit. He was heavily built, not tall . . .

Not Martin Fairstone.

'Who are you?' Siobhan hissed. She was holding his wrist high up his back, pressing forward on it. She heard car doors open and close, glanced up, saw a man and woman hurrying towards her.

'I just wanted a word,' her assailant gasped. 'I'm a reporter. Holly . . . Steve Holly.'

Siobhan let go the wrist. Holly cradled his hurt arm as he got to his feet.

'What's going on here?' the woman asked. Siobhan recognised her: Whiteread, the army investigator. Simms was with her, a thin smile on his face, nodding approval of Siobhan's reflexes.

'Nothing,' Siobhan told them.

'Didn't look like nothing.' Whiteread was staring at Steve Holly.

'He's a reporter,' Siobhan explained.

'If we'd known that,' Simms said, 'we'd've waited a bit longer before stepping in.'

'Cheers,' Holly muttered, rubbing his elbow. He looked from Simms to Whiteread. 'I've seen you before ... outside Lee Herdman's flat, if I'm not mistaken. I thought I knew all the CID faces.' He straightened up, held out a hand towards Simms, mistaking him for the superior. 'Steve Holly.'

Simms glanced towards Whiteread, alerting Holly immediately to his error. He swivelled slightly so the hand was facing the woman, and repeated his name. Whiteread ignored him.

'Do you always treat the fourth estate this way, DS Clarke?'

'Sometimes I go for a headlock instead.'

'That's a good idea, changing your attack,' Whiteread agreed.

'Means the enemy can't predict your move,' Simms added.

'Why do I get the feeling you three are taking the piss?' Holly asked.

Siobhan had bent down to retrieve her phone and book. She checked the phone for damage. 'What is it you want?'

'A quick couple of questions.'

'Concerning what exactly?'

Holly was staring at the army pair. 'Sure you want an audience, DS Clarke?'

'I've got nothing to say to you anyway,' Siobhan told him.

'How do you know until you've heard me out?'

'Because you're going to ask me about Martin Fairstone.'

'Am I?' Holly raised an eyebrow. 'Well, maybe that *was* the plan . . . but I'm also wondering why you're so jumpy, and why you don't want to talk about Fairstone.'

I'm jumpy because *of Fairstone*, Siobhan felt like shouting. But she sniffed dismissively instead. The Engine Shed was no longer an option; nothing to stop Holly following her there, taking the chair next to her . . . 'I'm going back in,' she said.

'Watch out nobody in there taps your shoulder,' Holly said. 'And tell DI Rebus I'm sorry . . .'

Siobhan wasn't going to fall for it. She turned towards the door, only to find Whiteread blocking her way.

'Mind if we have a word?' she asked.

'I'm on my lunch-break.'

'I could do with something myself,' Whiteread said, glancing towards her colleague, who nodded agreement. Siobhan sighed.

'You better come in then.' She pushed at the revolving door, Whiteread right behind her. Simms made to follow, but paused for a moment, turning his attention to the reporter.

'You work for a newspaper?' he asked. Holly nodded. Simms smiled at him. 'I killed a man once with one of those.' Then he turned and followed the women inside.

The canteen didn't have much left. Whiteread and Siobhan opted for sandwiches, Simms a heaped plate of chips and beans.

'What did he mean about Rebus?' Whiteread asked, stirring sugar into her tea.

'Doesn't matter,' Siobhan said.

'Sure about that?'

'Look . . .'

'We're not the enemy here, Siobhan. I know what it's

like: you probably don't trust officers at the next station, never mind outsiders like us. But we're on the same side.'

'I don't have a problem with that, but what just happened hasn't got anything to do with Port Edgar, Lee Herdman or the SAS.'

Whiteread stared at her, then gave a shrug of acceptance.

'So what was it you wanted?' Siobhan asked.

'Actually, we were hoping to talk to DI Rebus.'

'He's not here.'

'So they told us at South Queensferry.'

'But you still came?'

Whiteread made a show of studying her sandwich filling. 'Obviously, yes.'

'He wasn't here . . . but you knew I was?'

Whiteread smiled. 'Rebus trained for the SAS, but didn't make the grade.'

'So you've said.'

'Has he ever told you what happened?'

Siobhan decided not to answer, unwilling to admit that he'd never let her into that part of his history. Whiteread took her silence as answer enough.

'He cracked up. Left the army altogether, had a nervous breakdown. Lived beside a beach for a while, somewhere north of here.'

'Fife,' Simms added, mouth stuffed with chips.

'How come you know all this? It's supposed to be Herdman you're looking at.'

Whiteread nodded. 'Thing is, we didn't have Lee Herdman flagged.'

'Flagged?'

'As a potential psycho,' Simms said. Whiteread's eyes flared, and he swallowed hard, went back to his eating.

'Psycho's not the right word,' Whiteread corrected him for Siobhan's benefit.

'But you had John flagged?' Siobhan guessed.

'Yes,' Whiteread admitted. 'The breakdown, you see . . .

177

And then he became a policeman, his name appearing quite regularly in the media . . .'

And about to appear again, Siobhan was thinking. 'I still don't see what this has to do with the inquiry,' she said, hoping she sounded calm.

'It's just that DI Rebus may have insights that could prove useful,' Whiteread explained. 'DI Hogan certainly seems to think so. He's taken Rebus with him to Carbrae, hasn't he? To see Robert Niles?'

'Another of your spectacular failures,' Siobhan felt compelled to say.

Whiteread seemed content to accept the comment, putting most of the sandwich back down on her plate, lifting her cup instead. Siobhan's mobile rang. She checked its screen: Rebus.

'Sorry,' she said, getting up from the table, walking towards the drinks machine. 'How did it go?' she asked into the mouthpiece.

'We got a name: can you start running a check?'

'What's the name?'

'Brimson.' Rebus spelled it for her. 'First name Douglas. Address at Turnhouse.'

'As in the airport?'

'So far as we know. He was another of Niles's visitors . . .'

'And doesn't live far from South Queensferry, so chances are he might have known Lee Herdman.' Siobhan looked back to where Whiteread and Simms sat, talking to one another. 'I've got your army pals here. Want me to run this Brimson character past them, just in case he's ex-forces?'

'Christ, no. Are they listening in?'

'I was having lunch with them in the canteen. Don't worry, they're out of earshot.'

'What are they doing there?'

'Whiteread's got a sandwich, Simms is wolfing down a plate of chips.' She paused. 'But it's me they've been trying to grill.'

'Am I expected to laugh at that?'

'Sorry. Feeble effort. Has Templer spoken with you yet?'

'No. What sort of mood's she in?'

'I've managed to steer clear of her all morning.'

'She's probably been meeting the pathologists, prior to giving me a roasting.'

'Now who's the one making jokes?'

'I wish it was a joke, Siobhan.'

'How soon will you be back?'

'Not today, if I can help it. Bobby wants to talk to the judge.'

'Why?'

'To clear up a couple of points.'

'And that'll take you the rest of the day?'

'You've plenty to keep you busy without me there. Meantime, tell the Gruesome Twosome nothing.'

The Gruesome Twosome: Siobhan glanced over in their direction. They'd stopped talking, finished eating. Both were staring at her.

'Steve Holly's been sniffing around, too,' Siobhan told Rebus.

'I assume you kicked him in the balls and sent him on his way?'

'Not far off it, actually . . .'

'Let's talk again before the end of play.'

'I'll be here.'

'Nothing from the laptop?'

'Not so far.'

'Keep trying.'

The phone went dead, a merry-sounding series of bleeps telling Siobhan that Rebus had cut the connection. She walked back to the table, fixing a smile to her face.

'I've got to get back,' she said.

'We could give you a lift,' Simms suggested.

'I mean back upstairs.'

'You're finished at South Queensferry?' Whiteread asked.

'I just have some stuff here to be getting on with.'

'Stuff?'

'Odds and ends from before this all started.'

'Paperwork, eh?' Simms sympathised. But the look on Whiteread's face said she wasn't falling for it.

'I'd better see you out,' Siobhan added.

'What does a CID office look like?' Whiteread asked. 'I've often wondered . . .'

'I'll give you the tour sometime,' Siobhan answered. 'When we're not up to our eyes.'

It was an answer Whiteread was forced to accept, but Siobhan could see she liked it about as much as she would a Mogwai concert.

10

Lord Jarvies was in his late fifties. Bobby Hogan had filled Rebus in on family history during the drive back to Edinburgh. Divorced from his first wife, remarried, Anthony the only child from this second relationship. The family lived in Murrayfield.

'Plenty of good schools around there,' Rebus had commented, wondering at the distance between Murrayfield and South Queensferry. But Orlando Jarvies was a former pupil of Port Edgar. In his twenties, he'd even played for the Port Edgar FP rugby team.

'What position?' Rebus had asked.

'John,' Hogan had replied, 'what I know about rugby could be written on the leftovers of one of your cigarettes.'

Hogan had expected that they would find the judge at home, in shock and in mourning. But a couple of calls revealed that Jarvies was back at work, and therefore to be found in the Sheriff Court on Chambers Street, opposite the museum where Jean Burchill worked. Rebus considered calling her – there might be time for a quick coffee – but decided against. She was bound to notice his hands, wasn't she? Best to hang fire till they'd mended. He could still feel the handshake Robert Niles had pressed on him.

'You ever come up against Jarvies?' Hogan asked as he parked on a single yellow line, outside what had been the city's dental hospital, now transformed into a nightclub and bar.

'A few times. You?'

'Once or twice.'

'Give him any cause to remember you?'

181

'Let's find out, shall we?' Hogan said, placing a notice on the inside of the windscreen identifying the car as being 'on police business'.

'Might be cheaper to risk a ticket,' Rebus advised.

'How so?'

'Think about it.'

Hogan frowned in thought, then nodded. Not everyone who walked out of the courthouse would have reason to be enamoured of the police. A ticket might cost thirty quid (and could always be cancelled after a quiet word); scratched bodywork came in a little more expensive. Hogan removed the notice.

The Sheriff Court was a modern building, but its visitors were taking their toll. Dried spittle on the windows, graffiti on the walls. The judge was in the robing room, and that was where Rebus and Hogan were taken to meet with him. The attendant bowed slightly before he left.

Jarvies had just about finished changing out of his robes of office and back into a pinstripe suit, complete with watch-chain. His burgundy tie sported a perfect knot, and his shoes were highly polished black brogues. His face looked polished, too, highlighting a network of tiny red veins in either cheek. On a long table sat other judges' workday clothes: black gowns, white collars, grey wigs. Each set bore its owner's name.

'Take a seat, if you can find one,' Jarvies said. 'I won't be long.' He looked up, mouth hanging slightly open, as it often did when he was in the courtroom. The first time Rebus had given evidence in front of Jarvies, the mannerism had disconcerted him, making him think the judge had been about to interrupt. 'I do have another appointment, which is why I had to see you here or not at all.'

'Quite all right, sir,' Hogan said.

'To be honest,' Rebus added, 'with everything you've been through, we're surprised to see you here at all.'

'Can't let the bastards beat us, can we?' the judge

replied. It didn't sound like the first time he'd had to offer the explanation. 'So, what is it I can do for you?'

Rebus and Hogan shared a look, both finding it hard to believe the man in front of them had just lost a son.

'It's about Lee Herdman,' Hogan stated. 'Seems he was friends with Robert Niles.'

'Niles?' The judge looked up. 'I remember him ... stabbed his wife, didn't he?'

'Slit her throat,' Rebus corrected. 'He went to jail, but right now he's in Carbrae.'

'What we're wondering,' Hogan added, 'is whether you've ever had cause to fear a reprisal.'

Jarvies stood up slowly, took out his watch and flipped it open, checking the time. 'I think I see,' he said. 'You're seeking a motive. Isn't it enough to say that Herdman merely lost the balance of his mind?'

'That may end up as our conclusion,' Hogan conceded.

The judge was examining himself in the room's full-length mirror. There was a faint aroma in Rebus's nostrils, and at last he was able to place it. It was the smell of gentlemen's outfitters, shops he'd been taken to as a child on those occasions when his father was being measured for a suit. Jarvies patted down a single stray hair. There were touches of grey at the temples, but otherwise his hair was chestnut brown. Almost too brown, Rebus thought, wondering if some colouring had gone into it. The judge's haircut with its precise left parting gave the impression that no other style had been attempted since schooldays.

'Sir?' Hogan prompted. 'Robert Niles . . .?'

'I've never received any kind of threat from that direction, Detective Inspector Hogan. Nor had I heard the name Herdman until after the shootings.' He turned his head from the mirror. 'Does that answer your questions?'

'Yes, sir.'

'If Herdman had set out to target Anthony, why turn the gun on the other boys? Why wait so long after sentencing?'

'Yes, sir.'

'Motive isn't always the issue . . .'

Rebus's phone trilled suddenly, sounding out of place, a modern distraction. He smiled an apology and stepped into the red-carpeted hall-way.

'Rebus,' he said.

'I've just had a couple of interesting meetings,' Gill Templer said, straining to keep her temper in check.

'Oh, aye?'

'The forensics from Fairstone's kitchen show that he was probably bound and gagged. That makes it murder.'

'Or someone trying to give him a bloody good scare.'

'You don't sound surprised.'

'Nothing much surprises me these days.'

'You already know, don't you?' Rebus stayed silent; no point getting Dr Curt into trouble. 'Well, you can probably guess who the second meeting was with.'

'Carswell,' Rebus said. Colin Carswell: Assistant Chief Constable.

'That's right.'

'And I'm now to consider myself under suspension, pending investigation?'

'Yes.'

'Fine. Is that all you wanted to tell me?'

'You'll be required to attend an initial interview at HQ.'

'With the Complaints?'

'Something like this, it could even be the PSU.' Meaning the Professional Standards Unit.

'Ah, the Complaints' paramilitary wing.'

'John . . .' Her tone was a mixture of warning and exasperation.

'I'll look forward to talking to them,' Rebus said, ending the call. Hogan was stepping out of the robing room, thanking the judge for his time. He closed the door after him, spoke in an undertone.

'He's taking it well.'

'Bottling it up, more like,' Rebus said, falling into step. 'I've got a bit of news, by the way.'

'Oh?'

'I've been suspended from duty. I dare say Carswell's trying to find you right now to let you know.'

Hogan stopped walking, turned to face Rebus. 'As predicted by you at Carbrae.'

'I went back to a guy's house. Same night he died in a fire.' Hogan's gaze dropped to Rebus's gloves. 'Nothing to do with it, Bobby. Just a coincidence.'

'So what's the problem?'

'This guy had been hassling Siobhan.'

'And?'

'And it looks like he was tied to a chair when the fire started.'

Hogan puffed out his cheeks. 'Witnesses?'

'I was seen going into the house with him, apparently.'

Hogan's phone went off, different tone from Rebus's. Caller ID brought a twitch to Hogan's mouth.

'Carswell?' Rebus guessed.

'HQ.'

'Then that's who it is.'

Hogan nodded, dropped the phone back into his pocket.

'No point putting it off,' Rebus told him.

But Bobby Hogan shook his head. 'There's every point putting it off, John. Besides, they may be pulling you off casework, but Port Edgar isn't really a case, is it? Nobody's going to go to court. It's just housekeeping.'

'I suppose so.' Rebus gave a wry smile. Hogan patted his arm.

'Don't you worry, John. Uncle Bobby will look after you . . .'

'Thanks, Uncle Bobby,' Rebus said.

'. . . right up until the moment when the shit really does hit the fan.'

By the time Gill Templer got back to St Leonard's, Siobhan

had already tracked down Douglas Brimson. It hadn't been exactly onerous, due to the fact that Brimson was in the phone book. Two addresses and phone numbers: one home, the other business. Templer had disappeared into her office across the corridor, slamming the door after her. George Silvers had looked up from his desk.

'Sounds like she's on the war-path,' he'd said, pocketing his biro and preparing to beat a retreat. Siobhan had tried phoning Rebus, but he was busy. Busy warding off blows from the Chief Super's tomahawk, most probably.

With Silvers gone, Siobhan again found herself alone in the CID room. DCI Pryde was around somewhere; so was DC Davie Hynds. But both were managing to make themselves invisible. Siobhan stared at the screen of Derek Renshaw's laptop, bored to death of sifting its inoffensive contents. Derek, she was sure, had been a good kid, but dull with it. He'd already known the path his life would take: three or four years at uni, Business Studies with Computing, and then an office job, maybe in accountancy. Money to buy a waterfront penthouse, fast car and the best hi-fi system around . . .

But that future remained frozen, realised only in words on a screen, bytes of memory. The thought made her shiver. Everything changing in an instant . . . She held her face in her hands, rubbing her fingers over her eyes, knowing only one thing: she didn't want to be here when Gill Templer emerged from behind that door. Because for once, Siobhan suspected she would give her boss as good as she got, and maybe even a bit more besides. She wasn't in the mood to be anybody's victim. She looked at her phone, then at the notebook containing Brimson's details. Decided, she shut down the laptop, placing it in her shoulder-bag. Picked up her mobile and the notebook.

Walked.

Her one detour: a quick stop home, where she found her CD of *Come On Die Young*. She played the album as she drove, listening for clues. Not easy when so much of it was instrumental . . .

Brimson's home address turned out to be a modern bungalow on a narrow road between the airport and what had been Gogarburn Hospital. As Siobhan got out of her car, she could hear demolition work in the distance: Gogarburn was being dismantled. She thought the site had been sold to one of the major banks, to be transformed into their new headquarters. The house in front of her sat behind a tall hedge and green wrought-iron gates. She pushed open the gates and crunched across pink gravel. Tried the doorbell, then peered in through the windows either side. One belonged to a living room, the other a bedroom. The bed had been made, and the living room looked little used. A couple of magazines sat on the blue leather sofa, pictures of aeroplanes on their covers. The garden to the front was mostly paved, with just a couple of beds where roses waited to grow. A narrow path separated the bungalow from its garage, with another gate which opened when she turned the handle, allowing entry to the rear garden. It comprised a huge expanse of sloping lawn, at the bottom of which stretched what looked like acres of farmland. The timber-framed conservatory seemed a recent addition to the house. Its door was locked. Windows showed her a large, very white kitchen and another bedroom. She got no sense of family life: no garden toys, nothing to suggest a woman's touch. All the same, the place was kept in immaculate condition. Walking back down the path, she noticed a glass pane in the garage's side door. There was a car inside, one of the sportier Jaguars, but its owner definitely wasn't home.

She got back into her own car and headed for the airport, stopping in front of the terminal building. A security man warned her that parking wasn't allowed, but waved her on when she showed her ID. The terminal was busy: long queues for what looked like a package flight to the sun; business suits wheeling their cases briskly towards the escalator. Siobhan studied the signs, saw one for Information and headed that way, asking at the desk to speak to Mr Brimson. A quick clatter of a keyboard, then a shake of the head.

'I'm not getting that name.'

Siobhan spelled it for the woman, who nodded that she'd entered it correctly. She picked up her phone, spoke to someone. Her turn now to spell out the letters: B-r-i-m-s-o-n. She pulled her mouth down, again shaking her head.

'Sure he works here?' she asked.

Siobhan showed her the address, copied from the phone book. The woman smiled.

'That says "airfield", love,' she explained. 'That's what you want, not the airport.' She then gave directions, and Siobhan thanked her and left, face flushed from having made the mistake in the first place. The airfield was just that. It joined on to the airport, and could be reached by driving halfway around the perimeter. Light aircraft were hangared here, and, according to the sign on the gate, it was also home to a flying school. There was a phone number below: the number Siobhan had copied from the phone book. The high metal gate was padlocked, but there was an old-fashioned telephone receiver in a wooden box attached to a post. Siobhan picked it up, and heard the ringing tone.

'Hello?' A man's voice.

'I'm looking for Mr Brimson.'

'You've found him, sweetheart. What can I do for you?'

'Mr Brimson, my name's Detective Sergeant Clarke. I'm with Lothian and Borders Police. I was wondering if I could have a word with you.'

There was a moment's silence. Then: 'Just wait a tick. I'll have to unlock the gate.'

Siobhan started to say another thank you, but the phone was dead. She could see a few hangars, a couple of aeroplanes. One had a single propellor on its nose, the other boasted two, one on either wing. They looked like two-seaters. There were also a couple of squat prefabricated buildings, and it was from one of these that the figure emerged, hoisting itself into an open-topped, venerable-looking Land Rover. A plane coming in to land at the airport drowned out any sound of the engine starting. The Land Rover jolted forward, speeding the hundred or so yards to the gate. The man leapt out again. He was tall, tanned and muscular-looking. Probably just into his fifties, with a lined face which had cracked into a brief smile of introduction. A short-sleeved shirt, the same green-olive colour as the Land Rover, showed off silvery-haired arms. Brimson's thick head of hair was the same silver colour, and had probably been ash-blond in youth. The shirt was tucked into grey canvas trousers, showing the beginnings of a gut.

'Have to keep the place locked,' he started to explain, jangling a vast set of keys taken from the Land Rover's ignition. 'Security.'

She nodded her understanding. There was something immediately likeable about this man. Maybe it was his sense of energy and self-confidence, the way he rolled his shoulders as he walked up to the gate. That brief, winning smile.

But as he pulled open the gate for her, she noted that his face had become more serious. 'I suppose it's about Lee,' he said solemnly. 'Bound to happen sooner or later.' Then he motioned for her to drive in. 'Park by the office,' he said. 'I'll catch you up.'

As she drove past him, she couldn't help wondering about his choice of words.

Bound to happen sooner or later . . .

Seated opposite him in the office, she got the chance to ask.

'All I meant was,' he replied, 'you were bound to want to talk to me.'

'How so?'

'Because I'm guessing you want to know why he did it.'

'And?'

'And you'll be asking his friends if they can help.'

'You were a friend of Lee Herdman's?'

'Yes.' He frowned. 'Isn't that why you're here?'

'In a roundabout way, yes. We found out that both yourself and Mr Herdman paid visits to Carbrae.'

Brimson nodded slowly. 'That's clever,' he said. The kettle, having come to the boil, clicked off, and he leapt from his chair to pour water into two mugs of instant coffee, handing one to Siobhan. The office was tiny, just enough room for the desk and two chairs. The door led back to an anteroom with a few more chairs and a couple of filing-cabinets. There were posters on the walls – various forms of aircraft.

'You're a flying instructor, Mr Brimson?' Siobhan said, accepting the mug.

'Call me Doug, please.' Brimson sat back down. A figure appeared, framed by the window behind him. A rap of knuckles on the pane. Brimson turned his head, gave a wave, which the other man returned.

'That's Charlie,' he explained. 'Going for a spin. Works as a banker, says he'd swap jobs with me tomorrow if it meant he could spend more time in the sky.'

'You rent out your planes then?'

It took Brimson a moment to follow her question. 'No, no,' he said at last. 'Charlie has his own plane, he just keeps it here.'

'The airfield's yours though?'

Brimson nodded. 'In as much as I rent the actual ground from the airport. But, yes, all this is mine.' He opened his arms wide, offering another smile.

'And how long have you known Lee Herdman?'

The arms dropped, and the smile with them. 'A good few years.'

'Can you be more specific?'

'Pretty much since he moved here.'

'That would be six years then?'

'If you say so.' He paused. 'I'm sorry, I've forgotten your name . . .'

'Detective Sergeant Clarke. Were the two of you close?'

'Close?' Brimson shrugged. 'Lee didn't really let people get "close". I mean, he was friendly, liked meeting up, all that sort of thing . . .'

'But?'

Brimson frowned in concentration. 'I was never really sure what was going on in here.' He tapped his head.

'What did you think when you heard about the shooting?'

He shrugged. 'It was impossible to believe.'

'Did you know Herdman had a gun?'

'No.'

'He was interested in them though.'

'That's true . . . but he never showed me one.'

'Never talked about it?'

'Never.'

'So what did the two of you talk about?'

'Planes, boats, the services . . . I served seven years in the RAF.'

'As a pilot?'

Brimson shook his head. 'Didn't do much piloting back then. I was the electrics wizard, keeping the crates up in the air.' He leaned across the desk. 'Have you ever flown?'

'Just holiday trips.'

He wrinkled his face. 'I mean like Charlie there.' He hooked his thumb towards where a small plane was taxiing past the window, engines droning.

'I have enough trouble driving a car.'

'A plane's easier, believe me.'

'So all those dials and switches are just for show?'

He laughed. 'We could go right now, what do you say?'

'Mr Brimson . . .'

'Doug.'

191

'Mr Brimson, I don't really have time for a flying lesson right now.'

'Tomorrow then?'

'I'll think about it.' She couldn't help smiling, thinking that a thousand feet above Edinburgh might be safe from Gill Templer.

'You'll love it, that's a promise.'

'We'll see.'

'But you'll be off duty, right? Which means you'll be allowed to call me Doug?' He waited till she'd nodded. 'And what will I be allowed to call you, Detective Sergeant Clarke?'

'Siobhan.'

'An Irish name?'

'Gaelic.'

'Your accent's not . . .'

'My accent's not what I'm here to talk about.'

He raised his hands in mock surrender.

'Why didn't you come forward?' she asked. He seemed not to understand. 'After the shooting, some of Mr Herdman's friends called to talk to us.'

'Did they? What for?'

'All kinds of reasons.'

He considered his answer. 'I didn't see the point, Siobhan.'

'Let's save first names for later, eh?' Brimson tilted his head in apology. There was a sudden burst of static, then transistorised voices.

'The tower,' he explained, reaching down behind his desk to tweak the volume on the radio set. 'That's Charlie requesting a slot.' He glanced at his watch. 'Should be okay this time of day.'

Siobhan listened to a voice warning the pilot to watch out for a helicopter over the city centre.

'Roger, control.'

Brimson turned the volume lower still.

'I'd like to bring a colleague out here to talk to you,' Siobhan said. 'Would that be all right?'

Brimson shrugged. 'You can see how hectic life is around here. Only really busy at weekends.'

'I wish I could say the same.'

'Don't tell me you're not busy at weekends? Good-looking young woman like you?'

'I meant . . .'

He laughed again. 'I'm only teasing. No wedding ring though.' He nodded towards her left hand. 'Do you think I'd make the grade in CID?'

'I notice you don't wear a ring either.'

'Eligible bachelor, that's me. Friends say it's because I've got my head in the clouds.' He pointed upwards. 'Not too many singles bars up there.'

Siobhan smiled, then realised that she was enjoying the conversation – always a bad sign. There were questions she knew she should be asking, but they weren't coming into focus.

'Maybe tomorrow then,' she said, getting up from the chair.

'Your first flying lesson?'

She shook her head. 'Talking to my colleague.'

'But you'll come too?'

'If I can.'

He seemed satisfied, came around the desk, hand outstretched. 'Good to meet you, Siobhan.'

'Good to meet you, Mr . . .' She faltered as he raised a warning finger. 'Doug,' she relented.

'I'll see you out.'

'I can manage.' Opening the door, wanting a little more space between them than he was allowing.

'Really? You're good at picking locks then, are you?'

She remembered the padlocked gate. 'Right enough,' she said, following Doug Brimson outside just as Charlie's machine came to the end of its run-up and lifted its wheels clear of the ground.

'Has Gill tracked you down yet?' Siobhan asked, speaking into her phone as she drove back into the city.

'Affirmative,' Rebus replied. 'Not that I was hiding or anything.'

'So what's the outcome?'

'Suspended from duty. Except that Bobby doesn't see it that way. He still wants me helping out.'

'Which means you still need me, right?'

'I think I could just about drive myself if I had to.'

'But you don't have to . . .'

He laughed. 'I'm just teasing, Siobhan. The gig's yours if you want it.'

'Good, because I've tracked down Brimson.'

'I'm impressed. Who is he?'

'Runs a flying school out at Turnhouse.' She paused. 'I went to see him. I know I should have checked first, but your phone was engaged.'

'She's been out to see Brimson,' she heard Rebus tell Hogan. Hogan muttered something back. 'Bobby's of the opinion,' Rebus told her, 'that you should have sought permission before doing that.'

'Are those his exact words?'

'Actually, he rolled his eyes and uttered a few oaths. I'm choosing to extrapolate.'

'Thanks for saving my maidenly blushes.'

'So what did you get out of him?'

'He was friends with Herdman. They share similar backgrounds: army and RAF.'

'And how does he know Robert Niles?'

Siobhan's mouth twitched. 'I forgot to ask him that. I did say we'd go back.'

'Sounds like we'll have to. Did he offer anything at all?'

'Says he didn't know Herdman kept guns and doesn't know why he went to the school. What about Niles?'

'Sod all use to us.'

'So where do we go from here?'

'Let's rendezvous at Port Edgar. We need to have a proper talk with Miss Teri.' There was silence on the line, and Siobhan thought she'd lost him, but then he asked: 'Any more messages from our friend?'

Meaning the notes; keeping it vague in front of Hogan. 'There was another one waiting for me this morning.'

'Yes?'

'Much the same as the first.'

'Sent it to Howdenhall?'

'Didn't see the point.'

'Good. I'll want a look at it when we meet up. How long will you be?'

'Fifteen minutes, give or take.'

'A fiver says we beat you.'

'You're on,' Siobhan said, pressing her foot a little harder to the accelerator. It was a few moments before she realised she didn't know where Rebus had been calling from . . .

True to form, he was waiting for her in the car park of Port Edgar Academy, leaning against Hogan's Passat, one foot crossed over the other, arms folded.

'You cheated,' she said, getting out of her car.

'Caveat emptor. That's five quid you owe me.'

'No way.'

'You took the bet, Siobhan. A lady always pays up.'

She shook her head, reached into her pocket. 'Here's that letter, by the way,' she said, producing the envelope. Rebus held his hand out. 'Cost you a fiver to read it.'

Rebus looked at her. 'For the privilege of giving you my expert opinion?' His hand stayed outstretched, the envelope just out of reach. 'All right, it's a deal,' he said, curiosity winning in the end.

In the car, he read it through several times while Siobhan drove.

'A fiver wasted,' he finally offered. 'Who's Cody?'

'I think it means Come On, Die Young. It's a gang thing, from America.'

'How do you know that?'

'It's a Mogwai album. I loaned you their stuff.'

'Might be a name. Buffalo Bill, for example.'

'The connection being . . .?'

'I don't know.' Rebus refolded the note, examining its creases, peering inside the envelope.

'Good Sherlock Holmes impression,' Siobhan said.

'What else do you want me to do?'

'You could admit defeat.' She held her hand out. Rebus returned the note to her, tucked back in its envelope.

'Make my day . . . Dirty Harry?'

'That's my guess,' Siobhan agreed.

'Dirty Harry was a cop . . .'

She stared at him. 'You think someone I work with did this?'

'Don't say it hasn't crossed your mind . . .'

'It has,' she finally admitted.

'But it would have to be someone who knows you connect to Fairstone.'

'Yes.'

'And that brings it down to me and Gill Templer.' He paused. 'And I'm guessing you've not loaned her any albums of late.'

Siobhan shrugged, eyes back on the road ahead. She didn't say anything for a while, and neither did Rebus, until he checked an address in his notebook, leaned forward in his seat, and told her: 'We're here.'

Long Rib House was a narrow whitewashed structure which looked as though it might have been a barn some time in the past. It consisted of a single storey, but with an attic conversion indicated by a row of windows built out from the sloping red-tiled roof. A wooden gate barred the entrance, but it wasn't locked. Siobhan pushed it open, got back into the car, and drove up the few yards of gravel driveway. By the time she'd closed the gate again, the front door was open, a man standing there. Rebus was out of the car, introducing himself.

'And you must be Mr Cotter?' he guessed.

'William Cotter,' Miss Teri's father said. He was in his early forties, short and stocky with a fashionably shaven head. He shook Siobhan's hand when she offered it, but didn't seem put out that Rebus was keeping his own gloved hands firmly by his sides. 'You better come in,' he said.

There was a long carpeted hallway, decorated with framed paintings and a grandfather clock. Rooms off to right and left, the doors firmly closed. Cotter led them to the end of the corridor and into an open-plan living area with kitchen off. This had the look of a recent extension, French doors leading out to a patio, and offering a view across the expanse of rear garden towards another recent addition, wood-framed but with plenty of windows to show off its contents.

'Indoor pool,' Rebus mused. 'That must be handy.'

'Gets more use than an outdoor one,' Cotter joked. 'So what can I do for you?'

Rebus looked to Siobhan, who was casting an eye over the room, taking in the L-shaped cream leather sofa, the B&O hi-fi and flat-screen TV. The TV was switched on, sound muted. It was tuned to Ceefax, showing a screen of stock market fluctuations. 'It was Teri we wanted a word with,' Rebus said.

'Not in any trouble, is she?'

'Nothing like that, Mr Cotter. It's to do with Port Edgar. Just a few follow-up questions.'

Cotter narrowed his eyes. 'Maybe it's something I can help with . . .?' Angling for more information.

Rebus had decided to sit down on the sofa. There was a coffee table in front of him, newspapers spread out on it, open at the business pages. Cordless phone, and a pair of half-moon reading-glasses, empty mug, pen and A4 pad. 'You're in business, Mr Cotter?'

'That's right.'

'Mind if I ask what sort?'

'Venture capital.' Cotter paused. 'You know what that is?'

'Investing in start-ups?' Siobhan offered, staring out at the garden.

'More or less. I dabble in property, people with ideas . . .' Rebus made a show of taking in his surroundings. 'You're obviously good at it.' He waited for the flattery to sink in. 'Is Teri here?'

'Not sure,' Cotter said. He saw Rebus's look, and gave an apologetic smile. 'You're never sure with Teri. Sometimes she's quiet as the grave. Knock at her door, she doesn't answer.' He shrugged.

'Not like most teenagers then.'

Cotter shook his head.

'But then I got that impression when I met her,' Rebus added.

'You've spoken to her before?' Cotter asked. Rebus nodded. 'In full regalia?'

'I'm guessing she doesn't go to school like that.'

Cotter shook his head again. 'They're not even allowed nose-studs. Dr Fogg's strict about that sort of thing.'

'Could we maybe try her door?' Siobhan asked, turning to face Cotter.

'Can't do any harm, I suppose,' Cotter said. They followed him back down the hall and up a short flight of stairs. Again they were confronted with a long, narrow corridor, doors off. Again, all the doors were closed.

'Teri?' Cotter called as they reached the top of the stairs. 'You still here, love?' He bit this final word off, and Rebus guessed he'd been warned off using it by his daughter. They reached the final door, and Cotter put his ear to it, knocking softly.

'Could be dozing, I suppose,' he said in an undertone.

'Mind if I . . .?' Without waiting for an answer, Rebus turned the handle. The door opened inwards. The room was dark, gauzy black curtains drawn shut. Cotter flicked the light-switch. There were candles on every available surface. Black candles, many of them melted down to almost nothing. Prints and posters on the walls. Rebus recognised some by H.R. Giger, knew him because he'd designed an album for ELP. They were set in a kind of stainless-steel hell. The other pictures showed equally dark imaginings.

'Teenagers, eh?' was the father's only comment. Books by Poppy Z. Brite and Anne Rice. Another called *The Gates of Janus*, apparently written by 'Moors Murderer' Ian Brady. Plenty of CDs, all by noise merchants. The sheets on the single bed were black. So was the shiny duvet cover. The walls of the room were the colour of meat, the ceiling split into four squares, two black, two red. Siobhan was standing by a computer desk. The set-up on top of it looked high quality: flat-screen monitor, DVD hard disk, scanner and webcam.

'I don't suppose these come in black,' she mused.

'Otherwise Teri would have them,' Cotter agreed.

'When I was her age,' Rebus said, 'only Goths I knew of were pubs.'

Cotter laughed. 'Yes, Gothenburgs. They were community pubs, weren't they?'

Rebus nodded. 'Unless she's under the bed, I'm guessing she's not here. Any idea where we might find her?'

'I could try her mobile . . .'

'Would that be this one?' Siobhan said, holding up a small gloss-black phone.

'That's it,' Cotter agreed.

'Not like a teenager to leave their phone at home,' Siobhan mused.

'No, well . . . Teri's mum can be . . .' He twitched his shoulders, as if feeling a sudden discomfort.

'Can be what, sir?' Rebus prodded.

'She likes to keep tabs on Teri, is that it?' Siobhan guessed. Cotter nodded, relieved that she'd saved him the trouble of spelling it out.

'Teri should be home later,' he said, 'if it can wait.'

'We'd rather get it over and done with, Mr Cotter,' Rebus explained.

'Well . . .'

'Time being money and all that, as I'm sure you'd agree.'

Cotter nodded. 'You could try Cockburn Street. A few of her friends sometimes congregate there.'

Rebus looked to Siobhan. 'We should have thought of that,' he said. Siobhan's mouth gave a twitch of agreement. Cockburn Street, a winding conduit between the Royal Mile and Waverley Station, had always enjoyed a louche reputation. Decades back, it had been the haunt of hippies and drop-outs, selling cheesecloth shirts, tie-dye, and cigarette papers. Rebus had frequented a good secondhand record stall, without ever bothering with the clothes. These days, the new alternative cultures lionised the place. A good street for browsing, if your tastes inclined towards the macabre or the stoned.

As they walked back along the hallway, Rebus noticed that one door had a small porcelain plaque stating that this was 'Stuart's Room'. Rebus paused in front of it.

'Your son?'

Cotter nodded slowly. 'Charlotte . . . my wife . . . she wants it kept the way it was before the accident.'

'No shame in that, sir,' Siobhan offered, sensing Cotter's embarrassment.

'I suppose not.'

'Tell me,' Rebus said, 'did Teri's Goth phase start before or after her brother's death?'

Cotter looked at him. 'Soon after.'

'The pair of them were close?' Rebus guessed.

'I suppose so . . . But I don't see what any of this has to do with . . .'

Rebus shrugged. 'Just curious, that's all. Sorry: it's one of the pitfalls of the job.'

Cotter seemed to accept this, and led them back down the staircase.

'I buy CDs there,' Siobhan said. They were back in the car, heading for Cockburn Street.

'Ditto,' Rebus told her. And he'd often seen the Goths, taking up more than their fair share of pavement, spilling down the flight of steps to the side of the old *Scotsman* building, sharing cigarettes and trading tips on the latest bands. They started to appear as soon as school had finished for the day, maybe changing out of their uniform and into the regulation black. Make-up and baubles, hoping to fit in and stand out at the same time. Thing was, people were harder to shock these days. Once upon a time, collar-length hair would have done it. Then glam came along, followed by its bastard offspring, punk. Rebus still remembered one Saturday when he'd been out buying records. Starting the long climb up Cockburn Street and passing his first punks: all slouches and spiky hair, chains and sneers. It had been too much for the middle-aged woman behind him, who'd spluttered out the words 'Can't you walk like human beings?', probably making the punks' day in the process.

'We could park at the bottom of the road and walk up,' Siobhan suggested as they neared Cockburn Street.

'I'd rather park at the top and walk down,' Rebus countered.

They were in luck: a space opened up just as they approached, and they were able to park on Cockburn Street itself, only a few yards from where a bunch of Goths were milling around.

'Bingo,' Rebus said, spotting Miss Teri in animated conversation with two friends.

'You'll need to get out first,' Siobhan told him. Rebus saw the problem: there were sacks of rubbish sitting kerbside, awaiting collection and blocking the driver's-side door. He got out, holding the door open so Siobhan could slide across and make her exit. Feet were running down the pavement, and then Rebus saw one of the rubbish-bags disappear. He looked up and saw five youths hurtling past the car, dressed in hooded tops and baseball caps. One of them was swinging the rubbish-bag into the group of

Goths. The bag burst, spraying its contents everywhere. There were shouts, screams. Feet were swinging, as were fists. One Goth was sent flying head first down the stone steps. Another dodged into the roadway and was winged by a passing taxi. Bystanders were yelling warnings, shopkeepers coming to their doors. Someone called out to phone the police.

The fighting was spilling across the street, bodies pushed against windows, hands clawing at necks. Only five attackers to a dozen Goths, but the five were strong and vicious. Siobhan had run forward to tackle one of them. Rebus saw Miss Teri diving through a shop doorway, slamming the door after her. The door was glass, and her pursuer was looking around for something to throw through it. Rebus took a deep breath and hollered.

'Rab Fisher! Hey, Rab! Over here!' The pursuer stopped, looked in Rebus's direction. Rebus was waving a gloved hand. 'Remember me, Rab?'

Fisher's mouth twisted in a sneer. Another of his gang had recognised Rebus. 'Polis!' he yelled, the other Lost Boys heeding his call. They gathered in the middle of the road, chests pumping, breathing hard.

'Ready for that trip to Saughton, lads?' Rebus asked loudly, taking a step forwards. Four of them turned and ran, jogging downhill. Rab Fisher lingered, then gave the glass door a final stubborn kick before sauntering off to join his friends. Siobhan was helping a couple of the Goths to their feet, checking for injuries. There had been no knives or missiles; mostly it was only pride which had taken a beating. Rebus walked over to the glass door. Behind it, Miss Teri had been joined by a woman in a white coat, the kind worn by doctors and pharmacists. Rebus saw a row of gleaming cubicles; it was a tanning salon, brand new by the look of it. The woman was running a hand down Teri's hair, while Teri tried to wriggle free. Rebus pushed open the door.

'Remember me, Teri?' he said.

She studied him, then nodded. 'You're the policeman I met.' Rebus held out a hand towards the woman.

'You must be Teri's mother. I'm DI Rebus.'

'Charlotte Cotter,' the woman said, taking his hand. She was in her late thirties, with lots of wavy ash-blonde hair. Her face was lightly tanned, almost glowing. Looking at the two women, it was hard to see any similarity. If told they were related, Rebus might have guessed they were contemporaries: not sisters, but maybe cousins. The mother was an inch or two shorter than her daughter, slimmer and toned-looking. Rebus thought he knew now which member of the Cotter family made use of the indoor pool.

'What was all that about?' he asked Teri.

She shrugged. 'Nothing.'

'You get a lot of hassle?'

'They're always getting hassle,' her mother answered for her, receiving a glare for her trouble. 'Verbal abuse, sometimes more.'

'Like you'd know,' her daughter argued.

'I see things.'

'Is that why you opened this place? To keep an eye on me?' Teri had started playing with the gold chain around her neck. Rebus could see a diamond hanging from it.

'Teri,' Charlotte Cotter said with a sigh, 'all I'm saying is—'

'I'm going outside,' Teri muttered.

'Before you do,' Rebus interrupted, 'any chance I could have a word?'

'I'm not going to press charges or anything!'

'You see how stubborn she is?' Charlotte Cotter said, sounding exasperated. 'I heard you shout out a name, Inspector. Does that mean you know these thugs? You can arrest them . . .?'

'I'm not sure it would do any good, Mrs Cotter.'

'But you saw them!'

Rebus nodded. 'And now they've been warned. Could be

enough to do the trick. Thing is, it's not just chance that I was here. I wanted a word with Teri.'

'Oh?'

'Come on then,' Teri said, grabbing him by the arm. 'Sorry, Mum, got to go help the police with their inquiries.'

'Hang on, Teri . . .'

But it was too late. Charlotte Cotter could only watch as her daughter dragged the detective back outside and across the road to where the mood was lightening. Battle scars were being compared. One boy in a black trenchcoat was sniffing his lapels, wrinkling his nose to acknowledge that the coat would need a good wash. The rubbish from the torn bag had been gathered together – mostly by Siobhan, Rebus guessed. She was trying to elicit help in filling an intact bag, the gift of a neighbouring shop.

'Everybody okay?' Teri asked. There were smiles and nods. It looked to Rebus like they were enjoying the moment. Victims again, and happy with their lot. Like the punks and the woman, they had got their reaction. Still a group, but strengthened now: war stories they could share. Other kids – on their slow route home from school, still dressed in uniform – had stopped to listen. Rebus led Miss Teri back up the street and into the nearest watering-hole.

'We don't serve her kind!' the woman behind the bar snapped.

'You do when I'm here,' Rebus snapped back.

'She's underage,' the woman pressed.

'Then she'll take a soft drink.' He turned to Teri. 'What'll it be?'

'Vodka tonic.'

Rebus smiled. 'Give her a Coke. I'll have a Laphroaig with a splash of water.' He paid for the drinks, confident enough now to try bringing coins from his pocket as well as notes.

'How are the hands?' Teri Cotter asked.

'Fine,' he said. 'You can carry the drinks though.' They received a few stares as they made their way to a table. Teri seemed pleased with the reception, blowing a kiss at one man, who just sneered and looked away.

'You pick a fight in here,' Rebus warned her, 'you're on your own.'

'I can handle myself.'

'I saw that, way you ran to your mum's as soon as the Lost Boys arrived.'

She glowered at him.

'Good plan, by the way,' he added. 'Defence the better part of valour and all that. Is it true what your mum says, this sort of thing happens a lot?'

'Not as much as she seems to think.'

'And yet you keep coming to Cockburn Street?'

'Why shouldn't we?'

He shrugged. 'No reason. Bit of masochism never hurt anyone.'

She stared at him, then smiled, gazing down into her glass.

'Cheers,' he said, lifting his own.

'You got the quote wrong,' she said. ' "The better part of valour is discretion." Shakespeare, *Henry IV, Part One*.'

'Not that you and your pals could be described as discreet.'

'I try not to be.'

'You do a good job. When I mentioned the Lost Boys, you didn't seem surprised. Meaning you know them?'

She looked down again, the hair falling over her pale face. Her fingers stroked the glass, nails gloss black. Slender hands and wrists. 'Got a cigarette?' she asked.

'Light us a couple,' Rebus said, digging the pack out of his jacket pocket. She placed the lit cigarette between his lips.

'People will start to talk,' she said, exhaling smoke.

'I doubt it, Miss Teri.' He watched the door swing open, Siobhan walk in. She saw him, and nodded towards the toilets, holding up her hands to let him know she was going to wash them.

205

'You like being an outsider, don't you?' Rebus asked.

Teri Cotter nodded.

'And that's why you liked Lee Herdman: he was an outsider, too.' She looked at him. 'We found your photo in his flat. From which I assume you knew him.'

'I knew him. Can I see the photo?'

Rebus took it from his pocket. It was held inside a clear polythene envelope. 'Where was it taken?' he asked.

'Right here,' she said, gesturing towards the street.

'You knew him pretty well, didn't you?'

'He liked us. Goths, I mean. Never really understood why.'

'He had a few parties, didn't he?' Rebus was remembering the albums in Herdman's flat: music for Goths to dance to.

Teri was nodding, blinking back tears. 'Some of us used to go to his place.' She held up the photo. 'Where did you find this?'

'Inside a book he was reading.'

'Which book?'

'Why do you want to know?'

She shrugged. 'Just wondered.'

'It was a biography, I think. Some soldier who ended up doing himself in.'

'You think that's a clue?'

'A clue?'

She nodded. 'To why Lee killed himself.'

'Might be, I suppose. Did you ever meet any of his friends?'

'I don't think he had many friends.'

'What about Doug Brimson?' The question came from Siobhan. She was sliding on to the banquette.

Teri's mouth twitched. 'Yeah, I know him.'

'You don't sound enthusiastic,' Rebus commented.

'You could say that.'

'What's wrong with him?' Siobhan wanted to know. Rebus could see her prickling.

Teri just shrugged.

'The two lads who died,' Rebus said, 'ever see them at the parties?'

'As if.'

'Meaning what?'

She looked at him. 'They weren't the type. Rugby and jazz music and the Cadets.' As if this explained everything.

'Did Lee ever talk about his time in the army?'

'Not much.'

'But you asked him?' She nodded slowly. 'And you knew he had a thing about guns?'

'I knew he kept pictures . . .' She bit her lip, but too late.

'On the inside of his wardrobe door,' Siobhan added. 'It's not everyone who'd know that, Teri.'

'Doesn't mean anything!' Teri's voice had risen. She was playing with her neck-chain again.

'Nobody's on trial here, Teri,' Rebus said. 'We just want to know what made him do it.'

'How should I know?'

'Because you knew him, and it seems not many people did.'

Teri was shaking her head. 'He never told me anything. That was the thing about him – like he had secrets. But I never thought he'd . . .'

'No?'

She fixed her eyes on Rebus's, but said nothing.

'He ever show you a gun, Teri?' Siobhan asked.

'No.'

'Ever hint that he had access to one?'

A shake of the head.

'You say he never really opened up to you . . . what about the other way round?'

'How do you mean?'

'Did he ask about you? Maybe you spoke to him about your family?'

'I might have.'

207

Rebus leaned forward. 'We were sorry to hear about your brother, Teri.'

Siobhan, too, leaned forward. 'You probably mentioned the crash to Lee Herdman.'

'Or maybe one of your pals did,' Rebus added.

Teri saw that they were hemming her in. No escape from their stares and questions. She had placed the photo on the table, concentrating her attention on it.

'Lee didn't take this,' she said, as if trying to change the subject.

'Anyone else we should talk to, Teri?' Rebus was asking. 'People who went to Lee's little soirées?'

'I don't want to answer any more questions.'

'Why not, Teri?' Siobhan asked, frowning as though genuinely puzzled.

'Because I don't.'

'Other names we can talk to . . .' Rebus was saying. 'Might get us off your back.'

Teri Cotter sat for a moment longer, then rose to her feet and climbed on to the banquette, stepped on to the table and jumped down to the floor at the other side, the gauzy black layers of her skirts billowing out around her. Without looking back, she made for the door, opened it and banged it shut behind her. Rebus looked at Siobhan and gave a grudging smile.

'The girl has a certain style,' he said.

'We panicked her,' Siobhan admitted. 'Pretty much as soon as we mentioned her brother's death.'

'Could be they were just close,' Rebus argued. 'You're not really going for the assassin theory?'

'All the same,' she said. 'There's something . . .' The door opened again, and Teri Cotter strode towards the table, leaning on it with both hands, her face close to her inquisitors.

'James Bell,' she hissed. 'There's a name for you, if you want one.'

'He went to Herdman's parties?' Rebus asked.

Teri Cotter just nodded, then turned away again. The regulars, watching her make her exit, shook their heads and went back to their drinks.

'That interview we listened to,' Rebus said, 'what was it James Bell said about Herdman?'

'Something about going water-skiing.'

'Yes, but the way he said it: "we'd met socially", something like that.'

Siobhan nodded. 'Maybe we should have picked up on it.'

'We need to talk to him.'

Siobhan kept nodding, but she was looking at the table. She peered beneath it.

'Lost something?' Rebus asked.

'No, but you have.'

Rebus looked too, and it dawned on him. Teri Cotter had taken her photograph with her.

'Think that was why she came back?' Siobhan guessed.

Rebus shrugged. 'I suppose it counts as her property . . . a memento of the man she's lost.'

'You think they were lovers?'

'Stranger things have happened.'

'In which case . . .'

But Rebus shook his head. 'Using her womanly wiles to persuade him to turn assassin? Do me a favour, Siobhan.'

'Stranger things have happened,' she echoed.

'Speaking of which, any chance of you buying me a drink?' He held up his empty glass.

'None whatsoever,' she said, getting up to leave. Glumly, he followed her out of the bar. She was standing by her car, seemingly transfixed by something. Rebus couldn't see anything worthy of note. The Goths were milling around as before, minus Miss Teri. No sign of the Lost Boys either. A few tourists stopping for photographs.

'What is it?' he asked.

She nodded towards a car parked opposite. 'Looks like Doug Brimson's Land Rover.'

209

'You sure?'

'I saw it when I was out at Turnhouse.' She looked up and down Cockburn Street. Brimson wasn't anywhere to be seen.

'It's in worse shape than my Saab,' Rebus commented.

'Yes, but you don't have a Jag garaged at home.'

'A Jag and a clapped-out Land Rover?'

'I reckon it's an image thing . . . boys and their toys.' She looked up and down the street again. 'Wonder where he is.'

'Maybe he's stalking you,' Rebus suggested. He saw the look on her face, and shrugged an apology. She turned her attention to the car again, certain in her mind that it was his. Coincidence, she told herself, that's all it is.

Coincidence.

But all the same, she jotted down the number.

11

That evening, she settled down on her sofa, trying to get interested in anything on the TV. Two gaudily dressed presenters were telling their victim that her clothes were all wrong for her. On another channel, a house was being 'decluttered'. Which left Siobhan the choice of a grey-looking film, a dreary comedy series or a documentary about cane toads.

All of which served her right for not bothering to stop off at the video shop. Her own collection of films was small – 'select', as she preferred to call it. She'd watched each one half a dozen times at least, could recite dialogue, knew exactly what was coming in every scene. Maybe she would put some music on, turn the TV to mute and invent her own script for the boring-looking film. Or even for the cane toads. She'd already skimmed a magazine, picked up a book and put it down again, eaten the crisps and chocolate she'd bought at the garage when she'd stopped for petrol. There was a half-finished chow mein on the kitchen table, which she might get round to microwaving. Worst of all, she'd run out of wine, nothing in the flat but empty bottles awaiting the recycling run. She had gin in the cupboard, but nothing to mix it with except Diet Coke, and she wasn't *that* desperate.

Not yet, anyway.

There were friends she could phone, but she knew she wouldn't make great company. There was a message on her answering-machine from her friend Caroline, asking if she fancied a drink. Blonde and petite, Caroline always attracted attention when the two of them went out together. Siobhan had decided not to return the call just yet. She was too tired, and with the case buzzing around her head, refusing to leave her alone. She'd made herself coffee, taking a mouthful before realising she hadn't boiled the kettle. Then she'd spent a couple of minutes searching the kitchen for sugar, before remembering she didn't take sugar. Hadn't taken it in coffee since she'd been a teenager.

'Senile dementia,' she'd muttered aloud. 'And talking to yourself: another symptom.'

Chocolate and crisps weren't on her panic-free diet. Salt, fat and sugar. Her heart wasn't exactly racing, but she knew she had to calm down somehow, had to relax and start winding down as bedtime approached. She'd stared out of her window for a while, checking on the neighbours across the street, pressing her nose to the glass as she looked down two storeys to the passing traffic. It was quiet outside, quiet and dark, the pavement picked out by orange street-lamps. There were no bogeymen; nothing to be scared of.

She remembered that a long time ago, back in the days when she'd still taken sugar in her coffee, she'd been afraid of the dark for a while. Around the age of thirteen or fourteen: too old to confide in her parents. She would spend her pocket money on batteries for the torch she kept on all night, keeping it beneath the covers with her, holding her breath in an attempt to pick out the breathing of anyone else in the room. The few times her parents caught her, they just thought she was staying up late to read. She could never be sure which was the right thing to do: leave the door open, so you could make a run for it, or close it to keep out intruders? She checked beneath her bed two or three times each day, though there was little enough room under there: it was where she stored her albums. The thing was, she never had nightmares. When she did eventually drop off to sleep, that sleep was deep and cleansing. She never suffered panic attacks. And eventually, she forgot why she'd ever been afraid in the first place. The torch went back in its drawer. The money she'd been wasting on batteries she now started spending on make-up.

She could never be sure which came first: did she discover boys, or did they discover her?

'Ancient history, girl,' she told herself now. There were no bogey men out there, but precious few knights either, tarnished or otherwise. She walked over to her dining-table, looked at her notes on the case. They were laid out in no order whatsoever – everything she'd been given that first day. Reports, autopsy and forensics, photos of crime scene and victims. She studied the two faces, Derek Renshaw and Anthony Jarvies. Both were handsome, in a bland sort of way. There was a haughty intelligence to Jarvies's heavy-lidded stare. Renshaw looked a lot less sure of himself. Maybe it was a class thing, Jarvies's breeding showing through. She reckoned Allan Renshaw would have been proud of the fact that his son boasted a judge's son as a friend. It was why you sent your kids to private school, wasn't it? You wanted them to meet the right sort of people, people who might prove useful in future. She knew fellow officers, not all of them on CID salaries, who scrimped to send their offspring to the kinds of schools they themselves had never been offered the chance of. The class thing again. She wondered about Lee Herdman. He'd been in the army, the SAS . . . ordered about by officers who'd been to the right schools, who spoke the right way. Could it be as simple as that? Could his attack have been motivated by nothing more than bitter envy of an elite?

There's no mystery . . . Remembering her own words to Rebus, she laughed out loud. If there was no mystery, what was she worrying about? Why was she slogging her guts out? What was to stop her putting it all to one side and relaxing?

'Bugger it,' she said, sitting down at the table, pushing away the paperwork, and pulling Derek Renshaw's laptop towards her. She booted it up, plugging it into her phone

213

line. There were e-mails to be gone through, enough to keep her awake half the night if need be. Plenty of other files, too, that she hadn't checked yet. She knew the work would calm her. It would calm her because it was work.

She decided on some decaf, this time remembering to switch the kettle on. Took the hot drink through to the living room. The password 'Miles' got her on-line, but the new e-mails were junk. People trying to sell insurance or Viagra to someone they couldn't know was dead. There were a few messages from people who'd noted Derek's absence from various message boards and chat rooms. Siobhan thought of something and dragged the icon to the top of the screen, clicking on 'Favourite Places'. Up came a list of sites, shortcuts to addresses Derek had used regularly. The chat rooms and messageboards were there, along with the usual suspects: Amazon, BBC, Ask Jeeves . . . But one address was unfamiliar. Siobhan clicked on it. Connection took only a few moments.

WELCOME TO MY DARKNESS!

The words were in dull red, the colour pulsing with life. The rest of the screen was a blank background. Siobhan moved the cursor on to the letter W and double-clicked. Connection took a little longer this time, the screen changing to a picture of a room's interior. The image was fairly indistinct. She tried altering the screen's contrast and brightness, but the problem was with the image itself, little she could do to improve it. She could make out a bed, and a curtained window behind it. She tried moving the cursor around the screen, but there was no hidden marker for her to click on. This was all there was. She was sitting back, arms folded, wondering what it might mean, wondering what interest the image could have had for Derek Renshaw. Maybe it was his room. Maybe the 'darkness' was another side to his character. Then the screen changed, a strange yellow light passing across it. Interference of some kind? Siobhan sat forward, grasping the edge of her table. She knew what it was now. It was a car's headlights, brief illumination from behind the curtains. Not a picture then, not a captured still.

'Webcam,' she whispered. She was watching a real-time broadcast of somebody's bedroom. Moreover, she knew now whose bedroom it was. Those headlights had done just enough. She got up, found her telephone and made the call.

Siobhan plugged everything in and rebooted the computer. The laptop was on a chair – not enough cable to stretch from Rebus's telephone socket to his dining-table.

'All very mysterious,' he said, fetching through a tray – mugs of coffee for the pair of them. She could smell vinegar: a fish supper probably. Thinking of the chow mein waiting for her at home, she realised how similar they were – takeaway food, no one to go home to . . . He'd been drinking beer, an empty bottle of Deuchar's on the floor by his chair. And listening to music: the Hawkwind anthology she'd bought him last birthday. Maybe he'd put it on specially, to make her think he hadn't forgotten.

'Almost there,' she said now. Rebus had turned off the CD and was rubbing his eyes with his ungloved, hot-looking hands. Nearly ten o'clock. He'd been asleep in his chair when she'd phoned, quite content to stay there till morning. Easier than getting undressed. Easier than un-tying shoelaces, fiddling with buttons. He hadn't bothered tidying up. Siobhan knew him too well. But he'd closed the kitchen door so she wouldn't see the dirty dishes. If she saw them, she'd offer to wash up for him, and he didn't want that.

'Just need to connect . . .'

Rebus had brought one of the dining-chairs over to sit on. Siobhan was kneeling on the floor in front of the laptop. She angled its screen a little, and he nodded to let her know he could see it.

WELCOME TO MY DARKNESS!

'Alice Cooper fan club?' he guessed.

'Just wait.'

'Royal Society for the Blind?'

'If I so much as smile, you have permission to hit me over the head with the tray.' She sat back a little. 'There . . . now take a look.'

The room was no longer completely dark. Candles had been lit. Black candles.

'Teri Cotter's bedroom,' Rebus stated. Siobhan nodded. Rebus watched the candles flicker.

'This is a film?'

'It's a live feed, as far as I know.'

'Meaning?'

'There was a webcam attached to her computer. That's where the picture's coming from. When I first watched, the room was dark. She must be home now.'

'Is this supposed to be interesting?' Rebus asked.

'Some people like it. Some of them *pay* to watch stuff like this.'

'But we're getting a show for free?'

'Seems like.'

'You reckon she switches it off when she comes in?'

'Where would the fun be in that?'

'She keeps it on all the time?'

Siobhan shrugged. 'Maybe we're going to find out.'

Teri Cotter had entered the frame, moving jerkily, the camera presenting a series of stills broken up by momentary delays.

'No sound?' Rebus enquired.

Siobhan didn't think so, but she tried turning up the volume anyway. 'No sound,' she acknowledged.

Teri had seated herself cross-legged on her bed. She was dressed in the same clothes as when they'd met. She seemed to be looking towards the camera. She leaned forwards and stretched out on her bed, supporting her chin on her cupped hands, face close to the camera now.

'Like one of those old silent films,' Rebus said. Siobhan

didn't know if he was referring to the picture quality or lack of sound. 'What exactly are we supposed to be doing?'

'We're her audience.'

'She knows we're here?'

Siobhan shook her head. 'Probably no way of knowing who's watching – if anyone.'

'But Derek Renshaw used to watch?'

'Yes.'

'You think she knows?'

Siobhan shrugged, sipped the bitter-tasting coffee. It wasn't decaf, and she might suffer for it later, but she didn't care.

'So what do you think?' he asked.

'It's not so unusual for young girls to be exhibitionists.' She paused. 'Not that I've come across anything like this before.'

'I wonder who else knows about this.'

'I doubt her parents do. Is it something we need to ask her?'

Rebus was thoughtful. 'How would people get here?' He pointed towards the screen.

'There are lists of home pages. She'd just have to provide a link, maybe a description.'

'Let's take a look.'

So Siobhan quit the page and went hunting through cyberspace, typing in the words 'Miss' and 'Teri'. Page after page of links came up, mostly for porn sites and people called Terry, Terri and Teri.

'This could take a while,' she said.

'So this is what I've been missing out on, not having a modem?'

'All human life is here, most of it ever so slightly depressing.'

'Just what's needed after a day at the coal-face.'

Her face creased in what could almost have passed for a smile. Rebus made a show of reaching for the tea-tray.

'Here we go, I think,' Siobhan said a couple of minutes

later. Rebus looked at where she was underlining some words with her finger.

Myss Teri – visit my 100% non-pornographic (sorry, guys!) home page!

'Why "Myss"?' Rebus asked.

'Could be all the other spellings were already taken. My e-mail's "66Siobhan".'

'Because sixty-five Siobhans got there ahead of you?'

She nodded. 'And I thought I had an uncommon name.' Siobhan had clicked on the link. Teri Cotter's home page started to load. There was a photo of her in full Goth mode, palms held either side of her face.

'She's drawn pentagrams on her hands,' Siobhan noted. Rebus was looking: five-pointed stars, enclosed by circles. There were no other photos, just some text outlining Teri's interests, which school she attended, and an invitation to 'come worship me, Cockburn Street most Saturday afternoons . . .' There was an option of sending her an e-mail, adding comments to her guest book, or clicking on various links, most of which would send the visitor to other Goth sites, but one of which was marked 'Dark Entry'.

'That'll be the webcam,' Siobhan said. She tried the link, just to be sure. The screen changed back to the same red words: WELCOME TO MY DARKNESS! Another click and they were in Teri Cotter's bedroom again. She'd changed position so that she had her head against the bedboard, knees tucked in front of her. She was writing something in a loose-leaf binder.

'Looks like homework,' Siobhan said.

'Could be her potions book,' Rebus suggested. 'Anyone accessing her home page would know her age, which school she goes to, and what she looks like.'

Siobhan was nodding. 'And where to find her on a Saturday afternoon.'

'A dangerous pastime,' Rebus muttered. He was thinking of her potential as prey to any of the hunters out there.

'Maybe that's why she likes it.'

Rebus rubbed his eyes again. He was remembering his first meeting with her. The way she'd said she was jealous of Derek and Anthony . . . and her parting remark: *You can see me whenever you like* . . . He knew now what those words had been hinting at.

'Seen enough?' Siobhan asked, tapping the screen.

He nodded. 'Initial thoughts, DS Clarke?'

'Well . . . *if* she and Herdman were lovers, and *if* he was the jealous type . . .'

'That only works if Anthony Jarvies knew about the site.'

'Jarvies and Derek were best friends: what are the chances Derek didn't let him in on it?'

'Good point. We'll need to check.'

'And talk to Teri again?'

Rebus nodded slowly. 'Can we open the visitors' book?'

They could, but it didn't have much to say. No obvious notes from either Derek Renshaw or Anthony Jarvies, just waffle from some of Miss Teri's admirers, the majority of whom seemed to be based abroad, if their English was anything to go by. Rebus watched Siobhan as she shut the laptop down.

'Did you run that number-plate?' he asked.

She nodded. 'Last thing I did before clocking off. It was Brimson's.'

'Curiouser and curiouser . . .'

Siobhan folded the screen shut. 'How are you coping?' she asked. 'I mean, dressing and undressing?'

'I'm all right.'

'Not sleeping in your clothes?'

'No.' He tried to sound indignant.

'So I can expect to see a clean shirt tomorrow?'

'Stop mothering me.'

She smiled. 'I could run you another bath.'

'I can manage.' He waited till her eyes met his. 'Cross my heart.'

'And hope to die?'

Which took him back to his first meeting with Teri Cotter . . . asking him about deaths he'd witnessed . . . wanting to know what it felt like to die. With a website which would be as good as an invitation to some sick minds.

'There's something I want to show you,' Siobhan said, rummaging in her bag. She produced a book, showed him the cover: *I'm A Man* by Ruth Padel. 'It's about rock music,' she explained, opening it at a marked page. 'Listen to this: "the heroism dream begins in the teenage bedroom".'

'Meaning what?'

'She's talking about how teenagers use music as a kind of rebellion. Maybe Teri's using her actual bedroom.' She flicked to another page. 'And there's something else . . . "the gun is male sexuality in jeopardy".' She looked at him. 'Makes sense to me.'

'You're saying Herdman was jealous after all?'

'You've never been jealous? Never flown into a rage?'

He thought for a moment. 'Maybe once or twice.'

'Kate mentioned a book to me. It was called *Bad Men Do What Good Men Dream*. Maybe Herdman's rage took him too far.' She held a hand to her mouth, stifling a yawn.

'Time you got to bed,' Rebus told her. 'Plenty of time in the morning for amateur analysis.' She unplugged the laptop, gathered up the cables. He saw her out, then watched from his window as she made it to the safety of her car. Suddenly, a man's figure appeared at her driver's-side door. Rebus turned and ran for the stairs, took them two at a time. Hauled open the front door. The man was saying something, voice raised above the ticking engine. He was holding something to the windscreen. A newspaper. Rebus grabbed his shoulder, feeling a jab of fire from his fingers. Turned him around . . . recognised the face.

It was the reporter, Steve Holly. Rebus realised that what he was holding was probably the next morning's edition.

'Very man I wanted to see,' Holly said, shrugging himself free and offering a grin. 'Nice to see CID making home visits to each other.' He turned to glance at Siobhan, who had cut her engine and was stepping from the car. 'Some might think it a bit late in the evening for chit-chat.'

'What do you want?' Rebus asked.

'Just after a comment.' He held up the paper's front page so Rebus could make out the headline: HELL HOUSE COP MYSTERY. 'We're not printing any names as yet. Wondered if you wanted to put your side of the story. I understand you're on suspension, subject to an internal inquiry?' Holly had folded the paper and produced a micro-recorder from his pocket. 'That looks nasty.' He was nodding towards Rebus's ungloved hands. 'Burns take a while to heal, don't they?'

'John . . .' Siobhan warning him not to lose his head. Rebus pointed a blistered finger at the reporter.

'Stay away from the Renshaws. You hassle them, you'll have me to deal with, understood?'

'Then give me an interview.'

'Not a chance.'

Holly looked down towards the paper he was holding. 'How about this for a headline: "Cop Flees Murder Scene"?'

'It'll look good to my lawyers when I sue you.'

'My paper's always open to a fair fight, DI Rebus.'

'Then that's a problem,' Rebus said, smothering the tape-recorder with his hand. 'Because I *never* fight fair.' Spitting the words out, showing Holly two rows of bared teeth. The reporter pressed his finger to a button, stopping the tape.

'Nice to know where we stand.'

'Lay off the families, Holly. I mean it.'

'In your sad, misguided way, I'm sure you do. Sweet dreams, Detective Inspector.' He bowed slightly in Siobhan's direction, then strode off.

'Bastard,' Rebus hissed.

'I wouldn't worry about it,' Siobhan said soothingly. 'Only a quarter of the population reads his paper anyway.' She climbed back into her car, turned the ignition and reversed out of the parking space. Gave a little wave as she drove away. Holly had disappeared round a corner, heading for Marchmont Road. Rebus climbed his stairwell, went indoors and found his car keys. Put his gloves back on. Double-locked the door on the way out.

The streets were quiet, no sign of Steve Holly. Not that he was looking for him. He got into his Saab and tried gripping the steering-wheel, turning it left and right. He thought he could manage. He drove down Marchmont Road and on to Melville Drive, heading towards Arthur's Seat. He didn't bother putting any music on, thought instead of everything that had happened, letting conversations and images swirl around.

Irene Lesser: *You might want to talk to someone . . . a long time to be carrying any baggage . . .*

Siobhan: quoting from that book.

Kate: *Bad Men Do . . .*

Boethius: Good men suffer . . .

He didn't think of himself as a bad man, but knew he probably wasn't a good one either.

'I'm A Man': title of an old blues song.

Robert Niles, leaving the SAS, but without having been switched off first. Lee Herdman, too, had carried 'baggage' with him. Rebus felt that if he could understand Herdman, maybe he would understand himself better, too.

Easter Road was quiet, bars still serving, a queue beginning to form in the chip shop. Rebus was headed for Leith Police Station. The driving was okay, the pain in his hands bearable. The skin there seemed to have grown taut, as if from sunburn. He saw a space kerbside, not fifty yards from the front door of the station, and decided to take it. Got out and locked the car. There was a camera crew across the street, probably wanting the station in the background as the presenter did his piece. Then Rebus saw who it was: Jack Bell. Bell, turning his head, recognised Rebus, pointed to him before turning back to the camera. Rebus caught his words:

'. . . while CID officers like the one behind me continue to mop up, without ever offering workable solutions . . .'

'Cut,' the director said. 'Sorry, Jack.' He nodded towards Rebus, who had crossed the road and was standing directly behind Bell.

'What's going on?' Rebus asked.

'We're doing a piece on violence in society,' Bell snapped, annoyed at the interruption.

'I thought maybe it was a self-help video,' Rebus drawled.

'What?'

'A guide to kerb-crawling, something like that. Most of the girls work down that way now,' Rebus added, nodding in the direction of Salamander Street.

'How dare you!' the MSP spluttered. Then he turned to the director. 'Symptomatic, you see, of the very problem we're tackling. The police have ceased to be anything other than petty-minded and spiteful.'

'Unlike yourself, I'm sure,' Rebus said. He noticed for the first time that Bell was holding a photograph. Bell held it up in front of him.

'Thomas Hamilton,' he stated. 'No one thought him exceptional. Turned out he was evil incarnate when he walked into that school in Dunblane.'

'And how could the police have prevented that?' Rebus asked, folding his arms.

Before Bell could answer, the director had a question for Rebus. 'Were any videos or magazines found in Herdman's home? Violent films, that sort of thing?'

'There's no sign he was interested in anything like that. But so what if he was?'

The director just shrugged, deciding he wasn't going to get what he wanted from Rebus. 'Jack, maybe you could do a quick interview with . . . sorry, I didn't catch your name.' He smiled at Rebus.

'My name's Fuck You,' Rebus said, returning the smile.

Then he crossed the road again and pushed open the door of the police station.

'You're a disgrace!' Jack Bell was shouting at him. 'An absolute disgrace! Don't think I won't take this any further . . .!'

'That you making friends again?' the desk sergeant asked.

'I seem to be blessed that way,' Rebus informed him, climbing the stairs to the CID office. Overtime was available on the Herdman case, which meant a few souls were still working, even at this hour. Tapping reports into computers, or sharing gossip over hot drinks. Rebus recognised DC Mark Pettifer, and walked over to him.

'Something I need, Mark,' he said.

'What's that then, John?'

'The loan of a laptop.'

Pettifer smiled. 'Thought your generation preferred quill and parchment.'

'One other thing,' Rebus added, ignoring this. 'It has to be Internet-ready.'

'I think I can sort you something out.'

'While you're doing that . . .' Rebus leaned in closer, dropping his voice. 'Remember when Jack Bell got pulled in for kerb-crawling? That was some of your lads, wasn't it?'

Pettifer nodded slowly.

'I don't suppose there'd be any paperwork . . .?'

'I wouldn't think so. He was never charged, was he?'

Rebus was thoughtful. 'What about the guys who stopped his car: any chance I could have a word?'

'What's this all about?'

'Just say I'm an interested party,' Rebus said.

But as it turned out, the young DC who'd dealt with Bell had moved stations and was now based at Torphichen Street. Rebus eventually got a mobile number for him. His name was Harry Chambers.

'Sorry to bother you,' Rebus said, having introduced himself.

'No bother, I'm just walking home from the boozer.'

'Hope you had a good night.'

'Pool competition, I made the semis.'

'Good for you. The reason I'm calling is Jack Bell.'

'What's the oily bastard gone and done now?'

'He keeps getting under our feet at Port Edgar.' It was the truth, if not the whole truth. Rebus didn't think he needed to explain his desire to prise Kate away from the MSP.

'Then make sure to wipe your shoes on him,' Chambers was saying. 'About all he's good for.'

'I'm sensing a slight antagonism, Harry.'

'After the kerb-crawling thing, he tried to get me knocked back to uniform. And all that guff he came out with: first he was on his way home from somewhere . . . then, when he couldn't back that up, he was "researching" the need for a tolerance zone. Aye, that'll be right. The hoor he was talking to, she told me they'd already agreed a price.'

'Reckon it was his first trip down that way?'

'No idea. Only thing I do know – and I'm being as objective as possible here – is that he's a sleazy, lying, vindictive bastard. Why couldn't that guy Herdman have done us all a favour and popped him instead of those poor bloody kids . . .?'

Back home, Rebus tried to remember Pettifer's instructions as he set up the computer. It wasn't the newest model. Pettifer's comment: 'If it seems sluggish, just feed in another shovelful of coal.' Rebus had asked him how old the machine was. Answer: two years, and already near as dammit obsolete.

Rebus decided that something so venerable should be cherished. He gave the keyboard and screen a wipe with a damp cloth. Like him, it was a survivor.

'Okay, old-timer,' he told it, 'let's see what you can do.'

After a frustrating few minutes, he put in a call to Pettifer, eventually finding him on his mobile – in his car and on his way home to bed. More instructions . . . Rebus kept the line open until he was sure he'd succeeded.

'Cheers, Mark,' he said, cutting the connection. Then he dragged his armchair over so that he could sit in relative comfort.

Seated, one leg crossed over the other, arms folded, head tilted slightly to one side.

Watching Teri Cotter as she slept.

Day Four

Friday

12

'You slept in your clothes,' Siobhan commented, picking him up the next morning.

Rebus ignored her. There was a tabloid on the passenger seat, same one Steve Holly had brandished the previous night.

HELL HOUSE COP MYSTERY

'It's slim stuff,' Siobhan reassured him. And so it was. High on conjecture, low on facts. All the same, Rebus had ignored phone calls at 7, 7.15 and 7.30 a.m. He knew who it would probably be: the Complaints, trying to book an appointment for his persecution. He managed to turn the pages by dint of wetting the fingers of his gloves. 'Rumours are flying at St Leonard's,' Siobhan added. 'Fairstone was gagged and tied to a chair. Everyone knows you were there.'

'Did I say I wasn't?' She looked at him. 'It's just that I left him alive, nodding off on his sofa.' He turned a few more pages, seeking refuge. Found it in the story of a dog who'd swallowed a wedding ring – the one shaft of light in a paper full of grim little headlines: pub stabbings, celebs being outed by their mistresses, Atlantic oil slicks and American tornadoes.

'Funny how a daytime TV host merits more column inches than an ecological disaster,' he commented, folding the paper and tossing it over his shoulder. 'So where are we headed?'

'I thought maybe a face-to-face with James Bell.'

'Good enough.' His mobile rang, but he left it in his pocket.

'Your fan club?' Siobhan guessed.

'I can't help being popular. How come you know the goss at St Leonard's?'

'I went there before I came to pick you up.'

'A glutton for punishment.'

'I was using the gym.'

'Not a word I've come across before.'

She smiled. When her own phone sounded, she looked to Rebus again. He shrugged, and she checked the number on her screen.

'Bobby Hogan,' she told Rebus, answering the call. He could hear only her side of the conversation. 'We're on our way . . . why, what's happened?' A glance in Rebus's direction. 'He's right here . . . not sure his phone's charged up . . . yes, I'll tell him.'

'Time you got one of those hands-free jobs,' Rebus told her as she ended the call.

'Is my driving that bad?'

'I meant so I could listen in.'

'Bobby says the Complaints are looking for you.'

'Really?'

'They asked him to pass on the message. Seems you're not answering your phone.'

'I'm not sure it's charged up. What else did he say?'

'Wants to meet us at the marina.'

'Did he say why?'

'Maybe he's treating us to a day's cruising.'

'That'll be it. A thank you for all our diligence and hard work.'

'Just don't be surprised if the skipper turns out to be from Complaints . . .'

'You saw this morning's paper?' Bobby Hogan asked. He was leading them along the concrete pier.

'I saw it,' Rebus admitted. 'And Siobhan passed on your message. None of which explains what we're doing here.'

'I've also had a call from Jack Bell. He's toying with

making an official complaint.' Hogan glanced at Rebus. 'Whatever it was you did, please keep it up.'

'If that's an order, Bobby, then I'm happy to oblige.'

Rebus saw that there was a cordon at the top of the wooden ramp leading down to the pontoons where the yachts and dinghies were moored. Three uniforms standing guard beside a sign saying 'Berth Holders Only'. Hogan lifted the tape so they could pass through, leading them down the slope.

'Something we shouldn't have missed.' Hogan frowned. 'For which I take responsibility, naturally.'

'Naturally.'

'Seems Herdman owned another boat, something a bit bigger. Sea-going.'

'A yacht?' Siobhan guessed.

Hogan nodded. They were passing a series of anchored vessels, bobbing up and down. That same clanking sound from the rigging. Gulls overhead. There was a stiff breeze, and occasional salt spray. 'Too big for him to store in his shed. He obviously used it, otherwise it'd be kept ashore.' He indicated the shoreline, where a series of boats sat on blocks, well away from the ageing effects of sea-water.

'And?' Rebus asked.

'And see for yourself . . .'

Rebus saw. He saw a crowd of figures, recognised a couple of them as coming from Customs and Excise. Knew what that meant. They were examining something which had been laid out on a folded sheet of polythene. Shoes were being pressed to the corners of the polythene to stop it blowing away.

'Sooner we get this lot indoors the better,' one officer was saying. Another was arguing that Forensics should take a look first, before quitting the locus. Rebus stood behind one of the crouched figures, and saw the haul.

'Eckies,' Hogan explained, sliding his hands into his trouser pockets. 'We reckon about a thousand. Enough to keep a few all-night raves going.' The ecstasy tablets were in twelve or so translucent blue plastic bags, the kind you might use to store scraps of food in a freezer. Hogan tipped a few on to his palm. 'Anything from eight to ten grand's worth at street prices.' The pills had a greenish tinge to them, each one half the size of the painkillers Rebus had taken that morning. 'There's some cocaine, too,' Hogan continued for Rebus's benefit. 'Only a grand or so's worth, maybe for personal use.'

'We found traces of coke in his flat, didn't we?' Siobhan asked.

'That's right.'

'And where was this lot?' Rebus enquired.

'Stored in a locker below deck,' Hogan said. 'Not very well hidden.'

'Who found it?'

'We did.'

Rebus turned towards the voice. Whiteread was walking down the short plank connecting yacht to pontoon, a smug-looking Simms right behind her. She made a show of brushing dust from her hands.

'Rest of the boat looks clean, but your officers might want to check anyway.'

Hogan nodded. 'Don't worry, we will.'

Rebus was standing in front of the two army investigators. Whiteread met his stare.

'You seem happy enough,' Rebus said. 'Is that because you found the drugs, or were able to put one over on us?'

'If you'd done your job in the first place, DI Rebus . . .' Whiteread left it for Rebus to fill in the rest of the sentiment.

'I'm still asking myself the "how?"'

Whiteread's mouth twitched. 'There were records in his office. After which it was just a matter of talking to the marina manager.'

'You searched the boat?' Rebus was studying the yacht. It looked well-used. 'On your own, or did you follow SOP?' SOP: Standard Operating Procedure. Whiteread's smile levelled out. Rebus turned his attention to Hogan. 'Jurisdiction, Bobby. You might want to ask yourself why they went ahead with the search without contacting yourself first.' He pointed towards the two investigators. 'I trust them about as much as I'd trust a junkie with a chemistry set.'

'What gives you the right to say that?' Simms was smiling, but only with his mouth. He looked Rebus up and down. 'And talk about the pot calling the kettle black – it's not us being investigated for—'

'That's enough, Gavin!' Whiteread hissed. The young man fell silent. The whole marina seemed suddenly still and noiseless.

'This isn't going to help us,' Bobby Hogan said. 'Let's send the stuff for analysis . . .'

'I know who needs analysis,' Simms muttered.

'. . . and meantime put our heads together to see what all of this might add to the inquiry. That all right with you?' He was looking at Whiteread, who nodded, apparently content. But she shifted her eyes to Rebus, daring him to hold her gaze. He stared back at her, knowing his message was being reinforced.

I don't trust you . . .

They ended up in a convoy of cars, heading for Port Edgar Academy. There were fewer ghouls and news crews outside the gates, and no uniforms patrolling the perimeter to repel trespassers. The Portakabin had outgrown its usefulness, and someone had finally thought of annexing one of the classrooms in the school building. The school itself wouldn't reopen for a few days yet; even then, the crime scene would remain locked and unused. Everyone had gathered behind desks, where pupils would normally have been seated to listen to their geography teacher. There were maps on the walls, rainfall charts, pictures of tribesmen, bats and igloos. Some of the team preferred to stand, legs slightly apart, arms folded. Bobby Hogan stood in front of the pristine blackboard. Beside it was a marker-board bearing the single word 'Homework' followed by three exclamation marks.

'Could have been meant for us,' Hogan stated, tapping the board. 'Thanks to our friends from the armed forces here . . .' he nodded in the direction of Whiteread and Simms, who'd chosen to stand in the doorway, 'the case has taken a slight turn. A sea-going yacht and a quantity of drugs. What do we make of that?'

'Smuggling, sir,' a voice stated.

'Just to add one fact . . .' The speaker was standing at the back of the room: Customs and Excise. 'The majority of ecstasy coming into the UK originates in Holland.'

'So we need to take a look at Herdman's logs,' Hogan announced. 'See where he's been sailing to.'

'Logs can always be falsified, of course,' the Customs man added.

'We also need to talk to the Drugs Squad, see what they know about the ecstasy scene.'

'We're sure it's eckies, sir?' a voice piped up.

'Whatever it is, it's not sea-sickness pills.' There was some forced laughter at this.

'Sir, does this mean the case will be handed over to DMC?' DMC: Drugs and Major Crime.

'I can't answer that as yet. What we need to do is focus on the work we're already doing.' Hogan looked around the room, making sure he had everyone's attention. The only person not looking at him, he noted, was John Rebus. Rebus was staring at the two figures in the doorway, his eyebrows lowered in a thoughtful frown. 'We also need to go over that yacht with a fine-toothed comb, see if we managed to miss anything else.' Hogan saw Whiteread and Simms share a look. 'Right, any questions?' he asked. There were a few, but he dealt with them briskly. One officer wanted to know how much a yacht like Herdman's would cost. An answer had already been provided by the marina manager: for a forty-foot yacht, six berths, you'd need sixty thousand pounds. If you were buying second-hand.

'Which didn't come from his pension fund, trust me,' Whiteread commented.

'We're already looking at Herdman's various bank accounts and other assets,' Hogan told the room, glancing again in Rebus's direction.

'Mind if we're included in the search of the boat?' Whiteread asked. Hogan couldn't think of any reason to refuse, so just gave a shrug. As the meeting broke up, he found Rebus by his side.

'Bobby,' the voice reduced to a murmur, 'those drugs could be a plant.'

Hogan stared at him. 'To what possible purpose?'

'I don't know. But I don't trust—'

'You've made that abundantly clear.'

'Things were looking like winding down. This gives Whiteread and her lackey an excuse to stick around.'

'I don't see that.'

'You forget, I've dealt with their kind before.'

'No old scores to settle?' Hogan was trying to keep his voice down.

'It's not like that.'

'Then what is it?'

'An ex-soldier goes off on one, last people you'll see afterwards are his old employers. They don't want the publicity.' The two men were out in the corridor now. There was no sign of the army duo. 'More than that, they don't want any blame attaching. That's why they steer clear.'

'So?'

'So, the Gruesome Twosome are sticking to this like shit to a shoe-sole. There's got to be more to it.'

'More to it than what?' Despite his best endeavours, Hogan's voice had risen. People were looking towards them. 'Herdman paid for that boat somehow . . .'

Rebus shrugged. 'Just do me a favour, Bobby. Get hold

of Herdman's army record.' Hogan stared at him. 'I'm willing to bet Whiteread's got a copy with her. You could ask to see it. Tell her you're just curious. She might be willing.'

'Jesus Christ, John . . .'

'You want to know why Herdman did what he did? That's why you brought me here, unless I'm mistaken.' Rebus looked around, to make sure no one was within earshot. 'First time I met them, they were crawling all over Herdman's boat-shed. Next thing, they're snooping around his yacht. Now they're heading back there. It's like they're looking for something.'

'What?'

Rebus shook his head. 'I don't know.'

'John . . . Complaints and Conduct are just about to start crawling all over *you*.'

'So?'

'So is there any way you could be . . . I don't know . . .'

'You think I'm reading too much into it?'

'You're under a lot of stress.'

'Bobby, you either think I'm up to the job, or you don't.' Rebus folded his arms. 'Which is it?' Rebus's mobile was trilling again.

'You going to answer that?' Rebus shook his head. Bobby Hogan sighed. 'Okay, I'll talk to Whiteread.'

'Don't mention my name. And don't seem too worried about getting hold of the files. You're just curious, that's all.'

'I'm just curious,' Hogan echoed.

Rebus gave him a wink and moved off. Siobhan was waiting at the entrance to the school.

'Are we going to talk to James Bell?' she asked.

Rebus nodded. 'But first, let's see how good a detective you really are, DS Clarke.'

'I think we both know the answer.'

'Okay then, smartie-pants. You're army personnel, fairly

senior level, and you're dispatched from Hereford to Edinburgh for a week or so. Where do you base yourself?'

Siobhan thought about it as she got into her car. She slid the key into the ignition and turned to Rebus. 'Redford Barracks maybe? Or the Castle: there's a garrison there, isn't there?'

Rebus nodded: they were decent enough answers. He just didn't think they were right. 'Does Whiteread look as though she roughs it? Besides, she'd want to stick close to the action.'

'Fair enough: a local hotel then.'

Rebus nodded. 'That's what I reckon. Either that or bed and breakfast.' He gnawed at his bottom lip.

'The Boatman's has a couple of rooms, doesn't it?'

Rebus nodded slowly. 'Let's start there then.'

'Am I allowed to ask why?'

Rebus shook his head. 'Less you know, the better – that's a promise.'

'You don't think you're in enough trouble?'

'Room for a bit more, I think.' He tried a reassuring wink, but Siobhan looked far from convinced.

The Boatman's wasn't yet open for business, but when the barman recognised Siobhan, he let them in.

'It's Rod, isn't it?' Siobhan said. Rod McAllister nodded. 'This is my colleague, DI Rebus.'

'Hello,' McAllister said.

'Rod knew Lee Herdman,' Siobhan reminded Rebus.

'Did he ever sell you any eckies?' Rebus asked.

'Pardon?'

Rebus just shook his head. Now that they were inside the bar, he breathed deeply: last night's beer and cigarettes, failing to be masked by furniture polish. McAllister had been busy with paperwork, piled on top of the bar. He was running a hand beneath his baggy T-shirt, scratching his chest. The T-shirt had faded badly, its seam broken at one shoulder.

'You a Hawkwind fan?' Siobhan asked. McAllister

looked down at the front of the shirt. The faint print showed the cover of *In Search of Space*. 'We won't keep you,' Siobhan went on. 'Just wondered if you had a couple of guests—'

Rebus butted in to provide the names, but McAllister shook his head. He was looking at Siobhan, didn't seem interested in Rebus.

'Anywhere else in the town that might put up visitors?' Siobhan asked.

McAllister scratched at his stubble, reminding Rebus that the shaving he himself had carried out this morning had been tentative at best.

'There's a few,' McAllister admitted. 'You said someone might come to talk to me about Lee . . .?'

'Did I?'

'Well, it's just that nobody has.'

'Any idea why he did it?' Rebus asked abruptly. McAllister shook his head. 'Then let's concentrate on those addresses, shall we?'

'Addresses?'

'B and Bs, other hotels . . .'

McAllister understood. Siobhan took out her notebook, and he started reciting the names. After half a dozen, he shook his head to let them know he was finished. 'Might be more,' he admitted with a shrug.

'Enough to be going on with,' Rebus said. 'We'll let you get back to the important work, Mr McAllister.'

'Right . . . thanks.' McAllister made a little bow, and held the door open for Siobhan. Outside, she consulted her notebook.

'This could take all day.'

'If we want it to,' Rebus said. 'Looks like you've got an admirer.'

She looked up in the direction of the hotel window, saw McAllister's face there. He shrank back, turned away. 'You could do a lot worse – just imagine, never having to pay for another drink in your life . . .'

'Something you've striven towards.'

'That's a low blow. I pay my share.'

'If you say so.' She waved the notebook at him. 'There's an easier route, you know.'

'Name it.'

'Ask Bobby Hogan. He's bound to know where they're staying.'

Rebus shook his head. 'Best keep Bobby out of it.'

'Why am I getting such a bad feeling about this?'

'Let's get back in the car and you can start making those calls.'

Sliding into her seat, she turned to him. 'A sixty-grand yacht – where did the money come from?'

'Drugs, obviously.'

'You think so?'

'I think it's what we're supposed to be thinking. Nothing we've learned about Herdman makes him look like a drug baron.'

'Except his magnetic attraction for bored teenagers.'

'Didn't they teach you anything at college?'

'Such as?'

'Not jumping to conclusions.'

'I forgot – that's your department.'

'Another one below the belt. Careful or the referee will step in.'

She stared at him. 'You know something, don't you?'

He held her stare and shook his head slowly. 'Not until you make those calls . . .'

13

They got lucky: the third address was a hotel just outside town, overlooking the Road Bridge. Its car park was blustery and deserted. Two telescopes were waiting forlornly for tourists. Rebus tried one, but couldn't see anything.

'You have to put money in,' Siobhan explained, indicating the coin-slot. Rebus didn't bother, made for reception instead.

'You should wait out here,' he warned her.

'And miss all the fun?' She followed him in, trying not to show how worried she was. He was on painkillers . . . and looking for trouble. A bad combination. She'd seen him cross the line before, but he'd always been in control. But with his hands still blistered and pink, and the Complaints about to investigate him for involvement in a possible murder . . . There was a member of staff behind the reception desk.

'Good morning,' the woman said brightly.

Rebus already had his ID out. 'Lothian and Borders Police,' he said. 'You've got a woman called Whiteread staying here.'

Fingers clacked against a computer keyboard. 'That's right.'

Rebus leaned across the desk. 'I need access to her room.'

The receptionist looked confused. 'I'm not . . .'

'If you're not in charge, can I speak with whoever is?'

'I'm not sure . . .'

'Or you could save us the trouble and just give me a key.'

The woman looked more flustered than ever. 'I'll have to find my supervisor.'

'You do that then.' Rebus placed his hands behind his back, as though impatient. The receptionist picked up her phone, tried a couple of numbers, but didn't find who she was looking for. The lift sounded, doors slid open. One of the cleaners got out, carrying a duster and an aerosol. The receptionist put down the phone.

'I'll just have to find her.' Rebus sighed and checked his watch. Then stared at the receptionist's back as she pushed open some swing doors and disappeared. He leaned over the desk again, this time pulling the computer screen around so he could see it.

'Room 212,' he told Siobhan. 'You staying here?'

She shook her head, followed him to the lift. He pushed the button for the second floor. The doors closed with a dry, rasping sound.

'What if Whiteread comes back?' Siobhan asked.

'She's busy searching the yacht.' Rebus looked at her and smiled. A bell sounded and the doors shuddered open. As Rebus had hoped, the cleaning staff were still working this floor: a couple of their carts were parked in the corridor. Sheets and towels were piled up, waiting to be taken away for laundry. He had his story ready: forgotten something . . . key down in reception . . . any chance you could open the door for me? If that didn't work, maybe a fiver or a tenner would. But his luck was in: the door to 212 stood wide open. The maid was in the bathroom. He put his head around the door.

'Had to pop back for something,' he told her. 'Just you carry on.' Then he scanned the bedroom. The bed had been made. Personal items sat on the dressing-table. Clothes hung in the narrow wardrobe. Whiteread's suitcase was empty.

'She probably takes everything with her,' Siobhan whispered. 'Keeps it in the car.'

Rebus paid her no heed. He checked beneath the bed,

went through both clothes drawers, and slid open the drawer to the bedside cabinet, revealing a Gideon Bible.

'Just like Rocky Raccoon,' he muttered to himself. Then he straightened up. There was nothing here. He'd seen nothing in the bathroom either, when he'd peered around its door. But now he was staring at another door ... a connecting door. He tried the handle, and it opened, leading to another door, with no handle Rebus's side. Which didn't matter: it was already open an inch. Rebus pushed it, and found himself in the next bedroom along. Clothes strewn over both available chairs. Magazines on the bedside cabinet. Ties and socks spilling from an oversized black nylon sports holdall.

'Simms's room,' Rebus commented. And there on the dressing-table, a brown manila file. Rebus turned it over, picked out the words CONFIDENTIAL and PERSONNEL. Picked out the name LEE HERDMAN. Simms's idea of security: placing it face down so no one would see what it was.

'You want to read it here?' Siobhan asked. Rebus shook his head: had to run to forty or fifty sheets.

'Reckon our receptionist would copy it for us?'

'I've got a better idea.' Siobhan lifted the file. 'There was a sign in Reception for a business suite. I'm guessing they'll have a photocopier.'

'Then let's go.' But Siobhan was shaking her head.

'One of us stays here. Last thing we want is the cleaner disappearing, leaving the place locked tight behind her.'

Rebus saw the reasonableness of this, and nodded. So Siobhan took the file, while Rebus made a cursory examination of Simms's room. The mags were the usual men's fare: *FHM, Loaded, GQ*. Nothing under the pillows or mattress. None of Simms's clothes had made it as far as the chest of drawers, though a couple of shirts and suits hung in the wardrobe. Connecting doors ... he didn't know what, if anything, to read into that. Whiteread's door had been kept closed, meaning Simms couldn't get into her room. But Simms had left his own door an inch or two open ... Inviting her to join him some night? In his bathroom: toothpaste and battery-operated brush. He'd brought his own shampoo: anti-dandruff. Twin-bladed razor and a can of shaving-foam. Back in the bedroom, Rebus looked more closely at the black holdall. Five pairs of socks and underpants. Two shirts hanging up, two more on the chairs. Making five shirts in total. A week's worth. Simms had packed for a week's trip. Rebus was thoughtful. An ex-soldier goes on a killing spree, the army sends two investigators to make sure nothing links back to the killer's past. Why send two people? And would they require a full week at the scene? What kind of people would you send? Psychologists maybe, to look into the killer's state of mind. Neither Whiteread nor Simms struck him as having any experience of psychology, or any interest in Herdman's state of mind.

They were hunters, maybe hunter-gatherers: Rebus was convinced of it.

There was a soft tapping at the door. Rebus checked the spy-hole: it was Siobhan. He let her in, and she put the file back on the dressing-table.

'Pages in the right order?' Rebus asked.

'Good as gold.' She had the copied sheets in a padded yellow envelope. 'We ready to leave?'

Rebus nodded, and followed her to Simms's door. But then he stopped, turned back. The file was lying face up. He turned it over, gave the room a final look around, and left.

They'd offered the receptionist a smile as they'd passed her. A smile, but no words.

'Think she'll tell Whiteread?' Siobhan had asked.

'I doubt it.' And he'd shrugged, because even if she did, there was nothing Whiteread could do about it. There'd been nothing in her room for anyone to find, and nothing was missing. While Siobhan drove them along the A90 towards Barnton, Rebus got started on the file. A lot of it was chaff: various test scores and reports; medical stuff; results from promotion boards. Pencilled marginalia commented on Herdman's strengths and weaknesses. His physical stamina was questioned, but his career was textbook stuff: tours of duty in Northern Ireland, the Falklands, the Middle East; training exercises in the UK, Saudi Arabia, Finland, Germany. Rebus turned a page, and found himself staring at a sheet blank save for a few typed words: REMOVED BY ORDER. There was a scribbled signature, and a stamped date, going back only four days. The date of the killings. Rebus turned to the next page, and found himself reading about Herdman's closing few months in the army. He had told his employers that he wouldn't be signing up again – a copy of his letter was enclosed. Moves had been made to entice him to stay, but to no avail. After which, the file descended into a bureaucracy of form-filling. Events taking their course.

'Did you see this?' Rebus said, tapping the words REMOVED BY ORDER.

Siobhan nodded. 'What does it mean?'

'It means something's been taken out, probably locked away somewhere in SAS HQ.'

'Sensitive information? Not for Whiteread and Simms's eyes?'

Rebus was thoughtful. 'Maybe.' He flicked back a page, concentrated on the final paragraphs. Seven months before Herdman had walked away from the SAS, he'd been part of a 'salvage team' on Jura. On first glancing down the page, Rebus had seen the word Jura and assumed it referred to an exercise. Jura: a narrow island off the west coast. Isolated, just the one road and some mountains. Real wilderness country. Rebus had done some training there himself, back in his army days. Long marshy hikes, broken up with rock climbing. He remembered the range of hills: the 'Paps of Jura'. Recalled the short ferry crossing to Islay, and how, at the end of the exercise, they'd all been taken to a distillery there.

But Herdman hadn't been there on an exercise. He'd been part of a 'salvage team'. Salvaging what exactly?

'Any further forward?' Siobhan asked, braking hard as the dual carriageway ended. Ahead of them lay a tailback from the Barnton roundabout.

'I'm not sure,' Rebus admitted. Nor was he sure how he felt about Siobhan's involvement in his little spot of subterfuge. He should have made her stay in Simms's room. That way, it would have been his face the staff member in the business suite would remember. His description they would give to Whiteread if she ever came sniffing . . .

'Was it worth it then?' Siobhan was asking.

He just shrugged, growing thoughtful as they took a left at the roundabout, watching as she pulled up at a driveway, then turned the car into it. 'Where are we?' he asked.

'James Bell's house,' she told him. 'Remember? We were going to talk to him?'

Rebus just nodded.

The house was modern and detached, with small windows and harled walls. Siobhan pressed the bell and waited. The door was opened by a tiny woman in her well-preserved fifties, with piercing blue eyes and her hair tied back with a black velvet bow.

'Mrs Bell? I'm DS Clarke, this is DI Rebus. We were wondering if we could have a word with James.'

Felicity Bell examined both IDs, then stepped back to allow them inside. 'Jack's not here,' she said, in a voice devoid of energy.

'It's your son we wanted to see,' Siobhan explained, voice dropping for fear of scaring this small, harried-looking creature.

'But all the same . . .' Mrs Bell looked around her wildly.

She'd brought them into the living room. In an attempt to calm her, Rebus lifted a family photo from the windowsill.

'You've got three children, Mrs Bell?' he asked. She saw what he was holding, stepped forward to pluck it from his grasp, and did her best to put it back in the exact spot it had come from.

'James is the last,' she said. 'The others are married . . . flown the nest.' She made a little flapping movement with one hand.

'The shooting must have been a terrible shock,' Siobhan said.

'Terrible, terrible.' The wild look had come back into her eyes.

'You work at the Traverse, don't you?' Rebus asked.

'That's right.' She didn't seem surprised that he would know this about her. 'We've got a new play just starting . . . really, I should be there to help out, but I'm needed here, you see.'

'What's the play?'

'It's a version of *The Wind in the Willows* . . . do either of you have children?'

Siobhan shook her head. Rebus explained that his daughter was too old.

'Never too old, never too old,' Felicity Bell said in her quavering voice.

'I take it you're staying home to look after James?' Rebus said.

'Yes.'

'So he's upstairs, is he?'

'In his room, yes.'

'And would he be able to spare us a couple of minutes, do you think?'

'Well, I don't know . . .' Mrs Bell's hand had gone to her wrist at Rebus's mention of 'minutes'. Now she decided that she'd better look at her watch. 'Gracious, nearly lunchtime already . . .' She made to wander out of the room, perhaps in the direction of the kitchen, but then remembered these two strangers in her midst. 'Maybe I should call Jack.'

'Maybe you should,' Siobhan conceded. She was studying a framed photo of the MSP, triumphant on election night. 'We'd be happy to speak to him.'

Mrs Bell looked up, focusing on Siobhan. Her eyebrows drew together. 'What do you need to speak to him for?' She had a clipped, educated Edinburgh accent.

'It's James we want to talk to,' Rebus explained, taking a step forwards. 'He's in his room, is he?' He waited till she'd nodded. 'And that's upstairs, I take it?' Another nod. 'Then here's what we'll do.' He had laid a hand on her bone-thin arm. 'You go get the lunch started, and we'll find our own way. Less fuss all round, don't you think?'

Mrs Bell seemed to take this in only slowly, but at last she beamed a smile. 'Then that's what I'll do,' she said, retreating into the hall. Rebus and Siobhan shared a look, then a nod of agreement. The woman was not cooking with a full set of saucepans. They climbed the stairs, found what they took to be James's room: stickers placed on the door in childhood had been scraped off. Nothing on it now but old concert tickets, mostly from English cities – Foo Fighters in Manchester; Rammstein in London; Puddle of Mudd in Newcastle. Rebus knocked, but got no answer. He turned the handle and opened the door. James Bell was sitting up in bed. White sheets and duvet, stark white walls with no ornamentation. Pale green carpet half-covered with throw-rugs. Books were crammed into bookshelves. Computer, hi-fi, TV . . . CDs scattered around. Bell wore a black T-shirt. He had his knees up, propping a magazine. He turned the pages with one hand, the other arm being strapped across his chest. His hair was short and dark, face pale, one cheek picked out by a mole. Few signs of teenage rebellion in this room. When Rebus had been in his teens, his own bedroom had been little more than a series of hiding-places: scud mags under the carpet (the mattress wouldn't do, it got turned occasionally), cigarettes and matches behind one leg of the wardrobe; a knife tucked away beneath the winter jumpers in the bottom drawer of the chest. He got the feeling that if he looked in the drawers here, he'd find clothes; nothing under the carpet but thick underlay.

Music was leaking from the headphones James Bell wore. He still hadn't looked up from his reading. Rebus guessed he thought his mother had come in, and was studiously ignoring her. The facial similarity between son and father was remarkable. Rebus bent down a little, angling his face, and James finally looked up, eyes widening in surprise. He slipped off the headphones, turned the music off.

'Sorry to interrupt,' Rebus said. 'Your mum said we should just come up.'

'Who are you?'

'We're detectives, James. Wondered if you could give us a moment of your time.' Rebus was standing by the bed, being careful not to kick over the large bottle of water by his feet.

'What's going on?'

Rebus had lifted the magazine from the bed. It was about gun collecting. 'Funny subject,' he said.

'I'm trying to find the one he shot me with.'

Siobhan had taken the magazine from Rebus. 'I think I can understand that,' she said. 'You want to know all about it?'

'I didn't get much of a look at it.'

'You sure about that, James?' Rebus asked. 'Lee Herdman collected gun stuff.' He nodded towards the magazine, which Siobhan was now flicking through. 'That one of his?'

'What?'

'Did he let you borrow it? We hear you knew him a bit better than you've been letting on.'

'I never said I didn't know him.'

' "We'd met socially" – your exact words, James. I heard

them on the tape. You make it sound like you'd bump into him in the pub or the newsagent's.' Rebus paused. 'Except that he'd told you he was ex-SAS, and that's more than just a casual comment, isn't it? Maybe you were talking about it at one of his parties.' Another pause. 'You used to go to his parties, didn't you?'

'Some. He was an interesting guy.' James glared at Rebus. 'I probably said that on the tape, too. Besides, I told the police all this already, told them how well I knew Lee, and that I went to his parties . . . even about that time he showed me the gun . . .'

Rebus's eyes narrowed. 'He showed you?'

'Christ, haven't you listened to the tapes?'

Rebus couldn't help but glance towards Siobhan. Tapes plural . . . they'd only bothered listening to the one. 'Which gun was this?'

'The one he kept in his boathouse.'

'Did you think it was real?' Siobhan asked.

'It looked real.'

'Anyone else there at the time?'

James shook his head.

'You never saw the other one, the pistol?'

'Not until he shot me with it.' The teenager looked down at his injured shoulder.

'You and two others,' Rebus reminded him. 'Am I right to say that he didn't know Anthony Jarvies and Derek Renshaw?'

'Not that I know of.'

'But he left you alive. Are you just lucky, James?'

James's fingers hovered just above his wound. 'I've been wondering about that,' he said quietly. 'Maybe he recognised me at the last moment . . .'

Siobhan cleared her throat. 'And have you been wondering why he did it in the first place?'

James nodded slowly, but didn't say anything.

'Maybe,' Siobhan continued, 'he saw something in you he didn't see in the others.'

'They were both pretty active in the CCF, could be it had something to do with that,' James offered.

'How do you mean?'

'Well . . . Lee was in the army half his life . . . and then they kicked him out.'

'He told you that?' Rebus asked.

James nodded again. 'Maybe he had this grudge. I've said he didn't know Renshaw and Jarvies, but that doesn't mean he hadn't seen them around . . . maybe in their uniforms. Some kind of . . . trigger?' He looked up, smiled. 'I know – I should leave the cod psychology to the cod psychologists.'

'You're being very helpful,' Siobhan said, not because she believed it necessarily, but because she thought he was looking for some sliver of praise.

'The thing is, James,' Rebus said, 'if we could understand why he'd left you alive, we'd maybe know why the others had to die. Do you see?'

James was thoughtful. 'Does it really matter, in the end?'

'We think it does.' Rebus straightened up. 'Who else did you see at these parties, James?'

'You're asking for names?'

'That's the general idea.'

'It wasn't always the same people.'

'Teri Cotter?' Rebus hinted.

'Yes, she was there sometimes. Always brought a few Goths with her.'

'You're not a Goth yourself, James?' Siobhan asked.

He gave a short laugh. 'Do I look like one?'

She shrugged. 'The music you listen to . . .'

'It's just rock music, that's all.'

She lifted the small machine attached to his headphones. 'MP3 player,' she commented, sounding impressed. 'What about Douglas Brimson, ever see him at the parties?'

'Is he the guy who flies planes?' Siobhan nodded. 'I spoke to him one time, yes.' He paused. 'Look, these weren't really "parties", not like the organised sort. It was just people dropping in, having a drink . . .'

'Doing drugs?' Rebus asked casually.

'Sometimes, yes,' James admitted.

'Speed? Coke? A bit of E?'

The teenager snorted. 'A couple of joints passed round if you were lucky.'

'Nothing harder?'

'No.'

There was a knock at the door. It was Mrs Bell. She looked at the two visitors as though she'd forgotten all about them. 'Oh,' she said, confused for a moment. Then: 'I've made some sandwiches, James. What would you like to drink?'

'I'm not hungry.'

'But it's lunchtime.'

'Do you want me puking up, Mum?'

'No . . . of course not.'

'I'll tell you when I'm hungry.' His voice had hardened: not because he was angry, Rebus thought, but because he was embarrassed. 'But I'll have a mug of coffee, not too much milk in it.'

'Right,' his mother said. Then, to Rebus: 'Would you like a . . .?'

'We're just on our way, thanks all the same, Mrs Bell.' She nodded, stood for a moment as though forgetting what she'd been about to do, then turned and left, her feet making no sound on the carpet.

'Your mother's all right, is she?' Rebus asked.

'Are you blind?' James shifted position. 'A lifetime with my dad . . . it's no wonder.'

'You don't get on with your father?'

'Not particularly.'

'You know he's started a petition?'

James screwed up his face. 'Fat lot of good it'll do.' He was silent for a moment. 'Was it Teri Cotter?'

'What?'

'Was she the one who told you I went to Lee's flat?' The detectives stayed silent. 'Wouldn't put it past her.' He shifted again, as if trying to get comfortable.

'Want me to help you?' Siobhan offered.

James shook his head. 'I think I need some more painkillers.' Siobhan found them by the other side of the bed, sitting in their silver strip of foil on a readied chess board. She gave him two tablets, which he washed down with water.

'One more question, James,' Rebus said, 'then we'll leave you to it.'

'What?'

Rebus nodded towards the foil. 'Mind if I nick a couple of tabs? I've run out . . .'

Siobhan had half a bottle of flat Irn-Bru in her car. Rebus took a mouthful after each tablet.

'Careful they don't turn into a habit,' Siobhan said.

'What did you reckon to back there?' Rebus asked, changing the subject.

'He could be on to something. Combined Cadet Force . . . kids running around in uniforms.'

'He also said Herdman was kicked out of the army. Not true, according to his file.'

'So?'

'So either Herdman lied to him or young James made it up.'

'Active fantasy life?'

'You'd need one in a room like that.'

'It was certainly . . . tidy.' Siobhan started the engine. 'You know what he was saying about Miss Teri?'

'He was right: it *was* her who told us.'

'Yes, but more than that . . .'

'What?'

She put the car in gear and started off. 'Just the way he spoke . . . You know that old thing about someone protesting too much?'

'Making out he doesn't like her because he really likes her?' Siobhan nodded. 'Reckon he knows about her little website?'

'I don't know.' Siobhan finished her three-point turn.

'Should have asked him.'

'What's this?' Siobhan asked, peering through the windscreen. A patrol car, its blue light flashing, was blocking the entrance to the driveway. As Siobhan put the brakes on, the back door of the patrol car opened and a man in a grey suit got out. He was tall, with a shiny bald dome of a head and large, heavy-lidded eyes. He held his hands together in front of him, feet apart.

'Don't worry,' Rebus told Siobhan. 'It's just my twelve o'clock appointment.'

'What appointment?'

'The one I never got round to making,' Rebus told her, opening his door and stepping out. Then he leaned back in. 'With my own personal executioner . . .'

14

The bald man was called Mullen. He was from the Professional Standards Unit of the Complaints. Up close, his skin had a slightly scaly quality, not, Rebus thought, unlike that of his own blistered hands. His elongated ear lobes had probably brought him a few 'Dumbo'-sourced nicknames at school, yet it was his fingernails that fascinated Rebus. They were almost too perfect: pink and shiny and unridged, with just enough white cuticle. During the hour-long interview, Rebus was tempted more than once to add a question of his own and ask if Mullen ever visited a manicurist.

But in fact all he'd done was ask if he could get a drink. The aftertaste of James Bell's painkillers lingered in his mouth. The tablets themselves had done their job – certainly better than the scabby wee pills he himself had been prescribed. Rebus was feeling at one with his world. He didn't even mind that Assistant Chief Constable Colin Carswell, all haircut and eau de Cologne, was sitting in on the interview. Carswell might hate his guts, but Rebus couldn't find it in himself to blame him for it. Too much history between them for that. They were in an office at Police HQ on Fettes Avenue, and it was Carswell's turn to have a go at him.

'What the hell did you think you were doing last night?'

'Last night, sir?'

'Jack Bell and that TV director. They're both demanding an apology.' He wagged a finger at Rebus. 'And you're going to do it in person.'

'Would you rather I dropped my trousers and bent over for them?'

Carswell's face seemed to swell with rage.

'Once again, DI Rebus,' Mullen interrupted, 'we find ourselves returning to the question of what you thought you might hope to gain by going along to a known criminal's home for a night-time beverage.'

'I thought I might gain a free drink.'

Carswell expelled a slow hiss of air. He'd uncrossed and recrossed his legs, unfolded and refolded his arms, many dozens of times in the course of the interview.

'I suspect there was more to your visit than that.'

Rebus just shrugged. He wasn't allowed to smoke, so was playing with the half-empty packet instead, opening and closing it, sending it spinning across the table with the flick of a finger. He was doing this because he could see how much it annoyed Carswell.

'What time did you leave Fairstone's house?'

'Some time before the fire broke out.'

'You can't be more specific?'

Rebus shook his head. 'I'd been drinking.' Drinking more than he should . . . much, much more. He'd been a good boy since, trying to atone.

'So, some time after you left,' Mullen continued, 'someone else arrived – unseen by neighbours – and proceeded to gag and tie Mr Fairstone, before turning on the heat beneath a chip-pan and then departing?'

'Not necessarily,' Rebus felt obliged to state. 'The chip-pan could already have been on.'

'Did Mr Fairstone say he was going to make some chips?'

'He might have mentioned being a bit peckish . . . I can't be sure.' Rebus straightened in his chair, feeling vertebrae click. 'Look, Mr Mullen . . . I can see that you've got a fair amount of circumstantial evidence sitting here . . .' He tapped the manila file, not unlike the one which had sat on Simms's dressing-table . . . 'which tells you that I was the last person to see Martin Fairstone alive.' He paused. 'But that's *all* it tells you, wouldn't you agree? And I'm not denying the fact.' Rebus sat back and waited.

'Except the killer,' Mullen said, so softly he might have been speaking to himself. 'What you should have said was: "I was the last person to see him alive, except his killer."' He glanced up from beneath his drooping eyelids.

'That's what I meant to say.'

'It's not what you said, DI Rebus.'

'You'll have to excuse me then. I'm not exactly a hundred per cent . . .'

'Are you on drugs of some kind?'

'Painkillers, yes.' Rebus held up his hands to remind Mullen of why.

'And you took the most recent dose when?'

'Sixty seconds before clapping eyes on you.' Rebus let his eyes widen. 'Maybe I should have mentioned at the start . . .?'

Mullen slapped the desk with both palms. 'Of course you should!' He wasn't talking to himself any more. He let his chair fall backwards as he got to his feet. Carswell had risen, too.

'I don't see . . .'

Mullen leaned across the desk to switch off the tape-recorder. 'You can't hold an interview with someone who's under the influence of prescribed drugs,' he explained, for the ACC's benefit. 'I thought everyone knew that.'

Carswell started muttering something about how he'd just forgotten, that was all. Mullen was glaring at Rebus. Rebus gave him a wink.

'We'll talk again, Detective Inspector.'

'Once I'm off the medication?' Rebus pretended to guess.

'I'll need the name of your doctor, so I can ask when that's likely to be.' Mullen had opened the file, his pen poised over an empty sheet.

'It was the Infirmary,' Rebus stated blithely. 'I can't remember the doctor's name.'

'Well then, I'll just have to find out.' Mullen closed the file again.

'Meantime,' Carswell piped up, 'I don't need to remind you about making that apology, or that you're still on suspension?'

'No, sir,' Rebus said.

'Which rather begs the question,' Mullen said quietly, 'of why I found you in the company of a fellow officer at Jack Bell's house.'

'I was hitching a lift, that's all. DS Clarke had to stop off at Bell's place to talk to the son.' Rebus gave a shrug, while Carswell expelled more air.

'We *will* get to the bottom of this, Rebus. You can be sure of that.'

'I don't doubt it, sir.' Rebus was the last of the three to rise to his feet. 'Well, I'll leave you to it then. Enjoy the bottom when you get there . . .'

Siobhan, as he'd guessed, was waiting with her car outside. 'Nicely timed,' she said. The back of the car was full of carrier-bags. 'I waited ten minutes to see if you'd tell them straight off.'

'And then went to do some shopping?'

'Supermarket at the top of the road. I was going to ask if you fancied coming round for dinner tonight.'

'Let's see how the rest of the day pans out.'

She nodded agreement. 'So when did the question of the painkillers arise?'

'About five minutes ago.'

'You left it a while.'

'Wanted to see if they'd anything new to tell me.'

'And did they?'

He shook his head. 'Doesn't look like they consider you a suspect though,' he told her.

'Me? Why should they?'

'Because he was stalking you . . . because every cop knows the old chip-pan trick.' He shrugged.

'Any more of that and the dinner invite's cancelled.' She

started driving them out of the car park. 'Next stop Turnhouse?' she asked.

'You think I need to be on the next plane out of here?'

'We were going to talk to Doug Brimson.'

Rebus shook his head. 'You talk to him. Drop me off somewhere first.'

She looked at him. 'Where?'

'Any place on George Street will do.'

She was still looking. 'Suspiciously close to the Oxford Bar.'

'That wasn't what I had in mind, but now that you come to mention it . . .'

'Drink and tranqs don't mix, John.'

'It's an hour and a half since I took those pills. Besides, I'm on suspension, remember? I'm allowed to misbehave.'

Rebus was waiting for Steve Holly in the back room of the Oxford Bar.

It was one of the city's smaller pubs: just the two rooms, neither much bigger than the lounge of a normal semi-detached house. The front room was usually busy, in that three or four bodies could make it seem so. The back room had tables and chairs, and Rebus had positioned himself in the darkest corner, furthest from the window. The walls were the same jaundiced colour they'd been when he'd first found the place, three decades back. The stark, old-fashioned interior had the power to intimidate newcomers, but Rebus wasn't betting on it having any such effect on the journalist. He'd called the tabloid's Edinburgh office – only a ten-minute walk from the bar. His message had been curt: 'I want to talk to you. Oxford Bar. Now.' Cutting the connection before Holly could start a conversation. Rebus knew he would come. He'd come because he would be intrigued. He'd come because of the story he'd broken. He'd come because that was his job.

Rebus heard the door open and close. He wasn't worried about the occupants of the other tables. Anything they happened to overhear, they would keep to themselves. It was that kind of place. Rebus hoisted what was left of his pint. His grip was improving. He could pick a glass up one-handed, flex his wrist without the pain becoming unbearable. He was steering clear of whisky: Siobhan had given him good advice, and for once he would heed it. He knew he needed his wits about him. Steve Holly wasn't going to want to play on Rebus's terms.

Feet on the steps, a shadow preceding Holly's entrance into the back room. He peered into the afternoon gloom, squeezing between chairs as he approached the table. He was carrying what looked like a glass of lemonade, maybe with a vodka added for good measure. He gave a slight nod, stayed standing until Rebus gestured for him to sit. Holly did so, checking to left and right, unhappy about sitting with his back to the bar's other denizens.

'Nobody's going to leap from the shadows and chib you,' Rebus reassured him.

'I suppose I should be congratulating you,' Holly said. 'I hear you're managing to get right up Jack Bell's nose.'

'And I notice your paper's supporting his campaign.'

Holly's mouth twitched. 'Doesn't mean he's not a prick. You lot should have stuck to your guns, that time you caught him with the prossie. Better yet, you should have phoned my paper, we'd have come down and got some snaps of him *in flagrante*. Have you met the wife?' Rebus nodded. 'Bananas, she is,' the reporter continued. 'Nervous wreck by all accounts.'

'She stood by him though.'

'That's what MPs' wives do, isn't it?' Holly said dismissively. Then: 'So, to what do I owe the honour? Decided to put your side of the story?'

'I need a favour,' Rebus said, placing his gloved hands on the table.

'A favour?' Rebus nodded. 'In return for what exactly?'

'Special relationship status.'

'Meaning?' Holly lifted his glass to his mouth.

'Meaning whatever I get on the Herdman case, you get first shout.'

Holly snorted. Had to wipe some of his drink from around his mouth. 'You're on suspension, as far as I know.'

'Doesn't stop me keeping my ear to the ground.'

'And what exactly is it you can tell me about Herdman that I can't get from a dozen of my other sources?'

'Depends on that favour. It's one thing I've got that they haven't.'

Holly rolled some more of his drink around the inside of his mouth. Then he swallowed, smacked his lips.

'Trying to throw me off the scent, Rebus? I've got you by the short and curlies over Marty Fairstone. Everyone knows it. And now *you're* asking favours?' He chuckled, but there was no humour in his eyes. 'You should be begging me not to rip your gonads right off.'

'Think you've got the balls for it?' Rebus said, finishing his own drink. He slid the empty glass across the table towards the journalist. 'Pint of IPA, when you're ready.' Holly looked at him, then smiled with half his mouth and rose to his feet, manoeuvring his way back through the chairs. Rebus lifted the lemonade glass and sniffed: vodka, definitely. He managed to light a cigarette, had smoked half of it by the time Holly returned.

'Barman's got an attitude, hasn't he?'

'Maybe he doesn't like what you said about me,' Rebus explained.

'So go to the Press Complaints Commission.' Holly handed the pint over. He'd brought another vodka and lemonade for himself. 'Only I don't see you doing that,' he added.

'That's because you're not worth the effort.'

'And this is the guy who wants a favour doing?'

'A favour you haven't bothered listening to yet.'

'Well, here I am . . .' Holly opened his arms wide.

'A salvage operation of some kind,' Rebus said quietly. 'It

happened on Jura, June of ninety-five. I need to know what it was for.'

'Salvage?' Holly frowned, his instincts aroused. 'A tanker? Something like that?'

Rebus shook his head. 'On land. The SAS were brought in.'

'Herdman?'

'He might have been involved.'

Holly chewed on his bottom lip as if trying to dislodge the hook Rebus had landed there. 'What's it got to do with anything?'

'We won't know that till we take a look.'

'And if I agree, what do I get out of it?'

'Like I said, first go at any story.' Rebus paused. 'I might also have access to Herdman's army files.'

Holly's eyebrows rose perceptibly. 'Anything good in them?'

Rebus shrugged. 'At this stage, I couldn't possibly comment.' Reeling the reporter in . . . knowing full well there was little in the file to interest any tabloid reader. But then how was Steve Holly to know that?

'Well, we could have a shufti, I suppose.' Holly was rising to his feet again. 'No time like the present.'

Rebus studied his beer glass, still three-quarters full. Holly had yet to start on his own second drink. 'What's the rush?' he said.

'You don't think I came here to pass the time of day with you?' Holly said. 'I don't like you, Rebus, and I certainly don't trust you.' He paused. 'No offence.'

'None taken,' Rebus said, rising to follow the reporter out of the bar.

'By the way,' Holly said, 'something that's been bugging me . . .'

'What?'

'I was talking to a guy, and he said he could kill someone with a newspaper. You ever heard of that?'

Rebus nodded. 'A magazine's better, but a paper might just do it.'

Holly looked at him. 'So how does it work? Smothering or what?'

Rebus shook his head. 'You roll it up, tight as you can, then you use it on the throat. Enough force, you'll crush the windpipe.'

Holly was staring. 'You learned that in the army?'

Rebus nodded again. 'As did whoever you were talking to.'

'It was a bloke at St Leonard's . . . him and some stroppy-looking woman.'

'Her name's Whiteread; his is Simms.'

'Army investigators?' Holly nodded to himself, as though it all made sense. Rebus stopped himself from smiling: putting Holly on to Whiteread and Simms was most of his plan.

They were outside the pub now, and Rebus expected that they'd be walking to the newspaper office, but Holly had turned left rather than right, pointing his ignition key at the line of cars parked kerbside.

'You drove?' Rebus said, as the locks clunked open on a silver-grey Audi TT.

'It's what your legs are for,' Holly informed him. 'Now get in.'

Rebus slid into what space there was, thinking that an Audi TT was the car Teri Cotter's brother had been driving, the night he'd died, with Derek Renshaw sitting in the passenger seat, same seat Rebus was in now . . . remembering the photos of the crash, Stuart Cotter's rag-doll body . . . He watched as Holly slipped a hand beneath the driver's seat, sliding out a thin black laptop computer. He placed it across his legs, opening it and holding his mobile phone in one hand while he operated the keyboard with the other.

'Infra-red connection,' he explained. 'Gets us on-line in a hurry.'

'And why are we going on-line?' Rebus had to push back a sudden memory of his night-time vigil at Miss Teri's website, embarrassed that he'd allowed himself to be drawn into her world.

'Because that's where my paper has most of its library. I just enter the password . . .' Holly stabbed half a dozen keys, Rebus trying to see what they were. 'No peeking, Rebus,' he warned. 'There's all sorts of stuff on here: clippings, dropped stories, archives . . .'

'Lists of the cops you pay for information?'

'Would I be that stupid?'

'I don't know: would you?'

'When people talk to me, they know I can keep a secret. Those names go to my grave.'

Holly turned his attention back to the screen. Rebus had no doubt this machine was state of the art. Connection had been fast, and now pages were popping up in the blink of an eye. The laptop Rebus had borrowed was, as Pettifer had said, coal-fired by comparison.

'Search mode . . .' Holly was talking to himself. 'We enter the month and year, keywords Jura and salvage . . . and see what Brainiac comes up with.' He hit a final key and sat back, turning again towards Rebus to measure how impressed he was. Rebus was hellish impressed, but hoping it didn't show.

The screen had changed again. 'Seventeen items,' Holly said. 'Christ, yes, I remember this.' He angled the screen a little, and Rebus leaned towards him so that he could see what was there. And suddenly Rebus remembered it, too, remembered the incident, but hadn't registered it as happening on Jura. An army helicopter, half a dozen top brass on board. Killed outright, along with the pilot, when the chopper had crashed. Speculation at the time that it had been downed. Jubilation in some quarters in Northern Ireland – a splinter Republican group taking early credit. But in the end, 'pilot error' had been given as the cause.

'No mention of the SAS,' Holly pointed out.

Instead, a vague mention of a 'rescue team', sent to locate the debris and, more importantly, the bodies. Whatever was left of the chopper would be taken away for analysis, the bodies sent for autopsy prior to the funerals. An inquiry was set in motion, its findings a long time coming.

'Pilot's family weren't happy,' Holly said, racing through time to the end of the investigation. Memories tarnished by that conclusion: 'pilot error'.

'Go back again,' Rebus said, annoyed that Holly was a faster reader than him. Holly obliged, the screen switching in an instant.

'So Herdman was part of the rescue team?' Holly observed. 'Makes sense, army sending in their own . . .' He turned to Rebus. 'What point is it you're supposed to be making?'

Rebus didn't want to give him much more, so said he wasn't sure.

'Then I'm wasting my time here.' Holly hit another button, blacking out the screen. Then he twisted his body so he was facing Rebus. 'So what if Herdman was on Jura? What the hell's it got to do with what went on in that school? You going for the stress/trauma angle?'

'I'm not sure,' Rebus repeated. He stared at the reporter. 'But thanks anyway.' He pushed open the door and started levering himself out of the low-built seat.

'Is that it?' Holly spat. 'I show you mine and you bottle out?'

Rebus leaned back down into the car. 'Mine's more interesting than yours, pal.'

'You didn't need me for this,' Holly said, glancing towards his laptop. 'Half an hour with a search engine and you'd've learned as much.'

Rebus nodded. 'Or I could have asked Whiteread and Simms, only I don't think they'd have been quite as accommodating.'

Holly blinked. 'Why not?'

Bait taken, Rebus just winked and slammed shut the door, walked back into the Ox, where Harry was about to pour his drink down the sink.

'Let me relieve you of that,' Rebus said, stretching out his hand towards the barman. He heard the roar of the Audi's engine, Steve Holly making a quick and angry getaway. Rebus wasn't bothered. He had what he needed.

A helicopter crash. Top brass involved. Now *there* was something to whet the appetite of a couple of army investigators. What was more, when Holly had flicked back through the screens, Rebus had registered the news that a few of the locals on the island had helped with the search, men who knew the Paps of Jura well. One of them had even been interviewed, giving his description of the crash site. His name was Rory Mollison. Rebus finished off the pint, standing at the bar, his eyes staring at the TV without taking any of it in. A kaleidoscope of colours, that was all it meant to him. His mind was elsewhere, crossing land and then water, gliding over hilltops . . . Sending the SAS to pick up bodies? Jura wasn't exactly the most mountainous terrain, certainly a long way short of the peaks you'd find in the Grampians. Why send such a specialised team?

Gliding over moor and glen, inlets and sheer cliff faces . . . Rebus fumbled for his phone, pulled off his glove with his teeth and punched numbers with his thumbnail. Waited for Siobhan to pick up.

'Where are you?' he said.

'Never mind that: what the hell are you doing talking to Steve Holly?'

Rebus blinked, ran to the door and pulled it open. She was standing right in front of him. He put the phone back in his pocket. As if in a mirror image, she did the same with hers.

'You're tailing me,' he said, trying to sound appalled.

'Only because you need tailing.'

'Where were you?' He started pulling the glove back on. She nodded towards North Castle Street. 'Car's parked

265

just around the corner. Now, to return to my original question . . .'

'Never mind that. At least this means you've not been back to the airfield.'

'Not yet, no.'

'Good, because I want you to talk to him.'

'Who? Brimson?' She watched him nod. 'And after that, you'll tell me what you were doing with Steve Holly?'

Rebus looked at her, then nodded again.

'And this'll be over a drink, which you're going to buy me?'

The look became a glare. Siobhan had taken the phone back out of her pocket, and was waving it in Rebus's face.

'All right,' he growled. 'Just call the guy, okay?'

Siobhan checked in her notebook, finding Brimson's details, started punching numbers. 'What exactly is it that I'm telling him?'

'Charm offensive: you need a big favour. Maybe more than one actually . . . But for starters, you can ask him if there's a landing-strip anywhere on Jura . . .'

When Rebus arrived at Port Edgar Academy, he saw that Bobby Hogan was remonstrating with Jack Bell. Bell wasn't alone: he had the same camera crew with him. Plus, he had one hand clamped around Kate Renshaw's fore-arm.

'I think we've every right,' the MSP was saying, 'to see where our loved ones were gunned down.'

'With respect, sir, that classroom remains a crime scene. No one goes in without good reason.'

'We're the family, which I'd have thought was the best reason there was.'

Hogan pointed to the crew. 'Pretty extended family, sir . . .'

The director had noticed Rebus's approach. He tapped Bell's shoulder. Bell turned, his face forming a cold smile.

'You'll have come to apologise?' he guessed.

Rebus ignored him. 'Don't go in there, Kate,' he said, standing directly in front of her. 'It can't do any good.'

She couldn't meet his gaze. 'People need to know.' She spoke in an undertone, Bell nodding in agreement.

'Maybe so, but what they don't need is a publicity stunt. It just cheapens everything, Kate, you must see that.'

Bell had turned his attention back to Hogan. 'I must insist that this man be removed from here.'

'Must you?' Hogan echoed.

'He is already on record as having uttered abusive comments at my crew and myself . . .'

'Plenty more where that came from,' Rebus stated.

'John . . .' Hogan's eyes warning him to calm down. Then: 'I'm sorry, Mr Bell, but I really can't allow filming inside that room.'

'What if there's no camera?' the director offered. 'Sound only?'

Hogan was shaking his head. 'You're not going to move me on this.' He folded his arms, as if to signal an end to the discussion.

Rebus was still concentrating on Kate, trying for eye contact. She seemed to be finding something fascinating in the near-distance. The gulls on the playing-field perhaps, or the rugby posts . . .

'Well, where can we film?' the MSP was asking.

'Outside the gates, same as everyone else,' Hogan replied. Bell exhaled furiously.

'You can be sure your obstructiveness will be noted,' he warned.

'Thank you, sir,' Hogan said, keeping his voice level while his eyes burned.

The common room had been emptied: no chairs, hi-fi or magazines. The principal, Dr Fogg, was standing in the doorway, hands held before him, palms pressed together. He was dressed in a sober charcoal suit, white shirt, black tie. His eyes had dark rings around them, hair speckled

267

with dandruff. He sensed Rebus behind him, and turned, offered a watery smile.

'Trying to decide what use might best be made of the room,' he explained. 'The chaplain thinks it could be turned into a sort of chapel, something the pupils could use for contemplation.'

'It's an idea,' Rebus said. The principal had moved aside so Rebus could enter the room. Blood had dried into the walls and floor. Rebus tried to side-step the stains.

'You could always lock it, leave it a few years. Kids will all have moved on by then . . . few coats of paint, new carpet . . .'

'Hard to look that far ahead,' Fogg said, managing another smile. 'Well, I'll leave you to . . . to your . . .' He made a little bow and turned away, walking back towards his office.

Rebus was staring at the blood spatter pattern on one wall. This was where Derek had been standing. Derek, part of his family, now obliterated.

Lee Herdman . . . Rebus was trying to visualise him, waking up that morning and reaching for a gun. What had happened? What in his life had changed? Were demons dancing around his bed when he awoke? Were the voices teasing him? The teenagers he'd befriended . . . had something broken that spell? Fuck you, kids, I'm coming for you . . . Driving into the school grounds, stopping the car rather than actually parking it. In a rush, leaving his driver's door wide open. In through the side entrance, no cameras to catch him . . . Up the corridor and into this room. Here I am, kids. Anthony Jarvies, shot through the head. He'd probably been first. All the army teaching told you to aim for the centre of the chest: bigger target, harder to miss and usually deadly. But Herdman had opted for the head . . . Why? That first shot had lost him the element of surprise. Maybe Derek Renshaw had been in movement, receiving a shot to the face for his trouble. James Bell ducking down, one bullet to the shoulder, squeezing his eyes tight shut as Herdman turned the gun on himself . . .

The third head-shot, this time to his own temple.

'Why, Lee? That's all we want to know,' Rebus whispered into the silence. He walked to the door, turned, entered the room again, holding out his right gloved hand as though it were the weapon. Swivelled from one firing position to another. He knew that the forensics team would be doing much the same, albeit in front of their computers. Reconstructing the scene in the room, computing the angles of bullet-entry, positioning the gunman for each shot. Every shred of evidence added its own sentence to the story. Here's where he was standing . . . then he turned, moved forward . . . If we match angle of entry to the blood spatter pattern . . .

Eventually, they would know every move Herdman had made. They would have brought the scene vividly to life with their graphics and ballistics. And none of it might make them any the wiser about the only question that mattered.

The why.

'Don't shoot,' a voice said from the doorway. It was Bobby Hogan, standing with arms raised. He had with him two figures Rebus knew. Claverhouse and Ormiston. Claverhouse, tall and lanky, was a detective inspector; Ormiston, shorter and stocky with a permanent sniffle, was a detective sergeant. Both worked for Drugs and Major Crime, and had close links to the Assistant Chief Constable, Colin Carswell. In fact, on a bad day Rebus might have called them Carswell's hatchet men. He realised that he still had his gun-hand out, so lowered it.

'I hear the fascist look's in this year,' Claverhouse said, indicating Rebus's leather gloves.

'Making you fashionable year in and year out,' Rebus retorted.

'Now, children,' Hogan warned. Ormiston was peering at the blood on the floor, rubbing the tip of his shoe over it.

'So what brings you sniffing around?' Rebus asked, eyes on Ormiston as the stocky man rubbed the back of his hand across his nostrils.

'Drugs,' Claverhouse said. With all three buttons of his suit-jacket closed, he resembled a shop-window mannequin.

'Looks like Ormy's been sampling the goods.'

Hogan bowed his head to try to hide a smile. Claverhouse swivelled towards him. 'I thought DI Rebus was out on his ear.'

'News travels fast,' Rebus said.

'Aye, especially good news,' Ormiston snapped back.

Hogan straightened up. 'Do the three of you want detention?' No one replied. 'To answer your question, DI Claverhouse, John's here in a purely advisory capacity, due to his army background. He's not "working" per se . . .'

'No change there then,' Ormiston muttered.

'And the kettle's trailing the pot one–nil at half-time,' Rebus informed him.

Hogan held up a hand. 'And that's a yellow card from the referee. Any more shite and you're out of here, I mean it!' His voice had hardened. Claverhouse's eyes flickered, but he didn't say anything. Ormiston had his nose all but pressed to one of the bloodstains on the wall.

'Right . . .' Hogan said into the silence, sighing heavily. 'So what is it you've got for us?'

Claverhouse took this as his cue. 'Looks like the stuff you found on the boat is checking out: ecstasy and cocaine. The cocaine's pretty high-grade. Maybe it was due to be cut a bit further . . .'

'Crack?' Hogan asked.

Claverhouse nodded. 'It's taken hold in a few places – fishing towns up north, some of the housing schemes here and in Glasgow . . . A grand's worth of good stuff can turn into ten when it's cut.'

'There's also a bundle of hash going around,' Ormiston added.

Claverhouse glared at him, not wanting to have his thunder stolen. 'Ormy's right, there's plenty of hash on the streets.'

'What about ecstasy?' Hogan asked.

Claverhouse nodded. 'We thought it was coming up from Manchester. Could be we were wrong.'

'From Herdman's logs,' Hogan said, 'we know he's been to and fro to the continent. Seems to stop off at Rotterdam.'

'Lot of E factories in Holland,' Ormiston stated casually. He was still studying the wall in front of him, hands in pockets and leaning back on his heels, as if concentrating on the exhibit at a gallery. 'Lot of cocaine over there, too.'

'And Customs weren't suspicious of these jaunts to Rotterdam?' Rebus asked.

Claverhouse shrugged. 'Those poor buggers are stretched to breaking point. No way they can check up on everybody hopping over to Europe, especially in these days of open borders.'

'So what you're saying is, you let Herdman slip through your net?'

Claverhouse's eyes met Rebus's. 'Like Customs, we depend on intelligence gathering.'

'Not much sign of that around here,' Rebus countered, shifting his gaze from Claverhouse to Ormiston and back again. 'Bobby, have Herdman's finances been looked into?'

Hogan nodded. 'No evidence of sudden large deposits or withdrawals.'

'Dealers steer clear of banks,' Claverhouse stated. 'Hence the need for money laundering. Herdman's boat business would do just fine.'

'What about Herdman's autopsy?' Rebus asked Bobby Hogan. 'Any sign that he was a drug user?'

Hogan shook his head. 'Blood tests negative.'

'Dealers aren't always users,' Claverhouse intoned. 'The big players are in it for the money. Past six months, we busted one operation carrying a hundred and thirty thousand tabs of E, street value of a million and a half, forty-four kilos' worth. Four kilos of opium was intercepted after being flown in from Iran.' He stared at Rebus. 'That was a Customs bust, based on intelligence.'

'And how much did we find on Herdman's boat?' Rebus asked. 'A drop in the ocean, if you'll pardon the expression.' He had started to light a cigarette, but caught Hogan's look, eyes casting around the room. 'It's not a church, Bobby,' he said, finishing what he'd started. He didn't think Derek or Anthony would mind. Didn't care what Herdman thought . . .

'For personal use perhaps,' Claverhouse offered.

'Except he didn't use.' Rebus blew smoke down his nostrils in Claverhouse's direction.

'Maybe he had friends who did. I hear he used to host a few parties . . .'

'We've not spoken to anyone who says he gave them coke or eckies.'

'As if they'd want to advertise the fact,' Claverhouse snorted. 'Fact is, I'm astonished you can find anyone who'll admit to having known the bastard.' He stared down at the bloodstained floor.

Ormiston ran a hand beneath his nose again, then let out a huge sneeze, further mottling the wall.

'Ormy, you insensitive bastard,' Rebus hissed.

'He's not the one flicking fag-ash on the floor,' Claverhouse growled.

'The smoke tickles my nose,' Ormiston was saying. Rebus had strode over to stand next to him. 'That was somebody from my fucking family!' he snarled, pointing at the pattern of blood.

'I didn't mean it.'

'What did you just say, John?' Hogan's voice was a low rumble.

'Nothing,' Rebus said. But it was too late. Hogan was standing right beside him, sliding hands into pockets, expecting an explanation. 'Allan Renshaw's a cousin of mine,' Rebus admitted.

'And you didn't feel that was information I might need to know?' Hogan's face was puce with anger.

'Not really, Bobby, no.' Over Hogan's shoulder, Rebus could see a huge grin spreading across Claverhouse's narrow face.

Hogan removed his hands from his pockets, tried clenching them behind his back, but found the manoeuvre unsatisfactory. Rebus knew where Bobby really wanted those hands. He wanted them around Rebus's neck.

'It doesn't change anything,' he argued. 'Like you said, I'm here as an advisor, that's all. We're not building a court case, Bobby. No lawyer's going to be able to use me as a technicality.'

'Bastard was a drug smuggler,' Claverhouse interrupted. 'There must be associates out there for us to catch. One of them gets a bright enough brief . . .'

'Claverhouse,' Rebus said wearily. 'Do the world a favour and' – his voice a sudden howl – *'just shut the fuck up!'*

Claverhouse started forward, Rebus ready to meet him, Hogan stepping between them, though in the certain knowledge of being as useful as chocolate handcuffs. Ormiston's role was spectator; no way he'd interrupt unless his partner was coming off worst.

'Phone call for DI Rebus!' A sudden shout from the open doorway, Siobhan standing there, holding out a mobile phone. 'I think it's urgent: the Complaints.'

Claverhouse stepped back, allowing Rebus clear passage. He even made a mocking motion with his arm, signalling 'after you'. And the grin was back on his face. Rebus looked down to where Bobby Hogan still had a handful of the front of his suit-jacket. Hogan let go, and Rebus walked to the doorway.

'Want to take it outside?' Siobhan suggested. Rebus nodded, held out his hand for the phone. But she was keeping it, walking with him all the way out of the building. She looked around, saw that they were at a safe distance, and held the phone out to him.

'Better make it look like you're talking,' she warned. Rebus held the phone to his ear. Nothing there at all.

'No call?' he asked. She shook her head.

'Just thought you needed rescuing.'

He managed a smile, keeping the phone to his ear. 'Bobby knows about the Renshaws.'

'I know. I heard.'

'Spying on me again?'

'Not much going on in the geography class.' They were heading towards the Portakabin. 'So what do we do now?'

'Whatever it is, it better be away from here . . . give Bobby time to cool off.' Rebus looked back towards the school. Three figures were watching from the doorway.

'And Claverhouse and Ormiston time to crawl back under their rock?'

'You're reading my mind.' He paused. 'So what am I thinking now?'

'You're thinking we could go for a drink.'

'This is uncanny.'

'And you're also thinking of paying, as a way of saying thanks for saving your arse.'

'That is the incorrect answer. Still, as Meat Loaf used to say . . .' They'd reached her car. He handed back her phone. 'Two out of three ain't bad.'

15

'So if no money turned up in Herdman's bank,' Siobhan
said, 'we can scratch him as a hired killer.'

'Unless he turned the money into drugs,' Rebus replied,
for the sake of argument. They were in the Boatman's,
drinking with the late-afternoon crowd. Suits and labour-
ers who'd finished work for the day. Rod McAllister was
behind the bar yet again. Rebus had asked jokingly if he
was a permanent feature.

'Day shift,' McAllister had replied unsmilingly.

'You're a real asset to the place,' Rebus had added,
accepting his change.

Now he sat with a half-pint of beer and the remains of a
glass of whisky. Siobhan was drinking a garishly coloured
mixture of lime juice and soda.

'You really think Whiteread and Simms might have
planted those drugs?'

Rebus shrugged. 'There isn't much I wouldn't put past
the likes of Whiteread.'

'Based on . . .?' He looked at her. 'I mean,' she went on,
'you've always stayed pretty tight-lipped about your army
years.'

'Not the happiest of my life,' he admitted. 'I saw guys
broken by the system. Fact of the matter is, I only just
about held on to my own sanity. When I left, I had a
nervous breakdown.' Rebus swallowed back the memories.
He thought of all the comfortable clichés: what's done is
done . . . you can't go living in the past . . . 'One guy – a
guy I was close to – he went to pieces during the training.

They turfed him out, but forgot to switch him off . . .' His voice trailed away.

'What happened?'

'He blamed me, came looking for revenge. Way before your time, Siobhan.'

'So you can understand why Herdman might lose it?'

'Maybe.'

'But you're not sure he did, are you?'

'There are usually warning signs. Herdman wasn't the archetypal loner. No arsenal in his home, just that one gun . . .' Rebus paused. 'We could do with knowing when he got hold of it.'

'The gun?'

Rebus nodded. 'Then we'd know whether he bought it with that one specific purpose.'

'Chances are, if he was smuggling drugs, he'd feel the need for some kind of protection. Might explain the Mac 10 in the boathouse.' Siobhan was following the progress of a young blonde woman who'd just entered the bar. The barman seemed to know her. He was pouring out her drink before she got to him. Bacardi and Coke, it looked like. No ice.

'Nothing came of all those interviews?' Rebus was asking.

Siobhan shook her head. He meant all the low-lifes and firearm merchants. 'The Brocock wasn't the most recent model. Thinking seems to be, he brought it north with him when he moved here. As for the machine-gun, who knows?'

Rebus was thoughtful, Siobhan watching as Rod McAllister leaned on the bar-top, resting his forearms there. Deep in conversation with the blonde . . . the blonde Siobhan knew from somewhere. He looked as contented as Siobhan had ever seen him, head tilted to one side. The woman was smoking, blowing ash-grey plumes ceiling-wards.

'Do me a favour, will you?' Rebus asked suddenly. 'Get on the phone to Bobby Hogan.'

'Why?'

'Because he probably doesn't want to speak to me right now.'

'And what is it I'm phoning him for?' Siobhan had her mobile out.

'To ask if Whiteread was forthcoming with Lee Herdman's army records. The answer's probably no, in which case he should have called the army direct. I want to know if they've come through.'

Siobhan was nodding, pushing buttons. The conversation from then on was one-sided.

'DI Hogan, it's Siobhan Clarke . . .' Listening, she looked up at Rebus. 'No, I've no idea what that was about . . . I think he was called to Fettes.' She widened her eyes questioningly, and Rebus nodded to let her know she'd said the right thing. 'What I was wondering was, did you get round to asking Ms Whiteread for the records on Herdman?' She listened to Hogan's reply. 'Well, John mentioned it to me, and I just thought I'd follow up . . .' She listened again, squeezing her eyes tight shut. 'No, he's not here listening in.' She'd opened her eyes again. Rebus winked, to let her know she was doing fine. 'Mmm . . . hmm . . .' She was listening to Hogan. 'Doesn't sound like she's being as co-operative as we'd have liked . . . Yes, I'll bet you told her.' A smile. 'What did she say?' More listening. 'And did you follow her advice? . . . So what did they say down at Hereford?' Meaning SAS HQ. 'So we're denied access?' Another look at Rebus. 'Well, he can be a difficult creature, we both know that.' Talking about Rebus now, Hogan probably saying that he would have told Rebus all this if the scene in the common room hadn't imploded. 'No, I'd no idea he was related to them.' Siobhan made an O of her mouth. 'Well, that's my story and I'm sticking to it.' Her turn to wink at Rebus. He drew a finger across his neck, but she shook her head. She was beginning to enjoy herself. 'And I'll bet you've got a few stories about him, too . . . I know he is.' A laugh. 'No, no, you're absolutely right. God, it's just as well he's not here . . .' Rebus made a move to snatch the phone from her, but she turned away from him. 'Really? Well, thanks. No, that's . . . Yes, yes, I'd like that. We'll maybe . . . yes, after this has all . . . I'll look forward to it. Bye, Bobby.'

She was smiling as she ended the call. Picked up her glass and took a sip.

'I think I got the gist of that,' Rebus muttered.

'I'm to call him "Bobby". He says I'm a good officer.'

'Jesus . . .'

'And he's invited me for a meal, once the case is finished.'

'He's a married man.'

'He's not.'

'Okay, his wife left him. He's old enough to be your dad, though.' Rebus paused. 'What did he say about me?'

'Nothing.'

'You laughed when he said it.'

'I was winding you up.'

Rebus glowered at her. 'I buy the drinks and you do the winding up? Is that the basis of our relationship?'

'I offered to cook you a meal.'

'So you did.'

'Bobby knows a nice restaurant in Leith.'

'Wonder which kebab shop he's meaning . . .'

She thumped his arm. 'Go get us another round.'

'After what I've just been through?' Rebus shook his head. 'Your shout.' He sat back in his chair, as if getting comfortable.

'If that's the way you want to play it . . .' Siobhan got to her feet. She wanted a closer look at the woman anyway. But the blonde was leaving, tucking cigarettes and lighter into her shoulder-bag, head dipped so that Siobhan could make out only part of her face.

'See you later!' the woman called.

'Aye, see you,' McAllister called back. He was wiping the bar-top with a damp cloth. The smile slid from his face at Siobhan's approach. 'Same again, is it?' he asked.

She nodded. 'Friend of yours?'

He'd turned away to measure out Rebus's whisky. 'In a way.'

'I seem to know her from somewhere.'

'Oh, aye?' He placed the drink in front of her. 'You want the half as well?'

She nodded. 'And another lime juice and . . .'

'. . . and soda. I remember. Nothing in the whisky, ice in the lime.' Another order was already coming from further down the bar: two lagers and a rum and black. He rang up Siobhan's drinks, was brisk with her change, and started on the lagers, making a show of being too busy for chit-chat. Siobhan stood her ground a few moments longer, then decided it wasn't worth it. She was halfway back to the table when she remembered. Brought up short, some of Rebus's beer trickled down the side of the glass, dripping on to the scuffed wooden floor.

'Whoa there,' Rebus cautioned, watching from his chair. She got the drinks to the table and set them down. Went to the window and looked out, but there was no sign of the blonde.

'I know who she was,' she said.

'Who?'

'The woman who just left. You must have seen her.'

'Long blonde hair, tight pink T-shirt, short leather jacket? Black ski-pants and heels slightly too high for their own good?' Rebus took a sip of beer. 'Can't say I noticed.'

'But you didn't recognise her?'

'Any reason I should?'

'Well, according to today's front page, you only went and torched her boyfriend.' Siobhan sat back, holding her own glass in front of her, waiting for her words to sink in.

'Fairstone's girlfriend?' Rebus said, eyes narrowing.

Siobhan nodded. 'I only saw her the once, the day Fairstone walked free.'

Rebus was looking towards the bar. 'You're sure it was her?'

'Fairly sure. When I heard her speak ... Yes, I'm positive. I saw her outside the court, when the trial finished.'

'Just that once?'

Siobhan nodded again. 'I wasn't the one who interviewed her about the alibi she gave her boyfriend, and she wasn't in court when I gave my evidence.'

'What's her name?'

Siobhan narrowed her eyes in concentration. 'Rachel something.'

'Where does Rachel something live?'

Siobhan shrugged. 'I'd guess not too far from her boyfriend.'

'Making this not exactly her local.'

'Not exactly.'

'Ten miles from her local, to be precise.'

'More or less.' Siobhan was still holding the glass; had yet to take her first sip.

'You had any more of those letters?'

She shook her head.

'Think she could be following you?'

'Not every minute of the day. I'd've spotted her.' Now Siobhan looked towards the bar, too. McAllister's flurry of activity had ended and he was back to washing glasses. 'Of course, it might not be me she came here to see ...'

Rebus got Siobhan to drop him off at Allan Renshaw's house. He told her she should go home; he'd take a taxi back into town, or get a patrol car to pick him up.

'I don't know how long I'll be,' he'd said. Not an official visit; just family. She'd nodded, driven off. He'd rung the doorbell with no success. Peered through the window. The boxes of snapshots were still spread out across the living room. No sign of life. He tried the door-handle, and it turned. The door was unlocked.

'Allan?' he called. 'Kate?'

He closed the door behind him. There was a buzzing noise from upstairs. He called out again, but without answer. Cautiously, he climbed the stairs. There was a metal step-ladder in the middle of the upstairs hall, leading up through an open hatch in the ceiling. Rebus took each rung slowly.

'Allan?'

There was a light on in the attic and the buzzing was louder. Rebus stuck his head through the hatch. His cousin was seated cross-legged on the floor, a control panel in his hand, mimicking the sound the toy racing-car made as it sped around the figure-of-eight track.

'I always let him win,' Allan Renshaw said, giving the first sign that he was aware of Rebus's appearance. 'Derek, I mean. We got him this for his Christmas one year . . .'

Rebus saw the open box, lengths of unused track spilling from it. Packing crates had been emptied, suitcases opened. Rebus saw women's dresses, children's clothes, a stack of old 45s. He saw magazines with long-forgotten TV stars on the front. He saw plates and ornaments, peeled from their protective newsprint. Some might have been wedding gifts, dispatched to darkness by changing fashions. A folded buggy waited to be claimed by the generation to come. Rebus had reached the top of the ladder, and settled his weight against the edge of the hatch. Somehow, amidst the clutter, Allan Renshaw had negotiated room for the race-track, his eyes following the red plastic car as it completed its endless circuits.

'Never saw the attraction myself,' Rebus commented. 'Same with train-sets.'

'Cars are different. You've got that illusion of speed . . . and you can race against everyone else. Plus . . .' Renshaw pushed his finger down harder on the accelerator button, 'if you take a bend too fast and crash . . .' His car spun from the track. He reached out for it, slid its guiding front-brush into the slot on the roadway. Pressed the button and sent it on its renewed journey. 'You see?' he said, glancing towards Rebus.

'You can always start again?' Rebus guessed.

'Nothing's changed. Nothing's broken,' Renshaw said, nodding. 'It's as if nothing happened.'

'It's an illusion then,' Rebus intimated.

'A comforting illusion,' his cousin agreed. He paused. 'Did I have a race-set when I was a kid? I don't remember . . .'

Rebus shrugged. 'I know I didn't. If they were around, they were probably too expensive.'

'The money we lash out on our kids, eh, John?' Renshaw produced the glimmer of a smile. 'Always wanting the best for them, never begrudging anything.'

'Must've been expensive, putting your two through Port Edgar.'

'Wasn't cheap. You've just got the one, is that right?'

'She's all grown now, Allan.'

'Kate's growing, too . . . moving on to another life.'

'She's got a head on her shoulders.' Rebus watched as the car tripped from the track again. It ended up near him, so he reached forward to replace it. 'That crash Derek was in,' he said. 'It wasn't his fault, was it?'

Renshaw shook his head. 'Stuart was a wild one. We're lucky Derek was all right.' He set the car moving again. Rebus had noticed a blue car in the box, and a spare controller sitting by his cousin's left shoe.

'We going to have a race then?' he asked, sliding further into the space, picking up the small black box.

'Why not?' Renshaw agreed, placing Rebus's car on the starting-line. He brought his own car to meet it, then counted down from five. Both cars jolted towards the first bend, Rebus's careering off straight away. He crawled over on hands and knees and fixed it back on to the track, just as Renshaw's car lapped him.

'You've had more practice than me,' he complained, sitting back down again. Draughts of warm air were gusting up through the open hatch, providing the attic with its only source of heat. Rebus knew that if he stood, there wouldn't be quite enough room for him. 'So how long have you been up here?' he asked. Renshaw ran a hand over what was now more beard than stubble.

'Since first thing,' he said.

'Where's Kate?'

'Out helping that MSP.'

'The front door isn't locked.'

'Oh?'

'Anyone could walk in.' Rebus had waited for Renshaw's car to catch up with him, and now they were racing again, crossing lanes at one point in the track.

'Know what I was thinking about last night?' Renshaw said. 'I think it was last night . . .'

'What?'

'I was thinking about your dad. I really liked him. He used to do tricks for me, do you remember that?'

'Producing pennies from behind your ear?'

'And making them disappear. He said he'd learned it in the army.'

'Probably.'

'He was in the Far East, wasn't he?'

Rebus nodded. His father had never said much about his wartime exploits. Mostly, all he'd shared were anecdotes, things they could laugh at. But later on . . . towards the end of his life, he'd let slip details of some of the horrors he'd witnessed.

These weren't professional soldiers, John, they were conscripts – men who worked in banks, shops, factories. War changed them, changed all of us. How could it not?

'Thing is,' Allan Renshaw continued, 'thinking about your dad got me thinking about you. Remember that day you took me to the park.'

'The day we played football?'

Renshaw nodded, gave a weak smile. 'You remember it?'

'Probably not as well as you.'

'Oh, I remember, all right. We were playing football, and then some guys you knew turned up, and I had to play by myself while you talked to them.' Renshaw paused. The cars crossed one another again. 'Coming back to you?'

'Not really.' But Rebus supposed it could be true. Whenever he'd gone home on leave, there'd been friends from school to catch up with.

'Then we started walking home. Or you and your pals did, me trailing behind, carrying the ball you'd bought us . . . Now this bit, this bit I'd pushed to the back of my mind . . .'

'What bit?' Rebus was concentrating on the race-track.

'The bit where we were passing the pub. You remember the pub on the corner?'

'The Bowhill Hotel?'

'That was it. We were passing, only then you turned to me, pointed at me, told me I'd to wait outside. Your voice was different, a lot harder, like you didn't want your pals to know *we* were pals . . .'

'You sure about this, Allan?'

'Oh, I'm sure. Because the three of you went inside, and I sat at the kerb and waited. I was holding on to the ball, and after a while you came out again, but just to hand me a bag of crisps. You went back inside, and then these other kids came up, and one of them kicked the ball out of my grasp, and they ran off, laughing and kicking it to each other. That's when I started crying, and still you didn't come out, and I knew I couldn't go in. So I got to my feet and walked back to the house by myself. I got lost once, but I stopped and asked someone.' The racing cars were speeding towards the point at which they would switch lanes. They arrived at the same time, met and bounced off the track, landing on their backs. Neither man moved. The attic was silent for a moment. 'You came home later,'

Renshaw continued, breaking the silence, 'and nobody said anything because I'd not said anything to them. But you know what really got me? You never asked what had happened to the ball, and I knew why you didn't ask. It was because you'd forgotten all about it. Because it wasn't important to you.' Renshaw paused. 'And I was just some little kid again, and not your friend.'

'Jesus, Allan . . .' Rebus was trying to remember, but there was nothing there. The day he'd thought he'd known had been sunshine and football, nothing else.

'I'm sorry,' he said at last.

Tears were dripping down Renshaw's cheeks. 'I was family, John, and you treated me like I was nothing.'

'Allan, believe me, I never—'

'Out!' Renshaw yelled, sniffing back more tears. 'I want you out of my house – now!' He'd risen stiffly to his feet. Rebus was up, too, the two men standing awkwardly, heads angled against the roofbeams, backs bent.

'Look, Allan, if it's any . . .'

But Renshaw had him by the shoulder, trying to manoeuvre him to the hatch.

'All right, all right,' Rebus was saying. He tried yanking himself free of the other man's grip, and Renshaw stumbled, one foot finding no purchase, sending him falling through the hatch. Rebus grabbed him by the arm, feeling his fingers burn as he tightened his grip. Renshaw scrabbled back upright.

'You okay?' Rebus asked.

'Didn't you hear me?' Renshaw was pointing at the ladder.

'Okay, Allan. But we'll talk again some time, eh? That's what I came here for: to talk, to get to know you.'

'You had your chance to get to know me,' Renshaw said coldly. Rebus was making his way back down the ladder. He peered up through the gap, but his cousin wasn't visible.

'Are you coming down, Allan?' he called. No response.

Then the buzzing sound again, as the red car recommenced its journey. Rebus turned and headed downstairs. Didn't really know what to do, whether it was safe to leave Allan like this. He walked into the living room, through to the kitchen. Outside, the lawn-mower had yet to move. There were sheets of paper on the table, computer print-outs. Petitions calling for gun control, for more safety in schools. No names as yet, just row after row of blank boxes. The same thing had happened after Dunblane. A tightening of rules and regulations. Result? More illegal guns than ever out there on the street. Rebus knew that in Edinburgh, if you knew where to go asking, you could get a gun in under an hour. In Glasgow, it was reckoned to take all of ten minutes. Guns were run like rental videos: you hired them for a day. If they came back unused, you got some money back. Used, and you didn't. A simple commercial transaction, not too far removed from Peacock Johnson's activities. Rebus thought about signing his name to the petition, but knew it would be an empty gesture. There were lots of newspaper cuttings and reprints of magazine articles: the effects of violence in the media. Kneejerk stuff, like saying a horror video could make two kids kill a toddler . . . He had a look around, wondering if Kate had left a contact number. He wanted to talk to her about her father, maybe tell her Allan needed her more than Jack Bell did. He stood at the foot of the stairs for a few minutes, listening to the noises in the attic, then checked the phone book for a taxi firm.

'Be with you in ten,' the voice on the phone told him. A cheery, female voice. It was almost enough to persuade him that there was another world than this . . .

Siobhan stood in the middle of her living room and looked around her. She walked over to the window and closed the shutters against the dying light. She picked up a mug and plate from the floor: toast crumbs identifying her last meal in the flat. She checked that there were no messages on her phone. It was Friday, which meant Toni Jackson and the other female officers would be expecting her, but the last thing she felt like was girlie bonhomie and the drunken eyeing-up of pub talent. The mug and plate took half a minute to wash and place on the draining-board. A quick look in the fridge. The food she'd bought, intending to cook a meal for Rebus, was still there, a few days shy of its 'best before' date. She closed the door again and went into her bedroom, straightened the duvet on her bed, confirmed that a laundry would be necessary this weekend. Then into the bathroom, a glance at herself in the mirror, before heading back into the living room, where she opened the day's post. Two bills and a postcard. The postcard was from an old college friend. They hadn't managed to see one another this year, despite living in the same city. Now the friend was enjoying a four-day break in Rome . . . probably already back, judging by the date on the card. Rome: Siobhan had never been there.

I walked into the travel agent, asked them what they had at short notice. Having a great time, chilling, doing the café thing, a bit of culture when the mood takes me. Love, Jackie.

She stood the card on her mantelpiece, tried remembering her last real holiday. A week with her parents? That weekend break in Dublin? It had been a hen party for one of the uniforms . . . and now the woman was expecting her first kid. She looked up at the ceiling. Her upstairs neighbour was thumping around. She didn't think he did it on purpose, but he walked like an elephant. She'd met him on the pavement outside when she was coming home, complaining that he'd just had to fetch his car from the council pound.

'Twenty minutes I left it, twenty on a single yellow . . . by the time I got back, it'd been towed . . . hundred and thirty quid, can you believe it? I almost told them it was more than the bloody thing's worth.' Then he'd stabbed a finger at her. 'You should do something about it.'

Because she was a cop. Because people thought cops could pull strings, get things sorted, change things.

You should do something about it.

He was raging all around his living room, a caged animal ready to hurl itself against the bars. He worked in an office on George Street: account executive, retail insurance. Not quite Siobhan's height, he wore glasses with narrow rectangular lenses. Had a male flatmate, but had stressed to Siobhan that he wasn't gay, information for which she had thanked him.

Stomp, thunk, plod.

She wondered if there was any purpose to his movements. Was he opening and closing drawers? Looking for the lost remote perhaps? Or was movement itself his purpose? And if so; what did that say about her own stillness, about the fact that she was standing here listening to him? One postcard on her mantelpiece . . . one plate and mug on the draining-board. One shuttered window, with a horizontal locking-bar which she never bothered fastening. Safe enough in here as it was. Cocooned. Smothered.

'Sod it,' she muttered, turning to make good her escape.

St Leonard's was quiet. She'd intended burning off some frustration in the gym, but instead got herself a can of something cold and fizzy from the machine and headed upstairs to CID, checking her desk for messages. Another letter from her mystery admirer:

DO BLACK LEATHER GLOVES TURN YOU ON?

Referring to Rebus, she surmised. There was a note for her to call Ray Duff, but all he wanted to say was that he'd managed to test the first of her anonymous letters.

'And it's not good news.'

'Meaning it's clean?' she guessed.

'As the proverbial whistle.' She let out a sigh. 'Sorry I can't be more helpful. Would buying you a drink help?'

'Some other time maybe.'

'Fair enough. I'll probably be here for another hour or two as it is.' 'Here' being the forensic lab at Howdenhall.

288

'Still working on Port Edgar?'

'Matching blood types, see whose spatters are whose.'

Siobhan was seated on the edge of her desk, phone tucked between cheek and shoulder as she sifted through the rest of the paperwork in her in-tray. Most of it concerned cases from weeks back . . . names she could barely remember.

'Better let you get back to it then,' she said.

'Keeping busy yourself, Siobhan? You sound tired.'

'You know what it's like, Ray. Let's have that drink sometime.'

'By then, I reckon we'll both need it.'

She smiled into the phone. 'Bye, Ray.'

'Take care of yourself, Shiv . . .'

She put the phone down. There it was again: somebody calling her Shiv, trying for a kind of intimacy they thought the foreshortening would bring. She'd noticed, though, that no one ever tried the same tack with Rebus, never called him Jock, Johnny, Jo-Jo, or JR. Because they looked at him or listened to him and knew he was none of those things. He was John Rebus. Detective Inspector Rebus. To his closest friends: John. Yet some of these same people would happily see her as 'Shiv'. Why? Because she was a woman? Did she lack Rebus's gravitas or sense of perpetual threat? Were they just trying to worm their way into her affections? Or would the conferring of a nickname make her seem more vulnerable, less edgy and potentially dangerous to them?

Shiv . . . It meant a knife, didn't it? American slang. Well, right now she felt just about as blunt as she ever had done. And here was another nickname walking into the room. DS George 'Hi-Ho' Silvers. Looking around as if for someone in particular. Spotting her, it took him a second to make up his mind that she might suit his particular requirements.

'Busy?' he asked.

'What does it look like?'

'Fancy a wee drive then?'

'You're not really my type, George.'

A snort. 'We've got a DP.' DP: Deceased Person.

'Where?'

'Over Gracemount way. Disused railway track. Looks like he fell from the footbridge.'

'An accident then?' Like Fairstone's chip-pan fire: another Gracemount accident.

Silvers shrugged his shoulders as far as he could within the confines of a suit-jacket which had fitted him with room to spare three years before. 'Story is, he was being chased.'

'Chased?'

Another shrug. 'That's as much as I know till we get there.'

Siobhan nodded. 'So what are we waiting for?'

They took Silvers's car. He asked her about South Queensferry, about Rebus and the house fire, but she kept her answers short. Eventually he got the message and turned on the radio, whistling along to trad jazz, possibly her least favourite music.

'You listen to any Mogwai, George?'

'Never heard of it. Why?'

'Just wondering . . .'

There was nowhere to park near the railway line. Silvers pulled up to the kerb, behind a patrol car. There was a bus stop, and behind it an area of grassland. They crossed it on foot, approaching a low fence overgrown with thistles and brambles. The fence was broken by a short metal stairway leading them on to the bridge across the railway, where sightseers from the local housing blocks had gathered. A uniformed officer was asking each one if they'd seen or heard anything.

'How the hell are we supposed to get down?' Silvers growled. Siobhan pointed to the far side, where a make-shift stile had been erected from plastic milk-crates and breeze-blocks, an old mattress folded across the top of the fence. When they reached it, Silvers took one look and decided it wasn't for him. He didn't say anything, just shook his head. So Siobhan clambered up and over, skidding down the steep embankment, digging her heels as far as possible into the soft ground, feeling nettles sting her ankles, briars snag at her trousers. Several figures had gathered around the prone body on the track. She recognised faces from Craigmillar Police Station, and the pathologist, Dr Curt. He saw her and smiled a greeting.

'We're lucky they haven't reopened this line yet,' he said. 'At least the poor chap's in one piece.'

She looked down at the twisted, broken body. His duffel coat had been thrown open, exposing a torso clad in a loose-fitting check shirt. Brown cord trousers and brown loafers.

'A couple of people called in,' one of the Craigmillar detectives was telling her, 'saying they'd seen him wandering the streets.'

'Probably not too unusual around here . . .'

'Except he looked like he was on the hunt for somebody. Kept a hand in one pocket, like he might be carrying.'

'And is he?'

The detective shook his head. 'Might be he dropped it when he was being chased. Local kids by the sound of it.'

Siobhan looked from the body to the bridge and back again. 'Did they catch him?'

The detective shrugged.

'So do we know who he is?'

'Video rental card in his back pocket. Name's Callis. Initial A. We've got someone checking the phone book. If that doesn't work, we'll get an address from the video shop.'

'Callis?' Siobhan's eyebrows creased. She was trying to remember where she'd heard that name . . . Then it hit her.

'Andy Callis,' she said, almost to herself.

The detective had heard her. 'You know him?'

She shook her head. 'But I know someone who might. If it's the same guy, he lives in Alnwickhall.' She was reaching for her mobile. 'Oh, and one other thing . . . if it *is* him, he's one of us.'

'A cop?'

She nodded. The detective from Craigmillar sucked air through his teeth, and stared up at the spectators on the bridge with a new sense of purpose.

16

There was nobody home.

Rebus had been watching Miss Teri's room for almost an hour. Dark, dark, dark. Just like his memories. He could not even recall which friends he'd met with that day in the park. Yet the scene had stayed with Allan Renshaw these past thirty-odd years. Indelible. It was funny, the things you couldn't help remembering, the ones you chose to forget. The little tricks your brain could play on you, sudden scents or sensations reviving the long-forgotten. Rebus wondered if perhaps Allan was angry with him because such anger was possible. After all, what point was there in getting angry with Lee Herdman? Herdman wasn't there to bear the brunt, while Rebus conspicuously was, as if conjured up for the very purpose.

The laptop kicked into screen-saver mode, shooting stars moving out of the far darkness. He hit the return key and was back in Teri Cotter's bedroom. What was he watching for? Because it satisfied the voyeur in him? He'd always enjoyed surveillances for the same reason: glimpses into secret lives. He wondered what Teri herself got out of it. She wasn't making money. There was no interaction as such, no way for the viewer to make contact with her, or for her to communicate with her audience. Why then? Because she felt the need to be on display? Like hanging out on Cockburn Street, stared at and sometimes set upon. She had accused her mother of spying on her, yet had made straight for her mother's door when the Lost Boys had attacked. Hard to know what to think about that particular relationship. Rebus's own daughter had lived her teenage years in London with her mother, remaining a mystery to him. His ex-wife would call him to complain about Samántha's 'attitude' or her 'moods', would let off steam at him and then put down the phone.

The phone.

His phone was ringing. His mobile phone. It was plugged into the wall, recharging. He picked it up. 'Hello?'

'I tried ringing your home phone.' Siobhan's voice. 'It was engaged.'

Rebus looked at the laptop, the laptop which was hooked up to his phone line. 'What's up?'

'Your friend, the one you were visiting that night you bumped into me . . .' She was on her mobile, sounded like she was outdoors.

'Andy?' he said. 'Andy Callis?'

'Can you describe him?'

Rebus froze. 'What's happened?'

'Look, it might not be him . . .'

'Where are you?'

'Describe him for me . . . that way you're not headed all the way out here for nothing.'

Rebus squeezed his eyes shut, saw Andy Callis in his living room, feet up in front of the TV. 'Early forties, dark-brown hair, five-eleven, probably twelve stone or there-abouts . . .'

She was silent for a moment. 'Okay,' she sighed. 'Maybe you should come after all.'

Rebus was already looking for his jacket. He remembered the laptop, broke the Internet connection.

'So where are you?' he asked.

'How are you going to get here?'

'My problem,' he told her, looking around for his car keys. 'Just give me the address.'

She was waiting for him kerbside, watched him pull on the handbrake and get out of the driver's seat.

'How are the hands?' she asked.

'They were fine before I got behind the wheel.'

'Painkillers?'

He shook his head. 'I can do without.' He was looking around at the scene. A couple of hundred yards or so up the road was the bus stop where his taxi had stopped for the Lost Boys. They started walking towards the bridge.

'He'd been stalking the place for a couple of hours,' Siobhan explained. 'Two or three people reported seeing him.'

'And did we do anything about it?'

'There wasn't a patrol car available,' she said quietly.

'If there had been, he might not be dead,' Rebus stated starkly. She nodded slowly.

'One of the neighbours heard shouts. She thinks some kids had started chasing him.'

'Did she see anyone?'

Siobhan shook her head. They were on the bridge now. The onlookers had started drifting away. The body had been wrapped in a blanket and loaded on to a stretcher, hitched to a length of rope with which to haul it up the embankment. A van from the mortuary had pulled up next to the stile. Silvers was standing there, chatting to the driver and smoking a cigarette.

'We've checked the Callises in the phone book,' he told Rebus and Siobhan. 'No sign of him.'

'Ex-directory,' Rebus said. 'Same as you and me, George.'

'You sure it's the same Callis?' Silvers enquired. There was a yell from below, the driver flicking away his cigarette so he could concentrate on his end of the rope. Silvers kept on smoking, not offering a hand until the driver asked for one. Rebus kept his own hands in his pockets. They felt like they were on fire.

'Heave away!' came the call. In under a minute, the stretcher was being carried over the fence. Rebus stepped forward, unwrapped the face. Stared at it, noting how peaceful Andy Callis looked in death.

'It's him,' he said, standing back again so the body could be loaded into the van. Dr Curt was at the top of the incline, having been helped by the Craigmillar detective. He was breathing hard, climbing over the stile with difficulty. When someone stepped forward to help, he spluttered that he could manage, his speech thick with effort.

'It's him,' Silvers was telling the new arrivals. 'According to DI Rebus, that is.'

'Andy Callis?' someone asked. 'Is he the guy from Firearms?'

Rebus nodded.

'Any witnesses?' the Craigmillar detective was asking.

One of the uniforms answered. 'People heard voices, nobody seems to've seen anything.'

'Suicide?' someone else asked.

'Or he was trying to escape,' Siobhan commented, noting that Rebus wasn't adding anything to the conversation, even though he'd known Andy Callis best. Or maybe *because* . . .

They watched the mortuary van bump over the uneven ground on its way back to the road. Silvers asked Siobhan if she was headed back. She looked at Rebus and shook her head.

'John'll give me a lift,' she said.

'Please yourself. Looks like Craigmillar'll be handling it anyway.'

She nodded, waiting for Silvers to leave. Then, left alone with Rebus: 'You okay?'

'I keep thinking of the patrol car that never came.'

'And?' He looked at her. 'There's more to it, isn't there?'

Eventually, he nodded slowly.

'Care to share it?' she asked.

He kept on nodding. When he moved off, she followed, back over the bridge, across the grass to where the Saab was sitting. It wasn't locked. He opened the driver's door, thought better of it and handed her the keys. 'You drive,' he said. 'I don't think I'm up to it.'

'Where are we going?'

'Just cruising around. Maybe we'll get lucky, find ourselves in Never Never Land.'

It took her a moment to decode the reference. 'The Lost Boys?' she said.

Rebus nodded, walked around the car to the passenger side.

'And while I'm driving, you'll be telling me the story?'

'I'll tell you the story,' he agreed.

And he did.

What it boiled down to was: Andy Callis and his partner on patrol in their car. Called to a nightclub on Market Street, just behind Waverley Station. It was a popular spot, people queuing to get in. One of them had called the police, reporting someone brandishing a handgun. Vague description. Teenager, green parka, three mates with him. Not in the queue as such, just walking past, pulling open his coat so people could see what was tucked into his waistband.

'By the time Andy got there,' Rebus said, 'there was no sign of him. He'd gone heading off down towards New Street. So that's where Andy and his partner went. They'd called it in and been authorised to unlock their guns . . . had them on their laps. Flak jackets on . . . Back-up was on its way, just in case. You know where the railway passes over the bottom of New Street?'

'At Calton Road?'

Rebus nodded. 'Stone railway arches. It's pretty gloomy down there. Not much in the way of street-lighting.'

Siobhan's turn to nod: it was a desolate spot all right.

'Lots of nooks and crannies, too,' Rebus continued. 'Andy's partner thought he spotted something in the shadows. They stopped the car, got out. Saw these four guys . . . probably the same ones. Kept their distance, asked if they were carrying any weapons. Ordered them to place anything on the ground. The way Andy told it, it was like shadows that kept shifting . . .' He rested his head against the back of the seat, closed his eyes. 'Wasn't sure if what he was looking at was a shadow or flesh and blood. He was unclipping his torch from his belt when he thought he saw movement, a hand stretching, pointing something. He aimed his own gun, safety off . . .'

'What happened?'

'Something fell to the ground. It was a pistol: a replica, as it turned out. But too late . . .'

'He'd fired?'

Rebus nodded. 'Not that he hit anyone. He was aiming at the ground. Ricochet could have gone anywhere . . .'

'But it didn't.'

'No.' Rebus paused. 'There had to be an inquiry: happens every time a weapon's discharged. Partner backed him up, but Andy knew the guy was just mouthing words. He started doubting himself.'

'And the guy with the gun?'

'Four of them. None would own up to carrying it. Three were wearing parkas, and the kid from the nightclub queue wasn't about to ID the carrier.'

'The Lost Boys?'

Rebus nodded. 'That's the neighbourhood name for them. They're the ones you ran into on Cockburn Street. The leader – his name's Rab Fisher – he went to court for carrying the replica, but the case was booted out . . . waste of the lawyers' time. And meanwhile, Andy Callis was playing it over and over again in his head, trying to sort out the shadows from the truth . . .'

'And this is the Lost Boys' patch?' Siobhan asked, peering out through the windscreen.

Rebus nodded. Siobhan was thoughtful, then asked: 'Where did the gun come from?'

'At a guess, Peacock Johnson.'

'Is that why you wanted a word with him that day he was brought into St Leonard's?'

Rebus nodded again.

'And now you want a word with the Lost Boys?'

'Looks like they've gone home for the night,' Rebus admitted, turning his head to watch from the passenger-side window.

'You think Callis came here on purpose?'

'Maybe.'

'Looking to confront them?'

'They got off scot-free, Siobhan. Andy wasn't too thrilled at that.'

She was thoughtful. 'So why aren't we telling all this to Craigmillar?'

'I'll let them know.' He felt her staring. 'Cross my heart.'

'It could have been an accident. That railway line would look like an escape route.'

'Maybe.'

'Nobody saw anything.'

He turned towards her. 'Spit it out.'

She sighed. 'It's just the way you keep trying to fight other people's battles for them.'

'Is that what I do?'

'Sometimes, yes.'

'Well, I'm sorry if that upsets you.'

'It doesn't upset me. But sometimes . . .' She swallowed back what she'd been about to say.

'Sometimes?' Rebus encouraged her.

She shook her head, exhaled noisily and stretched her back, working her neck. 'Thank God for the weekend. You got any plans?'

'Thought I might do some hill-walking . . . pump some iron at the gym . . .'

'Just a hint of sarcasm there?'

'Just a hint.' He'd spotted something. 'Slow down a bit.' He was turning to watch from the rear window. 'Back the car up.'

She did so. They were on a street of low-rise flats. A supermarket trolley, itself a long way from home, sat abandoned on the pavement. Rebus was looking down an alley between two blocks. One ... no, two figures. Just silhouettes, so close together they seemed to merge. Then Rebus realised what was happening.

'A good old-fashioned knee-trembler,' Siobhan commented. 'Who said the art of romance was dead?'

One of the faces had turned towards the car, noting the idling engine. A rough masculine voice called out: 'Enjoying the view, pal? Better than you're getting at home, eh?'

'Drive,' Rebus ordered.

Siobhan drove.

They ended up at St Leonard's, Siobhan explaining that her car was there, without elaborating any further. Rebus had told her he'd be okay to drive home: Arden Street was five minutes away. But by the time he parked outside his flat, his hands were burning. In the bathroom, he smeared more cream on, and took a couple of painkillers, hoping he'd be able to snatch a few hours' sleep. A whisky might help, so he poured a large measure and sat himself down in the living room. The laptop had gone from screen-saver to sleep mode. He didn't bother waking it, walked over to his dining-table instead. He had some stuff about the SAS laid out there, alongside the copy of Herdman's personnel file. He sat down in front of it.

Enjoying the view, pal?

Better than you're getting at home?

Enjoying the view ...?

Day Five

Monday

17

The view was magnificent.

Siobhan was in the front, next to the pilot. Rebus was tucked in behind, an empty seat next to him. The noise from the propellers was deafening.

'We could've taken the corporate plane,' Doug Brimson was explaining, 'but the fuel bill's massive, and it might've been too big for the LZ.'

LZ: landing zone. Not a term Rebus had heard since he'd left the army.

'Corporate?' Siobhan was asking.

'I've got a seven-seater. Companies hire me to fly them to meetings – otherwise known as "jollies". I lay on some chilled champagne, crystal glasses . . .'

'Sounds fun.'

'Sorry, all we've got today is a flask of tea.' He offered a laugh, turning to look at Rebus. 'I was in Dublin for the weekend, flew a bunch of bankers there for some rugby match. They paid for me to stay over.'

'Lucky you.'

'A few weekends back, it was Amsterdam: business-man's stag party . . .'

Rebus was thinking of his own weekend. When Siobhan had picked him up this morning, she'd asked what he'd done.

'Not much,' he'd said. 'You?'

'Ditto.'

'Funny, the guys down at Leith said you'd been dropping in.'

'Funny, they told me the same thing about you.'

'Enjoying it so far?' Brimson asked now.

'So far,' Rebus said. In truth, he had no great head for heights. All the same, he'd watched with fascination the aerial view of Edinburgh, amazed at how indistinguishable landmarks like the Castle and Calton Hill were from their surroundings. No mistaking the volcanic heft of Arthur's Seat, but the buildings suffered from a uniform grey colouring. Still, the elaborate patterning of the New Town's geometric streets was impressive, and then they were out over the Forth, passing South Queensferry and the road and rail bridges. Rebus sought Port Edgar School, saw Hopetoun House first and then the school building not half a mile distant. He could even make out the Portakabin. They were heading west now, following the M8 towards Glasgow.

Siobhan was asking Brimson if he did a lot of corporate work.

'Depends how the economy's doing. To be honest, if a company's sending four or five people to a meeting, it can be cheaper to charter than to fly regular business class.'

'Siobhan tells me you were in the forces, Mr Brimson,' Rebus said, leaning as far forward as his harness would allow.

Brimson smiled. 'I was RAF. What about you, Inspector? Forces background?'

Rebus nodded. 'Even trained for the SAS,' he admitted. 'Didn't quite make the grade.'

'Few do.'

'And some of those falter down the line.'

Brimson looked at him again. 'You mean Lee?'

'And Robert Niles. How did you come to know him?'

'Through Lee. He told me he visited Robert. I asked if I could go with him one day.'

'And after that, you started going on your own?' Rebus was remembering the entries in the visitors' log.

'Yes. He's an interesting chap. We seem to get along.' He

looked at Siobhan. 'Fancy taking over the controls while I chat with your colleague?'

'No fear . . .'

'Another time maybe. I think you'd like it.' He gave her a wink. Then, to Rebus: 'The army seems to treat its Old Boys pretty shabbily, wouldn't you say?'

'I don't know. There's support available when you hit civvy street . . . wasn't in my day.'

'High rate of marriage failures, breakdowns. More Falklands veterans have taken their own lives than were killed in the actual conflict. A lot of homeless people are ex-forces . . .'

'On the other hand,' Rebus said, 'the SAS is big business these days. You can sell your story to a publisher, sell your services as a bodyguard. Way I hear it, all four SAS squadrons are below quota. Too many are leaving. Suicide rate's lower than the average, too.'

Brimson didn't appear to be listening. 'One guy jumped out of a plane a few years back . . . maybe you heard about that, too. Recipient of the QGM.'

'Queen's Gallantry Medal,' Rebus explained, for Siobhan's benefit.

'Tried stabbing his ex-wife, thinking she was trying to kill him. Suffered depression . . . Couldn't take it any more, went into freefall, if you'll pardon the pun.'

'It happens,' Rebus said. He was remembering the book in Herdman's flat, the one Teri's photo had fallen from.

'Oh, it happens all right,' Brimson was continuing. 'The SAS chaplain who took part in the Iranian Embassy siege, he ended up committing suicide. Another ex-SAS man shot his girlfriend with a gun he'd brought back from the Gulf War.'

'And something similar happened to Lee Herdman?' Siobhan asked.

'Seems like,' Brimson said.

'Why pick on that school though?' Rebus continued. 'You went to a few of his parties, didn't you, Mr Brimson?'

'He threw a good party.'

'Always used to be plenty of teenagers hanging around.'

Brimson turned again. 'Is that a question or a comment?'

'Ever see any drugs?'

Brimson seemed to be concentrating on the control panel in front of him. 'Maybe a bit of pot,' he finally conceded.

'Is that as strong as it got?'

'It's as much as I saw.'

'Not quite the same thing. Did you ever hear a rumour that Lee Herdman might be dealing?'

'No.'

'Or smuggling?'

Brimson looked towards Siobhan. 'Shouldn't I have a solicitor present?'

She gave a reassuring smile. 'I think the Detective Inspector's just making conversation.' She turned to Rebus. 'Isn't that right?' Her eyes telling Rebus to go easy.

'That's right,' he said. 'Just a bit of chat.' He tried not to think about the hours of lost sleep, his stinging hands, Andy Callis's death. Concentrated instead on the view from his window, the changing landscape. They'd be over Glasgow soon, and then out into the Firth of Clyde, Bute and Kintyre . . .

'So you never associated Lee Herdman with drugs?' he asked.

'I never saw him with anything stronger than a joint.'

'That's not exactly answering my question. What would you say if I told you drugs had been found on one of Herdman's boats?'

'I'd say it's none of my business. Lee was a friend, Inspector. Don't expect me to play along with whatever game it is you're—'

'Some of my colleagues think he was smuggling cocaine and ecstasy into the country,' Rebus stated.

'It's not my problem what your colleagues think,' Brimson muttered, sinking into silence.

'I saw your car on Cockburn Street last week,' Siobhan said, trying for a change of subject. 'Just after I'd been out to Turnhouse to see you.'

'I'd probably stopped off at the bank.'

'This was gone closing time.'

Brimson was thoughtful. 'Cockburn Street?' Then he nodded to himself. 'Some friends have got a shop there. I think I popped in.'

'Which shop is it?'

He looked at her. 'It's not really a shop as such. One of those tanning places.'

'Owned by Charlotte Cotter?' Brimson looked amazed. 'We interviewed the daughter. She's a pupil at the school.'

'Right.' Brimson nodded. He'd been flying with a headset on, one of the ear protectors pushed away from his ear. But now he fixed it on, and angled the mic towards his mouth. 'Go ahead, Tower,' he said. Then he listened as the control tower at Glasgow Airport told him which route to take so as to avoid an incoming flight. Rebus was staring at the back of Brimson's head, thinking to himself that Teri hadn't mentioned him being a friend of the family . . . hadn't sounded as if she liked him at all . . .

The Cessna banked steeply, Rebus trying not to grip his arm-rest too tightly. A minute later, they were passing over Greenock, and then the short stretch of water which separated it from Dunoon. The countryside below was growing wilder: more forests, fewer settlements. They crossed Loch Fyne and were out into the Sound of Jura. The wind seemed to pick up almost immediately, buffeting the plane.

'I've not been this way before,' Brimson admitted. 'Looked at the charts last night. Just the one road, up the eastern side of the island. Bottom half's mostly forest and some decent peaks.'

'And the landing strip?' Siobhan asked.

'You'll see.' He turned to Rebus again. 'Ever read any poetry, Inspector?'

'Do I look the type?'

'Frankly, no. I'm a great fan of Yeats. There's a poem of his I was reading the other night: "I know that I shall meet my fate, somewhere among the clouds above; those that I fight I do not hate, those that I guard I do not love."' He looked at Siobhan. 'Isn't that the saddest thing?'

'You think Lee felt that way?' she asked.

He shrugged. 'The poor bastard who jumped out of the plane did.' He paused. 'Know what the poem's called? "An Irish Airman Foresees His Death".' Another glance at the instrument panel. 'This is us over Jura now.'

Siobhan looked out on to wilderness. The plane made a tight circuit, and she could see the coastline again, and a road running alongside it. As the plane made its descent, Brimson seemed to be checking the road for something . . . some marker perhaps.

'I don't see anywhere to land,' Siobhan said. But she noticed a man, who appeared to be waving both arms at them. Brimson took the plane back up, and made a further circuit.

'Any traffic?' he said, as they flew low over the road once more. Siobhan thought he must be talking to someone on the mic, some tower somewhere. But then she realised he was talking to her. And by 'traffic' he meant on the road beneath.

'You've got to be kidding,' she said, turning to see if Rebus shared her disbelief, but he seemed to be concentrating on guiding the plane down by willpower alone. The wheels rumbled as they hit tarmac, the plane bouncing once as if straining to be airborne again. Brimson had his teeth clenched, but was smiling, too. He turned to Siobhan as if in triumph, and taxied along the carriageway towards the waiting man, the man who was still waving his arms, and now guiding the small plane through an open gateway, leading to a field of stubble. They bumped over the ruts. Brimson cut the engines and slid off his head-phones.

There was a house next to the field, and a woman standing there watching them, nursing a baby over her shoulder. Siobhan opened her door, undid her harness and leapt out. The ground felt as if it were vibrating, but she realised it was her body, still shaken up from the flight.

'I've never landed on a road before,' a grinning Brimson was telling the man.

'It was that or the field,' the man said, in a thick accent. He was tall and muscular, with curly brown hair and bright pink cheeks. 'I'm Rory Mollison.' He shook Brimson's hand, then was introduced to Siobhan. Rebus, who was lighting a cigarette, nodded but didn't offer his own hand. 'You found the place all right then,' Mollison said, as if they'd arrived by car.

'As you can see,' Siobhan said.

'Thought it would work,' Mollison said. 'The SAS guys landed by helicopter. It was their pilot who told me the road would make a good landing-strip. No pot-holes, you see.'

'He was right,' Brimson said.

Mollison was the rescue team's 'local guide'. When Siobhan had asked her favour of Brimson – a plane-ride to Jura – he'd asked if she knew anywhere they could land. Rebus had passed along Mollison's name . . .

Siobhan waved at the woman, who waved back with no real enthusiasm.

'My wife Mary,' Mollison said. 'And our little one, Seona. Are you coming in for some tea?'

Rebus made a show of looking at his watch. 'Best if we get started, actually.' He turned to Brimson. 'You'll be all right here till we get back?'

'What do you mean?'

'We should only be a few hours . . .'

'Hang on, I'm coming, too. I don't suppose Mrs Mollison

309

wants me moping around here. And after flying you here, I don't see how you can turn me down.'

Rebus looked to Siobhan, then conceded with a shrug.

'You'll want to come in and get changed,' Mollison was saying. Siobhan lifted her backpack and nodded.

'Changed?' Rebus echoed.

'Climbing gear.' Mollison looked him up and down. 'Is that all you've brought?'

Rebus shrugged. Siobhan had opened her own pack to show hiking boots, cagoule, and flask. 'A regular Mary Poppins,' Rebus commented.

'You can borrow from me,' Mollison assured him, leading the three visitors towards the house.

'You're not a professional guide then?' Siobhan asked. Mollison shook his head.

'But I know this island like the back of my hand. I must have traversed every square inch of it these past twenty years.' They had taken Mollison's Land Rover as far as they could along muddy logging tracks, bumpy enough to shake the fillings from their teeth. Mollison was a skilled driver; either that or a madman. There were times when there seemed to be no track at all, and they were pitching wildly across the moss-covered forest floor, dropping down a gear to pass over rocky outcrops or through streams. But eventually even he had to concede defeat. It was time for them to walk.

Rebus was wearing a venerable pair of climbing boots whose leather had turned implacably hard, making it difficult for him to bend his feet at the toes. He had on waterproof trousers, splattered with old mud, and an oily Barbour jacket. With the car engine turned off, silence had returned to the woods.

'Ever see the first Rambo film?' Siobhan asked in a whisper. Rebus didn't think she was expecting an answer. He turned to Brimson instead.

'What made you leave the RAF?'

'I just got tired of it, I suppose. Tired of taking orders from people I didn't respect.'

'What about Lee? Did he ever say why he left the SAS?'

Brimson shrugged. His eyes were on the ground, watching for roots and puddles. 'Much the same thing, I'd guess.'

'But he never spelt it out?'

'No.'

'So what did the two of you find to talk about?'

Brimson glanced up at him. 'Plenty of things.'

'He was easy to get along with? No fallings-out?'

'We might have argued about politics once or twice . . . the way the world was headed. Nothing to make me think he was about to go off the rails. I'd have helped him if he'd hinted.'

Rails: Rebus thought of that word, saw Andy Callis's body being hauled up from the railway tracks. He wondered if his visits had helped, or had they merely been painful reminders of everything the man had lost? Then he remembered how Siobhan had been about to say something in the car last night. Maybe to do with why he felt he had to get involved in all these other lives . . . not always for the best.

'How far are we going?' Brimson was asking Mollison.

'Maybe an hour's hike, the same back.' Mollison had a knapsack slung over one shoulder. He looked at his companions, eyes lingering on Rebus. 'Actually,' he corrected himself, 'maybe an hour and a half.'

Rebus had already told Brimson part of the story back at the house, asking if Herdman had ever mentioned the mission to him. Brimson had shaken his head.

'I remember it from the papers though. People thought the IRA had blown the chopper out of the skies.'

Now, as they commenced the climb, Mollison was talking. 'That's what they told me we were looking for: evidence of a missile attack.'

'So they weren't interested in finding the bodies?'

Siobhan asked. She had changed into thick socks, tucking her trouser-bottoms into them. The boots looked new, or if not new then seldom worn.

'Oh, I think there was that, too. But they were more interested in why the crash happened.'

'How many of them were there?' Rebus asked.

'Half a dozen.'

'And they came straight to you.'

'I dare say they spoke to someone from Mountain Rescue, who told them I was as good a guide as they were going to get.' He paused. 'Not that there's much in the way of competition.' He paused again. 'They made me sign the Official Secrets Act.'

Rebus stared at him. 'Before or after?'

Mollison scratched behind one ear. 'Right at the start. They said it was standard procedure.' He looked at Rebus. 'Does that mean I shouldn't be talking to you?'

'I don't know . . . Did you find anything you think needs to be kept secret?'

Mollison considered his answer, then shook his head.

'Then it's all right,' Rebus told him. 'Probably just procedure after all.' Mollison set off again, Rebus keen to keep by his side, though the boots seemed to have other ideas. 'Has anyone been here since?' Rebus asked.

'We get plenty of walkers in the summer.'

'I meant from the army.'

Mollison's hand went to his ear again. 'There was one woman, middle of last year, I think it was . . . maybe more than that. She was trying to look like a tourist.'

'But not quite pulling it off?' Rebus suggested, going on to describe Whiteread.

'You've got her to a T,' Mollison admitted. Rebus and Siobhan shared a look.

'It may just be me,' Brimson said, pausing to catch his breath, 'but what has any of this got to do with what Lee did?'

'Maybe nothing,' Rebus conceded. 'But the exercise will do us good, all the same.'

As the walk continued, all of it uphill now, they fell quiet, saving energy. Eventually they emerged from the forest. The steep slope directly in front of them boasted only a few stunted trees. Grass, heather and bracken were broken by jagged stumps of rock. No more walking: if they wanted to go any further, it would be by climbing. Rebus craned his neck, seeking the distant summit.

'Don't worry,' Mollison said, 'we're not going up there.' He pointed upwards. 'Helicopter hit the rock-face about halfway to the top, came tumbling down here.' He waved an arm in the direction of the area around them. 'It was a big helicopter. Looked to me like it had too many propellers.'

'It was a Chinook,' Rebus explained. 'Two sets of rotor-blades, one lot at the front, one at the back.' He looked at Mollison. 'There must've been a lot of debris.'

'There was that. And the bodies . . . well, they were all over. One stuck on a ledge a hundred metres up. Myself and another fellow brought him down. They brought in a salvage team to take away what wreckage there was. But they had someone here to examine it. He didn't find anything.'

'Meaning it wasn't a missile?'

Mollison shook his head in agreement. He pointed back towards the tree-line. 'A lot of papers had been blown about. Mostly they were scouring the woods for them. Some of the sheets were stuck up trees. Would you believe they shimmied up to fetch them?'

'Did anyone say why?'

Mollison shook his head again. 'Not officially, but when the guys stopped to boil a brew – they were always doing that – I'd hear what they were saying. The helicopter was on its way to Ulster, majors and colonels on board. Had to be carrying documents they didn't want the terrorists to see. Might explain why they were carrying guns.'

'Guns?'

'The rescue team brought rifles with them. I thought it was a bit odd at the time.'

'Did you ever happen across any of these documents yourself?' Rebus asked. Mollison nodded.

'But I never looked at them. Just crunched them into a ball and brought them back.'

'Pity,' Rebus said, with the wryest smile he could manage.

'It's beautiful up here,' Siobhan said suddenly, shielding her eyes from the sun.

'It is, isn't it?' Mollison agreed, face breaking into a grin.

'Speaking of boiling a brew,' Brimson interrupted, 'got that flask of tea on you?' Siobhan opened her backpack and handed it over. The four of them passed the single plastic cup between them. It tasted the way tea always did from a flask: hot, but somehow not quite right. Rebus was walking around the area at the foot of the incline.

'Did anything strike you as strange?' he was asking Mollison.

'Strange?'

'About the mission . . . about the people or what they were up to?' Mollison shook his head. 'Did you get to know them at all?'

'We were only out here the two days.'

'You didn't know Lee Herdman?' Rebus had brought a photo with him. He handed it over.

'He's the one who shot the schoolkids?' Mollison waited for Rebus to nod, then stared at the photo again. 'I remember him, all right. Nice enough guy . . . quiet. Not exactly what you'd call a team player.'

'How do you mean?'

'He liked it best in the woods, tracking down the bits and pieces of paper. Every little scrap. The others joked about it. They'd have to call him two or three times when the tea was being poured.'

'Maybe he knew it wasn't worth hurrying for.' Brimson sniffed the surface of the cup.

'Are you saying I can't make tea?' Siobhan complained. Brimson held up his hands in surrender.

'How long were they here?' Rebus was asking Mollison.

'Two days. The salvage squad arrived on the second day. Took them another week to ship the wreckage out.'

'Did you get talking to them much?'

Mollison shrugged. 'Seemed nice enough lads. Very focused on their work.'

Rebus nodded and started walking into the forest. Not too far, but it was amazing how quickly you started to get the sense of being isolated, cut off from the still visible faces and still audible voices. What was that Brian Eno album? *Another Green World*. First there had been the world as seen from the air, and now this . . . equally alien and vibrant. Lee Herdman had walked into these woods and almost not come out again. His last mission before leaving the SAS. Had he learned something here? Found something?

Rebus had a sudden thought: you never really left the SAS. An indelible mark remained, just beyond your everday feelings and actions. You came to the realisation that there were other worlds, other realities. You'd had experiences beyond the usual. You'd been trained to see life as just another mission, filled with potential booby-traps and assassins. Rebus wondered how far he himself had been able to travel from his days in the Paras, and training for the SAS.

Had he been in freefall ever since?

And had Lee Herdman, like the airman of the poem, foreseen his own death?

He crouched down, ran a hand over the ground. Twigs and leaves, springy moss, a covering of native flowers and weeds. Saw in his mind's eye the helicopter hit the rock-face. Malfunction, or pilot error.

Malfunction, pilot error, or something more terrible . . .

Saw the sky explode as the fuel ignited, rotor blades

slowing, buckling. It would drop like a stone, bodies flying from it, concertinaing on impact. The dull thud of flesh hitting solid ground ... same noise Andy Callis's body would have made when it hit the railway line. The explosion sending the contents of the chopper bursting outwards, paper crisped at the edges or reduced to confetti. Secret papers, needing the SAS to recover them. And Lee Herdman busier than most as he plunged deeper and deeper into the woods. He recalled Teri Cotter's words about Herdman: *that was the thing about him ... like he had secrets*. He thought of the missing computer, the one Herdman had bought for his business. Where was it? Who had it? What secrets might it reveal?

'You okay?' Siobhan's voice. She was holding the cup, newly replenished. Rebus rose to his feet.

'Fine,' he said.

'I called you.'

'I didn't hear.' He took the cup from her.

'A touch of the Lee Herdmans?' she said.

'Could be.' He took a slurp of tea.

'Are we going to find anything here?'

He shrugged. 'Maybe it's enough just to see the place.'

'You think he took something, don't you?' Her eyes were on his. 'You think he took something, and the army want it back.' No longer a question, but a statement. Rebus nodded slowly.

'And this concerns us how?' she asked.

'Maybe because we don't like them,' Rebus answered. 'Or because whatever it is, they haven't found it yet, which means someone else might. Maybe someone found it last week ...'

'And when Herdman found out, he went berserk?'

Rebus shrugged again, handed back the empty cup. 'You like Brimson, don't you?'

She didn't blink, but couldn't hold his gaze.

'It's okay,' he said with a smile. She misread his tone, managed a glare.

'Oh, so I have your permission, do I?'

His turn to raise his hands in surrender. 'I just meant . . .' But he didn't think anything he said would help, so he let the words trail off. 'Tea's too strong, by the way,' he told her, making his way back towards the rock-face.

'At least I thought to bring some,' Siobhan muttered, tipping out the dregs.

On the flight back, Rebus sat silently in the back seat, though Siobhan had offered to swap. He kept his face to the window, as if transfixed by the passing views, giving Siobhan and Brimson the chance to talk. Brimson showed her the controls and how to use them, and made her promise to take a flying lesson from him. It was as if they'd forgotten about Lee Herdman, and maybe, Rebus was forced to reflect, they had a point. Most people in South Queensferry, even the families of the victims, just wanted to get on with their lives. What was past was past, and there was no changing it or making things right again. You had to let go sometime . . .

If you could.

Rebus closed his eyes against the sun's sudden glare. It bathed his face in warmth and light. He realised he was exhausted, in danger of dropping off to sleep; realised, too, that it didn't matter. Sleep was fine. But he awoke again minutes later with a start, having dreamed that he was alone in a strange city, clad only in an old-fashioned pair of striped pyjamas. Barefoot and with no money on him, seeking out anyone who might help, while all the time trying to look as if he fitted in. Peering through a café window, he'd spotted a man sliding a gun beneath a table, hiding it there on his lap. Rebus knowing he couldn't go in, not without money. So just standing there, watching with his palms pressed to the glass, trying not to make a fuss . . .

Blinking his eyes back into focus, he saw that they were over the Firth of Forth again, making their final approach. Brimson was talking.

'I often think about the damage a terrorist could do, even with something as small as a Cessna. You've got the dockyard, the ferry, road and rail bridges . . . airport near by.'

'They'd be spoilt for choice,' Siobhan agreed.

'I can think of bits of the city I'd rather see levelled,' Rebus commented.

'Ah, you're with us again, Inspector. I can only apologise that our company wasn't more sparkling.' Brimson and Siobhan shared a smile, letting Rebus know he hadn't been too sorely missed.

The landing was smooth, Brimson taxiing towards where Siobhan's car sat waiting. Climbing out, Rebus shook Brimson's hand.

'Thanks for letting me tag along,' Brimson said.

'It's me who should be thanking you. Send us the bill for your fuel and your time.'

Brimson just shrugged, turned to squeeze Siobhan's hand, holding on to it a little longer than necessary. Wagged a finger of his free hand at her.

'Remember, I'll be expecting you.'

She smiled. 'A promise is a promise, Doug. But meantime, I wonder if I can be cheeky . . .?'

'Go ahead.'

'I just wondered if I could take a peek at the corporate jet, to see how the other half lives.'

He stared at her for a moment, then smiled back. 'No problem. It's in the hangar.' Brimson started to lead the way. 'Coming, Inspector?'

'I'll wait here,' Rebus said. After they'd gone, he managed to get a cigarette lit, sheltering by the side of the Cessna. They reappeared five minutes later, Brimson's good humour evaporating as he saw the stub of Rebus's cigarette.

'Strictly forbidden,' he said. 'Fire hazard, you understand.'

Rebus gave a shrug of apology, nipped the cigarette and

crushed it underfoot. As he followed Siobhan to her car, Brimson was getting into the Land Rover, ready to drive to the gate and unlock it.

'Nice guy,' Rebus said.

'Yes,' Siobhan agreed. 'Nice guy.'

'You really think so?'

She looked at him. 'Don't you?'

Rebus shrugged. 'I get the feeling he's a collector.'

'Of what?'

Rebus thought for a moment. 'Of interesting specimens . . . people like Herdman and Niles.'

'He knows the Cotters, too, don't forget.' Siobhan's hackles weren't ready to go down just yet.

'Look, I'm not saying . . .'

'You're warning me off him, aren't you?'

Rebus stayed silent.

'Aren't you?' she repeated.

'I just don't want all that corporate jet glamour going to your head.' He paused. 'What was it like anyway?'

She glared at him, then relented. 'Smallish. Leather seats. They do champagne and hot meals on the flights.'

'Don't go getting any ideas.'

She gave a twitch of the mouth, asked where he wanted to go, and he told her: Craigmillar Police Station. The detective there was called Blake. He was a DC, less than a year out of uniform. Rebus didn't mind that: it meant he'd be keen to prove himself. So Rebus told him what he knew about Andy Callis and the Lost Boys. Blake kept a look of concentration on his face throughout, stopping Rebus from time to time and asking a question, noting everything on a lined A4 pad. Siobhan sat in the room with them, arms folded, mostly just staring at the wall ahead. Rebus got the feeling she was thinking of aeroplane rides . . .

At the end of the interview, Rebus asked if there'd been any progress. Blake shook his head.

'Still no witnesses. Dr Curt's doing the autopsy this

afternoon.' He checked his watch. 'I might head on down there. You're welcome to . . .'

But Rebus was shaking his head. He had no wish to see his friend dissected. 'Will you bring Rab Fisher in?'

Blake nodded. 'Don't worry about that, I'll have a word with him.'

'Don't expect much in the way of cooperation,' Rebus warned.

'I'll talk to him.' The young man's tone told Rebus that he was close to pushing too hard.

'Nobody likes to be told how to do their job,' Rebus acknowledged with a smile.

'At least not until after they've screwed it up.' Blake got to his feet, Rebus doing the same. The two men shook hands.

'Nice guy,' Rebus said to Siobhan, as they walked back to her car.

'Too cocky by half,' she responded. 'He doesn't think he's going to screw anything up . . . ever.'

'Then he'll learn the hard way.'

'I hope so. I really do.'

18

The plan had been for them to head back to Siobhan's flat, so she could cook the dinner she'd been promising. They were quiet in the car, and as they got to the junction of Leith Street and York Place, the lights were against them. Rebus turned to her.

'Drink first?' he suggested.

'With me as designated driver?'

'You could take a taxi home after, pick up the car in the morning . . .'

She was staring at the red light, making up her mind. When it turned green, she signalled to move into the next lane across, heading for Queen Street.

'I'll assume we're gracing the Ox with our precious custom,' Rebus said.

'Would anywhere else suit sir's stringent requirements?'

'Tell you what . . . we'll have one drink there, and after that you can choose.'

'Deal.'

So they had their one drink in the smoky front room of the Oxford Bar, the place loud with after-work chat, the late-afternoon drifting towards evening. Ancient Egypt on the Discovery Channel. Siobhan was watching the regulars: more entertaining than anything the TV could provide. She noticed that Harry, the dour barman, was smiling.

'He seems unusually chipper,' she commented to Rebus.

'I think young Harry's in love.' Rebus was trying to make his pint last: Siobhan still hadn't intimated whether they'd be sticking around for a second drink. She'd ordered a half of cider, already mostly gone. 'Want the other half of that?' he asked, nodding towards her glass.

'One drink, you said.'

'Just to keep me company.' He held his own glass aloft, showing how much was left. But she shook her head.

'I know what you're trying to do,' she told him. He attempted a look of shocked innocence, knowing it wouldn't fool her for a second. A few more regulars were squeezing into the mêlée. There were three women seated at a table in the otherwise empty back room, but none in the front bar save Siobhan. She wrinkled her nose at the crush and steady escalation in noise, put her glass to her lips and drained it.

'Come on then,' she said.

'Where?' Rebus affected a frown. But she just shook her head: not telling. 'My jacket's hanging up,' he told her. He'd taken it off in the hope of gaining a psychological advantage: a sign of how comfortable he felt here.

'Then get it,' she ordered. So he did, and gulped down the remains of his own drink before following her outside.

'Fresh air,' she was saying, breathing deeply. The car was parked on North Castle Street, but they walked past it, heading for George Street. Directly ahead of them, the Castle was illuminated against the ink-dark sky. They turned left, Rebus feeling a stiffness in both legs, the legacy of his trek across Jura.

'Long soak for me tonight,' he commented.

'Bet that was the most exercise you've taken this year,' Siobhan replied with a smile.

'This decade,' Rebus corrected her. She'd stopped at some steps and was heading down. Her chosen bar was tucked away beneath pavement level, a shop directly above it. The interior was chic, with subdued lighting and music.

'Your first time in here?' Siobhan asked.

'What do you think?' He was heading for the bar, but Siobhan tugged his arm and gestured towards a free booth.

'It's table service,' she said as they sat down. A waitress was already standing in front of them. Siobhan ordered a gin and tonic, Rebus a Laphroaig. When his malt arrived, he lifted the glass and peered at it, as if disapproving of the size of measure. Siobhan stirred her own drink, mashing the slice of lime against the ice-cubes.

'Want to keep the tab open?' the waitress asked.

'Yes, please,' Siobhan said. Then, when the waitress had gone: 'Are we any nearer finding out why Herdman shot those kids?'

Rebus shrugged. 'I think maybe we'll only know when we get there.'

'And everything up to that point . . .?'

'Is potentially useful,' Rebus said, knowing this wasn't how she'd have chosen to finish the sentence. He lifted his glass to his mouth, but it was already empty. No sign of the waitress. Behind the bar, one of the staff was mixing a cocktail.

'Friday night, out at that railway line,' Siobhan was saying, 'Silvers told me something.' She paused. 'He said the Herdman case was being handed over to DMC.'

'Makes sense,' Rebus muttered. But with Claverhouse and Ormiston running the show, there'd be no place for him or Siobhan. 'Didn't there used to be a band called DMC, or am I thinking of Elton John's record company?'

Siobhan was nodding. 'Run DMC. I think they were a rap band.'

'Rap with a capital C, most likely.'

'No match for the Rolling Stones certainly.'

'Don't knock the Stones, DC Clarke. None of the stuff you listen to would exist without them.'

'A point on which you've probably had many an argument.' She went back to stirring her drink. Rebus still couldn't see their waitress.

'I'm getting a refill,' he said, sliding out of the booth. He wished Siobhan hadn't mentioned Friday night. All weekend, Andy Callis hadn't been far from his thoughts. He kept thinking of how different sequences of events – tiny chinks of altered time and space – could have saved him. Probably could have saved Lee Herdman, too . . . and stopped Robert Niles killing his wife.

And stopped Rebus from scalding his hands.

Everything came down to the most minute contingencies, and to tinker with any single one of them was to change the future out of all recognition. He knew there was some argument in science, something to do with butterflies flapping their wings in the jungle . . . Maybe if he flapped his own arms he would end up getting served. The barman was pouring a bright pink concoction into a martini glass, turning away from Rebus to serve it. The bar was double-sided, dividing the room in half. Rebus peered across into the gloom. Not too many punters in the other half. A mirror-image of booths and squashy chairs, same decor and clientele. Rebus knew that he stood out by about thirty years. One young man had ranged himself across an entire banquette, arms stretched out behind him, legs crossed, looking cocksure and relaxed, wanting to be seen . . .

Seen by everyone but Rebus. The barman was ready to take Rebus's order, but Rebus shook his head, walked to the end of the bar and through the short corridor which led to the bar's other half. Across the floor until he was standing in front of Peacock Johnson.

'Mr Rebus . . .' Johnson's arms fell to his sides. He glanced to right and left, as if expecting Rebus to have reinforcements. 'The dapper detective, and no mistake. Looking for yours truly?'

'Not especially.' Rebus slid into the space across from Johnson. The young man's choice of Hawaiian shirt didn't look quite so garish in this light. A new waitress had appeared, and Rebus ordered a double. 'On my friend's tab,' he added, nodding across the table.

Johnson just shrugged magnanimously, and ordered

another glass of Merlot for himself. 'So this is by way of a pure and actual coincidence?' he asked.

'Where's your mongrel?' Rebus said, looking around.

'The wee evil fellow doesn't quite have the cachet for an establishment of this calibre.'

'You tie him up outside?'

Johnson grinned. 'I let him off the leash now and again.'

'An owner could get fined for that sort of thing.'

'He only bites when the Peacock gives the order.' Johnson finished the dregs of his wine, just as the new drinks arrived. The waitress put down a bowl of rice crackers between the two glasses. 'Cheers then,' Johnson said, hoisting the Merlot.

Rebus ignored this. 'I was just thinking of you actually,' he said.

'The purest of thoughts, I don't doubt.'

'Funnily enough, no.' Rebus leaned across the table, keeping his voice low. 'In fact, if you were a mind-reader, they'd have scared the shit out of you.' He had Johnson's attention now. 'Know who died last Friday? Andy Callis. You remember him, don't you?'

'Can't say I do.'

'He was the armed-response cop who stopped your friend Rab Fisher.'

'Rab's not so much a friend as a casual acquaintance.'

'Acquainted enough for you to sell him that gun.'

'A replica, if you don't mind me reminding you.' Johnson was diving into the bowl of snacks, holding his paw to his mouth and feeding them in morsel by morsel, so that bits flew out as he spoke. 'No case to answer, and I resent any implication to the contrary.'

'Except that Fisher was going around scaring people, and it nearly got him killed.'

'No case to answer,' Johnson repeated.

'And he turned my friend into a nervous wreck, and now that friend's dead. You sold someone a gun, and someone else ended up dying.'

'A replica, perfectly legitimate at this point in time and space.' Johnson was trying not to listen, making to grab another fistful of crackers. Rebus swiped at the hand, scattering the bowl and its contents. He grabbed the young man's wrist. Squeezed it hard.

'You're about as legitimate as every other bad bastard I've ever come across.'

Johnson was trying to free his hand. 'And you're pure as the driven, is that what you're saying? Everybody knows the lengths *you'll* go to, Rebus!'

'And what lengths are those?'

'Anything that'll get *me*! I know you tried fitting me up, saying I'm retooling deactivated guns.'

'Says who?' Rebus had released his grip.

'Says everyone!' There were flecks of saliva on Johnson's chin, bits of snack-food mixed in with them. 'Christ, you'd have to be deaf in this town not to hear.'

It was true: Rebus had been putting out feelers. He'd wanted Peacock Johnson. He'd wanted something – *something* – as repayment for Callis leaving the force. And though people had shaken their heads and muttered words like 'replicas' and 'trophies' and 'deactivated', Rebus had gone on asking.

And somehow, Johnson had got to hear of it.

'How long have you known?' Rebus asked now.

'What?'

'How long?'

But Johnson just picked up his glass, eyes beady, waiting for Rebus to try to knock it from his grasp. Rebus lifted his own glass, drained it in one burning mouthful.

'Something you ought to know,' he said, nodding slowly. 'I can hold a grudge for a lifetime: just you watch me.'

'Even though I've done nothing?'

'Oh, you'll have done *something*, believe me.' Rebus made to stand. 'I just haven't found out what it is yet, that's all.' He winked and turned away. Heard the table being pushed aside, looked round and Johnson was on his feet, fists clenched.

'Let's settle it now!' he was shouting. Rebus slipped his hands into his pockets.

'I'd prefer to wait for the court case, if that's all right with you,' he said.

'No way! I'm sick fed up of this!'

'Good,' Rebus said. He saw Siobhan emerging from the corridor, looking at him in disbelief. Probably thought he'd gone to the toilet. Her eyes said it all: *I can't leave you five damned minutes . . .*

'Any trouble here?' The question coming not from Siobhan but from some sort of doorman, thick-necked and wearing a tight black suit over a black poloneck. He was fitted with an earpiece and microphone. His shaven head shone beneath what light there was.

'Just a little argument,' Rebus assured him. 'In fact, maybe you can settle it: name of Elton John's old record label?'

The doorman looked nonplussed. The barman had his hand raised. Rebus nodded at him. 'DJM,' the barman said.

Rebus snapped his fingers. 'That's the one! Chalk up a drink for yourself, anything you like . . .' He headed for the corridor, pointed back towards Peacock Johnson. 'On that little bastard's tab . . .'

'You never talk much about your army days,' Siobhan said, bringing two plates through from the kitchen. Rebus had already been provided with a tray, knife and fork. Condiments were on the floor at his feet. He gave a nod of thanks, accepting the plate: a grilled pork chop with baked potato and a corn-cob.

'This looks great,' he said, lifting his wine-glass. 'Compliments to the chef.'

'I microwaved the potatoes, and the corn came out of the freezer.'

Rebus put a finger to his lips. 'Never give away your secrets.'

'A lesson you've taken to heart.' She blew on a forkful of pork. 'Want me to repeat the question?'

'Thing is, Siobhan, it wasn't a question.'

She thought back, and saw that he was right. 'Nevertheless,' she said.

'You want me to answer?' He watched her nod, then took a sip of his wine. Chilean red, she'd told him. Three quid a bottle. 'Mind if I eat first?'

'You can't eat and talk at the same time?'

'Bad manners, so my mum used to tell me.'

'You always listened to your parents?'

'Always.'

'And took their advice as gospel?' He nodded, chewing on some potato skin. 'Then how come we're talking and eating at the same time?'

Rebus washed the mouthful down with more wine. 'Okay, I give in. To answer the question you didn't ask, yes.' She was expecting more, but he was concentrating on his food again.

'Yes what?'

'Yes, it's true I don't talk much about my army days.'

Siobhan exhaled noisily. 'I'd get more chat out of one of the clients down at the mortuary.' She stopped, squeezed shut her eyes for a second. 'Sorry, I shouldn't have said that.'

'It's okay.' But Rebus's chewing had slowed. Two of the current 'clients': family member and ex-colleague. Strange to think of them lying on adjacent metal trays in the mortuary's chilled lockers. 'Thing about my army days is, I've spent years trying to forget them.'

'Why?'

'All sorts of reasons. I shouldn't have signed on the dotted line in the first place. Then I woke up and I was in Ulster, aiming a rifle at kids armed with Molotovs. Ended up trying for the SAS and getting my brain scrambled in the process.' He gave a shrug. 'That's about all there is to it.'

'So why did you join the police?'

He raised the glass to his mouth. 'Who else was going to take me?' He put the tray aside, leaned down to pour more wine. Raised the bottle towards Siobhan, but she shook her head. 'Now you know why they've never got me to front a recruiting drive.'

She looked at his plate. Most of the chop was still left. 'You going veggie on me?'

He patted his stomach. 'It's great, but I'm not that hungry.'

She thought for a moment. 'It's the meat, isn't it? It hurts your hands when you try to cut it.'

He shook his head. 'I'm just full, that's all.' But he could see she knew she was right. She started eating again, while he concentrated on the wine.

'I think you're a lot like Lee Herdman,' she said at last.

'A backhanded compliment if ever I heard one.'

'People thought they knew him, but they didn't. There was so much he managed to keep hidden.'

'And that's me, is it?'

She nodded, holding his stare. 'Why did you go back to Martin Fairstone's house? I get the feeling it wasn't just about me.'

'You "get the feeling"?' He peered down into his wine, seeing his reflection there, red-hued and wavering. 'I knew he'd given you that black eye.'

'Which gave you an excuse to go talk to him . . . but what was it you really wanted?'

'Fairstone and Johnson were friends. I needed some ammo on Johnson.' He paused, realising 'ammo' was not the most subtle choice of word.

'Did you get any?'

Rebus shook his head. 'Fairstone and Peacock had had a falling-out. Fairstone hadn't seen him in weeks.'

'Why had they fallen out?'

'He wouldn't say exactly. I got the feeling a woman might've been involved.'

'Does Peacock have a girlfriend?'

'One for every day of the year.'

'So maybe it was Fairstone's girlfriend?'

Rebus nodded. 'The blonde from the Boatman's. What was her name again?'

'Rachel.'

'And there's no good reason we can think of why she was in South Queensferry on Friday?'

Siobhan shook her head.

'But Peacock popped up in the town, too, night of the vigil.'

'Coincidence?'

'What else could it be?' Rebus asked wryly. He stood up, taking the bottle with him. 'You better help me out with this.' Came forward to pour some wine into her glass, then emptied what was left into his own. He stayed standing, walked over to her window. 'You really think I'm like Lee Herdman?'

'I don't think either of you ever really managed to leave the past behind.'

He turned to look at her. She raised an eyebrow, inviting a comeback, but he just smiled and turned back to stare out at the night.

'And maybe you're a bit like Doug Brimson, too,' she went on. 'Remember what you said about him?'

'What?'

'You said he collected people.'

'And that's what I do?'

'It might explain your interest in Andy Callis ... and why it pisses you off to see Kate with Jack Bell.'

He turned slowly to face her, arms folded. 'Does that make you one of my specimens?'

'I don't know. What do *you* reckon?'

'I reckon you're tougher than that.'

'You better believe it,' she said with just the hint of a smile.

When he'd called for the taxi, he'd given Arden Street as the destination, but that had been for Siobhan's benefit. He told the driver there'd been a change of plan: they'd be making a short stop at Leith Police Station before heading out to South Queensferry. At journey's end, Rebus asked for a receipt, thinking he could maybe charge it to the inquiry. He'd have to be quick though: he couldn't see Claverhouse giving the nod to a twenty-quid taxi ride.

He walked down the dark vennel, pushing open the main door. There was no police guard any more, no one checking the comings and goings at Lee Herdman's address. Rebus climbed the stairs, listening for noise from the other two flats. He thought he could hear a TV set. Certainly he could smell the aftermath of an evening meal. A growl from his stomach reminded him that he maybe should have tried to eat more of the pork, and hang the pain. He took out the key to Herdman's flat, the one he'd picked up at the station in Leith. It was a shiny, brand new copy of the original, and took a bit of manoeuvring before it would meet with the tumblers, opening the door for him. Once inside, he closed the door behind him and switched on the hall light. The place was cold. Electricity hadn't been disconnected yet, but someone had thought to turn off the central heating. Herdman's widow had been asked if she would come north to empty the flat of its contents, but she had declined. *What could that bastard have that I'd possibly want?*

A good question, and one Rebus was here to consider. Lee Herdman assuredly had had *something*. Something people had wanted. He studied the back of the door. Bolts top and bottom, and two mortice locks as well as the Yale. The mortices would deter housebreakers, but the bolts were for when Herdman was at home. What had he been so afraid of? Rebus folded his arms and took a few steps back. There was one obvious answer to his question. The drug-dealing Herdman had been afraid of a bust. Rebus had encountered plenty of dealers over the course of his career. Usually they lived in council flats on high-rise schemes, and their doors were steel-plated, offering considerably more resistance than Herdman's. It seemed to Rebus that Herdman's security measures were there to buy him a certain amount of time, and nothing more. Time, perhaps, to flush the evidence, but Rebus didn't think so. There was nothing about the flat to suggest that it had been used at any time as a drug factory. Besides, Herdman could boast so many other hiding places: the boathouse, the boats themselves. He had no need to use his flat for storage. What then? Rebus turned and walked into the living room, seeking and finding the light switch.

What then?

He tried to think of himself as Herdman, then realised he didn't need to. Hadn't Siobhan hinted as much? *I think you're a lot like Lee Herdman.* He closed his eyes, saw the room he was standing in as his own. This was his domain. He was in charge here. But say someone wanted in . . . some uninvited guest. He would hear them. Maybe they would try picking the locks, but the bolts would scupper them. So then they'd have to shoulder the door. And he'd have time . . . time to fetch the gun from wherever it was hidden. The Mac-10 was kept in the boathouse, in case anyone came there. The Brocock was kept right here, in the wardrobe, surrounded by pictures of guns. Herdman's little gun shrine. The pistol would give him the upper hand, because he didn't expect the visitors to be armed. They might have questions, might want to take him away, but the Brocock would deter them.

Rebus knew who Herdman had been expecting: maybe not Simms and Whiteread exactly, but people like them. People who might want to take him away for questioning . . . questions about Jura, the helicopter crash, the papers fluttering from the trees. Something Herdman had taken from the crash-site, could one of the kids have stolen it from him? Maybe at one of his parties? But the dead boys hadn't known him, hadn't come to his parties. Only James Bell, the sole survivor. Rebus sat down in Herdman's armchair, his palms resting against its arms. Shooting the other two in order to scare James? So that James would tell all? No, no, no, because then why would Herdman turn the gun on himself? James Bell . . . so self-contained and apparently unperturbable . . . flicking through gun magazines to study the model that had wounded him. He, too, was an interesting specimen.

Rebus rubbed his forehead softly with one gloved hand. He felt close to an answer, so close he could taste it. He stood up again, walking into the kitchen and opening the fridge. There was food in there: an unopened packet of cheese, some slices of bacon and a box of eggs. Dead man's food, he thought, I can't eat it. He went to the bedroom instead. Not bothering this time with the light: enough was spilling through the open doorway.

Who was Lee Herdman? A man who'd abandoned career and family to head north. Starting a one-man enterprise, living in a one-bedroom flat. Settling by the coast, his boats providing a means of escape whenever necessary. No close relationships. Brimson was about the only friend he seemed to have who was near his own age. He coveted teenagers instead: because they wouldn't be hiding anything from him; because he knew he could deal with them; because they'd be impressed by him. But not just any kids: they had to be outsiders, had to be cut from similar cloth . . . It struck Rebus that Brimson seemed to run a one-man show, too, and had few ties, if any at all. Spent as much time as he liked at one remove from the world. Ex-services, too.

Suddenly, Rebus heard a tapping. He froze, trying to place it. Coming from downstairs? No: the front door. Someone was knocking at the door. Rebus padded back down the hall and put his eye to the peep-hole. Recognised the face and opened up.

'Evening, James,' he said. 'Nice to see you back on your feet.'

It took James Bell a moment to place Rebus. He slowly nodded a greeting, looking past his shoulder and down the hall.

'I saw lights on, wondered if anyone was here.'

Rebus pulled the door open a little wider. 'Coming in?'

'Is it all right . . .?'

'There's nobody else here.'

'I just thought . . . maybe you're doing a search or something.'

'Nothing like that.' Rebus gestured with his head, and James Bell walked in. His left arm was in its sling, his right hand cradling it. A long black woollen Crombie-style coat was draped around his shoulders, flapping to show its crimson lining. 'What brings you here?'

'I was just walking . . .'

'You're a ways from home though.'

James looked at him. 'You've been to my house . . . maybe you can understand.'

Rebus nodded, closing the door again. 'Putting a bit of distance between your mum and yourself?'

'Yes.' James was looking around the hall, as if seeing it for the first time. 'And my dad.'

'Keeping busy, is he?'

'God knows.'

'I don't think I ever got round to asking . . .' Rebus said.

'What?'

'How many times you've been here.'

James shrugged with his right shoulder. 'Not that many.' Rebus was leading the way to the living room.

'You still haven't said why you're here.'

'I thought I had.'

'Not in so many words.'

'I suppose South Queensferry seemed as good a place as any for a walk.'

'You didn't walk here from Barnton though.'

James shook his head. 'I was hopping buses, just for the hell of it. One of them ended up bringing me here. When I saw the lights . . .'

'You wondered who was here? Who were you expecting to find?'

'Police, I suppose. Who else would be here?' He was studying the room. 'Actually, there was one thing . . .'

'Yes?'

'A book of mine. Lee borrowed it, and I thought I might retrieve it before everything gets . . . well, before the place is emptied.'

'Good thinking.'

James's hand went to his injured shoulder. 'Bloody thing itches, if you can believe that.'

'I can believe it.'

James smiled suddenly. 'I'm at a bit of a disadvantage here . . . I don't think I ever caught your name.'

'It's Rebus. Detective Inspector.'

The young man nodded. 'My dad's mentioned you.'

'Casting me in a flattering light, no doubt.' It was hard to meet the son's eyes without being tricked into seeing the father peering from behind them.

'I'm afraid he sees incompetence wherever he looks . . . kith and kin not excluded.'

Rebus had perched on the arm of the sofa, nodding towards the chair, but James Bell seemed happier on his feet. 'Did you ever find the gun?' Rebus asked. James seemed puzzled by the question. 'The time I visited,' Rebus explained. 'You had a gun magazine, looking for the Brocock.'

'Oh, right.' James nodded to himself. 'There were photos of it in the papers. My dad's been keeping all the stories, thinks he can spearhead a campaign.'

'You don't sound altogether approving.'

James's eyes hardened. 'Maybe that's because . . .' He broke off.

'Because what?'

'Because I've become useful to him, not for what I am but because of what happened.' His hand went to his shoulder again.

'You can never trust a politician,' Rebus commiserated.

'Lee told me something once. He said, "If you outlaw guns, the only people who have access to them are the outlaws."' James smiled at the memory.

'Seems he was an outlaw all right. Two unlicensed guns at the very least. Did he ever tell you why he felt the need to keep a gun?'

'I just thought he was interested in them . . . his background and everything.'

'You never got the sense that he was expecting trouble?'

'What sort of trouble?'

'I don't know,' Rebus conceded.

'You're saying he had enemies?'

'Ever wonder why he had so many locks on his door?'

James walked to the doorway and looked down the hall. 'I put that down to his background, too. Like when he went to the pub, he always sat in the corner, facing the door.'

Rebus had to smile, knowing he did the self-same thing. 'So he could check whoever came in?'

'That's what he told me.'

'The two of you sound as if you were pretty close.'

'Close enough for him to end up shooting me.' James's eyes went to his shoulder.

'Ever steal anything from him, James?'

The young man's brow furrowed. 'Why would I do that?'

Rebus just shrugged. 'Did you though?'

'Never.'

'Did Lee ever mention anything going missing? Ever seem agitated to you?'

The young man shook his head. 'I don't really see what you're getting at.'

'That paranoia of his, I just wondered how far it extended.'

'I didn't say he was paranoid.'

'The locks, the corner seat in the pub . . .'

'That just comes of being careful, wouldn't you say?'

'Maybe.' Rebus paused. 'You liked him, didn't you?'

'Probably more than he liked me.'

Rebus was remembering his last meeting with James Bell, and what Siobhan had said afterwards. 'What about Teri Cotter?' he asked.

'What about her?' James had taken a couple of steps back into the room, but seemed still restless.

'We think Herdman and Teri may have been an item.'

'So?'

'Did you know?'

James made to shrug with both shoulders, ended up flinching in pain.

'Forgot your wound for a moment there, eh?' Rebus commented. 'I remember you had a computer in your room. Ever visited Teri's website?'

'Didn't know she had one.'

Rebus nodded slowly. 'Derek Renshaw never mentioned it then?'

'Derek?'

Rebus was still nodding. 'Seems Derek was a bit of a fan. You were often in the common room, same time as him and Tony Jarvies . . . thought they might've talked about it.'

James was shaking his head, looking thoughtful. 'Not that I remember,' he said.

'Not to worry then.' Rebus made to stand up. 'This book of yours, can I help you look for it?'

'Book?'

'The one you're looking for.'

James smiled at his own stupidity. 'Yes, sure. That'd be

great.' He looked around the cluttered room, walked over to the desk. 'Hang on a sec,' he said, 'this is it.' He held up the paperback for Rebus to see.

'What's it about?'

'A soldier who went off the rails.'

'Tried killing his wife, then leapt from an aeroplane?'

'You know the story?'

Rebus nodded. James flicked through the book, then tapped it against his thigh. 'Reckon I've got what I came for,' he said.

'Anything else you want to take?' Rebus lifted a CD. 'It'll probably go into a skip, to be honest.'

'Will it?'

'His wife doesn't seem interested.'

'What a waste . . .' Rebus held out the CD, but James shook his head. 'I couldn't. It wouldn't seem right.'

Rebus nodded, remembering his own reticence in front of the fridge.

'I'll leave you to it, Inspector.' James tucked the book beneath his arm, stretched out his right hand for Rebus to shake. The coat slipped from his shoulder, crumpling to the floor. Rebus stepped around him and picked it up, replacing it.

'Thank you,' James Bell said. 'I'll see myself out.'

'Cheers, James. Good luck to you.'

Rebus waited in the living room, chin resting on one gloved hand as he listened to the front door open and then close. James was a long way from home . . . drawn by a light shining in a dead man's house. Rebus still wondered who the young man had expected to find . . . Muffled footsteps descending the stone stairs. Rebus crossed to the desk and shuffled through the remaining books. They all had a military theme, but Rebus was confident he knew which one the young man had taken.

The same one Siobhan had held up on their first visit to the flat.

The one from which Teri Cotter's photo had fallen . . .

Day Six

Tuesday

19

Tuesday morning, Rebus left his flat, walked to the foot of Marchmont Road, and proceeded across the Meadows, an area of grassland leading to the university. Students passed him, some of them on creaky bicycles. Others shuffled sleepily towards classes. The day was overcast, the sky's colour mirroring the slate-grey roofs. Rebus was headed for George IV Bridge. By now, he knew the drill at the National Library. The guard would allow you through, but you then had to climb the stairs and convince the librarian on duty that your need was desperate and no other library would do. Rebus showed his warrant card, explained what he wanted, and was directed towards the microfiche room. That was the way they kept the old papers nowadays: as rolls of microfilm. Years back, working one particular case, Rebus had taken a seat in the reading room, a servitor dutifully unloading a trolley of bound broadsheets on to the desk. Now, it was a case of switching on a screen, and threading a spool of tape through the machine.

Rebus had no specific dates in mind. He'd decided to go back a full month before the crash on Jura and just let the days roll across his vision, see what was happening back then. By the time he got to the day of the crash, he had a pretty good idea. The story had made the front page of the *Scotsman*, accompanied by photos of two of the victims: Brigadier General Stuart Phillips and Major Kevin Spark. A day later, Phillips being Scots-born, the paper ran a lengthy obituary, giving Rebus more than he needed to know about the man's upbringing and professional accomplishments. He checked the notes he'd been scribbling and wound the film to its end, replacing it with a roll from the previous two weeks, eventually spooling back to the date in his notes, the story about the IRA ceasefire in Northern Ireland, and the part being played in ongoing negotiations by Brigadier General Stuart Phillips. Preconditions being discussed; mistrustful paramilitaries on both sides; splinter groups to be appeased . . . Rebus tapped his pen against his teeth, until he noticed another user near by frowning. Rebus mouthed the word 'sorry' and cast his eyes over some of the other stories in the paper: earth summits, foreign wars, football reports . . . The face of Christ found in a pomegranate; a cat that got lost, but found its way back to its owners, even though they'd moved house in the interim . . .

The photo of the cat reminded him of Boethius. He went back to the main desk, asked where the encyclopaedias were kept. He looked up Boethius. Roman philosopher, translator, politician . . . accused of treason and while awaiting execution wrote *The Consolations of Philosophy*, in which he argued that everything was changeable and lacked any measure of certainty . . . everything except virtue. Rebus wondered if the book might help him comprehend Derek Renshaw's fate, and its effect on those closest to him. Somehow he doubted it. In his universe, the guilty too often went unpunished, while the victims went unnoticed. Bad things were always happening to good people, and vice versa. If God had planned things that way, the old bastard was blessed with a sick sense of humour. Easier to say that there was no plan, that random chance had taken Lee Herdman into that classroom.

But Rebus suspected that this wasn't true either . . .

He decided to head out on to George IV Bridge for coffee and a cigarette. He'd spoken to Siobhan first thing by telephone, letting her know he'd be busy in town and wouldn't be hooking up with her. She hadn't sounded too bothered; hadn't even seemed curious. She seemed to be drifting away from him, not that he could blame her. He'd always been a magnet for trouble, and her career prospects wouldn't exactly be enhanced by his proximity. All the same, he thought there was more to it than that. Maybe she really did see him as a collector, as someone who got too close to certain people, people he cared about or was interested in . . . uncomfortably close at times. He thought of Miss Teri's website, how it maintained an illusion that the viewer was connected to her. A one-way relationship: they could see her, but she couldn't see them. Was she another example of a 'specimen'?

Seated in the Elephant House coffee shop, sipping a large milky coffee, Rebus took out his mobile. He'd smoked a cigarette on the pavement before coming in: never knew these days whether smoking would be allowed indoors or not. He punched buttons with his thumbnail, connecting to Bobby Hogan's mobile.

'Goon Squad taken over yet, Bobby?' he asked.

'Not completely.' Hogan knowing who Rebus meant: Claverhouse and Ormiston.

'But they're in the area?'

'Pallying up to your girlfriend.'

It took Rebus a moment to work it out. 'Whiteread?' he guessed.

'That's the one.'

'Nothing Claverhouse would like more than hearing a few old stories about me.'

'Might explain the grin on his face.'

'Exactly how *persona non grata* do you reckon I am?'

'Nobody's said. Whereabouts are you anyway? Is that an espresso machine I can hear hissing in the background?'

'Mid-morning break, guv'nor, that's all. I'm digging into Herdman's time in the regiment.'

'You know I fell at the first hurdle?'

'Don't worry about it, Bobby. I couldn't see the SAS handing over his file without a bigger fight than we can put up.'

'So how are you managing to look into his army record?'

'Laterally, you might say.'

'Care to enlighten me further?'

'Not until I've found something useful.'

'John . . . the parameters of the inquiry are shifting.'

'In plain English, Bobby?'

'The "why" doesn't seem to matter so much any more.'

'Because the drugs angle's a lot more interesting?' Rebus guessed. 'Are you shutting me down, Bobby?'

'Not my style, John, you know that. What I'm saying is, it may be out of my hands.'

'And Claverhouse isn't running my fan club?'

'He's not even on the mailing list.'

Rebus was thoughtful. Hogan filled the silence. 'Way things are going, I might as well join you for that coffee . . .'

'You're being sidelined?'

'From referee to fourth official.'

Rebus had to smile at the image. Claverhouse as ref; Ormiston and Whiteread his linesmen . . . 'Any other news?' he asked.

'Herdman's boat, the one with the dope on it, seems that when he purchased it he paid the bulk in cash – dollars, to be precise. The international currency of illegal substances. More than a few trips to Rotterdam this past year, most he tried to keep hidden.'

'Looks good, doesn't it?'

'Claverhouse is wondering if there might be a porn angle, too.'

'The man's mind is a sewer.'

'He may have a point: plenty of hard-core to be found in places like Rotterdam. Thing is, our friend Herdman seems to have been a bit of a lad.'

Rebus's eyes narrowed. 'Defined as . . .?'

'We took his computer from home, remember?' Rebus remembered: it had already gone by the time he'd made his first visit to Herdman's flat. 'The boffins at Howdenhall were able to pinpoint sites he'd been using. A lot of them were aimed at peepers.'

'You mean voyeurs?'

'That's what I mean. Mr Herdman liked to *watch*. And how about this: some of the sites are registered in the Netherlands. Herdman paid his dues every month by credit card.'

Rebus was staring out of the window. It had started to rain, a softly angled drizzle. People were lowering their heads, walking faster. 'Ever heard of a porn baron paying to watch the stuff, Bobby?'

'First time for everything.'

'It's a non-starter, trust me . . .' Rebus paused, eyes narrowing. 'You've looked at these sites?'

'Duty-bound to study the evidence, John.'

'Describe them.'

'You after a cheap thrill?'

'For those I go to Frank Zappa. Humour me, Bobby.'

'A girl sits on a bed, she's wearing stockings, suspenders . . . all that sort of stuff. Then you type in whatever it is you want her to do.'

'Do we know what Herdman liked them to do?'

'Afraid not. Apparently there's only so much the boffins can extract.'

'You got a list of the sites, Bobby?' Rebus was forced to listen to a low chuckle on the line. 'I'm just hazarding a guess here, but was there one called Miss Teri's or Dark Entry?'

Silence at the other end, and then: 'How did you know?'

'I was a mind-reader in a previous life.'

'I mean it, John: how did you know?'

'See? I knew you were going to ask that.' Rebus decided to put Hogan out of his misery. 'Miss Teri is Teri Cotter. She's a pupil at Port Edgar.'

'And doing porn on the side?'

'Her site's not porn, Bobby . . .' Rebus broke off, but too late.

'You've seen it?'

'A webcam in her room,' Rebus admitted. 'Seems to run

twenty-four hours a day.' He winced, realising again that he'd said too much.

'And how long have you spent watching it, just so you could be sure?'

'I'm not certain it's got anything to do with—'

Hogan ignored him. 'I need to go to Claverhouse with this.'

'No, you don't.'

'John, if Herdman was obsessed with this girl . . .'

'If you're going to interview her, I want to be there.'

'I don't think you—'

'I *gave* you this, Bobby!' Rebus looked around, realising his voice had risen. He was seated at a communal counter beside the window. He caught two young women, office-workers on a break, just as they averted their eyes. How long had they been eavesdropping? Rebus lowered his voice. 'I need to be there. Promise me that, Bobby.'

Hogan's voice softened a little. 'For what it's worth, I promise. Doesn't mean Claverhouse will be so accommodating.'

'Sure you have to go to him with this?'

'What do you mean?'

'The two of us, Bobby, we could talk to her . . .'

'That's not how I work, John.' The tone stiffening again.

'I suppose not, Bobby.' Rebus had a thought. 'Is Siobhan there?'

'I thought she'd be with you.'

'No matter. You'll let me know about that interview?'

'Yes.' The word dissolving into a sigh.

'Cheers, Bobby. I owe you.' Rebus ended the call and walked away from what was left of his coffee. Outside, he lit another cigarette. The office girls were in a huddle, cupping hands to their mouths, maybe in case he could lip-read. They tried not to make eye contact with him. He blew smoke at the window and headed back to the library.

Siobhan had got to St Leonard's early, done some work in

346

the gym, and then headed to the CID suite. There was a large walk-in cupboard where old case-notes were stored, but when she examined the spines of the brown cardboard document-boxes, she realised one was missing. In its place was a slip of paper.

Martin Fairstone. Removed by order. Gill Templer's signature.

Stood to reason. Fairstone's death was no accident. A murder investigation was being instigated, linked to an internal inquiry. Templer would have removed the file so it could be passed on to whoever needed it. Siobhan closed the door again and locked it, then went into the corridor and listened at Gill Templer's door. Nothing but the distant trill of a telephone. She looked up and down the hall. There were bodies in the CID suite: DC Davie Hynds, and 'Hi-Ho' Silvers. Hynds was still too new to query anything she might do, but if Silvers spotted her . . .

She took a deep breath, knocked and waited, then turned the handle and pushed.

The door wasn't locked. She closed it behind her and tiptoed across her boss's office. There was nothing on the desk itself, and the drawers weren't big enough. She stared at the green four-drawer filing-cabinet.

'In for a penny,' she told herself, sliding open the top compartment. There was nothing inside. Plenty of paper-work in the other three, but not what she was looking for. She exhaled noisily and took another look around. Who was she kidding? There were no hiding places here. It was as utilitarian a space as was feasible. Once upon a time, Templer had nurtured a couple of plants on the window-sill, but even those had gone, either killed by neglect or binned during a sort-out. Templer's predecessor had lined his desk with framed photos of his extended family, but there was nothing here even to identify the occupant as a woman. Confident that she hadn't missed anything, Siobhan opened the door, only to find a frowning man standing there.

'The very person I wanted to see,' he said.

'I was just . . .' Siobhan glanced back into the room as if seeking a believable end to the sentence she'd started.

'DCS Templer's in a meeting,' the man explained.

'I'd gathered as much,' Siobhan said, regaining control of her voice. She clicked the door shut.

'By the way,' the man was saying, 'my name's—'

'Mullen.' Siobhan straightened her back, bringing her to within a few inches of his height.

'Of course,' Mullen said, displaying the thinnest of smiles. 'You were DI Rebus's driver the day I managed to run him to ground.'

'And now you want to ask me about Martin Fairstone?' Siobhan guessed.

'That's right.' He paused. 'Always supposing you can spare me a few minutes.'

Siobhan shrugged and smiled, as if to say that she could think of nothing more pleasant.

'If you'll follow me then,' Mullen said.

As they passed the open door of the CID suite, Siobhan glanced in, and saw that Silvers and Hynds were standing side by side. Both were holding their neckties above their heads, necks twisted, as though they were swinging from a noose.

The last they saw of their victim was her raised middle finger as it disappeared from view.

She followed the Complaints officer as he descended the staircase and, just before reaching the reception area, unlocked the door to Interview Room 1.

'I assume you had a good reason to be in DCS Templer's office,' he said, sliding out of his suit-jacket and placing it over the back of one of the room's two chairs. Siobhan sat down, watching him as he took his seat opposite, the chipped and biro-stained desk between them. Mullen leaned down and lifted a cardboard box from the floor.

'Yes, I had,' she said, watching him prise open the lid. The first thing she saw was a photo of Martin Fairstone, taken shortly after his arrest. Mullen took the picture out and held it in front of her. She couldn't help noticing that his nails were immaculate.

'Do you think this man deserved to die?'

'I've no real opinion,' she said.

'This is just between us, you understand?' Mullen lowered the photo a little so that the top half of his face appeared above it. 'No taping, no third parties . . . all very discreet and informal.'

'Is that why you took your jacket off, trying for informality?'

He chose not to answer. 'I'll ask you again, DS Clarke, did this man deserve his fate?'

'If you're asking me if I wanted him dead, the answer is "no". I've come across plenty of scumbags worse than Martin Fairstone.'

'You'd class him as what then: a minor irritation?'

'I wouldn't bother classifying him at all.'

'He died horribly, you know. Waking up to those flames and the choking smoke, trying to wrestle his way free from the chair . . . Not the way I'd choose to leave this life.'

'I'd guess not.'

They locked eyes, and Siobhan knew that any moment now he would get to his feet, start walking around, trying to unnerve her. She beat him to it, her chair scraping the floor as she rose. Arms folded, she walked to the furthest wall, so that her interrogator had to turn round to see her.

'You look like you might make the grade, DS Clarke,' Mullen said. 'Inspector within five years, maybe chief inspector before you're forty . . . that gives you a whole ten years to catch up on DCS Templer.' He paused for effect. 'All of that waiting for you, if you manage to steer clear of trouble.'

'I like to think I've got a pretty good navigation system.'

'I hope for your sake that you're right. DI Rebus, on the other hand . . . well, whatever compass he uses seems to point unerringly towards grief, wouldn't you say?'

'I've no real opinion.'

'Then it's time you did. A career like the one you seem destined for, you need to choose your friends with care.'

Siobhan paced to the other end of the room, turning when she reached the door. 'There must be plenty of candidates out there who'd want Fairstone dead.'

'Hopefully the inquiry will turn up lots of them,' Mullen said with a shrug. 'But meantime . . .'

'Meantime you want to give DI Rebus a going-over?' Mullen studied her. 'Why don't you sit down?'

'Do I make you nervous?' She leaned down over him, knuckles resting against the edge of the desk.

'Is that what you've been trying to do? I was beginning to wonder . . .'

She held his stare, then relented and sat down.

'Tell me,' he said quietly, 'when you first found out that DI Rebus had visited Martin Fairstone on the night he died, what were your thoughts?'

She offered a shrug, nothing more.

'One theory,' the voice intoned, 'is that someone could have been trying to give Fairstone a fright. It just went wrong, that's all. Could be that DI Rebus tried to get back into the house to save the man . . .' His voice trailed away. 'We had a call from a doctor . . . a psychologist, name of Irene Lesser. She had dealings recently with DI Rebus on another matter. She was thinking of making a complaint actually, something to do with a breach of patient confidentiality. At the end of her call, she offered the opinion that John Rebus is a "haunted" man.' Mullen leaned forward. 'Would you say he was haunted, DS Clarke?'

'He lets his cases get to him sometimes,' Siobhan conceded. 'I don't know if that's the same thing.'

'I think Dr Lesser meant that he has trouble living in the present . . . that there's a rage in him, something bottled up from years back.'

'I don't see where Martin Fairstone fits in.'

'Don't you?' Mullen smiled ruefully. 'Do you consider DI

Rebus a friend, someone you spend time with outside work?'

'Yes.'

'How much time?'

'Some.'

'Is he the kind of friend you'd take problems to?'

'Maybe.'

'But Martin Fairstone wasn't a problem?'

'No.'

'Not to you, at any rate.' Mullen let the silence lie between them, then leaned back in his chair. 'Do you ever feel the need to protect Rebus, DS Clarke?'

'No.'

'But you've been driving him around, while his hands mend.'

'Not the same thing.'

'Has he offered a believable explanation of how he managed to burn them in the first place?'

'He put them in water that was too hot for them.'

'I specified "believable".'

'I believe it.'

'You don't think it would be entirely in his nature for him to see you with a black eye, put two and two together, and go out hunting for Fairstone?'

'They sat in a pub together . . . I haven't heard anyone saying they were having a fight.'

'Not in public perhaps. But once DI Rebus had inveigled an invite back to the house . . . in the privacy of that place . . .'

Siobhan was shaking her head. 'That's not what happened.'

'I'd love to have your confidence, DS Clarke.'

'Would that mean swapping it for your smug arrogance?'

Mullen seemed to consider this. Then he smiled and placed the photograph back in its box. 'I think that's all for now.' Siobhan made no motion to leave. 'Unless there's something else?' Mullen's eyes glinted.

'Actually, there is.' She nodded towards the box. 'The reason I was in DCS Templer's office.'

Mullen looked at the box, too. 'Oh?' Sounding interested.

'It's nothing to do with Fairstone really. It's the Port Edgar inquiry.' She decided she had nothing to lose by telling him. 'Fairstone's girlfriend, she's been seen in South Queensferry.' Siobhan gave a surreptitious swallow before uttering her little white lie. 'DI Hogan wants her for interview, but I couldn't remember her address.'

'And it's in here?' Mullen patted the box, considered for a moment, and then prised open the lid again. 'Can't see the harm,' he said, pushing it towards her.

The blonde's name was Rachel Fox and she worked in a supermarket at the foot of Leith Walk. Siobhan drove down there, past the uninviting bars, secondhand shops and tattoo parlours. Leith, it seemed to her, was always on the verge of some renaissance or other. When the warehouses were turned into 'loft-style apartments', or a cinema complex opened, or the Queen's superannuated yacht was berthed there for tourists to visit, there was always talk of the port's 'rejuvenation'. But to her mind, the place never really changed: same old Leith, same old Leithers. She'd never felt apprehensive there, even at the dead of night when knocking on the doors of brothels and drug dens. But it could seem a spiritless place, too, where a smile might mark you as an outsider. There were no spaces in the supermarket car park, so she did a circuit, eventually noting that a woman was loading her boot with grocery bags. Siobhan waited, engine idling. The woman was shouting at a sobbing five-year-old. Two lines of light green mucus connected the boy's nostrils to his top lip. His shoulders were slumped, hiccuping with each sob. He was dressed in a puffy silver Le Coq Sportif jacket two sizes too big for him, so that he appeared to have no hands. When he began to wipe his nose on one sleeve, his mother erupted, shaking him. Watching, Siobhan realised that her fingers were gripping the door-handle. But she didn't get out of the car, knew her interference wouldn't make things any better for the child, and the woman wasn't suddenly going to see the error of her ways, just because a complete stranger bothered to give her a bollocking. The boot was being closed, the child pushed into the car. As the woman walked around to the driver's side, she looked at Siobhan and shrugged in what she thought was a sharing of her burden. *You know what it's like,* the shrug seemed to say. Siobhan just glared, the futility of the gesture lingering as she parked, grabbed a trolley, and wheeled it into the store.

What was she doing here anyway? Was she here because of Fairstone, or the notes, or because Rachel Fox had turned up at the Boatman's? Maybe all three. Fox was a checkout assistant, so Siobhan scanned the row of tills, and saw her almost immediately. She was wearing the same blue uniform as the other women, and had piled her hair atop her head, a ringlet hanging down over either ear. She had a vacant look on her face as she slid item after item over the barcode-reader. The sign above her till read 'Nine Items Or Less'. Siobhan made her way down the first aisle, couldn't find anything she needed. She didn't want to wait in the queues at the fish and meat counters. It would be just her luck if Fox took a break, or skipped out early. Two bars of chocolate went into the trolley, followed by kitchen towel and a tin of Scotch broth. Four items. At the top of the next aisle, she made sure Fox was still working the checkout. She was, and three pensioners were waiting their turn to pay. Siobhan added a tube of tomato purée to her provisions. A woman in an electric wheelchair whizzed past, her husband toiling to keep up. She kept yelling instructions to him: 'Toothpaste! The pump, mind, not the tube! And did you remember the cucumber?'

His sudden wince told Siobhan that he had in fact forgotten the cucumber, and would need to go back.

The other shoppers seemed to be moving at half-speed, as if trying to make the activity last longer than was strictly necessary. They'd probably end the trip with a visit to the in-store café – tea and a slice of cake, the cake to be chewed slowly, the tea sipped at. And then home to the afternoon cookery shows.

A packet of pasta. Six items.

Only one pensioner was now waiting at the express lane. Siobhan fell in behind him. He said hello to Fox, who managed a tired 'Hiya', cutting off any further conversation.

'Grand day,' the man said. His mouth seemed to be lacking the necessary dental plates, tongue protruding wetly. Fox just gave a nod, concentrating on processing his purchases as speedily as possible. Looking down at the conveyor belt, two things struck Siobhan. The first was that the gentleman had twelve items. The second, that like him she should have bought some eggs.

'Eight-eighty,' Fox said. The man's hand withdrew slowly from his pocket, counting out coins. He frowned and counted again. Fox held out her hand and took the money from him.

'Fifty pence short,' she informed him.

'Eh?'

'You're fifty pence short. You'll have to put something back.'

'Here, take this,' Siobhan said, adding another coin to the collection. The man looked at her, gave a toothless grin and a bow of his head. Then he lifted his bag and shuffled towards the exit.

Rachel Fox began dealing with her new customer. 'You're thinking "poor old soul",' she said without looking up. 'But he tries pulling that one every week or so.'

'More fool me then,' Siobhan said. 'It was worth it just to stop him doing another slow-motion recount.'

Fox glanced up, then back to the conveyor belt, then up again. 'I know you from somewhere.'

'Been sending me any letters, Rachel?'

Fox's hand froze on the pasta. 'How d'you know my name?'

'It's on your badge for one thing.'

But Fox knew now. Her eyes were heavily made-up. She narrowed them as she stared at Siobhan. 'You're that cop, tried to get Marty put away.'

'I gave evidence at his trial,' Siobhan conceded.

'Yeah, I remember you . . . Got one of your pals to torch him, too.'

'Don't believe everything the tabloids tell you, Rachel.'

'You were giving him hassle, weren't you?'

'No.'

'He talked about you . . . said you had it in for him.'

'I can assure you I didn't.'

'Then how come he's dead?'

The last of Siobhan's six items had gone through, and she was holding out a ten-pound note. The cashier at the next till had stopped serving and, like her customer, was now listening in.

'Can I talk to you someplace, Rachel?' Siobhan looked around. 'Somewhere more private.' But Fox's eyes were filling with tears. Suddenly she reminded Siobhan of the kid outside. In some ways, she thought, we just don't grow up. Emotionally, we never grow up . . .

'Rachel . . .' she said.

But Fox had opened the till to give Siobhan her change. She was shaking her head slowly. 'Got nothing to say to you lot.'

'What about the notes I've been getting, Rachel? Can you tell me about the notes?'

'I don't know what you're talking about.'

The sound of a motor told Siobhan that the woman in the wheelchair was right behind her. No doubt there were exactly nine items in her husband's trolley. Siobhan turned, and saw that the woman was cradling a hand-basket, with what looked like another nine items inside. The woman was glowering at Siobhan, wishing her gone.

'I saw you in the Boatman's,' Siobhan told Rachel Fox. 'What were you doing there?'

'Where?'

'The Boatman's . . . South Queensferry.'

Fox handed over Siobhan's change and receipt, gave a loud sniff. 'That's where Rod works.'

'He's a . . . friend . . . is he?'

'He's my brother,' Rachel Fox said. When she looked up at Siobhan, the water in her eyes had been replaced by fire. 'Does that mean you're going to want him killed, too? Eh? Does it?'

'Maybe we'll try another till, Davie,' the woman in the wheelchair told her husband. She was backing away as Siobhan snatched her carrier-bag and headed for the exit, Rachel Fox's voice following her all the way out:

'Murdering bitch! What had he ever done to you? Murderer! *Murderer!*'

She dumped the bag on the passenger seat, got in behind the steering-wheel.

'Nothing but a slut!' Rachel Fox was walking towards the car. 'Couldn't get a man if you tried!'

Siobhan turned the ignition, backed out of the space as Fox aimed a kick at the driver's-side headlamp. She was wearing trainers, and her foot glanced off the glass. Siobhan was craning her neck round, making sure she didn't hit anyone behind her. When she turned, Fox was wrestling with a line of parked trolleys. Siobhan moved the car forward, pushing the accelerator hard, hearing the clatter of the trolleys as they just missed her. Looked in the rearview and saw them blocking the road behind her, their leader bumping against a parked VW Beetle.

And Rachel Fox, still snarling, shaking both fists, then pointing a finger in the direction of the disappearing car, drawing the same finger across her throat. Nodding slowly, to let Siobhan know she meant it.

'Right you are, Rachel,' Siobhan muttered, turning out of the car park.

20

It had taken all of Bobby Hogan's powers of persuasion –
something he wasn't going to let Rebus forget. The look he
gave said it all: *Number one, you owe me; number two, don't
screw this up* . . .

They were in one of the offices at 'the Big House':
Lothian and Borders Police HQ in Fettes Avenue. This was
the home of Drugs and Major Crime, and as such Rebus
was here on sufferance. Rebus didn't know quite how
Hogan had persuaded Claverhouse to let him sit in on the
interview, but here they were. Ormiston was present too,
snuffling and screwing his eyes tight shut whenever he
blinked. Teri Cotter had come accompanied by her father,
and a female police constable was seated nearby.

'Sure you want your father present?' Claverhouse asked
matter-of-factly. Teri looked at him. She was in full Goth
camouflage, down to knee-length boots with multiple
shiny buckles.

'Way you make it sound,' Mr Cotter said, 'maybe I
should've brought my solicitor, too.'

Claverhouse just shrugged. 'I merely asked because I
don't want Teri getting embarrassed in front of you . . .' He
let his voice trail off, eyes fixing on Teri's.

'Embarrassed?' Mr Cotter echoed, looking in his daughter's direction, so that he missed it when Claverhouse
made a gesture with his fingers, as if typing on a keyboard.
But Teri saw it, and knew what it meant.

'Dad,' she said, 'maybe it'd be better if you waited
outside.'

'I'm not sure I—'

'Dad.' She laid her hand on his. 'It's fine. I'll explain later
. . . honest I will.' Her eyes boring into his.

'Well, I don't know . . .' Cotter looked around the room.

'It'll be fine, sir,' Claverhouse was reassuring him,
leaning back in his chair and crossing one leg over the
other. 'Nothing to worry about, just some background info
we think Teri can help us with.' He nodded towards
Ormiston. 'DS Ormiston can show you to the canteen, get
yourself a cup of something and we'll be finished here
before you know it . . .'

Ormiston looked unhappy, eyes flickering towards
Rebus and Hogan as if asking his partner why one of them
couldn't go in his place. Cotter was studying his daughter
again.

'I don't like leaving you here.' But his words had a
defeated sound to them, and Rebus wondered if the man
had ever stood up to either Teri or his wife. A man happiest
with rows of numbers, stock market movements; things he
felt he could predict and control. Maybe the car smash, the
death of his son, had robbed him of self-belief, showing
him up as powerless and puny in the face of random
chance. He was already rising to his feet, Ormiston meeting
him at the door, the two men exiting. Rebus thought
suddenly of Allan Renshaw, of the effect losing a son could
have on a father . . .

Claverhouse beamed a smile at Teri Cotter, who
responded by folding her arms defensively.

'You know what this is about, Teri?'

'Do I?'

Claverhouse repeated the typing motion with his fingers.
'You know what that means though?'

'Why don't you tell me.'

'It means you've got a website, Miss Teri. It means
people can watch your bedroom any hour of the day or
night. DI Rebus here seems to be one of your fans.'
Claverhouse nodded in Rebus's direction. 'Lee Herdman

was another.' Claverhouse paused, studying her face. 'You don't seem very surprised.'

She offered a shrug.

'Mr Herdman had a bit of a voyeur thing going.' Claverhouse glanced towards Rebus, as if wondering whether he might fit this category too. 'Quite a lot of sites he liked to go to, most of them he had to use his credit card . . .'

'So?'

'So you're giving it away for free, Teri.'

'I'm not like those sites!' she spat.

'Then what sort of site are you?'

She seemed about to say something, but bit it back.

'You like being watched?' Claverhouse guessed. 'And Herdman liked to watch. Seems the two of you were pretty compatible.'

'He'd screwed me a few times, if that's what you mean,' she said coldly.

'I might not have used quite those words.'

'Teri,' Rebus said, 'there's a computer Lee bought, we're having trouble tracing it . . . Is that because it's sitting in your bedroom?'

'Maybe.'

'He bought it for you, set it up for you?'

'Did he?'

'Showed you how to design a site, set up the webcam?'

'Why are you asking me if you already know?' Her voice had taken on an edge of petulance.

'What did your parents say?'

She looked at him. 'I've got money of my own.'

'They thought you'd paid for it? They didn't know about you and Lee?'

She gave him a look which confirmed how stupid his questions were.

'He liked watching you,' Claverhouse stated. 'Wanted to know where you were, what you were doing. That's why you set up the site?'

She was shaking her head. 'Dark Entry is for anyone who cares to look.'

'Was that his idea or yours?' Hogan asked.

She gave a shrill laugh. 'Am I supposed to be Red Riding Hood, is that it? With Lee as the big bad wolf?' She took a breath. 'Lee gave me the computer, said maybe we could keep in touch by webcam. Dark Entry was *my* idea. No one else's, just mine.' She pointed a finger at herself, finding a piece of bare flesh between her breasts. Her black lace top was low-cut. Her finger went to the diamond, hanging from its gold chain, and she played with it absent-mindedly.

'Did he give you that, too?' Rebus asked.

She peered down at the chain, nodded, folded her arms again.

'Teri,' Rebus said quietly, 'did you know who else was accessing your site?'

She shook her head. 'Being anonymous is part of the fun.'

'You were hardly anonymous. There was plenty of information to tell people who you were.'

She considered this and shrugged.

'Anyone from your school know about it?' Rebus asked.

Another shrug.

'I'll tell you one person who did know ... Derek Renshaw.'

Her eyes widened, mouth opening into an O.

'And Derek probably told his good friend Anthony Jarvies,' Rebus went on.

Claverhouse had straightened in his seat, holding up a hand. 'Wait a minute ...' He looked towards Hogan, who offered a shrug, then back to Rebus. 'This is the first I'm hearing about this.'

'Teri's site was bookmarked on Derek's computer,' Rebus explained.

'And the other kid knew, too? The one Herdman killed?'

Rebus shrugged. 'I'd say it's likely.'

Claverhouse bounded to his feet, rubbing at his jaw. 'Teri,' he asked, 'was Lee Herdman the jealous type?'

'I don't know.'

'He knew about your site ... I'm assuming you told him?' He was standing over her.

'Yes,' she said.

'How did he feel about that? I mean, about the fact that anyone – *anyone* – could watch you in your bedroom of a night?'

Her voice dropped to a whisper. 'You think that's why he shot them?'

Claverhouse leaned down over her, so his face was inches from hers. 'How does it look to you, Teri? Do you think it's possible?' He didn't wait for her reply, wheeled away on one heel and clapped his hands together. Rebus knew what he was thinking: he was thinking that he personally, Detective Inspector Charlie Claverhouse, had just cracked the case, on his first day in charge. And he was wondering how soon he could go trumpeting his triumph to his senior officers. He went to the door and threw it open, looking up and down the corridor, disappointed to find it empty. Rebus took the opportunity to rise from his own chair and place himself in Claverhouse's. Teri was staring into her lap, one finger running up and down the chain again.

'Teri,' he said quietly, to get her attention. She looked at him, eyes red-rimmed behind the liner and mascara. 'You okay?' She nodded slowly. 'Sure of that? Anything I can fetch you?'

'I'm fine.'

He nodded, as if trying to convince himself. Hogan had shifted places, too, and was now standing next to Claver-house in the doorway, one calming hand on his shoulder. Rebus couldn't make out what they were saying, wasn't really interested.

'I can't believe that bastard was watching me.'

'Who? Lee?'

'Derek Renshaw,' she spat. 'He as good as killed my brother!' Her voice was rising. Rebus lowered his even further when he spoke.

'As far as I can see, he was in the car with your brother, but that doesn't mean he was responsible.' Unbidden, an image of Derek's father flashed into Rebus's head: a kid abandoned at the edge of the pavement, gripping a newly bought football for dear life while the dizzying world spun past. 'You really think Lee would walk into a school and kill two people because he was jealous?'

She thought about this, then shook her head.

'Me neither,' Rebus said. She looked at him. 'For one thing,' he went on, 'how could he have known? Doesn't look like he knew either of the victims. So how would he have been able to pick them out?' He watched her take this in. 'Shooting's a bit excessive, wouldn't you say? And in such a public place . . . he'd have to've been mad with jealousy. Out of his mind with it.'

'So . . . what did happen?' she asked.

Rebus looked towards the doorway. Ormiston had returned from the cafeteria, and was now being hugged by Claverhouse, who'd probably have lifted the larger man off his feet if he'd been able. Rebus caught a hissed *we did it*, followed by a cautious muttering from Hogan.

'I'm still not sure,' Rebus said, answering Teri's question. 'It's a pretty good motive, which is why you've made DI Claverhouse a happy man.'

'You don't like him, do you?' A smile flitted across her face.

'Don't worry: the feeling's entirely mutual.'

'When you clicked on Dark Entry . . .' She lowered her eyes again. 'Was I doing anything in particular?'

Rebus shook his head. 'The room was empty.' Didn't want her to know he'd watched her sleeping. 'Mind if I ask you something?' He looked towards the doorway again, checking no one was listening. 'Doug Brimson says he's a family friend, but I get the feeling he's not top of your hit parade?'

Her face sagged. 'My mum's having an affair with him,' she said dismissively.

'You sure?' She nodded, not making eye contact. 'Does your dad know?'

Now she did look up, horror-struck. 'He doesn't need to know, does he?'

Rebus considered this. 'Suppose not,' he decided. 'How did you find out?'

'Woman's intuition,' she said, with no trace of irony. Rebus sat back, deep in thought. He was thinking about Teri and Lee Herdman and Dark Entry, wondering if any or all of it was a way of getting back at the mother.

'Teri, you're sure you'd no way of knowing who was watching you on the webcam? None of the other kids at school ever hinted . . .?'

She shook her head. 'I get messages in my guest book, but never from anyone I know.'

'Are any of those messages ever . . . I don't know . . . off the wall?'

'That's the way I like them.' She angled her head slightly, trying for the persona of Miss Teri, but too late: Rebus had seen her as plain Teri Cotter, and that was who she'd remain. He stretched his own neck and back. 'Tell you who I saw last night,' he said chattily.

'Who?'

'James Bell.'

'So?' Inspecting her black gloss fingernails.

'So I was wondering . . . that photo of you . . . do you remember? You palmed it that day we were in the pub on Cockburn Street.'

'It belonged to me.'

'I'm not saying it didn't. I also seem to recall that as you lifted it, you were telling me how James used to turn up at Lee's parties.'

'Does he say he didn't?'

364

'On the contrary, the two of them seem to have known one another pretty well, wouldn't you say?'

The three detectives – Claverhouse, Hogan and Ormiston – were coming back into the room. Ormiston was patting Claverhouse's back, and with it his ego.

'He liked Lee,' Teri was saying, 'no doubt about that.'

'But was it mutual?'

Her eyes narrowed. 'James Bell ... he could have pointed Renshaw and Jarvies out to Lee, couldn't he?'

'Wouldn't explain why Lee then shot him too. Thing is ...' Rebus knew he had seconds before the interview was wrenched away from him again. 'That photo of you ... you said it was taken on Cockburn Street. What I'm wondering is, who took it?'

She seemed to be looking for the purpose behind the question. Claverhouse was standing in front of them, clicking his fingers to let Rebus know it was time to relinquish the chair. Rebus kept his eyes on Teri as he rose slowly to his feet.

'James Bell?' he asked her. 'Was that who it was?'

And she nodded, unable to think of any reason not to tell him.

'He came to see you in Cockburn Street?'

'He was taking shots of all of us – a school project ...'

'What's this?' Claverhouse said, bouncing down on to the chair with a grin.

'He was asking me about James Bell,' Teri told Claverhouse, matter-of-factly.

'Oh aye? What about him?'

'Nothing,' she said, sending a wink towards the retreating Rebus. Claverhouse twitched, turned in his seat, but Rebus offered nothing more than a smile and a shrug. When Claverhouse turned away again, Rebus made a downstroke in the air with his forefinger, letting Teri know he owed her one. He knew what Claverhouse would have done with the information: James Bell lends Lee Herdman a book, not realising there's a photo of Teri inside, maybe being used as a bookmark . . . Herdman finds it, and feels jealous . . . It gave him a reason to wound James: not a gross enough infringement to merit killing him, and besides, James was a friend . . .

As it was, Claverhouse would be wrapping the inquiry up today. Straight to the Assistant Chief Constable's office to ask for his gold star. The Portakabin at Port Edgar Academy would be emptied, officers returned to their normal duties.

Rebus back under suspension.

And yet none of it really added up. Rebus knew that now. Knew, too, that something was staring him in the face. Then he looked at Teri Cotter, playing with her chain again, and he knew exactly what it was. Porn and drugs weren't Rotterdam's only businesses . . .

Rebus reached Siobhan in her car.

'Where are you?' he asked.

'A90, heading for South Queensferry. What about you?'

'Sitting at a red light on Queensferry Road.'

'Driving *and* using your phone? The hands must be healing.'

'Getting there. What've you been up to?'

'Fairstone's girlfriend.'

'Any joy?'

'Of a sort. What about you?'

'Sitting in on an interview with Teri Cotter. Claverhouse thinks he's found his motive.'

'Oh yes?'

'Herdman was jealous because the two kids were logging on to Teri's site.'

'And James Bell just happened to get in the way?'

'I'm sure that's how Claverhouse will see it.'

'So what now?'

'Everything shuts down.'

'And Whiteread and Simms?'

'You're right. They won't like it.' He watched the light in front of him turn green.

'Because they'll go away empty-handed?'

'Yes.' Rebus thought for a moment, holding the phone between jaw and shoulder as he changed up through the gears. Then: 'So what's waiting for you in Queensferry?'

'The barman at the Boatman's, he's Fox's brother.'

'Fox?'

'Fairstone's girlfriend.'

'Explaining why she was in the bar . . .'

'Yes.'

'So you've talked to her?'

'We exchanged a few pleasantries.'

'Did she say anything about Peacock Johnson, whether his falling-out with Fairstone had anything to do with her?'

'I forgot to ask.'

'You forgot . . .?'

'Things got a bit fraught. I thought maybe I'd ask her brother instead.'

'You reckon he'd know if she had a thing going with Peacock?'

'Don't know till I ask.'

'Why don't we hook up? I was planning a trip to the marina.'

'You want to go there first?'

'Then we can end the day with a well-earned drink.'

'I'll see you at the boat yard then.'

She ended the call and came off the dual carriageway at the last slip-road before the Forth Road Bridge. Drove down the hill into South Queensferry and turned left on Shore Road. Her phone trilled again.

'Change of plan?' she asked into the mouthpiece.

'Not until we've got a plan to change, which is the very reason I'm calling.'

She recognised the voice: Doug Brimson. 'Sorry, I thought you were someone else. What can I do for you?'

'I was just wondering if you're ready to take to the skies again.'

She smiled to herself. 'Maybe I am.'

'Great. How about tomorrow?'

She considered for a moment. 'I could probably bunk off for an hour.'

'Late afternoon? Just before the sun goes down?'

'Okay.'

'And you'll take the controls this time?'

'I think I could be persuaded.'

'Great. How does sixteen hundred hours sound?'

'It sounds like four in the afternoon.'

He laughed. 'I'll see you then, Siobhan.'

'Goodbye, Doug.'

She placed the phone back on the passenger seat, staring at the sky through her windscreen. Imagined herself flying a plane . . . Imagined having a panic attack in the middle of it. But she didn't think she'd panic. Besides, Doug Brimson would be there with her. No need for her to worry.

She parked outside the marina's cafeteria, went in and reappeared with a Mars bar. She was binning the wrapper when Rebus's Saab arrived. He passed her and stopped at the far end of the car park, fifty yards closer to Herdman's shed. By the time he'd got out and locked his door, she'd caught him up.

'So what are we doing here?' she asked, swallowing the last cloying mouthful.

'Apart from ruining our teeth?' he said. 'I want one last look at the shed.'

'Why?'

'Just because.'

The doors to the boathouse were closed, but not locked. Rebus slid them open. Simms was crouching on the deck of the parked dinghy. He looked up at the interruption. Rebus nodded towards the crowbar in his hand.

'Taking the place apart?' he guessed.

'Never know what you'll find,' Simms said. 'Our record in that department is rather better than yours, after all.'

Hearing the voices, Whiteread had emerged from the office. She was holding a sheaf of papers.

'All getting a bit frantic, isn't it?' Rebus said, walking towards her. 'Claverhouse is getting ready to call it a day, and that's not what you'd call music to the ears, is it?'

Whiteread managed a thin, cold smile. Rebus wondered what it would take to faze her; thought he had a pretty good idea.

'I assume it was you who put that journalist on to us,' she said. 'He wanted to ask about a helicopter crash on Jura. Which got me wondering . . .'

'Do tell,' Rebus said.

'I had an interesting chat this morning,' she drawled, 'with a man called Douglas Brimson. Seems the three of you took a little trip together.' Her eyes flitted towards Siobhan.

'Did we?' Rebus said. He'd stopped walking, but White-read hadn't, not until her face was inches from his.

'He took you to Jura. From there, you went looking for a crash-site.' She was studying his face for any sign of weakness. Rebus's eyes flickered in Siobhan's direction. *Bastard didn't need to tell them!* A red tint had appeared on her cheeks.

'Did we?' was all Rebus could think to say.

Whiteread had risen on her toes, so her face was level with his. 'The thing is, DI Rebus, how could you possibly have known about that?'

'About what?'

'Only way you could have known was if you had access to confidential files.'

'Is that right?' Rebus watched Simms climb down from the boat, still holding the crowbar. He gave a shrug. 'Well, if these files you're talking about are confidential, I can't have seen them, can I?'

'Not without a spot of breaking and entering . . .'

Whiteread turned her attention to Siobhan. 'Not to mention photocopying.' She angled her head, pretending to examine the younger woman's face. 'Caught a touch of the sun, DS Clarke? Only, your cheeks seem to be burning.' Siobhan didn't move, didn't say anything. 'Cat got your tongue?'

Simms was smirking, enjoying the detectives' discomfort.

'I hear tell,' Rebus said to him, 'you're scared of the dark.'

'Eh?' Simms frowned.

'Explains why you like to keep your door ajar.' Rebus gave a wink, then turned back to Whiteread. 'I don't think you're going anywhere with this. Not unless you want everyone on the inquiry knowing why you're really here.'

'From what I hear, you're already on suspension. Could be facing a murder charge any time soon.' Whiteread's eyes were dark points of light. 'Added to which, the psychologist at Carbrae says you went behind her back, looked up records without permission.' She paused. 'Seems to me you're already shoulder-deep in shit, Rebus. I can't think why you'd want more trouble than you've already got. Yet here you are, ready and willing to pick a fight with me. Let me try to get through to you.' She leaned forward so her lips were an inch from his ear. 'You've not got a prayer,' she said quietly. She pulled back slowly, ready to measure his response. Rebus had one gloved hand held up. She wasn't sure what the gesture meant. A frown furrowed her brow. And then she saw what he was holding between thumb and middle finger. Saw it glint and sparkle in the light.

A single diamond.

'What the hell . . .?' Simms muttered.

Rebus closed his hand around the diamond.

'Finders keepers,' he said, turning, starting to walk away. Siobhan fell into step with him, waited till they were back outdoors before she spoke.

'What was all that about?'

'Just a fishing expedition.'

'But what does it mean? Where did the diamond come from?'

Rebus smiled. 'Friend of mine, he runs a jeweller's shop on Queensferry Street.'

'And?'

'I persuaded him to let me borrow it.' Rebus was tucking the diamond back into his pocket. 'Thing is, *they* don't know that.'

'But you're going to explain it to me, right?'

Rebus nodded slowly. 'Just as soon as I find out what I've caught with my hook.'

'John . . .' Half warning, half pleading.

'We going for that drink now?' Rebus asked.

She didn't reply; tried staring him out as they walked back to his car. She was still staring as he unlocked his door and got in. He started the engine, put it in gear, then wound down his window.

'I'll see you there then,' was all he said, making to drive off. Siobhan stood her ground, but he just gave her a wave. Cursing silently, she started stalking towards her own car.

21

Rebus was seated at a window table in the Boatman's, checking a text message from Steve Holly.

Wot u got 4 me? Mite av 2 refresh chip pan story if u dont help.

Rebus debated whether to reply or not, then started pressing keys:

jura crash herdman there took sth army want back u could ask whiteread again

He wasn't sure that Holly would understand, Rebus not having worked out how to add punctuation or capitals to his text messages. But it would keep the reporter busy, and if he did end up confronting Whiteread and Simms, so much the better. Let them think the world was closing in on them. Rebus picked up his half-pint and made a little toast to himself with it, just as Siobhan arrived. He'd been debating whether to pass on Teri's news: Brimson and her mum. Thing was, if he told her, she probably couldn't keep it to herself. Next time she met Brimson, he'd see it in her face, the way she spoke to him, a reluctance to meet his eyes. Rebus didn't want that, couldn't see it doing anyone any good, not at this juncture. Siobhan slung her bag on to the table, and looked towards the bar, where a woman she'd never seen before was pulling pints.

'Don't worry,' Rebus said. 'I had a word. McAllister's shift starts in a few minutes.'

'Just long enough for you to enlighten me then.' She slipped off her coat. Rebus was rising to his feet.

'Let me get you a drink first. What'll it be?'

'Lime and soda.'

'Nothing stronger?'

She frowned at his near-empty glass. 'Some of us are driving.'

'Don't worry, I'm only having the one.' He made his way to the bar, came back with two drinks: lime and soda for her, cola for him. 'See?' he said. 'I can be all smug and virtuous too, when I want to be.'

'Better that than drunk at the wheel.' She lifted the straw from her glass and deposited it in the ashtray, sat back and placed her hands on her thighs. 'Right then . . . I'm ready if you are.'

At which, the door creaked open.

'Speak of the devil,' Rebus said, as Rod McAllister walked in. McAllister saw that he was being stared at. When he looked, Rebus beckoned him over. McAllister was unzipping a scuffed leather jacket. He pulled the black scarf from around his neck and stuffed it into a pocket.

'I've got to start work,' he said, when Rebus patted an empty stool.

'This'll only take a minute,' Rebus offered with a smile. 'Susie won't mind.' He nodded towards the barmaid.

McAllister hesitated, then sat down, elbows pressing against his thin legs, hands cupped below his chin. Rebus mimicked the posture.

'It's about Lee then?' McAllister guessed.

'Not strictly speaking,' Rebus said. Then he glanced towards Siobhan.

'We may come back to that,' she told the barman. 'But right now, we're more interested in your sister.'

He looked from Siobhan to Rebus and then back again. 'Which one?'

'Rachel Fox. Funny you've got different surnames.'

'We haven't.' McAllister's eyes were still shifting between the two detectives, unable to decide who he should be addressing. Siobhan answered with a click of her fingers. He focused on her, narrowed his eyes slightly. 'She changed her name a while back, trying to get into modelling. What's she got to do with you lot?'

'You don't know?'

He shrugged.

'Marty Fairstone?' Siobhan prompted. 'Don't tell me she never introduced you?'

'Yeah, I knew Marty. I was gutted when I heard.'

'What about a fellow called Johnson?' Rebus asked. 'His nickname's Peacock . . . friend of Marty's . . .'

'Yeah?'

'Ever come across him?'

McAllister seemed to be thinking. 'Not sure,' he said at last.

'Peacock and Rachel,' Siobhan began, angling her head to catch his attention again, 'we think they might've had a thing going.'

'Oh aye?' McAllister raised an eyebrow. 'That's news to me.'

'She never mentioned him?'

'No.'

'The pair of them have been hanging about the town.'

'Plenty of people hanging about recently. Take you two, for example.' He sat back, stretching his spine, glancing at the clock above the bar. 'Don't want to get in Susie's bad books . . .'

'Rumour is, Fairstone and Johnson had a falling-out, maybe over Rachel.'

'Oh aye?'

'If you're finding the questions too awkward, Mr McAllister,' Rebus said, 'feel free to say . . .'

Siobhan was staring at McAllister's T-shirt, revealed now that he wasn't slouched forward any more. It showed an album cover, an album she knew.

'Mogwai fan, eh, Rod?'

'Anything that's loud.' McAllister examined his shirt.

'It's their *Rock Action* album, isn't it?'

'That's the one.'

McAllister made to stand up, turning towards the bar. Siobhan locked eyes with Rebus and nodded slowly. 'Rod,' she said, 'that first time we met . . . you remember I gave you my card?'

McAllister nodded, walking away from her. But Siobhan was on her feet, following him, her voice rising.

'It had the St Leonard's address on it, didn't it, Rod? And when you saw my name, you knew who I was, didn't you? Because Marty had mentioned me . . . or maybe it was Rachel. You remember that Mogwai album, Rod, the one before *Rock Action*?'

McAllister had lifted the hatch so he could move behind the bar. He slammed it shut after him. The barmaid was staring at him. Siobhan lifted the hatch.

'Hoi, staff only,' Susie said. But Siobhan wasn't listening, was hardly aware that Rebus had risen from his chair and was approaching the bar. She grabbed McAllister by the sleeve of his jacket. He tried to shake her off, but she turned him to face her.

'Remember what it was called, Rod? It was *Come On Die Young*. C.O.D.Y., Rod. Same letters as on your second note.'

'Get the fuck off me!' he yelled.

'Whatever it is between you,' Susie was saying, 'take it outside.'

'It's a serious offence, Rod, sending threats like that.'

'Let go of me, you bitch!' He jerked his arm free, then swung it, catching her on the side of her face. She crashed into the gantry, sending bottles flying. Rebus had reached over the bar and grabbed McAllister by his hair, pulling his head down until it connected hard with the slop-tray. McAllister's arms were thrashing, his voice a wordless bellow, but Rebus wasn't about to let go.

'Any cuffs?' he asked Siobhan. She stumbled from behind the bar, glass crunching underfoot, ran to her bag, emptying its contents on to the table until she found the handcuffs. McAllister caught her a couple of good ones to

375

the shins with the heels of his cowboy boots, but she squeezed the cuffs tight, knowing they'd hold. She moved away from him, feeling dizzy, not knowing if it was concussion, adrenaline, or the fumes from half a dozen smashed spirits bottles.

'Call it in,' Rebus hissed, still not letting go of his prisoner. 'A night in the cells won't do this bastard any harm at all.'

'Here, you can't do that,' Susie complained. 'Who's going to cover his shift?'

'Not our problem, love,' Rebus told her, offering what he hoped might be taken for an apologetic smile.

They'd taken McAllister to St Leonard's, booked him into the only empty cell left. Rebus had asked Siobhan if they'd be charging him formally. She'd shrugged.

'I doubt he'll be sending any more notes.' One side of her face was still raw from where he'd connected, but it didn't look like it would bruise.

In the car park, they went their separate ways. Siobhan's parting words: 'What about that diamond?' Rebus waving to her as he drove off.

He made for Arden Street, ignoring the ringing of his mobile: Siobhan, wanting to put that question to him again. He couldn't find a parking space, decided he was too hyped up anyway for a quiet night at home. So he kept driving, cruising the city's south side until he found himself in Gracemount, back at the bus shelter where he'd confronted the Lost Boys what seemed like half a lifetime ago. Had it really only been Wednesday night? The shelter was deserted now. Rebus parked kerbside anyway, let his window down an inch and smoked a cigarette. He didn't know what he'd do with Rab Fisher if he found him; knew he wanted a few answers about Andy Callis's death. The episode in the bar had given him a taste. He looked at his hands. They were still tingling from contact with McAllister, but it wasn't altogether an unpleasant feeling.

Buses came, but didn't linger: no one was getting on or off. Rebus started the ignition and headed into the mazy housing schemes, covering every possible route, sometimes finishing in a cul-de-sac and having to reverse out. There were kids playing a game of football in the near-dark on a stunted patch of parkland. Others skateboarding towards an underpass. This was their territory, their time of day. He could ask about the Lost Boys, but knew that these kids learned the rules young. They wouldn't grass up the local gang, not when their chief aspiration in life was probably membership of the same. Rebus parked again outside a low-rise block, smoked another cigarette. He'd need to find a shop soon, somewhere he could stock up. Or head for a pub, where one of the drinkers would doubtless sell him a job-lot cheap, no questions asked. He checked the radio to see if anything bearable was being broadcast, but all he could find were rap and dance. There was a tape in the player, but it was Rory Gallagher, *Jinx*, and he wasn't in the mood. Seemed to remember one of the tracks was called 'The Devil Made Me Do It'. Not much of a defence these days, but plenty of others had come along in Old Nick's place. No such thing as an inexplicable crime, not now there were scientists and psychologists who'd talk about genes and abuse, brain damage and peer pressure. Always a reason . . . always, it seemed, an excuse.

So why had Andy Callis died?

And why had Lee Herdman walked into that classroom?

Rebus smoked his cigarette in silence, took the diamond out and looked at it, pocketed it at a sound from outside: one kid wheeling another past in a supermarket trolley. They both stared at him, as if he were the oddity here, and maybe he was. A couple of minutes later, they were back again. Rebus wound his window all the way down.

'Looking for something, mister?' The trolley-pusher was nine, maybe ten, head shaved, cheekbones prominent.

'Supposed to be meeting Rab Fisher.' Rebus pretended to look at his watch. 'Bastard hasn't shown up.'

The boys were wary, but not as wary as they would become in a year or two.

'Seen him earlier,' the trolley passenger said. Rebus decided to skip the grammar lesson.

'I owe him some cash,' he explained instead. 'Thought he'd be here.' Making a show now of looking all around, as though Fisher might suddenly appear.

'We could get it to him,' the trolley-pusher said.

Rebus smiling. 'Do I look like my head zips up the back?'

'Up to you.' The kid offering a shrug.

'Try two streets that way.' His passenger pointing ahead and right. 'We'll race you.'

Rebus turned the ignition again. Didn't want to race. He'd be conspicuous enough without a shopping-cart rattling along at his side. 'Bet you could find me some ciggies,' he said, picking a five-pound note from his pocket. 'Cheap as you like, and the change is all yours.'

The note was plucked from his hand. 'What's with the gloves, mister?'

'No fingerprints,' Rebus said with a wink, pushing the accelerator.

But nothing was happening two streets away. He came to a junction and looked left and right, saw another car parked by the kerb, a huddle of figures leaning down into it. Rebus paused at the Give Way, thinking the car was being broken into. Then he realised: they were talking to the driver. Four of them. Just the one head visible inside the car. Looked like the Lost Boys, Rab Fisher doing all the talking. The car's engine was a low growl, even in neutral. Souped up, or missing its exhaust-pipe. Rebus suspected the former. The car had been worked on: big brake-light in its back window, spoiler attached to the boot. The driver was wearing a baseball cap. Rebus wanted him to be a victim, mugged or threatened . . . something that would give Rebus the excuse to go storming in. But that wasn't the scenario here. He could hear laughter, got the feeling some anecdote was being shared.

One of the gang looked in his direction, and he realised he'd been sitting too long at the empty junction. He turned on to the new road, parked with his back to the other car, fifty yards further along. Pretended to be looking up at the block of flats . . . just a visitor, here to pick up a pal. Two impatient blasts of his horn to complete the effect, the Lost Boys giving him a moment's notice before dismissing him. Rebus put his phone to his ear, as if making a call to his missing friend . . .

And watched in his rear-view.

Watched Rab Fisher gesticulating, animating his story, the driver someone he was keen to impress. Rebus could hear music, a rumble of bass, the driver's radio tuned to one of the stations Rebus had rejected. He was wondering how long he could carry on the pretence. And what if the trolley twosome really did bring him some cigarettes?

But now Fisher was straightening up, backing away from the car-door, which was opening, the driver getting out.

And Rebus saw who it was: Evil Bob. Bob with his own car, acting big and tough, shoulders rolling as he walked around to the boot, unlocking it. There was something inside he wanted them all to see, the gang forming a tight semi-circle, blocking Rebus's view.

Evil Bob . . . Peacock's sidekick. But not acting the sidekick now, because though he might not be the brightest light on the Christmas tree, he was higher up that tree than a bauble like Fisher.

Not acting . . .

Rebus was remembering something from the interview room at St Leonard's, the day the low-lifes were being grilled. Bob, muttering about never having seen a panto, sounding disappointed. Bob, the big kid, hardly a grown-up at all. Which was why Peacock kept him around, treating him almost as a pet, a pet who did tricks for him.

And now Rebus had another face in his mind, another scene. James Bell's mother, *The Wind in the Willows* . . .

Never too old ... Wagging her finger at him. *Never too old* ...

He gave a final, apparently despairing look out of his side-window, then drove off, revving hard as if annoyed by his pal's no-show. Turned at the next junction and then slowed again, pulled in and made a call on his mobile. Scribbled down the number he was given, made a second call. Then did a circuit, no sign of the trolley or his money, not that he was expecting either. Ended up at another Give Way, a hundred yards in front of Bob's car. Waited. Saw the boot being slammed shut, the Lost Boys making their way back to the pavement, Bob getting behind the steering-wheel. He had an air-horn, it played 'Dixie' as he dropped the hand-brake, tyres squealing, sending up wisps of smoke. He was heading for fifty as he passed Rebus, 'Dixie' blaring again. Rebus started to follow.

He felt calm, purposeful. Decided it was time for the last cigarette in the pack. And maybe even a few minutes of Rory Gallagher, too. Remembered seeing Rory in the seventies, Usher Hall, the place filled with tartan shirts, faded denims. Rory playing 'Sinner Boy', 'I'm Movin' On' ... Rebus had one sinner boy in his sights, hopeful of snaring two more.

Rebus eventually got what he was hoping for. Having chanced his luck at a couple of amber traffic-lights, Bob was forced to stop for a red. Rebus drove up behind him, then passed and stopped, blocking the road. Opened the driver's door and got out, as 'Dixie' sounded its warning. Bob looked angry, came out of the car ready for trouble. Rebus had his hands up in surrender.

'Evening, Bo-bo,' he said. 'Remember me?'

Bob knew him now all right. 'The name's Bob,' he stated.

'Right you are.' The lights had turned green. Rebus waved for the cars behind to come around them.

'What's this all about?' Bob was asking. Rebus was

inspecting the car, a prospective buyer's once-over. 'I've no' done nothing.'

Rebus had reached the boot. He tapped it with his knuckles. 'Care to give me a quick tour of the exhibit?'

Bob's jaw jutted. 'Got a search warrant?'

'Think somebody like me bothers with the niceties?' The baseball cap was shading Bob's face. Rebus bent at the knees so he was looking up into it. 'Think again.' He paused. 'But as it happens . . .' He straightened. 'All I want is for the pair of us to go somewhere.'

'I've no' done nothing,' the young man repeated.

'No need to fret . . . the cells are jam-packed at St Leonard's as it is.'

'So where are we going?'

'My treat.' Rebus nodded towards his Saab. 'I'm going to park kerbside. You pull in behind and wait for me. Got that? And I don't want to see you with your mobile in your hand.'

'I've no'—'

'Understood,' Rebus interrupted. 'But you're about to do *something* . . . and you'll like it, I promise you.' He held up a finger, then retreated to his car. Evil Bob parked behind him, good as gold, and waited while Rebus got into the passenger seat, telling him he could drive.

'Drive where though?'

'Toad Hall,' Rebus said, pointing towards the road ahead.

22

They'd missed the first half of the show, but their tickets for the second half were waiting at the Traverse box office. The audience comprised families, a busload of pensioners, and what looked like at least one school trip, the children wearing identical pale blue jumpers. Rebus and Bob took their seats at the back of the auditorium.

'It's not a panto,' Rebus told him, 'but it's the next best thing.' The lights were just going down for the second half. Rebus knew he'd read *The Wind in the Willows* as a kid, but couldn't remember the story. Not that Bob seemed to mind. His caginess soon melted away as the lights illuminated the scenery and the actors bounded onstage. Toad was in jail as proceedings opened.

'Fitted up, no doubt,' Rebus whispered, but Bob wasn't listening. He clapped and booed with the kids, and by the climax – weasels put to flight by Toad and his allies – was on his feet, bellowing his support. He looked down at the still-seated Rebus and a huge grin spread across his face.

'Like I say,' Rebus offered as the house lights went up and kids began pouring out of the auditorium, 'not quite pantomime, but you get the idea.'

'And this is all because of what I said that day?' With the play over, some of Bob's mistrust was returning.

Rebus shrugged. 'Maybe I just don't see you as a natural-born weasel.'

Out in the foyer, Bob stopped, looking all around him, as though reluctant to leave.

'You can always come back,' Rebus told him. 'Doesn't have to be a special occasion.'

Bob nodded slowly, and allowed Rebus to lead him into the busy street. He already had his car keys out, but Rebus was rubbing his gloved hands together.

'A bag of chips?' he suggested. 'Just to round the evening off . . .'

'I'm buying,' Bob was quick to stress. 'You stumped up for the seats.'

'Well, in that case,' Rebus said, 'I'm bumping my order to a fish supper.'

The chip shop was quiet: pubs hadn't started emptying yet. They carried the warm, wrapped packages back to the car and got in, windows steaming up as they sat and ate. Bob gave a sudden, open-mouthed chuckle.

'Toad was an arse, wasn't he?'

'Reminded me of your pal Peacock actually,' Rebus said. He'd removed his gloves so they wouldn't get greasy; knew Bob wouldn't see his hands in the dark. They'd bought cans of juice. Bob slurped from his, not saying anything. So Rebus tried again.

'I saw you earlier with Rab Fisher. What do you make of him?'

Bob chewed thoughtfully. 'Rab's okay.'

Rebus nodded. 'Peacock thinks so too, doesn't he?'

'How would I know?'

'You mean he hasn't said?'

Bob concentrated on his food, and Rebus knew he'd found the chink he was looking for. 'Oh, aye,' he went on, 'Rab's rising in Peacock's estimation all the time. Ask me, he's just been lucky. See that time we lifted him for the replica gun? Case got tossed, and that makes it look like Rab outwitted us.' Rebus shook his head, trying not to let thoughts of Andy Callis cloud his concentration. 'But he didn't, he just got lucky. When you're lucky like that though, people start to look up to you . . . They reckon you're more sussed than others.' Rebus paused to let this sink in. 'But I'll tell you something, Bob, whether the guns are real or not isn't the issue. The replicas look too good, no way for us to tell they're not real. And that means sooner or later a kid's going to get himself killed. And his blood'll be on your hands.'

Bob had been licking ketchup from his fingers. He froze at the thought. Rebus took a deep breath and gave a sigh, leaning back against the head-rest. 'Way things are headed,' he added lightly, 'Rab and Peacock are just going to get closer and closer . . .'

'Rab's okay,' Bob repeated, but the words had a new hollowness to them.

'Good as gold, Rab is,' Rebus conceded. 'He buy whatever you were selling?'

Bob gave him a look, and Rebus relented. 'Okay, okay, none of my business. Let's pretend you don't have a gun or something wrapped in a blanket in your boot.'

Bob's face tightened.

'I mean it, son.' Rebus laying some stress on the *son*, wondering what sort of father Bob had known. 'No good reason why you should open up to me.' He picked out another chip, dropped it into his mouth. Gave a satisfied grin. 'Is there anything better than a good fish supper?'

'Cracking chips.'

'Almost like home-made.'

Bob nodded. 'Peacock makes the best chips I know, crispy at the edges.'

'Peacock does a bit of cooking, eh?'

'Last time, we had to go before he'd finished . . .'

Rebus stared ahead as the young man crammed home more chips. He picked up his can and held it, just for something to do. His heart was pounding, felt like it was squeezing itself into his windpipe. He cleared his throat. 'Marty's kitchen, was it?' he asked, trying to keep his voice level. Bob nodded, scouring the corners of the carton for crumbs of batter. 'I thought they'd fallen out over Rachel?'

'Yeah, but when Peacock got the phone call—' Bob stopped chewing, horror filling his eyes, realising suddenly that this wasn't just another chat with a pal.

'What phone call?' Rebus asked, allowing the chill to creep into his voice.

Bob was shaking his head. Rebus pushed open his door, snatched the keys from the ignition. Out of the car, scattering chips on the road, round to the back, opening the boot.

Bob was next to him. 'You can't! You said . . .! You bloody said . . .!'

Rebus pushing aside the spare tyre, revealing the gun, not wrapped in anything. A Walther PPK.

'It's a replica,' Bob stuttered. Rebus felt its heft, gave it a good look.

'No it's not,' he hissed. 'You know it and I know it, and that means you're going to jail, Bob. Next night at the theatre for you will be in five years' time. Hope you enjoy it.' He kept one hand on the gun, placed the other on Bob's shoulder. 'What phone call?' he repeated.

'I don't know.' Bob sniffing and trembling. 'Just some guy in a pub . . . next thing, we're in the car.'

'Some guy in a pub saying what?'

Shaking his head violently. 'Peacock never said.'

'No?'

The head going from side to side, eyes suddenly tearful. Rebus gnawed at his bottom lip, looked around. Nobody was paying much attention: buses and taxis on Lothian Road, a bouncer in the doorway of a nightclub nine or ten doors up. Rebus wasn't really seeing any of it, mind spinning.

Could have been any of the drinkers in the pub that night, spotting him having a long talk with Fairstone, the two men seeming too pally . . . thinking Peacock Johnson might be interested. Peacock, who'd once known Fairstone as a friend. Then the falling-out over Rachel Fox. And . . . And what? Peacock worried that Martin Fairstone had turned grass? Because Fairstone knew something Rebus might be interested in.

The question was, what?

'Bob.' Rebus's voice all balm now, trying to soothe and

calm. 'It's all right, Bob. Don't worry about it. Nothing to worry about. I just need to know what Peacock wanted with Marty.'

Another shake of the head; not so violent now, resignation taking hold. 'He'll kill me,' he stated quietly. 'That's what he'll do.' Staring at Rebus, eyes an accusation.

'Then you need me to help you, Bob. You need me to start being your friend. Because if you'll let that happen, it'll be Peacock in jail, not you. You'll be right as rain.'

The young man paused, as though taking this in. Rebus wondered what a halfway decent defence counsel would do to him in court. They'd question his ability and his wits, argue that he didn't make a competent witness.

But he was all Rebus had.

They drove the route back to Rebus's car in silence. Bob parked his own car on a side road, then got into Rebus's.

'Best if you kip at my place tonight,' Rebus explained. 'That way we both know you're safe.' *Safe*: a nice euphemism. 'Tomorrow, we'll have a chat, okay?' *Chat*: another euphemism. Bob nodded, not saying anything. Rebus found a parking space at the top of Arden Street, then led Bob down the pavement towards the tenement's main door. Pushed the door open, and noticed the light in the stairwell wasn't working. Realising too late what it might mean . . . hands grabbing him by the lapels, hurling him against the wall. A knee sought his groin, but Rebus was wise to the move, twisted his lower half so the blow connected with his thigh. He thudded his own forehead into his attacker's face, connecting with a cheekbone. One of the hands was at his throat, seeking the carotid artery. Pressure there, and Rebus would start to lose consciousness. He clenched his fists, went for kidney blows, but the attacker's leather jacket took most of the brunt.

'There's someone else,' a woman's voice hissed.

'What?' The attacker was male, English.

'Someone's with him!'

The pressure on Rebus's throat eased, the attacker backing off. Sudden torchlight illuminated the half-open door, Bob standing there, mouth gaping.

'Shit!' Simms said.

Whiteread was carrying the torch. She shone it in Rebus's face. 'Sorry about that . . . Gavin can get a bit too zealous at times.'

'Apology accepted,' Rebus said, getting his breathing back under control. Then he swung a punch. But Simms was quick, dodged out of its way and held his own fists up.

'Boys, boys,' Whiteread chided them. 'We're not in the playground now.'

'Bob,' Rebus ordered, 'up here!' He started climbing the stairs.

'We need to talk.' Whiteread spoke calmly, as though nothing had just happened. Bob was moving past her, making to follow Rebus.

'We really do need to talk!' she called, angling her head upwards, able to make out Rebus's silhouette as he reached the first landing.

'Fine,' he said eventually. 'But put the lights back on first.'

He unlocked his door, motioned Bob down the hall, showing him the kitchen and the bathroom, then the spare bedroom, single bed prepared for visitors who seldom came. He touched the radiator. It was cold. Crouched down and turned the thermostat.

'It'll warm up soon enough.'

'What was going on back there?' Bob sounded curious, but not altogether concerned. A lifetime's experience of keeping out of other people's business.

'Nothing for you to worry about.' When Rebus stood again, blood rushed into his ears. He steadied himself. 'Best if you wait in here while I talk to them. D'you want a book or something?'

'A book?'

'To read.'

'I've never been a great one for reading.' Bob sat down on the edge of the bed. Rebus could hear his front door closing, which meant Whiteread and Simms were in the hall.

'Just wait here then, okay?' he told Bob. The young man nodded, studying the room as if it were a cell. Punishment rather than refuge.

'No TV?' he asked.

Rebus left the room without answering. Motioned with his head for Whiteread and Simms to follow him into the living room. The photocopy of Herdman's file was on the dining-table, but Rebus didn't mind them seeing it. He poured himself a glass of malt, not bothering to share. Downed it as he stood by the window, where he could watch their reflections.

'Where did you get the diamond?' Whiteread began, holding her hands in front of her.

'That's what it's all about, isn't it?' Rebus smiled to himself. 'The reason Herdman took so many precautions . . . he knew you'd come back some day.'

'You found it on Jura?' Simms guessed. He looked calm, unruffled.

Rebus shook his head. 'I just worked it out, that's all. Knew if I waved a diamond at you, you'd start jumping to conclusions.' He raised his empty glass towards Simms. 'Which you've just done . . . cheers for that.'

Whiteread narrowed her eyes. 'We've confirmed nothing.'

'You came running here . . . confirmation enough in my book. Plus you were in Jura last year, failing to pass yourself off as a tourist.' Rebus poured himself another drink, took a sip. This one was going to last him. 'Army brass, negotiating an end to hostilities in Northern Ireland . . . stood to reason there'd be a price attached. Paying off the paramilitaries. Those guys are greedy, weren't about to go broke. The government was buying them off with diamonds. Only the stash went down with that helicopter, SAS sent on a mission to retrieve them. Armed to the teeth in case the terrorists came looking for them too.' Rebus paused. 'How am I doing so far?'

Whiteread hadn't moved. Simms had seated himself on an arm of the sofa, picking up a discarded Sunday supplement, rolling it into a tube. Rebus pointed at him.

'Going to crush my windpipe, Simms? There's a witness next door, remember.'

'Maybe just wishful thinking,' Simms answered, eyes burning, voice cold. Rebus turned his attention back to Whiteread, who was over by the table, one hand resting on Herdman's personnel file. 'Reckon you can curb your monkey's zeal?'

'You were spinning us a story about diamonds,' she said, not about to have her attention deflected.

'I never saw Herdman as a drug smuggler,' Rebus continued. 'Did you plant that stuff on his boat?' She shook her head slowly. 'Well, someone did.' He thought for a moment, took another sip. 'But all those trips across the North Sea . . . Rotterdam's a good place to trade diamonds. Way I see it, Herdman found the diamonds but wasn't about to own up to it. Either lifted them at the time, or hid them and came back later, sometime after his sudden decision not to re-enlist. Now, the army's wondering what did happen to that stash, and Herdman's suddenly flagged himself up. He's got some money, buys himself a boat business . . . but you can't prove anything.' Paused to take another sip. 'Reckon by now there's much left, or has he spent it?' Rebus thought of the boats: paid for with cash . . . dollars, the currency of the diamond exchange. And of the diamond around Teri Cotter's neck, which had proved the catalyst he'd been looking for. He'd given Whiteread time to answer, but she was staying quiet. 'In which case,' he said, 'your business here was damage limitation, make sure there's nothing anyone's going to find that would lift the lid on the whole thing. Every government says it: we don't negotiate with terrorists. Maybe not, but we did once try buying them out . . . and wouldn't that make a juicy story in the papers.' He stared at Whiteread above the rim of his glass. 'That's about it, isn't it?'

'And the diamond?' she asked.

'Borrowed from a friend.'

She was silent for the best part of a minute, Rebus content to bide his time, thinking that if he hadn't brought Bob home . . . well, things might not have gone nearly so well for him. He could still feel Simms's fingers around his neck . . . throat tight when he swallowed the whisky.

'Has Steve Holly been back in touch?' Rebus asked into the silence. 'See, anything happens to me, all of this goes to him.'

'You think that's enough to protect you?'

'Shut up, Gavin!' Whiteread snapped. Slowly, she folded her arms. 'What are you going to do?' she asked Rebus.

He shrugged. 'It's none of my business, far as I can see. No reason I should do anything, provided you can keep monkey-boy here on his chain.'

Simms had risen to his feet, a hand reaching inside his jacket. Whiteread spun round and slapped his arm away. The move was so fast, if Rebus had blinked he'd have missed it.

'What I want,' he said quietly, 'is for the pair of you to be gone by morning. Otherwise I have to start thinking about talking to my friend from the fourth estate.'

'How do we know we can trust you?'

Rebus gave another shrug. 'I don't think either of us wants it in writing.' He put down his glass. 'Now, if we're all through, I've got a guest I need to see to.'

Whiteread looked towards the door. 'Who is he?'

'Don't worry, he's not the talkative kind.'

She nodded slowly, then made as if to leave.

'One thing, Whiteread?' She paused, turned her head to face him. 'Why do you think Herdman did it?'

'Because he was greedy.'

'I meant, why did he walk into that classroom?'

Her eyes seemed to gleam. 'Why should I care?' And with

390

that she walked from the room. Simms was still staring at Rebus, who gave him a cheeky wave before turning to face the window again. Simms drew the automatic pistol from his jacket and took aim at the back of Rebus's head. Made a soft whistling sound between his teeth and then put the gun back in its holster.

'One day,' he said, voice barely above a whisper. 'You won't know when or where, but I'll be the last face you see.'

'Great,' Rebus exhaled, not bothering to turn round. 'I get to spend my last moments on earth staring at a complete arsehole.'

He listened to the footsteps retreat down the hall, the slamming shut of the door. Went to the doorway to check they'd really gone. Bob was standing just outside the kitchen.

'Made myself a mug of tea. You're out of milk, by the way.'

'The servants are on their day off. Try to get some shut-eye. Long day ahead.' Bob nodded and went to his room, closing the door after him. Rebus poured himself a third drink, definitely the last. Sat down heavily in his armchair, stared at the rolled-up magazine on the sofa opposite. Almost imperceptibly, it was starting to uncurl. He thought of Lee Herdman, tempted by the diamonds, burying them, then walking out of the woods with a shrug of his shoulders. But maybe feeling guilty afterwards, and fearful, too. Because the suspicion would linger. He'd probably been interviewed, interrogated, maybe even by Whiteread. The years might pass, but the army would never forget. Last thing they liked was a loose end, especially one that could turn as if by magic into a loose cannon. That fear, pressing down on him, so that he kept friends to a minimum . . . kids were all right, kids couldn't be his pursuers in disguise . . . Doug Brimson was apparently okay, too . . . All those locks, trying to shut out the world. Little wonder he snapped.

But to snap the way he did? Rebus still didn't get it, couldn't see it as plain jealousy.

James Bell, photographing Miss Teri on Cockburn Street . . .

Derek Renshaw and Anthony Jarvies, logging on to her website . . .

Teri Cotter, curious about death, ex-soldier for a lover . . .

Renshaw and Jarvies, close friends; different from Teri, different from James Bell. Jazz fans, not metal; dressing in their combat uniforms and parading at school, playing sports. Not like Teri Cotter.

Not at all like James Bell.

And when it came down to it, what, apart from their forces background, did Herdman and Doug Brimson have in common? Well, for a start, both knew Teri Cotter. Teri with Herdman, her mother seeing Brimson. Rebus imagined it as a weird sort of dance, the kind where you kept swapping partners. He rested his face in his hands, blocking out the light, smelling glove-leather mixing with the fumes from his whisky glass as the dancers spun around in his head.

When he blinked his eyes open again, the room was a blur. Wallpaper came into focus first, but he could see bloodstains in his mind, classroom blood.

Two fatal shots, one wounding.

No: *three* fatal shots . . .

'No.' He realised he'd said the word out loud. Two fatal shots, one wounding. Then another fatal shot.

Blood spraying the walls and floor.

Blood everywhere.

Blood, with its own stories to tell . . .

He'd poured the fourth whisky without thinking, raised the glass to his lips before he caught himself. Tipped it back carefully into the neck of the bottle, pushed the stopper home. Went so far as to replace the bottle on the mantelpiece.

Blood, with its own stories to tell.

He picked up his phone. Didn't think there'd be anyone at the forensic lab this time of night, but made the call anyway. You never could tell: some of them had their own little obsessions, their own little puzzles to solve. Not because the case demanded it, or even out of a sense of professional pride, but for their own, more private needs.

Like Rebus, they found it hard to let go. He no longer knew if this was a good or a bad thing; it was just the way it was. The phone was ringing, no one answering.

'Lazy bastards,' he muttered to himself. Then he noticed Bob's head, peeping round the door.

'Sorry,' the young man said, shuffling into the room. He'd taken his coat off. Baggy grey T-shirt beneath, showing flabby, hairless arms. 'Can't really settle.'

'Sit down if you like.' Rebus nodded towards the sofa. Bob took a seat, but looked awkward. 'TV's there if you want it.'

Bob nodded, but his eyes were wandering. He saw the shelves of books, walked over to take a look. 'Maybe I'll . . .'

'Help yourself, take anything you fancy.'

'That show we saw . . . you said it's based on a book?'

Rebus's turn to nod. 'I've not got a copy though.' He listened to the ringing-tone for another fifteen seconds, then gave up.

'Sorry if I'm interrupting,' Bob said. He still hadn't touched any of the books, seemed to be regarding them as some rare species, to be stared at but not handled.

'You're not.' Rebus got to his feet. 'Just wait here a minute.' He went into the hall, unlocked a cupboard door. There were cardboard boxes high up, and he lifted one down. Some of his daughter's old stuff . . . dolls and paint-boxes, postcards and bits of rock picked up on seaside walks. He thought of Allan Renshaw. Thought of the ties which should have bound the two of them, ties too easily loosed. Allan with his boxes of photographs, his attic store of memories. Rebus put the box back, brought down the one next to it. Some of his daughter's old books: little Ladybird offerings; some paperbacks with the covers scribbled on or half torn off; and a favoured few hardbacks. Yes, here it was: green dust-jacket, yellow spine with a drawing of Mr Toad.

Someone had added a speech-bubble and in it the words 'poop-poop'. He didn't know if the handwriting was his daughter's or not. Thought again of his cousin Allan, trying to put names to the long-dead faces in the photos.

Rebus put the box back where he'd found it, locked the cupboard, and took the book into the living room.

'Here you go,' he told Bob, handing it over. 'Now you can find out what we missed in the first act.'

Bob seemed pleased, but held the book warily, as if unsure how best to treat it. Then he retreated back to his room. Rebus stood by the window, staring out at the night, wondering if he, too, had missed something . . . not in the play, but right back at the start of the case.

Day Seven

Wednesday

23

The sun was shining when Rebus woke up. He checked his watch, then swivelled out of bed and got dressed. Filled the kettle and switched it on, gave his face a wash before treating it to a once-over with the electric razor. Listened at the door to Bob's bedroom. No sound. He knocked, waited, then shrugged and went into the living room. Called the forensic lab, still no answer.

'Lazy sods.' Speaking of which . . . This time, he banged harder on Bob's door, then opened it an inch. 'Time to face the world.' The curtains were open, the bed empty. Cursing under his breath, Rebus walked in, but there were no feasible hiding places. The copy of *The Wind in the Willows* was lying on the pillow. Rebus pressed his palm to the mattress, thought he could still feel some warmth there. Back in the hall, he saw that the door wasn't properly closed.

'Should have locked us in,' he muttered, going to push it shut. He'd get his jacket and shoes on and go out hunting again. Doubtless Bob would head for his car first of all. After which, if he had any sense at all, he'd take the road south. Rebus doubted he'd have a passport. He wished he'd thought to take down Bob's licence plate. It would be traceable, but it would take time . . .

'Hang on though,' he said to himself. He went back to the bedroom, picked up the book. Bob had used the fly-leaf as a page-marker. Why would he have done that unless . . .? Rebus opened the front door and stepped out on to the landing. Feet were shuffling up the steps.

'Didn't wake you, did I?' Bob said. He lifted a carrier-bag

for Rebus to see. 'Milk and tea-bags, plus four rolls and a packet of sausages.'

'Good thinking,' Rebus said, hoping he sounded calmer than he felt.

Breakfast over, they headed in Rebus's car to St Leonard's. He was trying not to make it seem like a big deal. At the same time, there was no disguising the fact that they were going to be spending most of the day in an interview room, tapes loaded into the dual voice recorder, with another tape for the video.

'Can of juice or anything before we get started?' Rebus asked. Bob had brought a morning tabloid with him, and had it spread out on the desk, lips moving as he read. He shook his head. 'I'll be back in a sec then,' Rebus told him, opening the door and closing it, locking it after him. He climbed the stairs to the CID suite. Siobhan was at her desk.

'Busy day ahead?' he asked her.

'I've got my first flying lesson this afternoon,' she said, looking up from her computer.

'Courtesy of Doug Brimson?' Rebus studied her face as she nodded. 'How're you feeling?'

'No visible signs of damage.'

'Has McAllister been let out of the cells yet?'

Siobhan looked up at the clock above the door. 'I suppose I better do that.'

'Not charging him then?'

'You think I should?'

Rebus shook his head. 'But before you let him waltz out, maybe you should ask him a few things.'

She rested against the back of her chair and stared up at him. 'Like what?'

'I've got Evil Bob downstairs. He says Peacock Johnson started the fire. Stuck the heat under the chip-pan and left it.'

Her eyes widened slightly. 'Does he say why?'

'My idea is, he thought Fairstone had turned grass. Already no love lost between them, then someone calls Johnson and says I'm having a friendly drink with Fairstone.'

'And he murdered him for *that*?'

Rebus shrugged. 'Must've had cause to worry.'

'But you don't know why?'

'Not yet. Maybe it was just meant to scare Fairstone off.'

'You reckon this Bob character's the missing link?'

'I think he can be persuaded.'

'How does Rod McAllister enter this food-chain of yours?'

'We won't know that until you use your brilliant detective powers on him.'

Siobhan started sliding her mouse around its mat, saving what she was working on. 'I'll see what I can do. You coming with me?'

He shook his head. 'I need to get back to the interview room.'

'This talk you're having with Johnson's sidekick . . . is it formal?'

'Informally formal, you might say.'

'Then you should have someone else present.' She looked at him. 'Go by the rule-book for once in your life.'

He knew she was right. 'I could wait till you've finished with the barman,' he suggested.

'Kind of you to offer.' She looked around the suite. DC Davie Hynds was taking a call, writing something down as he listened. 'Davie's your man,' she said. 'Bit more flexible than George Silvers.'

Rebus looked towards Hynds's desk. He'd finished the call and was putting the receiver down with one hand while still scribbling with the other. He saw that he was being stared at, looked up and lifted one eyebrow questioningly. Rebus crooked a finger, beckoning him over. He didn't know Hynds well; hadn't really worked with him much. But he trusted Siobhan's judgement.

'Davie,' he said, laying a companionable arm on the younger man's shoulder, 'take a walk with me, will you? I need to fill you in on the guy we're about to interview.' He paused. 'Best bring that notebook with you . . .'

Twenty minutes in, however, and with Bob still giving them general background, there was a knock at the door. Rebus opened it, saw a female uniform standing there.

'What is it?' he asked.

'Call for you.' She pointed back towards reception.

'I'm busy here.'

'It's DI Hogan. He says it's urgent, and you're to be pulled out of anything short of triple-bypass surgery.'

Despite himself, Rebus smiled. 'His exact words?' he guessed.

'Exact words,' the female officer echoed. Rebus turned back into the room, told Hynds he wouldn't be long. Hynds switched off the machines.

'Get you anything, Bob?' Rebus asked.

'I'm thinking maybe you should get me my lawyer, Mr Rebus.'

Rebus stared at him. 'That'll be Peacock's lawyer too, will it?'

Bob considered this. 'Maybe not just yet,' he said.

'Not just yet,' Rebus agreed, leaving the interview room. He told the officer he could find reception without her help, and entered the comms room, crossing the floor and through an open doorway. Picked up the handset that was lying on the desk.

'Hello?'

'Christ, John, have you gone into purdah or something?' Bobby Hogan sounded not altogether pleased. Rebus was watching the bank of screens in front of him. They showed half a dozen views of St Leonard's, exterior and interior, the viewpoints flickering every thirty seconds or so, shifting from one camera to another.

'What can I do for you, Bobby?'

'Forensics have finally come back to us on the shoot-ings.'

'Oh, aye?' Rebus winced. He'd meant to try phoning them again.

'I'm headed down there. Suddenly remembered that I'd have to drive straight past St Leonard's.'

'They've found something, haven't they, Bobby?'

'They say they've got a bit of a puzzle,' Hogan agreed. Then he broke off. 'You knew, didn't you?'

'Not in so many words. It's to do with the locus, am I right?' Rebus stared at one of the screens. It showed Detective Chief Superintendent Gill Templer entering the building. She carried a briefcase, with a heavy-looking satchel slung over one shoulder.

'That's right. A few . . . anomalies.'

'Good word that: anomalies. Covers a multitude of sins.'

'I just wondered if you fancied coming with me.'

'What does Claverhouse say?'

There was a pause on the line. 'Claverhouse doesn't know,' Hogan said quietly. 'The call came direct to me.'

'Why haven't you told him, Bobby?'

Another pause. 'I don't know.'

'Maybe a certain fellow officer's pernicious influence?'

'Maybe.'

Rebus smiled. 'Pick me up when you're ready, Bobby. Depending on what Forensics have got to tell us, I might have a few questions for them myself.'

He opened the interview room door, beckoned for Hynds to step into the corridor. 'We'll just be a minute, Bob,' he explained. Closed the door and faced Hynds, arms folded.

'I need to go to Howdenhall. Orders from above.'

'Want him put in the cells till you . . .?'

But Rebus was already shaking his head. 'I want you to keep going. I shouldn't be too long. If it gets sticky, call me on my mobile.'

'But . . .'

'Davie,' Rebus laid a hand on Hynds's shoulder, 'you're doing fine in there. You'll manage without me.'

'But there needs to be another officer present,' Hynds objected.

Rebus looked at him. 'Has Siobhan been coaching you, Davie?' He pursed his lips, thought for a moment and then nodded. 'You're right,' he said. 'Ask DCS Templer if she'll sit in with you.'

Both eyebrows shot up, connecting with Hynds's fringe. 'The boss won't . . .'

'Yes she will. Tell her it's about Fairstone. Believe me, she'll be only too happy to oblige.'

'She'll need to be briefed first.'

The hand which had been resting on Hynds's shoulder now patted it. 'You do it.'

'But, sir . . .'

Rebus shook his head slowly. 'This is your chance to show what you can do, Davie. Everything you've learned from watching Siobhan.' Rebus removed his hand and bunched it into a fist. 'Time to start using it.'

Hynds pulled himself a little more upright as he nodded his agreement.

'Good lad,' Rebus said. He turned to leave, but stopped in his tracks. 'Oh, and Davie?'

'Yes?'

'Tell DCS Templer she needs to act mumsy.'

'Mumsy?'

Rebus nodded. 'Just tell her,' he said, making for the exit.

'Forget the XJK. Anything from Porsche can leave the Jags standing.'

'I think the Jaguar's a better-looking car though,' Hogan argued, causing Ray Duff to look up from his work. 'More classical.'

'Old-fashioned, you mean?' Duff was sorting out a large number of crime scene photos, spreading them across every available wall-surface. The room they were in looked like a disused school laboratory, with four free-standing workbenches at its centre. The photos showed the Port Edgar classroom from every conceivable angle, concentrating on the bloodied walls and floor and the positioning of the bodies.

'Call me a traditionalist,' Hogan said, folding his arms in the hope this would put an end to yet another of Ray Duff's discussions.

'Go on then: top five British cars.'

'I'm not that much of a buff, Ray.'

'I like my Saab,' Rebus added, responding to Hogan's scowl with a wink.

Duff made a noise at the back of his throat. 'Don't get me started on the Swedes . . .'

'Okay, how about we concentrate on Port Edgar instead?' Rebus was thinking of Doug Brimson, another Jag-fancier.

Duff was looking around, locating his laptop. He plugged it into a socket on one of the benches and gestured for the two detectives to join him as he switched it on.

'Just while we're waiting.' he said, 'how's Siobhan doing?'

'Fine,' Rebus assured him. 'That little difficulty of hers . . .'

'Yes?'

'Resolved.'

'What difficulty?' Hogan asked. Rebus ignored the question.

'She's having a flying lesson this afternoon.'

'Really?' Duff raised an eyebrow. 'That doesn't come cheap.'

'I think it's a freebie, courtesy of a guy who owns an airfield and a Jag.'

'Brimson?' Hogan guessed. Rebus nodded.

'My offer to her of a ride in my MG pales by comparison,' Duff grumbled.

'You can't compete with this guy. He's got one of those corporate jets.'

Duff whistled. 'Must be loaded then. Those can set you back a few mill.'

'Aye, right,' Rebus said dismissively.

'I'm serious,' Duff said. 'And that's secondhand.'

'You mean millions of pounds?' This from Bobby Hogan. Duff nodded. 'Business must be good, eh?'

Yes, Rebus was thinking, so good Brimson could afford a day off for a trip to Jura . . .

'Here we go,' Duff was saying, drawing their attention back to the laptop. 'Basically, this has everything I need.' He ran an admiring finger along the edge of the screen. 'There's a simulation we can run . . . shows the pattern you'd expect to get when a gun is fired from whatever distance, whatever angle to the head or body.' He clicked a few more buttons and Rebus heard the whirr of the laptop's CD drive. The graphics appeared, a skeletal figure standing side on to a wall. 'See here?' Duff was saying. 'Subject is twenty centimetres from the wall, bullet is fired from a distance of two metres . . . entry and exit and . . . boom!' They watched as a line seemed to enter the skull, reappearing as a fine speckling. Duff's finger moved across the touch-pad, highlighting the marked area of wall, which then was magnified on-screen.

'Gives us a pretty good picture,' he said with a smile.

'Ray,' Hogan said quietly, 'just so you know, DI Rebus here lost a family member in that room.'

Duff's smile melted away. 'I didn't mean to make light of . . .'

'Maybe if we could just cut to the chase,' Rebus replied coolly. He didn't blame Duff: how could he? The man hadn't known. But anything to speed things up.

Duff plunged his hands into the pockets of his white lab-coat and turned towards the photographs.

'We need to look at these now,' he said, eyes on Rebus.

'That's fine,' Rebus agreed with a nod. 'Let's just get it done, eh?'

The early animation had left Duff's voice when he spoke now. 'First victim was the one nearest the door. That was Anthony Jarvies. Herdman walks in and aims at the person nearest him – stands to reason. From the evidence, the two were just under two metres apart. No real sense of an angle . . . Herdman was about the same height as his victim, so the bullet takes a lateral path through the skull. Blood spatter pattern is pretty much what we'd expect to find. Then Herdman turns. Second victim is a little further away, maybe three metres. Herdman may have closed that gap before firing, but probably not by much. This time the bullet angles down through the skull, indicating that Derek Renshaw was maybe trying to duck out of the way.' He looked at his audience. 'With me so far?' Rebus and Hogan nodded, and the three men moved along the wall. 'Blood-stains on the floor are explicable, nothing out of place.' Duff paused.

'Until now?' Rebus guessed. The scientist nodded.

'We've got a lot of data on firearms, what sort of damage they do to the human body, and to anything else they come in contact with . . .'

'And James Bell is proving a puzzle?'

Duff nodded. 'A bit of a puzzle, yes.'

Hogan looked from Duff to Rebus and back again. 'How so?'

'In Bell's statement he says he was hit while in movement. Basically, he was diving for the floor. He seemed to think this might explain why he wasn't killed. He also said that Herdman was about three and a half metres away when he fired.' He crossed to the computer again, and brought a 3-D simulation on to the screen, showing the classroom and pointing to the positions of gunman and schoolboy. 'Again, the victim is of similar height to Herdman. But this time, the angle of the shot appears to be upwards.' Duff paused to let this sink in. 'As if the person doing the firing was the one crouching down.' He bent low at the knees and pointed an imaginary pistol, then straightened and crossed to another of the benches. There was a light-box sitting on it, and he switched it on, illuminating a set of X-rays showing the route the bullet had taken in ripping through James Bell's shoulder. 'Entry wound at the front, exit at the back. You can see the trajectory quite clearly.' He traced it for them with his finger.

'So Herdman was crouching down,' Bobby Hogan said, with a shrug of the shoulders.

'I get the feeling Ray's just warming up,' Rebus said quietly, thinking that he wouldn't have too many questions for the scientist after all.

Duff returned Rebus's look and went back to the photographs. 'No blood spatter pattern,' he said, circling the area of the wall. Then he held up a hand. 'Actually, that's not strictly true. There's blood present, but it's such a fine diffusion you can't really make it out.'

'Meaning what?' Hogan asked, not bothering to hide his impatience.

'Meaning James Bell wasn't standing where he said he was at the time he was shot. He was much further into the room, which means closer to Herdman.'

'Yet there's still that upward trajectory to the shot?' Rebus noted.

Duff nodded, then pulled open a drawer and brought out a bag. It was clear polythene, edged with brown paper. An evidence bag. Folded up inside lay a bloodstained white shirt, the bullet hole at the shoulder clearly visible.

'James Bell's shirt,' Duff stated. 'And here we find something else . . .'

'Powder burns,' Rebus said quietly. Hogan turned to him.

'How come you already know all this?' he hissed.

Rebus shrugged. 'I've got no social life, Bobby. Nothing to do with myself but sit and think about things.' Hogan glowered, letting Rebus know this was well short of an acceptable answer.

'DI Rebus is spot on,' Duff said, gaining their attention again. 'You wouldn't expect powder burns on the bodies of the first two victims. They were shot from a distance. You only get powder burns when the gun is close to the skin or, say, the victim's clothes . . .'

'Did Herdman himself have powder burns?' Rebus asked.

Duff nodded. 'Consistent with placing the pistol to his temple and firing.'

Rebus went back along the display of photos, taking his time. They weren't really telling him anything, which in a way was the whole point. You had to peer beneath their surface to begin to glimpse the truth. Hogan was scratching the nape of his neck.

'I'm not really getting this,' he said.

'It's a puzzle,' Duff agreed. 'Hard to square the witness's account with the evidence.'

'Depends which way you look at it, though, Ray, am I right?'

Duff fixed eyes with Rebus and nodded. 'There's always a way to explain things.'

'Take your time then.' Hogan slapped his hands down on the workbench. 'I had nothing better to do with myself today anyway.'

'Just got to look at it a different way, Bobby,' Rebus told him. 'James Bell was shot at point-blank range . . .'

'By someone the approximate size of a garden gnome,' Hogan said dismissively.

Rebus shook his head. 'It's just that Herdman couldn't have done it.'

Hogan's eyes widened. 'Wait a second . . .'

'Isn't that right, Ray?'

'It's one conclusion, certainly.' Duff was rubbing the underside of his jaw.

'Couldn't have done it?' Hogan echoed. 'You're saying there was someone else in there? An accomplice?'

Rebus shook his head. 'I'm saying it's possible – maybe even probable – that Lee Herdman only killed one person in that room.'

Hogan's eyes narrowed. 'And who would that be?'

Rebus turned his attention to Ray Duff, who supplied the answer.

'Himself,' Duff stated, as though it were the simplest explanation in the world.

24

Rebus and Hogan sat in Hogan's idling car. They'd been silent for a few minutes. The passenger-side window was open, and Rebus was smoking, while Hogan's fingers drummed against the steering-wheel.

'How do we play this?' Hogan asked. This time round, Rebus had an answer.

'You know my preferred technique, Bobby,' he said.

'Bull in a china shop?' Hogan guessed.

Rebus nodded slowly, finishing his cigarette and flicking the butt on to the roadway. 'It's served me well enough in the past.'

'But this is different, John. Jack Bell's an MSP.'

'Jack Bell's a clown.'

'Don't underestimate him.'

Rebus turned to face his colleague. 'Having second thoughts, Bobby?'

'I just wonder if we shouldn't . . .'

'Cover our arses?'

'Unlike you, John, I've never been an aficionado of china shops.'

Rebus stared out through the windscreen. 'I'm going in there anyway, Bobby. You know that. Whether you're with me or not is up to you. You can always call Claverhouse and Ormiston, let them know the score. But I need to hear it for myself.' He turned again to stare at Hogan, eyes shining. 'Sure I can't tempt you?'

Bobby Hogan ran his tongue around his lips, clockwise, then anti-clockwise. His fingers tightened around the steering-wheel.

'Hell with it,' he said. 'What's a bit of broken crockery between friends?'

The door to the Barnton house was opened by Kate Renshaw.

'Hiya, Kate,' Rebus said, face stony, 'how's your dad?'

'He's all right.'

'Not think you'd be better off spending a bit more time with him?'

She'd opened the door wide to let them in, Hogan having phoned ahead to say they were coming.

'I'm doing something useful here,' Kate argued.

'Bolstering a kerb-crawler's career?'

Her eyes flashed fire, but Rebus ignored them. Through glass doors to the right, he could see the dining room, its table spread with the paperwork from Jack Bell's campaign. Bell himself was descending the staircase, rubbing his hands together as though he'd just washed them.

'Officers,' he said, not bothering to sound welcoming. 'I hope this won't take long.'

'Same here,' Hogan countered.

Rebus looked around. 'Is Mrs Bell in the house?'

'She's out visiting. Was there something in particular . . .?'

'Just wanted to tell her I saw *Wind in the Willows* last night. Cracking show.'

The MSP raised an eyebrow. 'I'll pass on the message.'

'You told your son to expect us?' Hogan asked.

Bell nodded. 'He's watching TV.' He gestured towards the living room. Without waiting to be asked, Hogan walked over to the door and opened it. James Bell was lying along the cream leather sofa, shoes off, head resting on the hand of his good arm.

'James,' his father said, 'the police are here.'

'So I see.' James swivelled his feet back on to the carpet.

'Hello again, James,' Hogan said. 'I think you know DI Rebus . . .'

410

James nodded.

'Mind if we sit down?' Hogan asked, aiming the question at son rather than father. Not that Hogan was about to wait for permission. He made himself comfortable in an armchair, while Rebus was content to stand by the fireplace. Jack Bell sat down next to his son, and placed a hand on James's knee, which the young man swatted away. James leaned down and picked up a glass of water from the floor, lifted it to his lips and sipped.

'I'd still like to know what's going on,' Jack Bell said impatiently: a busy man, a man who had better things to do with his time. Rebus's mobile sounded, and he mouthed an apology as he brought it out of his pocket. Looked at the display and saw who was calling. Apologised again as he stood up and left the room.

'Gill?' he said into the mouthpiece. 'How's Bob coming along?'

'Since you ask, he's a fund of good stories.'

Rebus looked into the dining room. There was no sign of Kate. 'He didn't know the chip-pan was meant to go on fire.'

'Agreed.'

'So what else has he said?'

'He seems to have taken against Rab Fisher, without realising how much he's implicating his friend Peacock in the process.'

Rebus's eyes narrowed. 'How so?'

'The reason Fisher was walking up and down nightclub queues, letting people get a glimpse of the gun he was carrying . . .'

'Yes?'

'He was trying to sell drugs.'

'Drugs?'

'Working for your friend Johnson.'

'Peacock's sold some hash in the past, but not enough to merit an assistant.'

411

'Bob's not spelling it out, but I think we might be talking crack.'

'Jesus . . . so who was his source?'

'I'd have thought that was obvious.' She gave a short laugh. 'Your other friend, the one with the boats.'

'I don't think so,' Rebus stated.

'Remind me, wasn't cocaine found on his boat?'

'All the same . . .'

'Well, someone else then.' She took a deep breath. 'Anyway, it's a good start, wouldn't you say?'

'Must be the woman's touch.'

'He just needs someone to mother him, John. Thanks for the tip.'

'Does this mean I'm out of the woods?'

'It means I need to bring Mullen in, let him hear what we've got.'

'But you don't think I killed Martin Fairstone?'

'Let's just say I'm wavering.'

'Thanks for backing me up, boss. Let me know if you get anything else, will you?'

'I'll try. What are you up to? Anything new I should be starting to worry about?'

'Maybe . . . Watch the sky over Barnton for fireworks.' He cut the call, made sure his phone was switched off, and went back into the room.

'I assure you, we'll be as quick as we can,' Hogan was saying. Then he looked up at Rebus. 'Now I'm going to hand over to my colleague.' Rebus pretended to take his time over forming his first question, then stared hard at James Bell.

'Why did you do it, James?'

'What?'

Jack Bell shifted forwards. 'I think I must protest at your tone . . .'

'Sorry about that, sir. I get a bit agitated sometimes when someone's been lying to me. Not just to me, but to everyone: the whole inquiry, his parents, the media . . .

everyone.' James was staring back at him. Rebus folded his arms. 'See, James, we're beginning to piece together what really happened in that classroom, and I've got news for you. When you fire a gun, there are traces left on your skin. They can last weeks, last through a dozen washings and scrubbings. On your shirt-cuffs, too. Remember, we've still got the shirt you were wearing.'

'What the hell are you saying?' Jack Bell snarled, face filling with blood. 'Do you expect me to let you walk into my house and accuse an eighteen-year-old boy of . . .? Is that the way you work in the police force these days?'

'Dad . . .'

'It's because of me, isn't it? You're trying to get at me through my son. Just because you made a horrific mistake which nearly cost me my job, my marriage . . .'

'Dad . . .' James's voice had risen a fraction.

'Now this terrible tragedy occurs and all you can do is—'

'There's no vendetta here, sir,' Hogan was protesting.

'Even though the arresting officer in Leith swears he had you bang to rights,' Rebus couldn't help adding.

'John . . .' Hogan warned.

'You see?' Jack Bell's voice was a tremor of anger. 'You see the way it is, and always will be? Because you're too arrogant to—'

James leapt to his feet. *'Will you shut the fuck up? For once in your bloody life, will you just shut the fuck up?'*

Silence in the room, even though the words seemed to hang in the air, reverberating. James Bell sat back down again slowly.

'Maybe,' Hogan said quietly, 'if we could let James have his say.' Directing his words at the MSP, who seemed stunned, eyes on a son he'd never known existed, someone suddenly revealed to him.

'You can't talk to me like that.' Looking at James, voice barely audible.

'I thought I just did,' James told his father. Then, eyes focused on Rebus, 'Let's get this over with.'

Rebus moistened his lips. 'Right now, James, probably the only thing we can prove is that you were shot at point-blank range – contrary to the story you've been sticking to thus far – and that the angle of the shot would suggest that you did it yourself. However, you've also admitted knowing of at least one of Lee Herdman's guns, which is why I think maybe you took the Brocock intending to shoot and kill Anthony Jarvies and Derek Renshaw.'

'They were wankers, the pair of them.'

'And that constitutes a good enough reason?'

'James,' Jack Bell warned, 'I don't want you saying anything to these men.'

His son ignored him. 'They had to die.'

Bell's mouth opened, but no sound came out. James concentrated on the water glass, turning it and turning it.

'Why did they have to die?' Rebus asked quietly.

James shrugged. 'I've already said.'

'You didn't like them?' Rebus suggested. 'And that's all there is to it?'

'Plenty of my peers have killed for less. Or haven't you been watching the news? America, Germany, Yemen . . . Sometimes it's enough that you don't like Mondays.'

'Help me understand, James. I know you had different taste in music . . .'

'Not just in music: in everything!'

'A different outlook on life?' Hogan suggested.

'Maybe,' Rebus said, 'a part of you wanted to impress Teri Cotter, too.'

James glared at him. 'Leave her out of this.'

'That's not easy to do, James. After all, Teri'd told you she was obsessed with death, hadn't she?' James said nothing. 'I think you'd become a bit infatuated with her.'

'How would you know?' the teenager sneered.

'Well, for a start, you made that trip to Cockburn Street to take her picture.'

'I took a lot of photos.'

'But you kept hers in that book you loaned to Lee. You

414

didn't like it that she'd slept with him, did you? Didn't like it when Jarvies and Renshaw told you they'd found her website, watching her in her bedroom.' Rebus paused. 'How am I doing?'

'You know a lot, Inspector.'

Rebus shook his head. 'But there's so much I don't know, James. And I'm hoping maybe you'll fill in the gaps.'

'You don't have to say anything, James,' his father croaked. 'You're a minor . . . there are laws to protect you. You've suffered a trauma. No court in the land would . . .' He looked across at the detectives. 'Surely he should have a solicitor present?'

'I don't want one,' James snapped.

'But you must.' The father sounded aghast.

The son sneered. 'It's not about you any more, Dad, do you see? It's all about me now. I'm the one who's going to put you back on the front pages, but for all the wrong reasons. And in case you hadn't noticed, I'm not a minor – I'm eighteen. Old enough to vote, old enough to do lots of things.' He seemed to wait for a retort which did not come, then turned his attention back to Rebus. 'What is it you need to know?'

'Am I right about Teri?'

'I knew she was sleeping with Lee.'

'When you gave him that book . . . you left her photo there deliberately?'

'I suppose so.'

'Hoping he'd see it, and do what?' Rebus watched as James shrugged. 'Maybe it was enough that he would know you liked her too.' Rebus paused. 'Why that particular book though?'

James looked at him. 'Because Lee wanted to read it. He knew the story, how the guy had jumped to his death from a plane. He wasn't . . .' James seemed unable to find the words he needed. He took a deep breath. 'He was a deeply unhappy man, you must realise that.'

'Unhappy in what way?'

The word came to James. 'Haunted,' he said. 'That's the sense I always got. He was haunted.'

There was silence in the room for a moment, broken by Rebus: 'You took the gun from Lee's flat?'

'That's right.'

'He didn't know?'

A shake of the head.

'You knew about the Brocock?' Bobby Hogan asked, just about keeping his voice under control. James nodded.

'So how come he turned up at the school?' Rebus asked.

'I left him a note. Didn't expect him to find it so soon.'

'What was your plan then, James?'

'Just walk into the common room – usually only the two of them there – and kill them.'

'In cold blood?'

'That's right.'

'Two kids who'd done you no harm?'

'Two less on the planet.' The teenager shrugged. 'I don't see typhoons and hurricanes, earthquakes and famine . . .'

'And that's why you did it, because it wouldn't matter?'

James was thoughtful. 'Maybe.'

Rebus looked down at the carpet, trying to control the rage growing within him. *My family . . . my blood . . .*

'It all happened so fast,' James was telling them. 'I was amazed how calm I felt. Bang bang, two bodies . . . Lee was walking in the door as I shot the second one. He just stood there, the pair of us did. Didn't know quite what to do.' He smiled at the memory. 'Then he held out his hand for the gun, and I handed it over.' The smile evaporated. 'Last thing I expected was for the stupid sod to point it at his own head.'

'Why do you think he did that?'

James shook his head slowly. 'I've been trying to work it out ever since . . . Do you know?' An imploring edge to the question; needing an answer. Rebus had a few theories: because the gun was his, and he felt responsible . . .

because the incident would bring whole teams of professionals sniffing around, including the army . . . because it was a way out . . .

Because he would no longer be haunted.

'You took the gun from him and shot yourself in the shoulder,' Rebus said quietly. 'Then placed it back in his hand?'

'Yes. The note I'd left for him, it was in his other hand. I took that, too.'

'What about fingerprints.'

'I did what they do in the films, wiped the pistol with my shirt.'

'But when you first walked in there . . . you must have been prepared for everyone to know you'd done it. Why the change of heart?'

The teenager shrugged. 'Because the chance presented itself maybe. Do we really know why we do what we do . . . in the heat of the moment?' He turned to his father. 'Instincts sometimes get the better of us. Those dark little thoughts . . .'

Which was when his father lunged at him, grabbing him around the neck, the two of them falling backwards over the sofa, crashing to the floor.

'You little bastard!' Jack Bell was yelling. 'Do you know what you've done? I'm ruined now! In tatters! Absolute fucking tatters!'

Rebus and Hogan separated them, the father still snarling and swearing, the son almost serene by comparison, and studying his father's incoherent ire as though it was a memory he would treasure in the years to come. The door had opened, Kate standing there. Rebus wanted to make James Bell fall down at her feet, beg forgiveness. She was taking in the scene, trying to make sense of it.

'Jack?' she asked softly.

Jack Bell looked at her, as if she was a stranger to him. Rebus was still holding the MSP in a bear-hug from behind.

'Get out of here, Kate,' he pleaded. 'Just go home.'

'I don't understand.'

James Bell, passive in Hogan's grasp, looked across to the doorway, then over to where his father and Rebus stood. A smile spread slowly across his face.

'Will you tell her, or shall I . . .?'

25

'I can't believe it,' Siobhan said, not for the first time. Rebus's phone call to her had lasted almost the whole of her drive from St Leonard's to the airfield.

'I'm having a hard time taking it in myself.'

She was on the A8, heading west out of the city. Looked in her mirror, then signalled, moving out to overtake a taxi. Businessman in the back of it, calmly reading a newspaper on his way to his flight. Siobhan felt like she needed to pull over on to the hard shoulder, bolt from her car and do some screaming, just to release whatever it was she was feeling. Was it the rush of getting a result? Two results really: the Herdman case and Fairstone's murder. Or was it the frustration of not being around at the time?

'He couldn't have shot Herdman too, could he?' she asked.

'Who? Young Master Bell?' She could hear Rebus turning from his phone to relay her question to Bobby Hogan.

'He leaves the note, knowing Herdman will follow him,' Siobhan was saying, mind rushing. 'Kills all three and turns the gun on himself.'

'It's a theory,' Rebus's voice crackled, sounding unconvinced. 'What's that noise?'

'My phone. It's telling me it needs a recharge.' She took the airport slip-road, the taxi still visible in her mirror. 'I could cancel, you know.' Meaning the flying lesson.

'What's the point? Nothing doing here.'

'You're heading for Queensferry?'

'Already there. Bobby's driving in through the school

gates as I speak.' He turned away from the phone again, said something to Hogan. Sounded like he was saying he wanted to be there when Hogan explained everything to Claverhouse and Ormiston. Siobhan caught the words 'especially that the drug-running's a non-starter'.

'Who put the drugs on his boat?' she asked.

'Didn't catch that, Siobhan.'

She repeated the question. 'You think Whiteread did it to keep the inquiry active?'

'I'm not sure even she has the clout for that sort of sting. We're rounding up the small-fry. Cars are already out looking for Rab Fisher and Peacock Johnson. Bobby's just about to deliver the news to Claverhouse.'

'I wish I could be there.'

'Catch us afterwards. We'll be adjourning to the pub.'

'Not the Boatman's though?'

'I thought maybe we'd try the place next door . . . just for a change.'

'I should only be an hour or so.'

'Take your time. I don't suppose we'll be going anywhere. Bring Brimson with you, if you like.'

'Should I tell him about James Bell?'

'That's up to you . . . papers will have it by the close of play.'

'Meaning Steve Holly?'

'Reckon I owe the sod that much. At least then Claverhouse doesn't get the pleasure of breaking the news.' He paused. 'Did you manage to put the frighteners on Rod McAllister?'

'He still denies writing the letters.'

'It's enough that you know . . . and that he knows you do. Feeling okay about the flying lesson?'

'I'll be fine.'

'Maybe I should alert air traffic control.' She could hear Hogan saying something in the background, and Rebus chuckling.

'What did he say?' she asked.

'Bobby reckons we might be better off warning the coastguard.'

'That's him crossed off my dinner list.'

She listened as Rebus relayed her message to Hogan. Then: 'Okay, Siobhan, that's us at the car park. Got to go deliver the news to Claverhouse.'

'Any chance of you keeping your composure?'

'Don't worry, I'll be cool, calm and collected.'

'Really?'

'Just as soon as I've rubbed his nose in the shit.'

She smiled, ended the call. Decided she might as well switch her phone off. Wouldn't be making calls at five thousand feet . . . Glanced at the dashboard clock and saw that she was going to be early. Didn't suppose Doug Brimson would mind. She tried to shake her head clear of everything she'd heard.

Lee Herdman didn't kill those kids.

John Rebus didn't torch Martin Fairstone's house.

She felt bad about having suspected Rebus, but it was his own fault . . . always so secretive. And Herdman, too, with his secret life, his daily fears. The media would be forced to eat humble pie, and would turn their fury on the easiest target available: Jack Bell.

Which almost counted as a happy ending . . .

As she arrived at the airfield gates, a car was just leaving. Brimson got out of the passenger side, offered a cautious smile as he undid the lock, pulled the gate open. Waited there as the car drove through, passing Siobhan at speed, a scowling face in its front seat. Brimson beckoned for Siobhan to drive in. She did so, then waited while the gate was locked again. Brimson opened the passenger-side door, got in.

'Wasn't expecting you quite yet,' he said.

Siobhan eased her foot from the clutch. 'Sorry about that,' she said quietly, staring through the windscreen. 'Who was your visitor?'

Brimson screwed up his face. 'Just someone interested in flying lessons.'

'Didn't seem the type somehow.'

'You mean the shirt?' Brimson laughed. 'Bit loud, wasn't it?'

'A bit.' They'd arrived at the office, Siobhan pulling on the handbrake. Brimson got out. She stayed where she was, watching him. He came round to her side of the car, opened the door, as if this was what she'd been waiting for. Avoiding eye contact.

'There's some paperwork,' he was saying. 'Liability waiver ... stuff like that.' He made towards the open doorway.

'Did your customer have a name?' she asked, following him in.

'Jackson ... Jobson ... something like that.' He'd entered his office, falling into his chair, hands sifting through paperwork. Siobhan kept on her feet.

'It'll be on the paperwork,' she said.

'What?'

'If he was here for lessons, I assume you've got his details?'

'Oh ... yes ... here somewhere.' He shuffled the sheets of paper. 'Time I got a secretary,' he said, attempting a grin.

'His name's Peacock Johnson,' Siobhan said quietly.

'Is it?'

'And he wasn't here for flying lessons. Did he want you to fly him out of the country?'

'You know him then?'

'I know he's a wanted man, responsible for the death of a petty criminal called Martin Fairstone. And now Peacock's panicking because he can't find his trusted lieutenant and probably knows we've got him.'

'All of which comes as news to me.'

'But you know who Johnson is ... and what he is.'

'No, I told you ... he just wanted flying lessons.'

Brimson's hands were busier than ever, sorting through the paperwork.

'I'll let you in on a secret,' Siobhan said. 'We've tied up the Port Edgar case. Lee Herdman didn't kill those kids; it was the MSP's son.'

'What?' Brimson didn't seem to be taking the news in.

'James Bell did it, then turned the gun on himself, after Lee had committed suicide.'

'Really?'

'Doug, are you looking for anything in particular, or trying to dig your way out of here through the desk?'

He looked up at her and grinned.

'I was telling you,' she went on, 'that Lee didn't kill those two boys.'

'Right.'

'Which means the only puzzle left is the drugs found on his boat. I'm assuming you knew about the yacht he kept moored shore-side?'

He could no longer hold her gaze. 'Why would I know anything about that?'

'Why wouldn't you?'

'Look, Siobhan . . .' Brimson made a show of checking his watch. 'Maybe we can leave the paperwork. Wouldn't do to miss our slot . . .'

She ignored this. 'The yacht looked good because Lee sailed to Europe, but now we know he was selling diamonds.'

'And buying drugs at the same time?'

She shook her head. 'You knew about his boat, and probably knew he went to the continent.' She'd taken a step towards the desk. 'It's the corporate flights, isn't it, Doug? Your own little trips to the continent, taking businessmen to meetings and on jollies . . . that's how you bring the drugs in.'

'It's all going to hell,' he said, almost too calmly. He'd leaned back in the chair, hands smoothing his hair, eyes staring ceilingwards. 'I told that stupid bastard never to come here.'

'You mean Peacock?'

He nodded slowly.

'Why plant the drugs?' Siobhan asked.

'Why not?' He gave another burst of laughter. 'Lee was dead. Way I saw it, it would focus attention on him.'

'Taking the heat off you?' She decided to sit down. 'Thing was, there was no heat *on* you.'

'Charlotte thought there was. You lot were sniffing into every nook and cranny, talking to Teri, talking to me . . .'

'Charlotte Cotter's involved?'

Brimson looked at her as though she were stupid. 'It's a cash business . . . all needs to be laundered.'

'Through the tanning salons?' Siobhan nodded, letting him know she understood. Brimson and Teri's mother: business partners.

'Lee wasn't squeaky clean, you know,' Brimson was saying. 'He was the one who introduced me to Peacock Johnson in the first place.'

'Lee knew Peacock Johnson? Is that where the guns came from?'

'That's one thing I was going to give you, only I couldn't see how . . .'

'What thing?'

'Johnson had these deactivated guns, needed someone to put the firing pins back, that sort of thing.'

'And Lee Herdman did it?' She thought of the well-stocked workshop at the boat-yard. Yes, a simple enough job, with the tools and the know-how. Herdman had had both.

Brimson was quiet for a moment. 'We could still go for that flight; shame to miss the slot.'

'I've not brought my passport.' She reached out a hand towards his phone. 'I need to make a call now, Doug.'

'I'd cleared our path, you know . . . cleared it with the

flight tower. I was going to show you so much . . .' She'd risen to her feet, lifted the receiver.

'Maybe another time, eh?'

The two of them knowing there would be no other time. Brimson's palms were flat against the desktop. Siobhan was holding the receiver to her ear, halfway through punching in the numbers. 'I'm sorry, Doug,' she said.

'Me too, Siobhan. Believe me, I'm as sorry as hell.'

He pushed up from the desk, lunged across it, sending all the paperwork flying as he came. She dropped the phone and took a step back, colliding with the chair behind her, tripping over it and hitting the floor, hands outstretched to cushion the blow.

Doug Brimson's whole weight landing on her, pinning her down, punching all the breath from her chest.

'Got to fly, Siobhan,' he snarled, gripping her by the wrists. 'Got to fly . . .'

26

'Happy, Bobby?' Rebus asked.

'Deliriously so,' Bobby Hogan replied. They were entering the bar on South Queensferry's waterfront. The meeting at the school could hardly have been better timed. They'd managed to interrupt a meeting between Claverhouse and Assistant Chief Constable Colin Carswell, Hogan taking a deep breath before stating that everything Claverhouse was saying was nonsense before going on to explain why.

At the end of the meeting, Claverhouse had walked out without any comment, leaving his colleague Ormiston to shake Hogan's hand, telling him he deserved the credit.

'Which doesn't mean you'll get it, Bobby,' Rebus had said. But he'd patted Ormiston's arm, to let him know the gesture was appreciated. He'd even asked him to join them for a drink, but Ormiston had shaken his head.

'I think you've just assigned me to solace duty,' he'd said.

So it was just Rebus and Hogan in the bar. As they waited their turn, Hogan seemed to deflate just a little. Usually at the end of a case, the whole team gathered in the murder room, while crates of beer were dragged in and opened. Maybe a bottle of fizz from the Brass. Whisky for the more traditionally minded. This didn't seem the same, just the two of them, the original team already dispersed . . .

'What'll it be?' Hogan asked, trying to sound breezy.

'Maybe a Laphroaig, Bobby.'

'The measures don't look generous.' Hogan had run an expert eye over the gantry. 'Better make it a double.'

'And decide right now who's the designated driver.'

Hogan's mouth twitched. 'I thought you said Siobhan was joining us.'

'That's cruel, Bobby.' Rebus paused. 'Cruel but fair.'

The barman was ready for them. Hogan ordered Rebus's whisky, and a pint of lager for himself. 'And two cigars,' he added, turning towards Rebus, seeming to study him. He rested his arm on the edge of the bar. 'Result like this, John, makes me think I want to go out while I'm winning.'

'Christ, Bobby, you're in your prime.'

Hogan snorted. 'Five years ago I'd have agreed with you.' He took a wad of notes from his pocket and extracted a ten. 'But this just about does it for me.'

'So what's changed?'

Hogan shrugged. 'A kid who can go and shoot two classmates, no real motive, I mean, none that makes any sense to me . . . It's a different world to the one I used to know, John.'

'Just means we're needed more than ever.'

Hogan snorted again. 'You really think so? You see yourself as being wanted, do you?'

'I didn't say "wanted"; I said *needed*.'

'And who needs us? People like Carswell, because we make him look good? Or Claverhouse, so he's not screwing up any more than he already is?'

'They'll do for a start,' Rebus said, smiling. His glass was placed in front of him, and he dribbled some water into it, just enough to take the edge off. Two thin cigars had arrived, and Hogan was unwrapping his.

'We still don't really know, do we?'

'Know what?'

'Why Herdman did it . . . topped himself.'

'Did you think we ever would? I had the feeling you brought me in because all the young folk around you were scaring you. You needed another dinosaur in the vicinity.'

'You're not a dinosaur, John.' Hogan lifted his glass, chinked it against Rebus's. 'Here's to the two of us.'

'Not forgetting Jack Bell, without whose presence James might have realised he could keep quiet and end up getting away with it.'

'Right enough,' Hogan said with a broad grin. 'Families, eh, John?' He started shaking his head.

'Families,' Rebus agreed, lifting the glass to his mouth.

When his phone sounded, Hogan told him to leave it. But Rebus checked the display, wondering if it might be Siobhan. It wasn't. Rebus motioned to Hogan that he was stepping back outside, where it was quieter. There was a beer garden to the front, just an area of tarmac with some tables. Too chill a breeze for anyone to be using them. Rebus lifted the phone to his ear.

'Gill?' he said.

'You wanted to be kept in touch.'

'Young Bob's still singing then?'

'I almost wish he'd stop,' Gill Templer said with a sigh. 'We've had his childhood, bullied at school, the time he wet himself . . . He keeps bouncing backwards and forwards, I never know if something happened last week or last decade. He says he wants to borrow *The Wind in the Willows* . . .'

Rebus smiled. 'It's at my flat. I'll fetch it for him.' Rebus heard the drone of a light aircraft in the distance. Peered up, shading his eyes with his free hand. The plane was over the Forth Road Bridge, too far away to tell if it was the same one they'd travelled to Jura in. Same sort of size, crawling almost lazily across the sky.

'What do you know about tanning parlours?' Gill Templer was asking.

'Why?'

'They keep cropping up. Some connection with Johnson and the drugs . . .'

Rebus kept watching the plane. It dipped suddenly, engine changing tone. Then it levelled off, wings tilting

428

from side to side. If it was Siobhan up there, she was learning the hard way.

'Teri Cotter's mother owns a few,' Rebus said into the phone. 'That's about as much as I know.'

'Could they be a front?'

'I wouldn't have thought so. I mean, where would she be getting . . .?' Rebus broke off. Brimson's car, parked in Cockburn Street where Teri's mum had one of her shops. Teri admitting to him that her mother was having an affair with Brimson . . .

Doug Brimson, friend of Lee Herdman. Brimson with his planes. Where the hell had he got the money for them? Millions, Ray Duff had said. It had hit a nerve at the time, but Rebus had become distracted by James Bell. Millions . . . the kind of money you could make from a few legitimate businesses, and dozens of illegal ones . . .

Rebus remembered what Brimson had said on the way back from Jura, with the Forth and Rosyth beneath: *I often think of the damage . . . even with something as small as a Cessna . . . dockyard . . . ferry . . . road and rail bridges . . . airport . . .* Rebus's hand fell. He squinted into the light.

'Jesus Christ,' he muttered.

'John? You still there?'

By the time she had the words out, he wasn't.

Ran back into the bar, dragged Hogan out. 'We need to get to the airfield!'

'What for?'

'No time!'

Hogan unlocking the car, Rebus getting behind the wheel. 'I'm driving!' Hogan not about to argue. Rebus sending the car screaming out of the car park, but then screeching to a halt, staring from the driver's-side window.

'Jesus, no . . .' Stumbling from the car, standing in the middle of the road, looking up. The plane had gone into a dive, but was coming out of it.

'What's going on?' Hogan yelled from the passenger seat.

Rebus got back behind the wheel, set off again. Following the plane's progress as it passed over the rail bridge, made a steep arc as it neared the Fife coastline and started back towards the bridges again.

'That plane's in trouble,' Hogan stated.

Rebus stopped the car again to watch. 'It's Brimson,' he hissed. 'He's got Siobhan with him.'

'Looks like it's going to hit the bridge!' Both men were out of the car. They weren't alone. Other drivers had stopped to watch. Pedestrians were pointing and muttering. The drone of the engine had grown louder, more discordant.

'Jesus,' Hogan gasped, as the plane flew underneath the rail bridge, mere feet from the surface of the water. It climbed steeply, almost vertically, levelled off, and then dived again. This time it went below the central span of the road bridge.

'Is he showing off or trying to scare the wits out of her?' Hogan said.

Rebus shook his head. He was thinking of Lee Herdman, the way he would try to scare his teenage water-skiers . . . testing them.

'Brimson's the one who planted those drugs. He's bringing them into the country on his plane, Bobby, and I get the feeling Siobhan knows that.'

'So what the hell is he doing now?'

'Scaring her maybe. I hope to hell that's all it is . . .' He thought of Lee Herdman, lifting a gun to his temple, and the ex-SAS man who jumped to his death from an aeroplane . . .

'Will they have parachutes?' Hogan was asking. 'Could she get out?'

Rebus didn't answer. His jaw was locked tight.

The plane was looping the loop now, but still far too close to the bridge. One wing clipped a suspension cable, sending the plane into a spiralling dive.

Rebus took an involuntary step forward, yelled out the

word 'No!' stretching it for the length of time it took the machine to hit the water.

'Hell's fucking bells,' Hogan cried. Rebus was staring at the spot . . . the plane already reduced to wreckage, wisps of smoke rising from it as the pieces began to disappear beneath the surface.

'We've got to get down there!' Rebus shouted.

'How?'

'I don't know . . . get a boat! Port Edgar . . . they've got boats!' They got back into the car and did a squealing U-turn, drove to the boat-yard where a siren was sounding, regular sailors already heading for the scene. Rebus parked, and they ran down to the jetty, past Herdman's boathouse, Rebus aware of movement at the corner of his eye, a flash of colour. Dismissing it in the urgency to reach the water's edge. Rebus and Hogan showed their ID to a man who was untying his speedboat.

'We need a lift.'

The man was in his late fifties, bald-headed with a silver beard. He looked them up and down. 'You need life-jackets,' he protested.

'No, we don't. Now just get us out there.' Rebus paused. 'Please.'

The man took another look at him, and nodded agreement. Rebus and Hogan clambered aboard, clinging on as the owner raced out of the harbour. Other small boats had already congregated around the slick of oil, and the lifeboat from South Queensferry was approaching. Rebus scanned the surface of the water, knowing it was futile.

'Maybe it wasn't them,' Hogan said. 'Maybe she didn't go.'

Rebus nodded in the hope that his friend might shut up. What debris there was was already spreading out, the tide and the swell from the various craft dispersing it. 'We need divers, Bobby. Frogmen . . . whatever it takes.'

'It'll be taken care of, John. Somebody else's job, not ours.' Rebus realised that Hogan's hand was squeezing his arm. 'Christ, and I made that stupid crack about the coastguard . . .'

'Not your fault, Bobby.'

Hogan was thoughtful. 'Nothing we can do here, eh?'

Rebus was forced to admit defeat: there was nothing they could do. They asked the skipper to take them back, which he did.

'Terrible accident,' he yelled above the noise of the outboard engine.

'Yes, terrible,' Hogan agreed. Rebus just stared at the choppy surface of the water. 'We still going to the airfield?' Hogan asked as they climbed back on to dry land. Rebus nodded, started striding towards the Passat. But then he paused outside Herdman's boathouse, and turned his head to look at the much smaller shed next door, the one with the car parked in front. The car was an old 7-series BMW, tarnished black. He didn't recognise it. Where had the flash of colour come from? He looked at the shed. Its door was closed. Had it been open when they'd arrived? Had the flash of colour flitted across the doorway? Rebus walked up to the door, gave it a push. It bounced back: someone behind it, holding it closed. Rebus stood back and gave the door an almighty kick, then shouldered it. It flew open, sending the man behind it sprawling.

Red short-sleeved shirt with palm trees on.

Face turning to meet Rebus's.

'Holy shit,' Bobby Hogan was muttering, studying the blanket on the ground, the array of weapons laid out on it. Two lockers stood gaping, emptied of their secrets. Pistols, revolvers, sub-machine-guns . . .

'Thinking of starting a war, Peacock?' Rebus said. And when Peacock Johnson scrambled forward, making towards the nearest gun, Rebus took a single step, swung back a foot, and kicked him straight in the middle of his face, throwing him back on to the floor again.

Johnson lay unconscious, spreadeagled. Hogan was shaking his head.

'How the hell did we miss this lot?' he was asking himself.

'Maybe because it was right under our noses, Bobby, same as everything else in this damned case.'

'But what does it mean?'

'I suggest you ask our friend here,' Rebus said, 'just as soon as he wakes up.' He turned to walk away.

'Where are you going?'

'The airfield. You stay here with him, call it in.'

'John . . . what's the point?'

Rebus stopped. He knew what Hogan meant: what's the point of going to the airfield? But then he started walking again; couldn't think of anything else to do. He punched Siobhan's number into his mobile, but a recording told him the number wasn't available and he should try again later. He punched it in again, same response. Dropped the tiny silver box on to the ground and stamped on it, hard as he could, with the heel of his shoe.

It was dusk by the time Rebus arrived at the locked gates.

He got out of the car and tried the entryphone, but no one was answering. He could see Siobhan's car through the fence, parked next to the office. The office door was standing open, as though someone had been in a hurry.

Or maybe struggling . . . not bothering to close it after them.

Rebus pushed at the gate, put his shoulder to it. The chain rattled, but wasn't going to yield. He stood back and kicked it. Kicked it again and again. Shouldered it, smashed his fists against it. Pressed his head to it, eyes squeezed shut.

'Siobhan . . .' His voice breaking.

He knew what he needed: bolt-cutters. A patrol car could bring some, if Rebus had any way of calling one.

Brimson . . . he knew it now. Knew Brimson was running drugs, had planted them on his dead friend's boat. He didn't know why, but he'd find out. Siobhan had discovered the truth somehow, and had died as a result. Perhaps she'd wrestled with him, explaining the erratic flight path. He opened his eyes wide, blinking back tears.

Staring through the gate.

Blinking his vision back into focus.

Because someone was there . . . A figure in the doorway, one hand to its head, another to its stomach. Rebus blinked again, making sure.

'Siobhan!' he yelled. She raised a hand, waved it. Rebus grabbed the fence and hauled himself on to it, shouted her name again. She disappeared back into the building.

His voice cracked. Was he seeing things now? No: she was out of the building again, getting into her car, driving the short distance to the gate. As she neared, Rebus saw that it really was her. And she was fine.

She stopped the car and got out. 'Brimson,' she was saying. 'He's the one with the drugs . . . in cahoots with Johnson and Teri's mother . . .' She'd brought Brimson's keys, was finding the right one to use on the padlock.

'We know,' Rebus told her, but she wasn't listening.

'Must've made a run for it . . . laid me out cold. I only came to when the phone started buzzing.' She yanked the padlock free, the chain coming with it. Pulled open the gate.

And was picked off the ground by Rebus, his hug enveloping her.

'Ow, ow, ow,' she said, causing him to ease off. 'Bit bruised,' she explained, her eyes meeting his. He couldn't help himself, planted his lips on hers. The kiss lingered, his eyes tight shut, hers wide open. She broke away, took a step back, tried to catch her breath.

'Not that I'm not overwhelmed or anything, but what's this all about?'

27

It was Rebus's turn to visit Siobhan in hospital. She'd been admitted for concussion, was due to stay the night.

'This is ridiculous,' she protested. 'I'm fine, really I am.'

'You'll stay where you are, young lady.'

'Oh yes? Like you did, you mean?'

As if to emphasise her point, the same nurse who had changed Rebus's dressings walked past, pushing an empty trolley.

Rebus pulled a chair across and sat down.

'You didn't bring anything then?' she asked.

Rebus shrugged. 'Been a bit rushed; you know how it is.'

'What's the story with Peacock?'

'He's doing a good impression of a clam. Not that it'll do him any good. Way Gill Templer sees it, Herdman wouldn't want the guns lying around in his own boathouse, so Peacock rented the one next door. That's where Herdman worked on them, reconditioning them, and they were stored in the shed. When he put a bullet to his head, things got too hot, no way Peacock could shift them . . .'

'But then he panicked?'

'Either that or he just wanted to tool himself up for what was to come.'

Siobhan closed her eyes. 'Thank God that didn't happen.'

They stayed quiet for a couple of minutes. Then: 'And Brimson?' she asked.

'What about him?'

'The way he decided to end it all . . .'

'I think he bottled it, right at the last.'

She opened her eyes again. 'Or came to his senses, couldn't bring himself to involve anyone apart from himself.'

Rebus shrugged. 'Whatever . . . he's another statistic for the armed forces to work on.'

'Maybe they'll try to say it was an accident.'

'Maybe it was at that. Could be he was planning to loop the loop and then smash on to the carriageway, go out in a blaze of mayhem.'

'I prefer my version.'

'Then you stick to it.'

'And what about James Bell?'

'What about him?'

'Reckon we'll ever understand how he could do it?'

Rebus shrugged again. 'All I know is, the papers are going to have a field day with his dad.'

'And that's good enough for you?'

'It'll do to be going on with.'

'James and Lee Herdman . . . I don't really get it.'

Rebus thought for a moment. 'Maybe James reckoned he'd found himself a hero, someone different from his dad, someone whose respect he'd give his eye-teeth for.'

'Or kill for?' Siobhan guessed.

Rebus smiled and stood up, patted her arm.

'You going already?'

He shrugged. 'Lots to be getting on with; we're an officer short at the station.'

'Nothing that can't wait till tomorrow?'

'Justice never sleeps, Siobhan. Which doesn't mean you shouldn't. Anything I can get you before I go?'

'A sense of having achieved something, maybe?'

'I'm not sure the vending machines are up to it, but I'll see what I can do.'

He'd done it again.

Ended up drinking too much . . . slumped on the toilet-seat back in his flat, jacket discarded on the hall floor. Leaning forward, head in hands.

Last time . . . Last time had been the night Martin Fairstone had died. Rebus had spent too long in too many pubs, tracking down his prey. A few more whiskies back at Fairstone's place, and a taxi home. Driver had had to wake him up when they reached Arden Street. Rebus reeking of cigarettes, wanting to slough it all off. Running a bath, just the hot tap, thinking he'd add cold later. Sitting on the lavatory, half-undressed, head in hands, eyes closed.

World tilting in the darkness, shifting on its axis, pitching him forward so his head thumped against the rim of the bath . . . waking on his knees, hands burning.

Hands hanging over the side of the bath, scalded by the rising water . . .

Scalded.

No mystery about it.

The sort of thing that could happen to anyone.

Couldn't it?

But not tonight. He got back to his feet, steadied himself, managed to make it through to the living room and into his chair, pushing it over to the window with his feet. The night was still and calm, lights on in the tenement windows across the way. Couples relaxing, checking on the kids. Singles awaiting pizza deliveries, or sitting down to the videos they'd rented. Students debating another night out at the pub, unstarted essays troubling them.

Few if any of them harbouring mysteries. Fears, yes; doubts, most certainly. Maybe even guilt about tiny mistakes and misdemeanours.

But nothing to trouble the likes of Rebus. Not tonight. His fingers patted the floor, feeling for the telephone. He sat with it in his lap, thinking of giving Allan Renshaw a call. There were things he had to tell him.

He'd been thinking about families: not just his own, but all those connected to the case. Lee Herdman, walking away from his family; James and Jack Bell, seemingly with nothing to connect them but blood; Teri Cotter and her mother . . . And Rebus himself, replacing his own family with colleagues like Siobhan and Andy Callis, producing ties that oftentimes seemed stronger than blood.

He stared at the phone in his lap, reckoned it was a bit late now to call his cousin. Shrugged and mouthed the word 'tomorrow'. Smiled at the memory of lifting Siobhan off her feet.

Decided to see if he could make it to his bed. The laptop was in 'sleep' mode. He didn't bother waking it; unplugged it instead. It could go back to the station tomorrow.

He came to a stop in the hallway and walked into the guest room, lifted the copy of *The Wind in the Willows*. He'd keep it near him so he wouldn't forget. Tomorrow he'd make a gift of it to Bob.

Tomorrow, God and the devil willing.

Epilogue

Jack Bell had spared no expense during the preliminary organisation of his son's defence. Not that James had seemed to notice. He'd remained adamant that he wasn't going to fight anything. He was guilty, and that was what he'd say in court.

Nevertheless, the solicitor engaged by Jack Bell was reckoned to be the best Scotland had to offer. He was based in Glasgow, and charged travelling time to Edinburgh at his standard rate. Immaculately dressed in chalk-stripe suit and burgundy bowtie, he smoked a pipe whenever such was permitted, and held the pipe in his left hand at what seemed all other times.

As he sat opposite Jack Bell now, one leg crossed over the other at the knee, he stared at a patch of wall just above the MSP's head. Bell had become used to his ways, and knew this was by no means an indication that the lawyer was distracted; rather, that he was focused on the matter at hand.

'We've got a case,' the lawyer said. 'A pretty good one, I'd say.'

'Really?'

'Oh, yes.' The lawyer examined the stem of his pipe, as if for flaws. 'It all boils down to this, you see – Detective Inspector Rebus belongs to Derek Renshaw's family . . . a cousin, to be precise. As a result of which, he should never have been let near the case.'

'Conflict of interests?' Jack Bell guessed.

'Self-evidently. You can't have a relation of one of the victims going in and questioning possible suspects. Then there's the matter of his suspension. You may not know this, but DI Rebus was being investigated by his own force at the time of the events at Port Edgar.' The lawyer's attention had shifted to the pipe's bowl, scrutinising its interior. 'A question of possible proceedings being taken against him in a murder case . . .'

'Better and better.'

'Nothing came of it, but all the same, one does have to wonder at the Lothian and Borders Police. I'm not sure that I've ever heard of an officer on suspension being able to move so freely around another ongoing inquiry.'

'It's irregular then?'

'Unheard of, I'd suggest. Which leads to very serious questions about the validity of much of the Crown's case.' The lawyer paused, tested the pipe between his teeth, his mouth forming a shape that might have been taken for a grin. 'There are so many possible objections and technicalities, the Crown might even be forced to concede without the need of anything other than a preliminary diet.'

'In other words, the case would be tossed out?'

'It's entirely feasible. I'd say we've got a very strong case.' The lawyer paused for effect. 'But only if James were to plead not guilty.'

Jack Bell nodded, and the two men's eyes met for the first time, then both heads turned to face James, who was seated across the table.

'Well, James?' the lawyer said. 'What do you think?'

The teenager seemed to be considering the offer. He returned his father's stare as if it were all the nourishment he needed and he had a hunger that would never be stilled.

READING
GROUP
NOTES

A QUESTION
OF BLOOD

© Rankin

ABOUT IAN RANKIN

Ian Rankin, OBE, writes a huge
proportion of all the crime novels sold
in the UK and has won numerous prizes,
including in 2005 the Crime Writers'
Association Diamond Dagger. His work
is available in over 30 languages, home
sales of his books exceed one million
copies a year, and several of the novels
based around the character of Detective
Inspector Rebus – his name meaning
'enigmatic puzzle' – have been
successfully transferred to television.

Introduction to DI John Rebus

The first novels to feature Rebus, a flawed
but resolutely humane detective, were not an
overnight sensation, and success took time
to arrive. But the wait became a period that
allowed Ian Rankin to come of age as a writer,
and to develop Rebus into a thoroughly
believable, flesh-and-blood character straddling
both industrial and post-industrial Scotland;
a gritty yet perceptive man coping with his
own demons. As Rebus struggled to keep
his relationship with daughter Sammy alive
following his divorce, and to cope with the
imprisonment of brother Michael, while all the
time trying to strike a blow for morality against
a fearsome array of sinners (some justified and
some not), readers began to respond in their
droves. Fans admired Ian Rankin's re-creation
of a picture-postcard Edinburgh with a vicious
tooth-and-claw underbelly just a heartbeat away,
his believable but at the same time complex
plots and, best of all, Rebus as a conflicted man
trying always to solve the unsolvable, and to do
the right thing.

As the series progressed, Ian Rankin refused
to shy away from contentious issues such as
corruption in high places, paedophilia and illegal

immigration, combining his unique seal of tight plotting with a bleak realism, leavened with brooding humour.

In Rebus the reader is presented with a rich and constantly evolving portrait of a complex and troubled man, irrevocably tinged with the sense of being an outsider and, potentially, unable to escape being a 'justified sinner' himself. Rebus's life is intricately related to his Scottish environs too, enriched by Ian Rankin's attentive depiction of locations, and careful regard to Rebus's favourite music, watering holes and books, as well as his often fraught relationships with colleagues and family. And so, alongside Rebus, the reader is taken on an often painful, sometimes hellish journey to the depths of human nature, always rooted in the minutiae of a very recognisable Scottish life.

The Oxford Bar – Rebus and many of the characters who appear in the novels are regulars of the Ox – as is Ian Rankin himself. The pub is now synonymous with the Rebus novels to the extent that one of the regular medical examiners called in to assist with investigations is named after the pub's owner, John Gates.

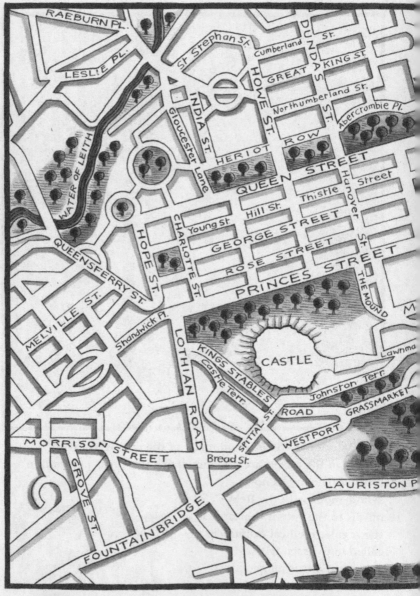

Edinburgh plays an important role throughout the Rebus
novels; a character itself, as brooding and as volatile as
Rebus. The Edinburgh depicted in the novels is far short of

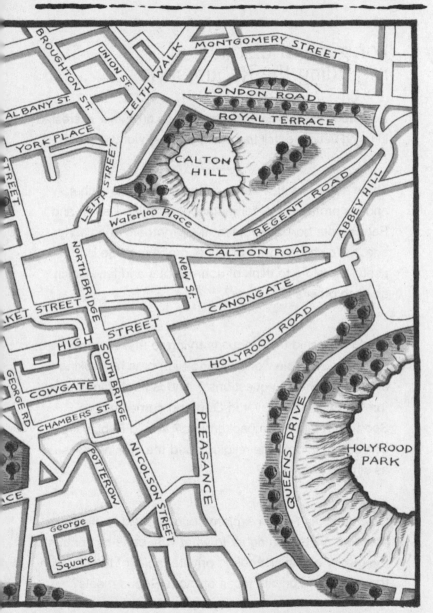

the beautiful city that tourists in their thousands flood to
visit. Hidden behind the historic buildings and elegant
façades is the world that Rebus inhabits.

For general discussion regarding the Rebus series

How does Ian Rankin reveal himself as an author interested in using fiction to 'tell the truths the real world can't'?

There are similarities between the lives of the author and his protagonist – for instance, both Ian Rankin and Rebus were born in Fife, lost their mothers at an early age, have children with physical problems – so is it useful therefore to think of John Rebus and Ian Rankin as each other's alter egos?

Could it be said that Rebus is trying to make sense in a general way of the world around him, or is he seeking answers to the 'big questions'? And is it relevant therefore that he is a believer in God and comes from a Scottish Presbyterian background? Would Rebus see confession in both the religious and the criminal sense as similar in any way?

How does Ian Rankin explore notions of Edinburgh as a character in its own right? In what way does he contrast the glossy public and seedy private faces of the city with the public and private faces of those Rebus meets?

How does Ian Rankin use musical sources – the Elvis references in *The Black Book*, for instance, or the Rolling Stones allusions in *Let It Bleed* – as a means of character development through the series? What does Rebus's own taste in music and books say about him as a person?

What do you think about Rebus as a character? If you have read several or more novels from the series, discuss how his character is developed.

If Rebus has a problem with notions of 'pecking order' and the idea of authority generally, what does it say about him that he chose careers in hierarchical institutions such as the Army and then the police?

How does Rebus relate to women: as lovers, flirtations, family members and colleagues?

Do the flashes of gallows humour as often shown by the pathologists but sometimes also in Rebus's own comments increase or dissipate narrative tension? Does Rebus use black comedy for the same reasons the pathologists do?

Do Rebus's personal vulnerabilities make him understanding of the frailties of others?

How does the characterisation of Rebus compare to other
long-standing popular detectives from British authors
such as Holmes, Poirot, Morse or Dalgleish? And are
there more similarities or differences between them?

A QUESTION OF BLOOD

Yet again Rebus finds himself in hot water: a man who'd been stalking DS Siobhan Clarke turns up burned to death; and Rebus has suspicious burn wounds on his own hands, which means that now he's facing the wrath of an internal inquiry. Meanwhile there's been a slaughter at a private school in South Queensferry, where an ex-Army gunman has killed two pupils and gravely wounded another. And the injured boy, James, has vociferous SMP Jack Bell as his father, a man with his own issues against the police. And to make matters worse, Rebus realises that he himself is related to one of the schoolboy victims.

As Miss Teri allows surreptitious webcam peeks into her bedroom and her Goth friends try to look enigmatic, and while the schoolboy Combined Cadet Force run around in military garb and the Lost Boys gang wanders the streets looking for trouble, Rebus begins to see that the world of teenagers is as alien to him as anything could be. As inexplicable perhaps as the need in 1995 for a covert SAS salvage operation on the remote Scottish Isle of Jura, something that gunman Lee Herdman may have talked about with friend Doug Brimson, a flying instructor who has caught Siobhan's eye and who seems to know rather too much about corporate jollies.

In *A Question of Blood* Rebus must ask himself about
how he treats his own family, and why he seems to be
carelessly discarding family ties. But as these bonds
loosen, he and Siobhan appear to be taking their
professional relationship to a new level.

Discussion points for
A Question of Blood

Ian Rankin says, '*The Rebus novels have always examined Edinburgh's dual identity, its Jekyll and Hyde nature. Private education is part of the city's fabric, but also a contentious issue in some quarters.*' How is this assertion explored?

What has happened to Rebus's relationship with Jean Burchill?

How is the price DCS Gill Templer is paying for climbing the career ladder showing? What does Siobhan feel about this? And what does it mean that Siobhan is now suffering from panic attacks?

'*Fear: the crucial word. Most people would live their whole lives untouched by crime, yet they still feared it, and that fear was real and smothering. The police force existed to allay such fears, yet too often was shown to be fallible, powerless, on hand only after the event, clearing up the mess rather than preventing it.*' Is this an overly cynical opinion of Rebus?

There is a parallel Army investigation, ostensibly into Lee Herdman's actions. What is actually whetting the two investigators' appetites? Is Rebus as irritated by their presence as he is by old adversaries Claverhouse and Ormiston, from Drugs and Major Crime? What do they all think of Rebus?

The title has a double meaning: blood as in lifeblood, and also as in familial ties. Consider the implications of this punning.

Rebus has lost touch with his brother Michael – why might this be?

Why did Lee Herdman act as he did?

Bearing in mind their similar Army backgrounds, is Lee Herdman the criminal that Rebus is arguably most like, personality-wise, throughout the Rebus series?

What is it about Wee Evil Bob that makes Rebus treat him with compassion? Is it an unrecognised fatherly impulse?

Does Siobhan have a poor instinct about men when it comes to her own personal relationships? How does she put herself in jeopardy?

Who is probably the most surprised at what happens after Rebus finds Siobhan alive?

Does Ian Rankin leave the climax open-ended as to what James Bell might do?

Is *A Question of Blood* a 'fun' book to read, as the author claims?

A QUESTION

OF BLOOD

YEAR PUBLISHED: 2003

BOOK THEMES

- *A Question of Blood* is the last book where Rebus is based in St Leonard's Police Station, because the real police station was believed to be shutting its CID unit. In reality it remained open and continues to operate to this day.

- With a shooting at a private school forming the main thrust of the plot, the book looks at the school system in Scotland.

- Rebus has an armed forces background, and Ian always kept an eye on news stories concerning the military – for example, whenever squaddies left the army and struggled to adapt to civilian life. This book ruminates on the theme of the outsider, and how easily a man can go off the rails.

IN THE NEWS . . .

- —North Korea withdraws with immediate effect from the Nuclear Non-Proliferation Treaty, drawing intense concern from neighbouring Asian countries.

- —After Saddam Hussein rejects US President George Bush's ultimatum to leave Iraq within fourty-eight hours, the US and Britain launch war against Iraq. Hussein is eventually arrested after eight months of evading capture.

- —Libya formally takes responsibility for the 1988 Lockerbie bombing, and agrees to pay $2.7 billion as compensation to the families of the 270 victims.

- —On 1 February, just sixteen minutes before touchdown, the US space shuttle Columbia disintegrates upon its re-entering the Earth's atmosphere. All seven crew members on board are killed.

- —Actor Arnold Schwarzenegger is elected Governor of California. He beats his closest challenger by more than one million votes.

- —A political storm rages around the 'Dodgy Dossier' that declares that Iraq could deploy weapons of mass destruction within forty-five minutes.

- —Dr David Kelly, the source who tips off the BBC to the 'sexed up' government report, is found dead from suspected suicide.

FILMS

- —Popular films include: *Lost in Translation, Pirates of the Caribbean: The Curse of the Black Pearl, The Lord of the Rings: The Return of the King, Finding Nemo, Master and Commander: The Far Side of the World, Love Actually.*

- —*Chicago* wins six Oscars from thirteen nominations, including Best Picture.

- —Roman Polanski wins Best Director for *The Pianist*, which also produces the Best Actor winner (Adrien Brody). Nicole Kidman wins Best Actress for her portrayal of Virginia Woolf in *The Hours.*

- —Polanski and Kidman both also triumph at the BAFTAs. *The Pianist* is awarded Best Film, and Daniel Day-Lewis wins Best Actor (*Gangs of New York*).

- —Despite *Chicago* and *Gangs of New York* receiving twenty-four BAFTA nominations between them, the pair of films combine for just three award wins, as six films win two trophies each.

MUSIC

- —Popular albums include: Outkast *Speakerboxxx/The Love Below*, The White Stripes *Elephant*, Beyoncé *Dangerously in Love*, Elbow *Cast of Thousands*, Neil Young and Crazy Horse *Greendale*.

- —The Eurovision Song Contest, held in Riga, Latvia, goes disastrously for the UK as their entry, Cry Baby by Jemini, earns zero points. The infamous 'nul points' finish was greeted with much consternation in the British media.

- —**Where Is The Love? makes stars out of The Black Eyed Peas, and is No.1 for six weeks towards the end of the year. Despite being the highest selling single of the year, the 650,000 copies sold is way down on figures from previous years.**

- —Michael Andrews featuring Gary Jules is a surprise Christmas No.1 with his cover of Tears for Fears's Mad World.

BOOKS

—Iain Banks's non-fiction book *Raw Spirit: In Search of the Perfect Dram*.

—Mark Haddon's mystery novel *The Curious Incident of the Dog in the Night-Time* is published to widespread acclaim.

—Terry Pratchett publishes his thirtieth and thirty-first Discworld novels: *The Wee Free Men* and *Monstrous Regiment*.

—After a three-year wait for fans, the next instalment in J. K. Rowling's Harry Potter series is released: *Harry Potter and the Order of the Phoenix*.

—Lynne Truss's punctuation guide *Eats, Shoots & Leaves* is a surprise bestseller.

—The Booker Prize is awarded to DBC Pierre for *Vernon God Little*.

—Zoë Heller's novel *Notes on a Scandal*.

—Monica Ali's novel *Brick Lane*.